A PLUME BOOK

OTHERWORLD NIGHTS

KELLEY ARMSTRONG is the number one *New York Times* bestselling author of the Otherworld series, as well as the young adult trilogy Darkest Powers, the Darkness Rising trilogy, and the Nadia Stafford series. She lives in rural Ontario, Canada.

OTHERWORLD NIGHTS

AN ANTHOLOGY

KELLEY ARMSTRONG

A PLUME BOOK

PLUME
Published by the Penguin Group
Penguin Group (USA) LLC
375 Hudson Street
New York, New York 10014

USA | Canada | UK | Ireland | Australia | New Zealand | India | South Africa | China
penguin.com
A Penguin Random House Company

First published by Plume, a member of Penguin Group (USA) LLC, 2014

Some of the stories in *Otherworld Nights* have been previously published online or
in obscure collections.

⫿ REGISTERED TRADEMARK—MARCA REGISTRADA

LIBRARY OF CONGRESS CATALOGING-IN-PUBLICATION DATA
Armstrong, Kelley.
Otherworld Nights : an anthology / Kelley Armstrong.
pages cm
ISBN 978-0-452-29834-7 (paperback)
   1. Fantasy fiction, American.   I. Title.
PS3551.R4678O84 2014
813'.54—dc23   2014030419

Printed in the United States of America
10 9 8 7 6 5 4 3 2 1

CONTENTS

INTRODUCTION

$\mathscr{T}$he Otherworld series may contain only thirteen novels, but the fictional world is much vaster than that, with dozens of short stories and novellas that I've written over the years—and continue to write now that the books are complete.

The short stories are scattered wide and far. Over the years, I've been asked to contribute stories to many anthologies, and I often wrote ones set in the Otherworld. Even the most devoted readers will have missed some.

My favorite form, though, is the novella—it allows more room for character work than a short story, but also allows for a more straightforward plot than a novel. There isn't much of a market for novellas, but I've been blessed to find Subterranean Press, which publishes limited-edition, illustrated novellas. The only disadvantage to that format? Not every reader wants to buy a limited-edition hardcover novella, as gorgeous as it may be!

For readers who've been clamoring for these shorts and novellas all in one place, I give you the first of three volumes of Otherworld short fiction. Yes, three—did I mention there were a lot of stories? Three won't even cover everything I've written for this world, and I also wanted to add a new novella to each volume.

For this first anthology, the focus is love, in its various forms—between lovers, between friends, between parents and children.

We start with "Demonology," where Adam's mother discovers what he is. This was originally an online story. Next is "Twilight," my unfortunately titled Cassandra story from *Many Bloody*

Returns. Then comes "Stalked," Clay's tale of his honeymoon with Elena. It's from *My Big Fat Supernatural Honeymoon* and was reprinted in the e-book *The Hunter and the Hunted*. "Chivalrous" is Reese's backstory from the long sold-out *Tales of Dark Fantasy 2*. "Lucifer's Daughter" is a Hope and Karl story originally printed in *Blood Lite 2*. Then we get the long novella *Hidden*, which was my Elena and Clay tale from Subterranean Press, published in 2012. "From Russia, with Love" was the Elena bonus story included with some versions of *Thirteen*. And finally, the new novella, *Vanishing Act*, is a Savannah and Adam story set after *Thirteen*.

If there are stories you're dying to see in the next two anthologies, let me know! In the meantime, I hope you'll enjoy your stay in these corners of the Otherworld.

OTHERWORLD *Nights*

DEMONOLOGY

*T*alia stared at the painting. A tiny fishing boat caught in a raging storm, swirling in an eddy, the crew members barely managing to keep it afloat . . . while a giant wave swelled behind them. *That's my life,* she thought. *I fight the storm and I keep fighting, but somehow, I never shake the feeling that a huge wave is gathering behind my back, waiting to make a mockery of my efforts.*

Her eight-year-old son, Adam, was sprawled across the office floor doing his homework with his blond head bent over the math workbook, pencil in his mouth, scowling at the numbers as if that could make them surrender their secrets. He'd been quiet for fifteen minutes now, a sure sign that he was dreading this appointment.

In her support group for parents of hyperactive children, the other mothers always rejoiced over their children's "quiet times," those rare occasions when their kids stopped bouncing and chattering and sat for more than a few minutes at a stretch. Talia never joined in. When Adam went quiet, it was a sure sign that something was bothering him. These days, he sank into those spells several times a week, more often if that week included appointments.

In the last three months, they'd been to at least a dozen doctors. General practitioners, specialists, psychiatrists, psychologists, social workers . . . a never-ending parade of professionals all claiming they could figure out what was wrong with Adam. Talia hated that phrase: "what was wrong with Adam."

There was nothing wrong with her son, and she told him that every day. But the fact that she needed to give constant reassurances proved that even Adam knew something *was* wrong. How many blood samples could a little boy give, how many questions could he answer, how many X-rays and tests could he undergo, before he stopped trusting his mother's reassurances?

"Mom?"

Talia looked over and met his brown eyes, the mirror image of her own.

"I'm thirsty."

She lifted her purse. "I brought juice boxes and animal crackers—"

"I'm *more* thirsty than that." He wrinkled his nose, freckles forming new constellations. Then he slanted a sly look her way. "I saw a pop machine down the hall."

"Did you, now? And let me guess. *That's* how thirsty you are: full-can-of-pop thirsty."

"Please?"

With a dramatic sigh, she opened her change purse and counted out enough for a soda and a candy bar. Yes, she was apologizing for the appointment with junk food, but sometimes you'd do just about anything to make the medicine go down easier. His grin as she handed over the money said she'd done the right thing, whatever the parenting books might tell her.

"Thanks, Mom."

He bounded for the door and nearly knocked over a student walking in. A blurted apology and a sheepish glance at Talia. Then, as he turned backward to the door, he froze, his gaze snagged on a photo. An aerial view of a forest fire. Adam had noticed it the moment he'd walked in. Yet now he stared as if seeing it for the first time.

"That's a neat photo, isn't it?" Talia said. "I wonder how they took it. From an airplane, I bet."

"Cool," Adam said, then tore his gaze away and took off, back on target.

Talia moved to the doorway. He shot her a look that said he was too old to have his mother watching out for him, but she stuck out her tongue and stood her ground.

As he ran down the hall, weaving through groups of students, her gaze slid back to the forest-fire photograph. Should she have commented on it like that? Most of the doctors she'd talked to would have said no, that she should either ignore his fascination or distract him from it. Maybe Talia was naive, but that didn't seem right to her. Treat it as normal—that's what she thought she should do. Act as if Adam's fixation with fire was neither positive nor negative, just a fact of his life, like another child's obsession with cars or trains.

Budding pyromania. That's what the experts called it. *Pyromania.* Talia could barely even think the word, as if that gave it a validity it didn't deserve. Yes, her son was fascinated by fire, but there was a huge difference between staring at a candle flame and lighting your bed on fire. Adam didn't start fires; he just liked to watch them. And yes, maybe that was a warning sign, but pyromania seemed a simplistic explanation that ignored so many other things.

When Adam struck out in anger, which was luckily very rare, his hands were hot enough to give a physical jolt, like touching fire itself. The last time he'd done that—three months ago, with a bully at school—he'd left a mark on the kid's skin. That's when the parade of experts had started.

Now, after months of searching, she'd ended up here. At the office of a different kind of doctor. A college professor. She looked at the nameplate again. Robert Vasic, PhD. Nothing to indicate his area of expertise or even his department. She could have looked that up. She should have. No one could accuse Talia of being anything less than thorough, especially when it came to her son's care.

But this time . . . When the nurse at the last specialist's office had taken her aside and slipped her Vasic's number, she'd made an appointment without even looking him up. She was that desperate.

"Do you think he forgot about us?"

Talia jumped and looked at the student Adam had nearly bowled over.

The young woman smiled. "Sorry, I was just wondering whether Dr. Vasic was going to show up. He can be a bit absentminded."

"Oh?" Talia said, trying to sound interested as she leaned to look for Adam.

"Last month, we were supposed to have a quiz, and he completely forgot about it." The girl grinned. "Not that anyone complained."

Adam was still at the vending machine, trying to make a decision.

"He's a great prof, though, isn't he? Enthusiasm makes all the difference, I think. Of course, it'd probably be hard to make something like that boring. When I told my mom I was studying demonology, she almost had a fit. She thought I was taking an occult class."

Talia stared at the young woman. Her mouth opened, but before she could speak, the student continued, "Then I told her he used to be a priest, and that made her happier. I think she figures we're learning about exorcisms and stuff. My aunt called last week, asking if I could take a look at my little cousin, check for signs of possession. I think she was joking . . . but I'm not sure."

Demonology? Former priest? Possession? Oh God, what had she done?

Talia caught sight of Adam bouncing back from the machines, pop can in one hand, candy bar in the other, his face beaming. She held up a finger, telling him to wait. Then she grabbed her purse and his homework, murmured something to the student about remembering another appointment, and raced out.

"Mom?" Adam said as she hurried to him. "What's—?"

"The appointment was canceled."

"So we don't have to stay?" A momentary shadow, then another sly look. "It's getting late to go back to school."

She put a hand against his back to steer him along the hall. "Definitely too late. But I think there's still time for the arcade, and I bet it isn't too busy at this time of day. No lineup for Pac-Man."

Another grin. "Cool."

They'd caught the attention of a slender, bearded middle-aged man. With his towheaded good looks and infectious grin, Adam often won the attention of strangers, but it was usually indulgent smiles and the occasional pat on the head. This man, who'd been rushing down the hall, had stopped and was frowning slightly, as if he recognized them.

"Ms. Lyndsay?"

She almost stopped. Almost turned. Then she realized this man must be Robert Vasic.

"Ms. Lyndsay?" he called after them.

She took Adam's arm, ignoring his protests, and steered him into a throng of students exiting a classroom. By the time they were through the crowd, Vasic was gone. She gave a soft sigh of relief, and hurried Adam to the exit.

That night, Talia dreamed of Adam's father, as she found herself doing more often these days, especially when her quest would smack into another dead end. It made sense, she supposed—that a single mother struggling with a parenting problem would reflect on her son's absent father. But there was never any anger to her dreams, no "Why am I stuck handling this alone?" bitterness. Instead, she dreamed of their meeting and of their night together.

From the start, she'd accepted that Adam was her sole responsibility. Had she been able to contact his father, she would have—it was only right. But that hadn't been an option, and she'd never wished it was otherwise.

She'd met him a month into her first college term. There'd been a lot of changes in that month, not all of them good, not all of them welcome. The biggest had been the end of a relationship. When she'd gone away to college, the guy she'd been dating since ninth grade had dumped her.

Maybe "dumped" wasn't the right word, as it implied a sudden, unexpected end to the relationship. Josh had warned her, starting the day she sent in her college application. *Leave for college, and we're through.* Like most of the boys in town, he already had a job lined up at the tire factory, and had his life lined up right behind it. Find a good job with good benefits, get married, start a family, like his father and his older brothers before him.

When he'd learned that Talia's plans didn't coincide with his, he'd given her his ultimatum. *Go to college and you lose me.* She hadn't believed him. When she was accepted, he'd sulked but continued dating her right until Labor Day weekend. She thought he'd changed his mind. Later she realized he just hadn't expected her to go through with it. When she did, he dumped her.

A month later, she'd come home for the weekend, planning to talk to him and work it out . . . only to discover he was dating Brandi Waters, who'd been after him since they were twelve. That was the end of her weekend home. And the end of Josh.

She'd caught the bus back to school, though she was sure she could have saved the fare and just kicked herself all the way back. Had she really gone home to try to make up with him? After what he did? She should have booted his ass to the curb the moment he'd given her that ultimatum.

When she got back to college that evening, she'd dropped off her suitcase at the dorm, then headed to the café to drown her sorrows in an herbal tea with scones and jam. They didn't have scones back in Springwater. They didn't have herbal tea, either. And they certainly didn't have any place like the Elysian Café, with its incense burners, abstract art, and Tuesday-night poetry readings. Most times, Talia found the place too So-Cal, but tonight anything that didn't remind her of home was exactly where she wanted to be.

She'd resisted the urge to bring schoolwork. This night was for wallowing, not studying. So she'd grabbed one of her roommate's novels. Stephen King's *Salem's Lot*. Vampires. If that wasn't wallowing, she didn't know what was.

She'd noticed him watching her as she sat down. He was a decent-looking guy. Not gorgeous, but Talia didn't go for gorgeous. He sat by the fireplace with his chair pulled up to the blaze as if he found the air-conditioning too much. She pegged him at a few years older than her, probably a grad student. Average height, average build, medium brown hair . . . average all around, really.

Only his eyes were noteworthy. A warm brown with coppery glints. When he smiled at her, she smiled back—polite, nothing more. Then she settled in with her book, tea, and scone.

After a few minutes of reading, a shadow passed over her table. She looked up to see the young man. He smiled. A cute, average sort of smile—friendly, nothing more.

"Vampires, hmmm?" he said, nodding at the book. "Do you like vampires?"

"I don't know. I've never met one."

He threw back his head and laughed as if this was the funniest thing he'd heard all day. His laugh was anything but average, as rich and vibrant as his copper-speckled eyes.

"That's not the most comfortable place for reading," he said, gesturing at her wooden chair. "The seats by the fire are much better."

"Sure, but they're always full—" She looked over. The chairs were empty, with only a jacket thrown over his to save his place. "Well, they were full when I came in."

"I scared everyone away for you."

She smiled. "Thanks. But I'm not sure—"

"You don't have to be sure," he said, his eyes dancing with amusement. "I'll just go back to my chair and move my coat over one for you, and if your chair here gets uncomfortable, you know where you can find something better."

With that, he tipped his head, the gesture oddly old-fashioned and courtly, then walked back to his chair by the fire.

Talia held out for ten more minutes. Then she looked at him, reading quietly, as anti-Josh as this café was anti-Springwater. She gathered her tea and her book, and went to join him.

They'd spent the evening talking. Just talking, about an endless array of topics. He seemed to know something about everything, but what he wanted to know most was more about her—her life, her interests, her goals. Of himself, he said very little, not even his name. It didn't matter. Talia was fascinated, and there was something fresh and exciting about being found fascinating in return. Nine years later, she could still see him, leaning forward, the fire making his eyes glitter.

They left only because the café closed at midnight. He offered to escort her back to her dorm. He actually said "escort," and she'd tried not to laugh, charmed in spite of herself. When they reached the building, they stopped under a tree to talk some more, and he'd kissed her.

In his kiss, there'd been something she'd never found with Josh, and when she'd closed her eyes, she'd seen fire, and felt it blazing through her. Then she did something that she still couldn't believe: she'd invited him to her room. Talia Lyndsay, the girl who'd made Josh wait almost three years before letting him go all the way, inviting a stranger into her bed. And, to this day, she didn't regret it.

That night . . . well, she'd had lovers since, but none had come close. He'd been perfect—patient yet passionate. Some nights she could still see the glimmer of his face in the candlelight, feel the heat of his fingers.

That was what she always remembered in these dreams. Those candles and that heat. She'd come from the bathroom to find that he'd lit every candle her New Age–obsessed roommate owned. She'd jokingly asked where he'd found the matches, because Sunny kept them hidden, but he'd only smiled and rose to meet her. And

his touch. Hot, his skin like someone with a fever, and his finger-
tips warmer still.

She'd asked him to wear a condom, and he'd produced one from
his wallet. She'd seen him put it on—she was sure she had. As for
what went wrong, she could only assume it had broken. She hadn't
noticed until the next morning, rising to find a still-damp spot
under her.

The last thing she remembered of their night was him lowering
her to the pillow, then staying there, watching her as her eyelids
flagged. Once, she'd forced them back open and had one last
glimpse of him, holding a candle to watch her face, his own shimmering against the flame. Then she'd drifted off, and when she
awoke, he was gone. A month later she missed her period and knew
he'd left something behind.

The day after she'd bolted from Dr. Vasic's office, Talia started
feeling foolish. That student had been laughing about her out-of-
touch mother jumping to conclusions . . . and Talia had done the
same thing. Put the words "ex-priest" and "demonology" together,
and she'd envisioned a man booted out of the Church for radical
views, a nut who'd see a child fascinated by fire and assume possession by hellfire imps. Just the kind of guy who'd make tenured professor at Stanford. Obviously, not.

So, Talia did what she should have done *before* making the
appointment. She researched him. And she found a man with a
solid academic record, lauded and admired by his peers.

After three nights of dreaming about Adam's father, she knew
her subconscious was telling her she'd run out of options. It was
time to take another look at Robert Vasic.

Two days later, Talia sat at the back of Vasic's lecture hall for his
huge first-year class. Getting in hadn't been difficult—she looked
young enough. Taking time off work hadn't been tough, either. She

was a horticulturist—a glorified gardener, as she joked—and self-employed, so her schedule was flexible. Busy, but flexible.

Talia couldn't believe not only that Stanford offered courses in demons but that they were so popular. By the end of the lecture, though, she understood why. Vasic was an outstanding teacher. He spoke with a quiet passion and a dry humor that had her suspecting he could have made even her plant physiology classes interesting.

At the end, she tried to merge into the rushing river of students.

"Ms. Lyndsay?"

Vasic's voice was soft yet strong enough to cut through the chatter. She could pretend she hadn't heard, but . . .

She backed into the classroom as Vasic stepped off the lecture platform and walked toward her.

"Did you enjoy the class?" he asked.

His voice was mild, no hint of mocking, but Talia's cheeks heated.

"It was very interesting, thank you."

"It can be, though it's never as interesting as some students hope. No satanic rituals. No demonic possession. No exorcisms."

Her face burned now.

"So how is young Adam?" he asked. "He looked quite happy the other day. Glad to miss an appointment, I'll bet. No doctors poking and prodding, asking questions, pestering him about his dreams, his thoughts, his feelings . . ."

"It's been difficult for him."

"I'm sure it has been." His eyes met hers. "For both of you." He paused. "May I buy you a coffee?"

Talia nodded, and let him lead the way.

They talked until their coffees went cold. Vasic asked questions, and Talia answered. It never felt like an interview, though. More like confession. Talia had never been to confession—she wasn't

Catholic—but she imagined this was what it would be like, talking to someone who seemed to have all the time in the world to listen and was genuinely interested in everything she had to say. With each scrap unloaded, the weight lifted.

She told him about Adam's father. All of it, most of which she'd never breathed to another soul. No matter how "liberated" you thought you were, there was shame in admitting you'd become pregnant at seventeen, in a one-night stand, and didn't even know the father's name.

But with Vasic, the confession came easily. He'd wanted to know everything about Adam's father, obviously looking for a genetic link, so she'd told him everything, right down to the silly fancies that ate at her brain—the images of fire, the heat of his touch. Vasic had seemed fascinated, pulling out every observation she'd made, until he seemed to cut himself short, dowsing his enthusiasm and forcing himself to move on.

One other topic had sparked that same excitement—her description of Adam's "abilities." That's what he called them, abilities not problems. He'd asked again how old Adam was. And when had this started? Had he burned anyone since the bully?

When they finished their coffees, Vasic leaned back in his chair as if digesting it all. His gaze flicked to the wall behind the counter. Talia followed it to a calendar that featured a photograph of a tornado. She'd seen Vasic notice it when they'd first walked in.

"First," he said as he tore his gaze back to Talia. "Let me reassure you. There is nothing wrong with Adam. He's not a 'budding pyromaniac' or any other label they've assigned. I've worked with cases like his before, children with behavioral anomalies that science can't explain. While his abilities may change as he grows, there is no cause for alarm. He will learn to manage them as we all learn to manage our special skills. That is where I can be of most assistance, Ms. Lyndsay. Helping you and Adam monitor and manage his skills."

Talia tensed. "How much is this—"

He cut her short with a small laugh. "My apologies if that sounded like a sales pitch. I'm an academic, Ms. Lyndsay, and I deal only in the currency of knowledge. Yes, I will keep notes on Adam for my research, but he will remain an anonymous subject, and I promise you that it will be strictly observational. I'll never subject him to any test or experiment for the sake of my work. My career is established. I'm not seeking to conduct groundbreaking studies, but simply to learn and to help others do the same."

"Learn about what? Does that mean you know what's—" She stopped, realizing she'd been about to say *what's wrong with Adam*. "You know what's happening with Adam? If you've seen this before—"

"If you're asking for a label, I can't provide one. I don't believe in them. What matters is that you have a very healthy, very special young boy and that none of that—his fascination with fire, his special abilities, those anomalies they found in his blood tests—is a cause for concern. We can continue to meet like this to monitor Adam's progress and make him comfortable with his skills."

She looked Vasic in the eye. "Do people buy that bullshit?"

He blinked and sat back.

"You said you've met other children like Adam. Do their parents fall for that? You pat them on the head, tell them everything is fine, and they go away happy?"

"A child's welfare is paramount—"

"I didn't need you to tell me that my son is fine. I *know* he is. What I want is an explanation. Not a label. An explanation."

"There's no need—"

"—to raise my voice? I've been searching for an answer for months, Doctor, and now you have it and you think you can just tell me everything is fine and I should be happy with that?" She paused, reining in her anger. "You said you wanted to meet Adam?"

Again, Vasic blinked, as if surprised by the change of tone and subject. Then he smiled and his eyes gleamed with barely contained enthusiasm. "Yes, certainly. I would very much like to meet him. He sounds . . . remarkable."

"He is." She took out her business card. "Here's my number. When you're willing to tell me what's going on, I'll bring him by your office."

She let the card flutter to the table, and strode from the coffee shop.

When a week passed with no word from Vasic, Talia began to second-guess herself. Maybe he hadn't been as interested in Adam as he'd seemed. Or maybe he really didn't know what was happening, only that he'd seen similar abilities before.

No, he *was* interested. There had been no mistaking the way his mild gaze had lit up when she'd asked whether he wanted to meet her son.

As for what was happening, he knew that, too. He wasn't just fishing with his questions, like the other doctors and specialists who'd randomly tossed out queries. He'd known exactly what to ask, including about Adam's father. *Especially* the questions about Adam's father. Nothing she'd said had shocked or surprised him . . . because he'd expected it.

After nine days with no call, Talia decided to light her own fire under Robert Vasic. First, she sent Adam to visit his great-great-aunt Peggy. Peg was like a second mother to Adam, and a fairy godmother to Talia. When Talia had been choosing colleges, her mother pushed her toward Berkeley, where her aunt Peg lived. Peg had offered to let Talia stay with her but had understood when Talia had wanted to try dorm life instead.

After Adam came, though, her aunt had been adamant that Talia would live with her. She would stay in school, while Peg—a retired schoolteacher—looked after Adam. When Talia had graduated, she hadn't left the area. After all Peg had done for them, Talia wasn't about to wrest her son away from the old woman.

Once Adam was at Aunt Peggy's, Talia made the call. Then she waited. Less than thirty minutes later, someone pounded at the front door. Didn't ring the bell or knock politely, but pounded. She opened it to see Vasic on her stoop, bareheaded in the rain, water streaming off his hair and beard, panting as if he'd run from the car and was unaccustomed to the exertion. Seeing him like that, she felt a little bad about what she'd done. But only a little, and only for a moment.

"Are you all right?" His eyes were dark with concern, and she felt another slight pang of remorse.

"I'm fine," she said.

As he searched her face, she knew she should try to seem more upset, even be crying, given what she'd told him on the phone. But making that call had drained her limited acting abilities.

"You should sit down," he said, taking her arm to guide her.

He thinks I'm in shock. She gently pulled from his grasp and led him to the kitchen.

"Where's Adam?" he asked.

"Staying at his aunt's."

A brief frown, as if surprised she wouldn't have him right there, at her side, after such a traumatic event.

"And the other boy?" he asked. "Is he all right? The burns . . . second-degree you said?"

She stared hard at Vasic. "Does that surprise you?"

He blinked.

"It doesn't, does it? You knew this could happen. These changes you mentioned, that's what you meant. That it would get worse. That he'd start inflicting real burns."

His gaze went to the patio doors. The rain beat against them, the harsh patter backlit by lightning and the rumble of distant thunder. "May we . . .?" He gestured at the doors. "Another room, perhaps. Less . . . distraction."

She took him into the living room. "You knew this could happen," she repeated before he could change the subject.

"Someday, yes. But not at this age. He's so young. I've never . . ." He took a deep breath. "I'm sorry, Ms. Lyndsay. That sounds inadequate, but I made an error in judgment, and I feel terrible about it. I knew Adam was displaying his pow— abilities at an early age, much younger than I usually see, but I misjudged the speed at which he could progress. I did intend to contact you, in a few months, after you'd had time to . . ."

"Calm down?" she said, crossing her arms. "Stop being such a demanding bitch?"

He flinched at her language.

She moved to the couch, subconsciously getting distance before letting loose the bomb. "Adam didn't burn anyone, Dr. Vasic. I just wanted to hear you admit that he could."

Vasic straightened sharply.

"You've just told me that my son could—will—someday be able to inflict serious damage with these 'abilities' of his. Now I think I have the right to know what's going on. If you refuse that, I can make things very unpleasant for you at Stanford—"

"There's no need to resort to threats, Ms. Lyndsay," Vasic said, his voice taking on an unexpected edge.

"I don't want to, but this is my son, and I need to know what he's going through."

He met her gaze. "What good will that do, Ms. Lyndsay? A label isn't going to give you a cure. There is none. It won't help you look after him and keep him safe, no better than you can do—and are doing—now. What will a label do for you? How will an explanation help?"

"It will help me understand my son."

"Will it?" His gaze bored into hers. "And what if this 'label' changed the way you saw Adam, changed your feelings for him?"

She met his gaze. "Not possible."

They argued for another hour. Three times Vasic said he was leaving. Once he got as far as the front stoop. But when Talia showed no signs of backing down and letting him help Adam without an explanation, he led her into the kitchen to stand by the patio doors.

For a minute, he just stared out at the storm. The look in his eyes sent a shiver down her spine. It was the same look Adam got when he stared into a fire.

"Do you like storms, Ms. Lyndsay?" Vasic asked softly.

"I . . . guess so. I'm not afraid of them, if that's what you mean."

"But they can be things to fear. Incredible power for destruction. Like fire. Beautiful from a distance, but devastating if uncontrolled. That's the key, to storms and fire. Control." He glanced over at her. "I can teach Adam to control his powers. As for the source of that power . . ." He looked her square in the eye. "I think you already know what it is; you're just too rational to believe it."

"I don't know what—"

"I'm talking about? Good. It's better that way. Safer. For you. There is absolutely no need for you to know the source of Adam's powers, Talia. You don't need to know that to help him. Knowing will change . . ." He looked back out the window. "Everything."

"I don't care."

He opened the patio doors and stepped outside. When he reached the far side of the plant-choked patio, he beckoned to her. She looked up at the rain.

"It's all right," he said. "Just step out."

She did, bracing for that first splash of rain. But it didn't come. She took another step. Still nothing. She made it to the middle of the porch and was still dry, while rain beat down all around her.

She looked up. There was nothing over her head. Nothing to shelter her. She turned toward Vasic.

"Put your hand out," he said softly.

She did, and felt the hard sting of the fast-falling rain against her palm. Then the rain softened, and turned cold. Ice-cold. Snow covered her hand. She stared at Vasic.

"Do you still want to know?" he asked.

"Yes."

"Then come inside and I'll tell you."

TWILIGHT

*A*nother life taken. Another year to live.

That is the bargain that rules our existence. We feed off blood, but for three hundred and sixty-four days a year, it is merely that: feeding. Yet before the anniversary of our rebirth as vampires, we must drain the lifeblood of one person. Fail and we begin the rapid descent into death.

As I sipped white wine on the outdoor patio, I watched the steady stream of passersby. Although there was a chill in the air—late autumn coming fast and sharp—the patio was crowded, no one willing to surrender the dream of summer quite yet. Leaves fluttering onto the tables were lauded as decorations. The scent of a distant wood fire was willfully mistaken for candles. The sun, almost gone despite the still-early hour, only added romance to the meal. All embellishments to the night, not signs of impending winter.

I sipped my wine and watched night fall. At the next table, a lone businessman eyed me. That was the sort of man I often had the misfortune to attract—middle-aged and prosperous, laboring under the delusion that success and wealth were such irresistible lures that he could allow his waist and jowls to thicken unchecked.

Under other circumstances, I might have returned the attention, let him lead me to some tawdry motel, then taken *my* dinner. He would survive, of course, waking weakened and blaming it on too much wine. A meal without guilt. Any man who took such a chance with a stranger—particularly when he bore a wedding band— deserved an occasional bout of morning-after discomfort.

He did not, however, deserve to serve as my annual kill. Yet I found myself toying with the idea more than I should have, prodded by a niggling voice that told me I was already late.

I stared at the glow over the horizon. The sun had set on the anniversary of my rebirth, and I hadn't taken a life. While I would hardly explode into dust at midnight, I would weaken as I began the descent into death. I could avoid that simply by fulfilling my bargain.

I measured the darkness, deemed it enough for hunting, then laid a twenty on the table and left.

A bell tolled ten. Two hours left. I chastised myself for being so dramatic. I loathe vampires given to theatrics—those who have read too many horror novels and labor under the delusion that's how they're supposed to behave. I despise any sign of it in myself, and yet, under the circumstances, perhaps it could be forgiven.

In all the years that came before this, I had never reached this date without fulfilling my obligation. I had chosen this vampiric life and would not risk losing it through carelessness.

Only once had I ever come close to my rebirth day without fulfilling the bargain, and then due to circumstances beyond my control. It had been 1867 . . . or perhaps 1869. I'd been hunting for my annual victim when I'd found myself tossed into a Hungarian prison.

I hadn't been caught at my kill—I'd never made so amateurish a mistake even when I'd been an amateur. The prison sojourn had been Aaron's fault, as such things usually were. We'd been hunting my victim when he'd come across a nobleman whipping a servant in the street. Naturally, Aaron couldn't ignore such an injustice. In the ensuing brawl, I'd been rousted with him and thrown into a pest-infested cell that wouldn't pass any modern health code.

Aaron had worked himself into a full-frothing frenzy, seeing my rebirth anniversary only days away while I languished in prison, waiting for justice that seemed unlikely to come swiftly. I hadn't been concerned. When one partakes of Aaron's company, one learns to expect such inconveniences. While he plotted, schemed, and swore he'd get us out in time, I simply waited.

We were released the day before my rebirth anniversary. I compensated for the trouble and delay by taking the life of a prison guard who'd enjoyed his work far more than was necessary.

This year, my only excuse was that I hadn't gotten around to it. As for why, I was somewhat . . . baffled. I am nothing if not conscientious about my obligations. Yet I'd been content to watch the days slip past and tell myself I would get around to it, as if it was no more momentous than a missed salon appointment. Even now, it was only an oddly cerebral concern. No matter. I would take care of it tonight.

As I walked, an old drunkard drew my gaze. I watched him totter into the shadows of an alley and thought, *There's a possibility* . . . I am usually quite finicky—refusing to feed off sleeping vagrants— yet as my annual kill, this one might do.

Every vampire deals with our "bargain" in the way that best suits his temperament and capacity for guilt and remorse. I cull from the edges—the sick, the elderly, those already nearing their end. I do not fool myself into thinking this is a just choice. There's no way to know whether that cancer-wracked woman might have been on the brink of remission or if that elderly man had been enjoying his last days to the fullest. I make the choice because it is one I can live with.

This old drunkard would do. As I watched him, I felt the gnawing in the pit of my stomach, telling me I'd already waited too long. I should follow him into that alley and get this over with. I *wanted* to get it over with—there was no question of that, no possibility I was conflicted on this point. Other vampires may struggle with our bargain. I do not.

Yet even as I visualized myself trailing the drunk into the alley, my legs didn't follow through. I stood there, watching him disappear into the darkness. Then I moved on.

A block farther, a crowd poured from a movie theater. As it passed, its life force enveloped me. I wasn't hungry, yet I could still feel that tingle of anticipation. I could smell their blood, hear the rush of it through their veins. The scent and sound of life.

Twenty steps later and they were still passing, an endless stream of humanity disgorged by a packed theater. How many seats were inside? Three hundred, three fifty? As many years as had passed since my rebirth?

One life per year. It seemed so moderate a price . . . until you looked back and realized you could fill a movie theater with your victims. A sobering thought, even for one not inclined to dwell on such things. No matter. There wouldn't be hundreds more. Not from this vampire.

Contrary to legend, our gift of longevity comes with an expiration date. Mine was drawing near. I'd felt a growing disinterest in all around me, though for me, disinterest wasn't new. I'd long since learned to keep my distance from a world that changed while I didn't.

After some struggle with denial, I'd accepted that I had begun the decline toward death. But it would be slow, and I still had years left, decades even. Or I would, if I could get past this silly bout of ennui and make my rebirth kill.

As the crowd dwindled, I watched them go and considered taking a life from them. A random kill. I'd done it once before, during a particularly bleak time when I hadn't been able to rouse enough feeling to care. Yet later I'd regretted it, having let myself indulge my darkest inclinations simply because I'd been in a dark place myself. Unacceptable. I wouldn't do it again.

I wrenched my gaze from the dispersing crowd. This was

ridiculous. I was no angst-ridden cinema vampire, bemoaning the choice she'd made in life. I was no flighty youngster, easily distracted from duty, abhorring responsibility. I was Cassandra DuCharme, senior vampire delegate to the interracial council. If any vampire had come to me with this problem—"I'm having trouble making my annual kill"—I'd have shown her the sharp side of my tongue, hauled her into the alley with that drunk, and told her, as Aaron might say, to "piss or get off the pot."

I turned around and headed back to the alley.

I'd gone only a few steps when I picked up a sense of the drunkard and excitement swept through me. I smiled. That was more like it.

The quickening accelerated as I slid into the shadows. My stride smoothed out, each step taken with care, rolling heel to toe, making no sound.

I spotted a recessed emergency exit a dozen feet ahead. A shoe protruded from the darkness. I crept forward until I spotted a dark form crumpled inside.

The rush of his blood vibrated through the air. My canines lengthened and I allowed myself one shudder of anticipation, then shook it off and focused on the sound of his breathing.

A gust whipped along the alley, scattering candy wrappers and leaflets, and the stink of alcohol washed over me. I caught the extra notes in his breathing—the deep, almost determined rhythm. Passed out drunk. He'd probably stumbled into the first semi-sheltered place he'd seen and collapsed.

That would make it easier.

So what was I waiting for? I should be in that doorway already, reveling in the luck of finding so easy a victim.

I shook the lead from my bones and crossed the alley.

The drunkard wore an army jacket, a real one if I was any judge. I resisted the fanciful urge to speculate, to imagine him as some shell-shocked soldier turned to drink by the horrors of war. More likely, he'd bought the jacket at a thrift shop.

His hair was matted, so filthy it was impossible to tell the original color. Above the scraggly beard, though, his face was unlined. Younger than I'd first imagined. Significantly younger.

That gave me pause, but while he was not the old drunkard I'd first imagined, he was certainly no healthy young man. I could sense disease and wasting, most likely cirrhosis. Not my ideal target, but he would do.

And yet . . .

Almost before I realized it, I was striding toward the road.

He wasn't right. If I made the wrong choice, I'd regret it. Better to let the pressure of this ominous date pass and find a better choice tomorrow. I headed for the park.

I stepped off the path. The ground was hard, so I could walk swiftly and silently.

My exit startled two young men huddled together. Their gazes tripped over me, eyes glittering under the shadows of their hoods, like jackals spotting easy prey. I met the stronger one's gaze. He broke first, grumbling deep in his throat. Then he shuffled back and waved his friend away as he muttered some excuse for moving on.

I watched them go, considering . . . then dismissing.

It was easy to separate one victim from a group. Not nearly so simple when the "group" consisted of only two people. As the young men disappeared into the shadows, I resumed my silent trek across the park.

My goal lay twenty paces away. He'd ignored a park bench under the light and instead had stretched out on top of a raised garden, hidden under the bushes and amidst the dying flowers.

He lay on his back with his eyes closed. His face was peaceful, relaxed. A handsome face, broad and tanned. He had thick blond hair and the healthy vitality of a young man in his prime. A big man, too, tall and solid, his muscular arms crossed behind his head, his slim hips and long denim-clad legs ending in work boots crossed at the ankles.

I circled north to sneak up behind his head. He lay completely motionless, even his chest was still, not rising and falling with the slow rhythm of breathing. I crossed the last few feet between us and stopped just behind his head. Then I leaned over.

His eyes opened. Deep brown eyes, the color of rich earth. He snarled a yawn.

"'Bout time, Cass," Aaron said. "Couple of punks been circling to see if I'm still conscious. Another few minutes and I'd have had to teach them to let sleeping vamps lie."

"Shall I go away, then? Let you have your fun?"

"Nah. They come back? We can both have fun." He heaved his legs over the side of the garden wall and sat up, shaking off sleep. Then, catching a glimpse of my face, his grin dropped into a frown. "You didn't do it, did you?"

"I couldn't find anyone."

"Couldn't find—?" He pushed to his feet, towering over me. "Goddamn it, what are you playing at? First you let it go until the last minute, then you 'can't find anyone'?"

I checked my watch. "It's not the last minute. I still have ten left. I trust that if I explode at midnight, you'll be kind enough to sweep up the bits. I would like to be scattered over the Atlantic, but if you're pressed for time, the river will do."

He glowered at me. "A hundred and twenty years together, and you never got within a week of your rebirth day without making your kill."

"Hungary. 1867."

"Sixty-eight. And I don't see any bars this time. So what's your excuse?"

"Among others, I was busy researching that council matter Paige brought to my attention. I admit I let things creep up on me this year, and a century ago that would never have happened, but while we were apart I changed—"

"Bullshit. You never change. Except to get more impervious, more pigheaded, and more cranky."

I started down the path. He muttered a few more descriptors behind me.

"You'd better be going off to find someone," he called after me.

"No, I'm heading home to bed. I'm tired."

"Tired?" He strode up beside me. "You don't get tired. You're—"

He stopped, mouth closing so fast his teeth clicked.

"The word is 'dying,'" I said. "And while that is true, and it is equally true that my recent inability to sleep is a symptom of that, tonight I am, indeed, tired."

"Because you're late for your kill. You can't pull this shit, Cassandra, not in your condition."

I gave an unladylike snort and kept walking.

His fingers closed around my arm. "Let's go find those punks. Have some fun." A broad, boyish grin. "I think one has a gun. Been a long time since I got shot."

"Another day."

"A hunt, then."

"I'm not hungry."

"Well, I am. Yeah, I know you wanted to do this alone. That's why I agreed to wait in the park. But you couldn't find someone suitable, so let me help. I know what you look for. We'll hunt together. I'll get a snack; you'll get another year. Fair enough?"

He tried to grin, but I could see a hint of panic behind his eyes. I felt an answering prickle of worry, but told myself I was being ridiculous. I'd simply had too much on my mind lately. I'd snap out of this embarrassing lethargy and make this kill. Soon.

"It's not the end of the world—or *my* world—if I don't take a life tonight, Aaron. You've been late yourself, when you couldn't find someone suitable. I haven't—and perhaps I'd simply like to know what that's like." I touched his arm. "At my age, new experiences are few and far between. I take them where I can."

He hesitated, then nodded, and accompanied me from the park.

Aaron followed me home. That wasn't nearly as exciting a prospect as it sounds. These days we were only friends. His choice.

When I first met Aaron, less than a year after his rebirth, he'd accused me of helping him in his new life because he looked like something to "decorate my bed with." True enough. Even as a human, I had never been able to muster more than a passing interest in men of my own social class. Too well mannered, too gently spoken, too *soft*. My tastes had run to stable boys and, later, to workingmen.

When I'd encountered Aaron as a newly reborn vampire—a big strapping farm boy with hands as rough as his manners—I will admit that my first thought was indeed carnal. He was younger than I liked, but I'd decided I could live with that.

So I'd trained him in the life of a vampire. In return, I'd received friendship, protection . . . and endless nights alone, frustrated beyond reason. It was preposterous, of course. I'd never had any trouble leading men to my bed, and there I was, reduced to chasing a virile young man who strung me along as if he were some coy maiden. I told myself it wasn't his fault—he was English. Thankfully, when he finally capitulated, I discovered he wasn't nearly as repressed as I'd feared.

Over a hundred years together. It was no grand romance. The word "love" never passed between us. We were partners in every sense—best friends, hunting allies, and faithful lovers. Then came the morning I woke, looked over at him, imagined *not* seeing him there, and went cold at the thought.

When you've lost everyone, you learn the danger of attachments. As a vampire, you must accept that every person you ever know will die, and you are the only constant in your life, the only person you can—and should—rely on. So I made a decision.

I betrayed Aaron. Not with another man. Had I done that, he'd simply have flown into a rage and, once past it, demanded to know what was really bothering me. What I did instead was a deeper betrayal, one that said, more coldly than I could ever speak the words, "I don't want you anymore." We'd ended up on the wrong side of an angry mob looking for a vampire and I'd given them Aaron. I'd let them take him and then I'd walked away and left him.

After over half a century apart, happenstance had brought us together again. We'd resisted the pull of that past bond, reminded ourselves of what had happened the last time, and yet, gradually, we'd drifted back into friendship. Only friendship. Sex was not allowed—Aaron's way of keeping his distance. Given the choice between having him as a friend and not having him in my life at all, I'd gladly choose the former . . . though that didn't keep me from hoping to change his mind.

That night, I slept. It was the first time I'd done more than cat-napped in over a year. While I longed to seize on this as some sign that I wasn't dying, I knew Aaron's assessment was far more likely—I was tired because I'd missed my annual kill.

Was this what happened, then, when we didn't hold up our end of the bargain? An increasing lethargy that would lead to death? I shook it off. I had no intention of exploring the phenomenon further. Come sunset, I would end this foolishness and take a life.

⁜

As I entered my living room that morning, I heard a dull slapping from the open patio doors. Aaron was in the yard, building a new retaining wall for my garden.

When he'd been here in the spring, he'd commented on the crumbling wall and said, "I could fix that for you." I'd nodded and said, "Yes, I suppose you could." Three more intervening visits. Three more hints about the wall. Yet I refused to ask for his help. I had lost that right when I betrayed him. So yesterday, he'd shown up on my doorstep, masonry tools in one hand, duffel bag in the other, and announced he was building a new wall for my rebirth day.

Had he simply decided my rebirth day made a good excuse? Or was there more than that? I watched Aaron through the patio doors. The breeze was chilly but the sun beat down, and he had his shirt off as he worked, oblivious to all around him. This was what he did for a living—masonry, the latest in a string of "careers." I chided him that, after two hundred years, one should have a healthy retirement savings plan. He only pointed the finger back at me, declaring that I also worked when I didn't need to. But I was self-employed, and selling art and antiques was certainly not in the same category as the physically demanding jobs he undertook. Yet another matter on which we disagreed—with vigor and enthusiasm.

I watched him for another minute, then headed for the kitchen to make him an iced tea.

I went out later to check a new shipment at an antique shop. When I got home, Aaron was sitting on the couch, a pile of newspapers on the table and one spread in his hands.

"I hope you didn't take those from my trash."

"I wouldn't have had to dig in your garbage if you'd recycle." He peered around the side of the paper. "That blue box in the garage? It's not for garden tools."

I waved him off. "Three hundred and fifty years and I have never been deprived of a newspaper or book for lack of paper in the world. I'm not going to start recycling now. I'm too old."

"Too stubborn." He gave a sly grin. "Or too lazy."

He earned a glare for that one. I walked over and snatched up a stray paper from the carpet before it stained.

"If you're that desperate for reading material, just tell me and I'll walk to the store and buy you a magazine."

He folded the paper and laid it on the coffee table, then patted the spot next to him. I hesitated, sensing trouble, and took a place at the opposite end of the couch. He reached over, his hand going around my waist, and dragged me over until I was sitting against him.

"Remember when we met, Cass?"

"Vaguely."

He laughed. "Your memory isn't *that* bad. Remember what you did for me? My first rebirth day was coming, and I'd decided I wasn't doing it. You found me a victim, a choice I could live with." With his free hand, he picked up a paper separated from the rest and dropped it onto my lap. "Found you a victim."

I sighed. "Aaron, I don't need you to—"

"Too late." He poked a calloused finger at the top article on the folded page. "Right there."

The week-old story told of a terminally ill patient fighting for the right to die. When I looked over at Aaron, he was grinning, pleased with himself.

"Perfect, isn't it?" he said. "Exactly what you look for. She wants to die. She's in pain."

"She's in a palliative care ward. How would I even get in there, let alone kill her?"

"Is that a challenge?" His arm tightened around my waist. "Because if it is, I'm up for it. You know I am."

He was still smiling, but behind it lurked a shadow of desperation. Again, his worry ignited mine. Perhaps this added incentive was exactly what I needed. It wouldn't be easy, but it could be interesting, particularly with Aaron's help.

Any other time, I'd have pounced on the idea, but now, even as I envisioned it, I felt only a spark of interest buried under an inexplicable layer of lethargy, even antipathy, and all I could think was, "Oh, but it would just be so much *work*."

My hackles rose at such indolence, but I squelched my indignation. I *was* determined to take a life tonight. I would allow nothing to stand in the way of that. Therefore, I could not enter into a plan that might prove too difficult. Better to keep this simple, so I would have no excuse for failure.

I laid the paper aside. "Are you hungry?"

A faint frown.

"Last night, you said you were hungry," I continued. "If you were telling the truth, then I presume you still need to feed, unless you slipped out last night."

"I didn't."

"Then we'll hunt tonight. But not"—a wave at the paper—"in a hospital."

It was almost dark, the sun only a red-tinged memory along the horizon. As I watched a flower seller clear her outdoor stock for the night, Aaron snapped his fingers.

"Flowers. That's what's missing in your house. You always have flowers."

"The last arrangement wilted early. I was going to pick up more when I was out today, but I didn't get the chance."

He seemed to cheer at that, as if reading some hidden message in my words.

"Here, then," he said. "I'll get some for you now."

I arched my brows. "And carry bouquets on a hunt?"

"Think I can't? Sounds like a challenge."

I smiled and laid my fingers on his forearm. "We'll get some tomorrow."

He took my hand and looped it through his arm as we resumed walking.

"We're going to Paris this spring," he said after a moment.

"Are we? Dare I ask what prompted that?"

"Flowers. Spring. Paris."

"Ah. A thoughtful gesture, but Paris in the spring is highly overrated. And overpriced."

"Too bad. I'm taking you. I'll book the time off when I get home, and call you with the dates."

When I didn't argue, he glanced over at me, then grinned and quickened his pace.

We bickered over the choice of victim. Aaron wanted to find one to suit my preference, but I insisted we select his type. Finally, he capitulated.

The disagreement dampened the evening's mood, but only temporarily. Once Aaron found a target, he forgot everything else.

In the early years, Aaron had struggled with vampiric life. He'd died rescuing a stranger from a petty thug. And his reward? After a life spent thinking of others, he'd been reborn as one who fed off them. Ironic and cruel.

Yet we'd found a way for him to justify—even relish—the harder facts of our survival. He fed from the dregs of society, punks and criminals like those youths in the park. For his annual kill, he condemned those whose crimes he deemed worthy of the harshest punishment. And so he could feel he did some good in this parasitic life.

As he said, I'd found his first victim. Now, two hundred years later, he no longer scoured newspapers or tracked down rumors, but seemed able to locate victims by intuition alone, as I could find the dying. The predatory instinct will adapt to anything that ensures the survival of the host.

Tonight's choice was a drug dealer with feral eyes and a quick switchblade. We watched from the shadows as the man threatened a young runner. Aaron rocked on the balls of his feet, his gaze fixed on that waving knife, but I laid my hand on his arm. As the runner loped toward the street, Aaron's lips curved, happy to see him go, but even happier with what the boy's safe departure portended—not a quick intervention but a true hunt.

We tracked the man for over an hour before Aaron's hunger won out. With no small amount of regret, he stopped toying with his dinner and I lured the drug dealer into an alleyway. An easy maneuver, as such things usually were with men like this—too greedy and cocksure to feel threatened by a middle-aged woman.

As Aaron's fangs sank into the drug dealer's throat, the man's eyes bugged, unable to believe what was happening. This was the most dangerous point of feeding—that split second where they felt our fangs and felt a nightmare come to life. The sedative in our saliva takes hold and when they pass out, those last few seconds are wiped from memory.

The man lashed out once, then slumped in Aaron's grasp. Still gripping the man's shirtfront, Aaron began to drink, gulping the blood. His eyes were closed, face rapturous, and I watched him, enjoying the sight of his pleasure, his appetite.

He'd been hungrier than he'd let on. Typical for Aaron, waiting that extra day or two, not to practice control or avoid feeding, but to drink heartily. Delayed gratification for heightened pleasure. I shivered.

"Cass?"

He licked a fallen drop from the corner of his mouth as he held the man out for me.

This was how Aaron liked to hunt: sharing victims. He always made the disabling bite, drank some, then let me feed to satiation. If I took too much for him to continue feeding safely, he'd find a second victim. There was no sense arguing that I could find my own food—he knew that but was compelled by a need to protect and provide.

"You go on," I said softly. "You're still hungry."

He thrust the man to me. "Yours."

His jaw set, and I knew his insistence had nothing to do with providing sustenance.

As Aaron held the man up for me, I moved forward. My canines lengthened, and I allowed myself a shudder of anticipation.

I lowered my mouth to the man's throat, scraped my canines over the skin, tasting, preparing. Then, with one swift bite, my mouth filled with—

I jerked back, almost choking. I resisted the urge to spit, and forced—with effort—the mouthful down, my stomach revolting in disgust.

It tasted like . . . blood.

When I became a vampire, I thought this would be the most unbearable part: drinking blood. But the moment that first drop had touched my tongue, I'd realized my worries had been for naught. There was no word for the taste; no human memory that came close. I can only say that it was so perfect a food that I could never tire of it nor wish for something else.

Before I'd completed the transition to vampire, I'd filled a goblet with cow's blood and forced it down, preparing for my new life. I could still taste the thick, metallic fluid that had coated my mouth and tongue, then sat in my stomach for no more than a minute before returning the way it had gone down. Now, after only a mouthful of this man's blood, I had to clamp my mouth shut to keep from gagging. Aaron dropped the man and grabbed for me. I waved him aside.

"I swallowed wrong."

I rubbed my throat, lips curving in a moue of annoyance, then looked around, and found the man at my feet. I steeled myself and bent. Aaron crouched to lift the man for me, but I motioned him back and shielded my face, so he wouldn't see my reaction. Then I forced my mouth to the man's throat.

The bleeding had already stopped. I bit his neck again, my nails digging into my palms, eyes closed, letting the disgusting taste fill my mouth, then swallowing. Drink, swallow. Drink, swallow. My nails broke my skin, but I felt no pain. I wished I could, if only to give me something else to think about.

It wasn't only the taste. That I could struggle past. But my whole body rebelled at the very sensation of the blood filling my stomach, screaming at me to stop, as if what I was doing was unnatural, even dangerous.

I managed one last swallow. And then . . . I couldn't. I simply couldn't. I hung there, fangs still in the man's neck, willing myself to suck, to fill my mouth, to finish this, mentally screaming, raging against the preposterousness of it. I was a vampire; I drank blood. And even if I didn't want to, by God, I would force every drop down my throat—

My stomach heaved. I swallowed hard.

I could sense Aaron behind me. Hovering. Watching. Worrying.

Another heave. If I took one more sip, I'd vomit and give Aaron reason to worry, to panic, and give *myself* reason to panic.

It was the victim's fault. God only knew what poisons this drug dealer had swimming through his veins, and while such things don't affect vampires, I am a delicate feeder. I've gone hungry rather than drink anything that tastes "off." There was no sense asking Aaron to confirm it—he could swill week-old blood and not notice.

I sealed the wound with my tongue and stepped back.

"Cass . . ." Aaron's voice was low with warning. "You need to finish him."

"I—"

The word "can't" rose to my lips, but I swallowed it back. I couldn't say that. Wouldn't.

"He isn't right," I said, then headed down the alley.

After a moment, I heard Aaron throw the unconscious man into a heap of trash bags and storm off in the opposite direction.

Any other man would have thrown up his hands and left me there. I arrived at my car to find Aaron waiting by the driver's door. I handed him the keys and got in the passenger's side.

At home, as I headed toward my bedroom, Aaron called after me. "I hope you're not going to tell me you're tired again."

"No, I'm taking a bath to scrub off the filth of that alley. Then, if you aren't ready to retire, we could have a glass of wine, perhaps light the fire. It's getting cool."

He paused, still ready for a fight, but finding no excuse in my words.

"I'll start the fire," he said.

No more than ten minutes after I got into the tub, the door banged open with such a crash that I started, sloshing bubbles over the side. Aaron barreled in and shoved a small book at me. My appointment book.

"I found this in your desk."

"Keen detective work. Practicing for your next council investigation?"

"*Our* next council investigation."

I reached for my loofah brush. "My mistake. That's what I meant."

"Is it?"

I looked up, trying to understand his meaning but seeing only rage in his eyes. He was determined to find out what had happened in that alley, and somehow this was his route there. My stomach clenched, as if the blood was still pooled in it, curdling. I wouldn't have this conversation. I wouldn't.

I sat up, letting the bubbles slide from me. Aaron's gaze dropped from my face. I tucked my legs under, took hold of the side of the tub, and started to rise. He let me get halfway up, then put his hand on my head and firmly pushed me down.

I reclined into the tub again, then leaned my head back, floating, breasts and belly peeking from the water. Aaron watched for a moment before tearing his gaze away with a growl.

"Stop that, Cass. I'm not going to run off and I'm not going to be distracted. I want to talk to you."

I sighed. "About my appointment book, I presume."

He lifted it. "Last week. On the day marked 'birthday.' Not your rebirth day, but the date you planned to make your kill. There's nothing else scheduled."

"Of course not. I keep that day open—"

"But you said you were busy. That's why you didn't do it."

"I said things came up."

"Such as . . . ?"

I raised a leg onto the rim and ran the loofah brush down it. Aaron's eyes followed, but after a second he forced his gaze back to mine and repeated the question.

I sighed. "Very well. Let's see. On that particular day, it was a midnight end-of-season designer clothing sale. As I was driving out of the city to make my kill, I saw the sign and stopped. By the time I left, it was too late to hunt."

He glowered at me. "That's not funny."

"I didn't say it was."

The glower deepened to a scowl. "You postponed your annual kill to *shop*? Bullshit. Yeah, you like your fancy clothes, and you're cheap as hell. But getting distracted by a clothing sale?" He snorted. "That's like a cop stopping a high-speed chase to grab doughnuts."

I went quiet, then said, as evenly as I could, "Perhaps. But I did."

He searched my gaze, finding the truth in my eyes. "Then something's wrong. Very wrong. And you know it."

I shuttered my gaze. "All I know is that you're making too big a deal of this, as always. You take the smallest—"

"Cassandra DuCharme skips her annual kill to go *shopping*? That's not small. That's apocalyptic."

"Oh, please, spare me the—"

He shoved the open book in my face. "Forget the sale. Explain the rest of it. You had nothing scheduled all week. There was no excuse. You didn't forget. You didn't get distracted." His voice dropped as he lowered himself to the edge of the tub. "You have no intention of taking a life."

"You . . . you think I'm trying to kill myself?" I laughed, the sound almost bitter. "Do you forget how I became what I am, Aaron? I *chose* it. I risked everything to get this life, and if you think I'd throw that away one minute before my time is up—"

"How you came into this life is exactly why you're hell-bent on leaving it like this. You cheated death. No, you *beat* it—by sheer goddamned force of will. You said, 'I won't die.' And now, when it's coming around again, you're damned well not going to sit back and let it happen. You chose once. You'll choose again."

I paused, looked away, then back at him. "Why are you here, Aaron?"

"I came to fix your wall—"

"At no prompting from me. No hints from me. You came of your own accord, correct?"

"Yeah, but—"

"If I'd planned to let myself die, that means you wouldn't have seen me again." I met his gaze. "Do you think I would do that? Of everyone I know in this world, would I leave you without saying good-bye?"

His jaw worked, but he said nothing. After a moment, he pushed to his feet and walked out.

⊹

I lay in bed, propped on my pillows, staring at the wall. Aaron was right. When the time came, I would leave this vampiric life as I'd come into it: by choice. But this was not that time. There was no doubt of that, no possibility that I was subconsciously trying to end my life.

When the time came, yes. But I would never be so irresponsible as to end my life before my affairs were in order. My estate would need to be disposed of in advance, given to those I wished to see benefit. Of equal concern was the discovery and disposal of my body. To leave that to chance would be unforgivably irresponsible.

I would make my peace with Aaron and make amends for my betrayal, or at the very least ensure he understood that the reason for it, the *failing* behind it, had been mine.

Then there was the council. Aaron was already my co-delegate, but I had to ready him to take my senior position and ready the vampire community to accept that change. Moreover, as the senior overall council member, it was my duty to pass on all I knew to Paige, as the keeper of records, something I'd been postponing, unwilling to accept that my time was ending.

Ending.

My stomach clenched at the thought.

I had never lacked for backbone and never stood for the lack of it in others. Now I needed to face and accept this reality. I was dying. Not beginning a lengthy descent, but at the end of the slope.

I now knew how a vampire died. A rebirth date came and we discovered, without warning, that we could not fulfill our end of the bargain. Not *would* not, but *could* not.

If I could not overcome this, I would die. Not in decades, but days.

Panic surged in me, coupled with an overwhelming wave of raw rage. Of all the ways to die, could any be more humiliating in its sublime ridiculousness? Not to die suddenly, existence snuffed out as my time ended. Not to die, beheaded, at the hands of an enemy. Not to grow ill and fade away. Not even to pass in my sleep. Such deaths couldn't be helped, and while I would have raged against that, the injustice of it, such a fate was nothing compared with this—to die because I inexplicably lacked the will to do something I'd done hundreds of times before.

That wasn't possible. I wouldn't *let* it be possible.

I would get out of this bed, find a victim, and force myself to drain his blood even if I vomited up every mouthful.

I envisioned myself standing, yanking on clothing, striding from the room . . .

Yet I didn't move.

My limbs felt leaden. Inside, I was spitting mad, snarling and cursing, but my body lay as still and calm as if I'd already passed.

I pushed down the burbling panic.

Consider the matter with care and logic. I should have taken Aaron's victim while I still had the strength, but now that I'd missed my opportunity, I couldn't chance waiting another day. I would rest for an hour or so, until Aaron had retired.

Better for him not to know. I wouldn't let him pity me, and coddle me simply because it was in his nature to help the sick, the weak, the needy. I would not be needy.

I'd stay awake and wait until the house grew quiet. Then I'd do this—alone.

I fixed my gaze on the light, staring at it to keep myself awake. Minutes ticked past. My eyes burned. My body begged for sleep. I refused. It threatened to pull me under even with my eyes open. I compromised. I'd close them for a moment's rest and then I'd leave.

I shut my eyes and all went dark.

⁜

I awoke to the smell of flowers. I usually had some in the house, so the smell came as no surprise, and I drowsily stretched, rested and refreshed.

Then I remembered I hadn't replaced my last flowers and I was seized by the sudden vision of my corpse lying on my bed, surrounded by funeral wreaths. I bolted upright and found myself staring in horror at a room of flowers . . . before realizing that the fact I was sitting upright would suggest I was not dead.

With a deep sigh, I looked around. Flowers did indeed fill my room. There were at least a dozen bouquets, each a riot of blooms, with no unifying theme of color, shape, or type.

My feet touched down on the cool hardwood as I crossed to a piece of paper propped against the nearest bouquet. An advertisement for flights to France. Beside another was a list of hotels. A picture of the Eiffel Tower adorned a third. Random images of Parisian travel littered the room, again with no obvious theme, simply pages hurriedly printed from websites. Typically Aaron. Making his point with all the finesse of a sledgehammer wielded with equal parts enthusiasm and determination.

Should I still fail to be swayed, he'd scrawled a note with letters two inches high, the paper thrust into a bouquet of roses. Paige had called. She needed my help. In smaller letters below, he informed me that today's paper carried another article on the palliative care patient who wanted to die.

I dressed, then tucked two of the pages into my pocket and slipped out the side door.

I didn't go to the hospital Aaron had suggested. It was too late for that. If I was having difficulty making this kill, I could not compound that by choosing one that would itself be difficult.

So I returned to the alley where I'd found—and dismissed—my first choice two nights ago. The drunkard wasn't there, of course.

No one was. So I traversed the maze of alleys and back roads in search of another victim. I couldn't wait for nightfall. I couldn't risk falling asleep again or I might not wake up.

When an exit door swung open, I darted into another doorway to avoid detection and spotted my victim. A woman, sitting in an alcove, surrounded by grocery bags stuffed with what looked like trash but which, I presumed, encompassed the sum of her worldly belongings. Behind me, whoever had opened that door tossed trash into the alley and slammed it shut again. The woman didn't move. She stared straight ahead, gaze vacant. Resting before someone told her to move on.

Even as I watched her, evaluated her, something deep in me threw up excuses. Not old enough. Not sick enough. Too dangerous a location. Too dangerous a time of day. Keep looking. Find someone better, someplace safer. But if I left here, left *her*, I would grow more tired, more distracted, and more uninterested with every passing hour.

She would do. She had to. For once, not a choice I could live with, but the choice that would let me live.

Unlike Aaron, I didn't like to let my victims see the specter of death approach, but today I had no choice. So I straightened and started toward her, as if it was perfectly natural for a well-dressed middle-aged woman to cut through alleyways.

Out of the corner of my eye, I saw her look up as I passed. She tensed, then relaxed, seeing no threat. I turned, as if just noticing her. Then, with a brisk nod, I took a twenty from my wallet.

A cruel ruse? Or making her last memory a pleasant one? Perhaps both. As expected, she smiled, her guard lowering even more. I reached down, but let go of the bill too soon. As it fluttered to the ground, I murmured an apology and bent as if to retrieve it, but she was already snatching it up. I kept bending, still apologizing . . . and sank my fangs into the back of her neck.

She gasped before the sedative took effect and then she fell forward. I tugged her into the alcove, propped her against the wall, and crouched beside her still form.

As my fangs pierced her jugular, I braced myself. The blood filled my mouth, as thick, hot, and horrible as the drug dealer's. My throat tried to seize up, rejecting it, but I swallowed hard. Another mouthful. Another swallow. Drink, swallow. Drink, swallow.

My stomach heaved. I pulled back from the woman, closed my eyes, lifted my chin, and swallowed the blood. Another heave, and my mouth filled, the taste too horrible to describe. I gritted my teeth and swallowed.

With every mouthful now, some came back up. I swallowed it again. Soon my whole body was shaking, my brain screaming that this wasn't right, that I was killing myself, drowning.

My stomach gave one violent heave, my throat refilling. I clamped my hand to my mouth, eyes squeezed shut as I forced myself to swallow the regurgitated blood.

Body shaking, I crouched over her again. I opened my eyes and saw the woman lying there. I couldn't do this. I couldn't—

One hand still pressed to my mouth, I tugged the pages from my pocket. I unfolded them and forced myself to look. Paige. The council. Paris. Aaron. I wasn't done yet. Soon . . . but not yet.

I squeezed my eyes shut, then slammed my fangs into the woman's throat and drank.

Her pulse started to fade. My stomach was convulsing now, body trembling so hard I could barely keep my mouth locked on her neck. Even as I pushed on, seeing the end in sight, I knew this wasn't success. I'd won only the first round of a match I was doomed to lose.

The last drops of blood filled my mouth. Her heart beat slower, and slower, then . . . stopped.

Another life taken. Another year to live.

STALKED

I had to get rid of the mutt.

Killing him would be easiest, but if Elena found out, she'd be pissed. Ten years from now, I'd still be hearing about it: "Clay couldn't even get through our honeymoon without killing someone."

She'd laugh when she said it . . . in ten years. Right now, she'd be furious.

She'd argue there were better ways to handle the situation. I disagreed. The mutt knew we were in St. Louis and that by sticking around, he was taking his life into his hands. If he'd skittered into the shadows and stayed out of our way, I'd have said, "Fuck it," and pretended not to notice. After all, it was my honeymoon.

Even if he'd just stood his ground and refused to hide, I wouldn't have made a big deal out of it. Beaten the crap out of him, yes. Had to. The Law was the Law, and it didn't matter if a mutt's instinct to protect his territory was as strong as any Pack wolf's. Let one mutt break the rules and next thing you knew, they'd be camping out back at Stonehaven, knocking on the door, asking if they could use the facilities.

But this mutt wasn't hiding or defending his territory. He was stalking Elena. He'd been following us all morning and was now sitting across the restaurant, gaze glued to Elena's ass as she bent over the buffet table.

When your mate is the only female werewolf, you get used to other wolves sniffing around. I'd spent the last eighteen years dealing with it or, more often, watching her deal with it. With Elena, interference is not appreciated. She can fight her own battles, and gets snippy if I rob her of the chance. But this was our honeymoon and damned if I was going to let this mutt spoil it. He had to be dealt with before Elena realized he was stalking her. The question was how.

When Elena walked back to the table, the mutt had the sense to busy himself gnawing on a sparerib.

"You okay?" she asked as she slid into her seat. "You've been quiet since the Arch."

She meant the Gateway Arch, one of St. Louis's tourist destinations, and where the mutt had started following us.

"Just hungry. I'm fine now."

"I should hope so. After three plates." She buttered her bread, then studied me. "Are you sure you're okay?"

"I don't know . . ." I pretended to ease back in my chair, then lunged and snagged bacon from her plate. I folded it into my mouth. "Nope, still hungry."

She brandished her fork. "Then get your own or—"

I snatched another slice, too slow this time, and she stabbed the back of my hand. I yelped.

"I warned you," she laughed.

The women at the next table stared in horror. Elena glanced their way. Five years ago, she would have blushed. Ten years ago, she would have found an excuse to leave. Today, she just murmured a rueful "Whoops" and dug into her potatoes.

I got another plate of food, avoiding the temptation to pass the mutt's table. He'd made a point of staying downwind outside and now sat partially obscured by a pillar, too far away for his scent to carry. For now, I'd let him think he was safe, undetected.

When I came back, Elena said, "I think I have an outing idea for us. Someone behind me in line was talking about a state park. Could be fun." Her blue eyes glittered. "Of course, we shouldn't go during the day when there are people around."

"Nope, we shouldn't." I speared a ham slab. "This afternoon, then?"

She grinned. "Perfect."

Planning our second run in as many days meant Elena was bored and trying very hard not to let me know it. When you're bored on your honeymoon, you know it's not going well.

The first couple of days had been great. With two-year-old twins at home, the only time we normally got away was when our Alpha, Jeremy, sent us to track down a misbehaving mutt. Being on a mission doesn't mean we can't enjoy ourselves. There's nothing like celebrating a successful hunt with sex. Or working out the frustration of a failed hunt with sex. Or dulling that edge of pre-hunt excitement with sex.

But there was also something to be said for skipping the whole "track, capture, and maim" part and being able to go straight to a hotel room and lock the door. Still, we could only stay in there for so long before we got restless, and when we came out, we'd discovered a problem with our honeymoon destination: there wasn't a helluva lot to do.

Back at the hotel, we called home and talked to the kids. Or they listened as we talked, and had their answers interpreted by Jeremy. As much as we loved our daily call, we spent most of it braced for the inevitable "Momma? Daddy? Home?" or in Kate's case: "Momma! Daddy! Home!" Jeremy managed to spare us this time, stopping as soon as Logan asked, "Momma where?" and bustling them off with his visiting girlfriend, Jaime.

Next, Jeremy and Elena would talk about the kids and discuss any new Pack or council business that had arisen. Normally, I'd listen in and offer my opinion—whether they wanted it or not—but today I told Elena I was going downstairs to grab a map and a bottle of water, and I took off.

⊹

While I was reasonably certain the mutt hadn't followed us from the restaurant, I wanted to scout to be absolutely sure. We'd walked to the Arch and then to the restaurant, meaning we'd had to walk back, which had given him the opportunity to follow. A cab would have solved that, but if I'd voluntarily offered to spend time trapped in a vehicle with a stranger, Elena would have been on the phone to Jeremy, panicked that the old wound in my arm was reinfected and I was sliding into delirium.

So I'd suggested we take the long route back. The mutt hadn't followed. Maybe he'd had second thoughts. If he'd heard the stories about me, he'd know he could be setting himself up for a long and painful death. But if he'd believed the stories, he should have hightailed it the moment he crossed our path. So while I hoped he was gone, I didn't trust he was.

I grabbed a brochure on state parks, stuffed it into my back pocket, then headed out the front door to circle the hotel. I got five steps before his scent hit me. I stopped to retie my sneaker and snuck a look around.

The bastard was right across the street. He sat on a bench facing the hotel, reading a newspaper. Cocky? Or just too young and inexperienced to know I could smell him from here?

I straightened and shielded my eyes, as if scanning the storefronts. When I turned his way, he very slowly lifted the paper to hide his face. Cocky. Shit.

Normally, I'm happy to show a young mutt how I earned my reputation. At that age, one good thrashing is all it takes. But damn it, this was my honeymoon.

I crossed the road and headed into the nearest service lane.

There were two ways the mutt could play this, depending on why he was stalking Elena. It could be his misguided way of challenging me. If that was his goal, he'd follow me down that service lane. Or he could *really* be after Elena. He wouldn't be the first mutt to think she might not object to a new mate.

I walked into the service lane then plastered myself against the wall, lost in its shadow, as I watched the hotel front door. After a few minutes, a car horn blasted and a figure darted between the heavy traffic. It was the mutt, heading straight for those doors.

I loped back down the service lane, circled around the block, then went in the hotel's side entrance. There he was, hovering near the check-in desk, sizing up the staff. Hoping to get our room number? Before I could step out, a pale blond ponytail bounced past on the other side of the lobby. Elena. I opened my mouth to hail her, then stopped. Better for her to keep walking and I'd catch up outside the front doors—

Shit. He'd walked *in* the front doors. His scent would still linger there, and Elena had a better sense of smell than any werewolf I knew. I started walking fast to cut her off. She caught sight of the brochure rack and veered that way.

"Elena!"

I yanked the park guide from my back pocket and waved it. I moved to the left, blocking her view of the mutt. While she couldn't smell him from that far away, she was in charge of the Pack's mutt dossiers and might recognize him.

"Got the maps," I said. "I was looking for water. I can't find a damn machine—"

She directed my attention to the gift shop.

"Shit. Okay, let's grab one and go."

Out of the corner of my eye, I saw the mutt watching us. Elena's gaze traveled across the lobby, as if sensing something. I took her elbow and wheeled her toward the gift shop.

She peeled my fingers from her arm. "I'm looking—"

"The gift shop's behind you."

"No kidding. I'm looking for the parking garage exit. I was going to say we can grab a drink on the way. It's too expensive here."

"Good. I mean, right. The stairs are back there, by the elevators."
She nodded and we headed that way.

The park wasn't busy, so avoiding humans was easy. That took some of the challenge out of a daytime run, but a new place to run is always good.

We spent most of the afternoon as wolves, exploring and playing, working up a sharp hunger for the hunt. We'd found a few deer trails, but all of our tearing around had scared the small herd into hiding. Probably just as well—in places like this, people pay attention to ripped-apart deer carcasses. We settled for rabbits—the fat, dull-witted sort you find in preserves with few natural predators.

The snack was enough to still the hunger pangs without making us sleepy, so we followed it with more games, these ones taking on an edge, the snarls sharper, the nips harder, fangs drawing blood, working up to the inevitable conclusion—a fast Change back and hard, raw sex that left us scratched and bruised, happy and drowsy, stretched on the forest floor, bodies apart, feet entwined.

I was on my back, shielding my eyes from the sun shifting through the trees, too lazy to move out of its way. Elena lay on her stomach as she watched an ant crawl across her open palm.

"What about a second stop for our honeymoon?" I asked.

Her nose scrunched in an unspoken *What?*

"Well, I know St. Louis isn't shaping up to be everything you'd hoped . . ."

"This afternoon was." She rubbed her foot against mine. "I'm having a good time, but if you're not . . ."

How the hell was I supposed to answer that? *No, darling, our honeymoon sucks. I'm bored, and I want to go somewhere else.*

If it had been true, I wouldn't have minded saying so, though I supposed, being a honeymoon, I'd have to phrase it more carefully.

Walking away from a threat set my teeth on edge but would be better than having this mutt ruin our honeymoon. Still, given the choice between staying and fighting this mutt or making Elena think I was having a shitty time, something told me option one was a whole lot safer.

"I'm fine," I said. "You just seemed a little . . . bored earlier."

Alarm brightened her eyes and she hurried to assure me she was having a good time. Which was a lie, and any other time she'd have had no problem saying she was bored. But a honeymoon was different. It was a ritual and, as such, came with rules, and admitting ours was boring broke them all.

Elena might squirm and chafe under the weight of human rules and expectations, but there was one aspect of them she embraced almost to the point of worship. Rituals. Like Christmas. Ask Elena to bring cookies for the parent-and-tot picnic and she'll buy them at the bakery, then dump them into a plastic container so they look homemade. But come mid-December, she'll whip herself into a frenzy of baking, loving every minute because that's part of Christmas.

When the subject of "making it official for the kids' sake" came up, I knew she'd want the ritual—a real wedding, the kind she'd dreamed of eighteen years ago when we'd bought the rings, her face alight with dreams of a white dress and a new life and happily ever after.

Instead of the happily ever after, she got a bite on the hand and the kind of new life that had once existed only in her nightmares.

I won't make excuses for what I did. The truth is that your whole life can change with one split-second decision and it doesn't matter if you told yourself you'd never do it, or if you stepped into that moment with no thought of doing it. All it takes is that one second of absolute panic when the solution shines right there in front of you, and you grab it . . . only to have it turn to ash in your hand. There is no excuse for what I did.

It took eleven years for her to forgive me. *Forgetting* what I'd done, though, was impossible. It was always there, lurking in the shadows of her memory.

When Elena vetoed a wedding, I thought it was just the weight of human mores again—that it didn't feel right when we already had kids. So I'd decided I'd give her one, as a surprise. Jeremy talked me out of it, and it was then, as he waffled and circled the subject of "why not," that I finally understood. There could be no wedding because every step—from sending invitations to walking down the aisle—would only remind her of the one she'd planned all those years ago, and the hell she'd gone through when it all fell apart.

But the honeymoon was one part of the ritual we hadn't discussed. So, if a wedding was out, the least I could do was give her a honeymoon.

So I'd planned everything. I'd picked St. Louis because she'd mentioned once that she'd like to go there. I'd made all the arrangements— my way of saying that I'd fucked up eighteen years ago and I was damned lucky we'd ever reached the stage where a honeymoon was even a possibility.

I gave her this honeymoon, and maybe it wasn't what she'd imagined, but at least I could make damned sure this mutt didn't ruin it completely.

The mutt resurfaced at dinner, spoiling my second meal in a day. Not just any meal this time, but a special one at a place so exclusive that I—well, Jeremy—had to reserve our table weeks ago. It was one of those restaurants where the lighting is so dim I don't know how humans can see what they're eating or *find* what they're eating—the tiny portions lost on a plate filled with inedible decorations. But it was romantic. At least, that's what the guidebook said.

I didn't know what was romantic about eating in the dark surrounded by strangers, but it matched Elena's expectations and that was all that mattered. She'd enjoy the fussy little portions, the fancy wines, the fawning waitstaff, then fill up on pizza in our room later. Which was fine by me . . . until the mutt showed up.

As I was returning from the bathroom, he stepped into the lobby to ask the maître d' for directions. Our eyes met. He smiled and sauntered back out.

I knew I should walk away. Take care of him later. But there was no way I could enjoy my dinner knowing he was prowling outside. And if I didn't enjoy it, Elena wouldn't enjoy it, and we'd get into a fight about why I'd take her someplace I'd hate only to sulk through the meal. I was determined to make it through this trip without any knockdown, drag-out fights . . . or at least not to cause any myself.

I waited until the maître d' escorted a couple into the dining room, then took off after the mutt.

I found him waiting for me in the lane behind the restaurant. He was leaning against the wall, arms crossed, eyes closed.

Who raises their kids like this? That was the problem with mutts. Not all mutts—I'll give them that. Some teach their sons basic survival, and a few do as good a job as any Pack wolf, but there are far too many who just don't give a damn. At least in a Pack, if your father doesn't teach you properly, someone else will.

Here stood a perfect example of poor mutt parenting skills—a kid stupid enough not only to challenge me but to feign confidence to the point of boredom, lowering his guard in hopes of looking "cool." Now I had to teach him a lesson, all because his father couldn't be bothered telling him I wasn't someone to fuck with.

Werewolves earn their reputations through endless challenges. Twenty-seven years ago, when I'd wanted to protect Jeremy on his rise to Alphahood, I didn't have time for those challenges. So I'd sealed my reputation with a single decisive act, one guaranteed to convince every mutt on the continent that this infamous child werewolf had grown into a raging lunatic. To get to Jeremy, they had to go through me, and after what I did, few dared try.

I could only hope this mutt just didn't realize whom he'd challenged, and once he did, a few abject apologies and a brief trouncing would set the matter straight and I could get back to my honeymoon.

I walked over and planted myself in front of him.

He opened his eyes, stretched, and faked a yawn. "Clayton Danvers, I presume?"

So much for that idea . . .

I studied him. After a moment, he straightened, shifting his weight and squirming like a freshman caught napping during my lectures.

"What?" he said.

I examined him head to foot, eyes narrowing.

"What?" he said again.

"I'm trying to figure out what you've got."

His broad face screwed up, lips pulling back, giving me a shot of breath that smelled like it'd never been introduced to mouthwash.

"So what is it?" I asked. "Cancer, hemorrhagic fever, rabies . . ."

"What the hell are you talking about?"

"You do have a fatal disease, right? You're about to die in horrible agony? 'Cause that's the only reason any mutt barely past his first Change would call me out. Looking for a quick end to an unbearable existence."

He let out a wheezing laugh. "Oh, that's a good one. Does that line usually work? Scare us off before you have to fight? Because *that's* the only reason a runt like you would have the reputation of a psycho killer."

He stepped closer, pulling himself up straight, just to prove, in case I hadn't noticed, that he had a good four inches and fifty pounds on me. Which did *not* make me a runt. I'd spent my childhood being small for my age, but I'd caught up to an average size.

Still, mutts like to point out that I'm not as big as my reputation, as if I've disappointed them.

"You do have a daddy, right?" I asked.

His face screwed up again. "What?"

"You have a father, don't you?"

"Is that some kind of Pack insult? Of course I have a father. Theo Cain. Maybe you've heard of him."

I knew the Cains. Killed one of them a few years ago in an uprising against the Pack. "And your daddy warned you about me? Told you about the pictures?"

"Pfft." He rolled his eyes. "Yeah, I've heard about those. Photos of some dude you carved up with a hatchet."

"Chainsaw."

"Whatever. It's bullshit."

I eased to the side, getting my nose away from his mouth. "And the witness? He's still alive, last I heard."

"Some guy you paid off."

"The pictures?"

"Photoshopped."

"It was almost thirty years ago."

"So?"

I shook my head. The problem with stupid people is you can't reason with them. Trying was a waste of my time, while my meal was getting cold and Elena was spending our romantic dinner alone.

Screw this.

I surveyed the dark service lane. There was never a convenient Dumpster when you needed one. I eyed the garbage cans, eyed Cain, sizing him up . . .

"So when do we fight?" he asked.

"What?"

"You know. Go mano a mano. Fight to the death. Your death, of course. I'm looking forward to enjoying the spoils." His tongue slid between his teeth. "Mmm. I gotta thing for blondes with tight little asses, and your girl is fine. Bet she'll fix up real nice."

"Fix up?"

"You know. Get some makeup on. Get rid of that ponytail. Trade the jeans for a nice miniskirt to show off those long legs. You gotta keep after chicks about things like that or they get comfortable, let it slide. Not that she isn't damned sweet right now, but with a little extra effort, she'd be hot."

I shook my head.

"What?" he said. "You've never tried?"

"Why would I?"

"Why *wouldn't* you?"

I opened my mouth, then shut it. Another waste of time. He wouldn't understand my point of view, no more than I understood his. "So you think if you kill me, you get Elena?"

"Sure, why not?"

"If it didn't require my death, I'd be tempted to go along with it, just to watch you tell her that."

"Whatever." He rolled on his heels. "Let's get this over with. I'm hoping you brought your chainsaw, 'cause otherwise this fight isn't going to be nearly as much fun as I was hoping, with your fucked-up arm and all."

I stopped, then slowly looked up, meeting his gaze. "My arm?"

"Yeah, Brian McKay said you busted his balls last year for having some sport with a whore. He said something was wrong with your arm. You kept using your other one. Tyler Lake says he did it, as payback for what you did to his brother."

"Yeah? Did he mention which arm it was? This one?"

I grabbed him by the throat and pinned him to the wall, hand tightening until his face purpled and his eyes bulged.

"Or was it this one?"

I slammed my fist into his jaw. Teeth and bone crackled. He tried to scream, but my hand against his windpipe stifled it to a whimper.

I dragged him down the wall until his face was level with mine, and leaned in, nose to nose. "I'd say that will teach you not to listen to rumors, but you're a bit thick, aren't you? I'm going to have to—"

A thump to my left stopped me short. The restaurant rear door swung open. We were behind it, a dozen feet away, out of sight. I held Cain still as I watched and listened, ready to drag him into the alley if a foot appeared under that door.

Garbage can lids clattered. The bins were right next to the door. No need to step outside. Just dump the trash—

Cain let out a high-pitched squeal—the loudest noise he could manage. Then he started banging at the boarded-up window beside him. I tightened my grip, my glower warning him to stop. A foot appeared under that door as someone stepped out. I dropped the mutt and dove around the corner.

"Hey! Hey, you there!"

I pressed up against the wall. Footsteps sounded. A man yelled at Cain, mistaking him for a drunk. The mutt mumbled something about being jumped, struggling to talk with a broken jaw.

I gritted my teeth. Ending a fight by alerting humans was bad enough. Trying to set them on my trail? That toppled into full-blown cowardice.

I shook it off and retreated before someone came looking for Cain's "mugger."

Back in the restaurant, I longed to visit the washroom and scrub Cain's stink off me. But I'd been gone too long already. So I grabbed a linen napkin from a wait station, dunked it into a glass of water, and carefully cleaned the blood from my hands as I strode through the dining room, then tossed the cloth onto an uncleared table.

Elena looked up from the last bites of her meal as I approached.

"Hey there," she said. "Thought you'd made a fast-food run on me."

"Nah." I took my suit coat from the chair and slipped it on, blocking the mutt's smell and covering the blood splatter. "Something didn't agree with me."

"Lunch, I bet. That's the thing about buffets—lots of food, none of it very good. So, is dessert out of the question?"

I shook my head. "Just give me a second to finish dinner."

Our hotel was a few blocks from the restaurant, so we'd walked. Heading back, I had to switch sides every time we turned a corner, staying downwind from Elena and keeping a foot's gap between us.

That worked only until we got to our room. She leaned against me as she pulled off her heels, then ran her hand up the back of my leg, grinning upside down, her hair fanning the floor. She swept it back as she stood, her hand sliding up my leg and into my back pocket.

"Pizza now?" she asked. "Or after we work up an appetite?"

I tugged her hand out, lacing my fingers with hers, elbow locked to keep her from getting close enough to smell Cain.

"Hold that thought," I said. "I'm going to grab a shower."

Her brows shot up. "Now?"

"That problem in the restaurant? I'm thinking it might be something I rolled in this afternoon. My leg's itching like mad. Let me scrub it off before I pass it along."

Her head tilted, the freckles across her nose bunching as she studied me, her bullshit meter wavering. Normal-Elena would have called me on it, but honeymoon-Elena wanted to avoid confrontation, so after a moment she shrugged.

"Take your time. I'll catch the news."

I ran my hands through my hair and lifted my face into the spray. My forearm throbbed as the hot water hit it. Tomorrow I'd pay for overworking the damaged muscle, but it was worth it if Cain took home proof that Clayton Danvers's arm was definitely *not* "fucked up."

For two years, I'd been careful in every fight, convinced no one would notice I was favoring my left. I should have known better. Like scavengers, mutts could sense weakness.

I squeezed the water from my hair as I moved out of the spray and looked down at the pitted rut of scar tissue. All these years of fighting without a permanent injury, and what finally does it? One little scratch from a rotting zombie. At the worst of the infection, I'd been in danger of losing my arm, so I couldn't complain about some muscle damage.

But if rumors were circulating, I had a problem. Was Theo Cain's son only the first in a new generation of mutts who'd heard the stories about me and fluffed them off as urban legends or, at least, ancient history?

I'd first cemented my reputation to protect Jeremy. Now I had fresh concerns—a mate, kids . . . and a fucked-up arm that was never going to get any better. So how was I going to convince a new generation of mutts that Clayton Danvers really was the raging psychopath their fathers warned them about?

I rubbed the facecloth over my chest, hard and brisk enough to burn. I didn't want to go through that shit again. What the hell would I do for an encore? What *could* I do that wouldn't have Elena bustling the twins off to a hotel while she reconsidered whether I was the guy she wanted raising her kids?

Elena understood why I'd taken a chainsaw to that mutt. If pressed, she might even grudgingly admit it had been a good idea. Anesthetic ensured the guy hadn't even suffered much—the point was only to make others think he had. Still, only in the last few years had she stopped twitching every time someone mentioned the photos. Admitting I might have been right didn't mean she wanted to *think* about what I'd done. And she sure as hell wouldn't want me doing it again.

I shut the taps and toweled off, scrubbing away any remaining trace of Cain.

As I got out, I could hear the television from the next room. The news wasn't over. Good. Elena would be engrossed in it, which meant I could have some fun distracting her, a sure way to clear my head of thoughts that didn't belong on a honeymoon.

I draped the towel around my shoulders, then eased open the door to get a peek at the playing field. Through the mirror, I could see the bed. An empty bed, the spread gathered and wrinkled where Elena had sprawled to watch the news.

A sportscaster was running through scores. Shit.

I tried to see the sitting area through the mirror, but the angle was wrong. It didn't matter. If she was finished with the news, I'd lost my chance to play. I gave my dripping hair one last swipe, tossed the towel on the bathroom floor, walked into the suite, and thumped onto the bed, springs squealing.

"All done. Still ready to work up that—?"

The room was empty.

I strode to the door, heart thudding as I sniffed for Cain. I knew my fears were unfounded. No way could he get Elena out of this room . . . not without blood spattered on the walls and carpet.

But what if he'd been lurking outside the door? If she'd heard him? She'd peeked out and he bolted? She'd give chase.

I opened the door and was crouching at the entrance when a yelp made me jump. Down the hall, a middle-aged woman stumbled back into her room, chirping to her husband. For a moment I thought, *Hell, I wasn't even sniffing the carpet yet.* Then I remembered I was naked.

I slammed the door and stalked into the bathroom for a towel. Humans and their screwed-up sensibilities. If that woman saw Elena dragged down the hall kicking and clawing, she'd tell herself it was none of her business. But God forbid she should catch a glimpse of a naked man. Probably on the phone to security right now.

Towel in place, I cracked open the door. When I was certain the hall was clear, I crouched to smell the carpet. No trace of Cain's scent. Holding the door open with my foot, I leaned into the hall for another sniff. Nothing.

Sloughing off the fear, I strode into the room to search for clues. The answer was right there, on the desk. A page ripped off the notepad, Elena's looping handwriting: *salty crab + no water = beverage run.*

Shit.

As I pulled on a T-shirt, I told myself Cain was long gone. I'd had him in a death hold before he could lay a finger on me. A sensible mutt would take it as a lesson in arrogance, swallow the humiliation, get out of town, and find a doctor to set his jaw before he was permanently disfigured. But a sensible mutt wouldn't have gotten himself into that scrape in the first place.

Cain would back off only long enough to pop painkillers. Then the humiliation would crystallize into rage. Too cowardly to come after me, he'd aim a sucker punch where he thought I was most vulnerable: Elena, who'd just strolled out alone into the night, having no idea that a mutt had been stalking her all day because I hadn't bothered to tell her.

Shit.

As I tugged on my jeans with one hand, I dialed Elena's cell phone with the other. Elena's dress, discarded on the chair, began to vibrate. Beneath it lay the purse she'd taken to dinner, open, where she'd grabbed her wallet, leaving the purse—and her cell phone—behind.

I grabbed my sneakers and raced out the door.

I didn't bother checking the gift shop. Elena had already decreed the water there too expensive. Jeremy and I might have had some lean times during my childhood, but Elena knew what it was like to wear three sweaters all winter because you couldn't afford a coat. Even if she could now afford to buy the whole damned gift shop, she wouldn't give them three bucks for water that cost half that down the block.

Normally, I respect that, but this was one time when I wished to hell she'd just spend the damned money.

I strode out the front doors, stopped, and inhaled. A couple glowered when they had to drop hands to walk around me. I scanned the road, sampling the air. Finally it came. Elena's faint scent on the wind. I hurried down the steps.

There was a convenience store on the corner, but Elena's trail crossed the road and headed down the very service lane where I'd waited for Cain that afternoon. What the hell was wrong with the shop on the corner? Was the water ten cents cheaper three blocks away? Goddamn it, Elena!

Even as I cursed her, I knew I was really angry with myself. I should have warned her about the mutt. If I'd honestly believed I could keep her in my sights twenty-four hours a day, then I was deluded. The late hour wouldn't stop Elena from running out for water. She was a werewolf; she didn't need to worry about muggers and rapists. But a pissed-off mutt twice her size?

I broke into a jog.

The moment I stepped into the alley, I smelled him. He must have been lying in wait outside the hotel, formulating a plan. Then his quarry had sailed out the front doors . . . and waltzed straight into the nearest dark laneway.

By the time he got over the shock at his good fortune, he'd lost his chance to catch her in the lane. She'd exited, walked a block, then . . . cut through an alley.

Goddamn it!

I raced to the alley and then pulled up short. Cain stood at the far end, his back to me, gaze fixed on Elena across the road.

I circled to the next road, hoping to cut him off. The streets and sidewalks were empty. Our hotel was in the business section of town. That had looked good when I'd picked it online—surrounded by restaurants and other conveniences. But we arrived to discover those conveniences weren't nearly so convenient when they closed at five, as the offices emptied.

When I peeked around the corner, I saw yet another quiet street, vacant except for a lone shopper gazing at the display of a closed clothing store. I had to do a double take to make sure it was Elena. It certainly looked like her—a tall, slender woman in jeans and sneakers, her pale blond hair hanging loose down the back of her denim jacket. But window-shopping? At a display of women's business clothes? This honeymoon was boring her even more than I'd feared.

As she studied the display, her gaze kept sliding to the right. I squinted to see what was drawing her attention, but the streetlights turned the glass into a mirror, reflecting . . . reflecting Cain.

She knew he was there. I exhaled in relief. The sound couldn't have been loud enough for Elena to hear, but she went still, then pivoted just enough to see me. She jerked her attention back to the window and motioned, palm out, for me to stay put.

A quick sequence of charade moves warned me there was a mutt in that alley, but she would handle it and I could settle into backup mode. Then, mid-motion, she stopped and gave a slow smile, her teeth glinting in the darkness. Seeing that smile, I knew what she was thinking before she glanced over, her lips forming the word.

"Play?"

My grin answered.

No game is fair—or much fun—when one of the parties doesn't realize he's playing. So Elena started by drumming her fingers against her leg, her head twisting his way, a subtle hint that she knew Cain was there and was growing impatient waiting for his next move.

She glanced over her right shoulder, hair sweeping back as her face tilted his way, and I didn't need to see her expression. I'd seen it often enough. Lips parted, eyes glittering beneath arched brows, a look that translated, in human or wolf, into: "Well, are you going to come get me or not?"

Cain slingshot from the alley so fast he stumbled. Elena laughed, a husky growl that made me lock my knees to keep from answering it myself. She took off, hair flashing behind her.

Cain teetered on the curb and stared after her in confusion and disappointment, the human telling him that a woman running in the other direction wasn't a good sign. She stopped at the next corner and turned to face him.

He stepped off the curb. She took a slow stride back. Another forward, another back, and it wasn't until the dance had gone on for nearly ten paces that the wolf instinct finally clicked on and he realized that, to her, running away meant not "I'm trying to escape" but "Catch me if you can."

His broad face split into a grin. He winced, slapping a hand to his broken jaw. When he looked up, Elena was gone. One panicked glance around, then he broke into a run.

Had Elena been a wolf playing this mating ritual for real, she'd have ditched Cain after five minutes, deciding he either wasn't interested enough or wasn't competent enough to track her, and either way wasn't worthy of her attention.

He kept losing her trail and backtracking. Or he'd glimpse a pedestrian down another road and take off that way before his nose told him it wasn't her. Without a Pack, a werewolf grows up immersed in human society, not trusting his wolf instincts, not knowing what to do with them. Cain seemed to be running on pure lust and enthusiasm, which, while amusing, wasn't much of a challenge . . . or much fun.

After he backtracked over my trail twice—luckily not noticing— Elena decided it was time to take this game to the next level before Cain realized there was a third player. She led him to a park down by the river and then darted into a cluster of shrubs to Change. Cain caught up quickly. After a few seconds of trying unsuccessfully to see her naked through the bushes, he tore off to find a Changing spot of his own.

I guarded Elena until I heard Cain's first grunt, assuring me he wasn't about to change his mind. Then I ducked into a hiding place and undressed.

When I came out, Elena was already lying in the shadows, tail flicking against the ground, eager to be off. Seeing me a dozen feet away, she let out a soft chuff, her blue eyes rolling, saying, "Settle in—this could take a while."

I was looking around when Cain's bushes erupted in a flurry of rustling, punctuated by very human grunts. He'd barely begun.

Elena's head slumped forward, muzzle resting on her forelegs as a sigh rippled through her flanks. I growled a laugh and loped off to set up the playing field.

I lay on a flat rock overlooking the path, my nose twitching as the river scents wafted past, making me salivate at the smell of fish. I hooked my forepaws over the rock and stretched, my back arching, nails extending, foot pads scraping against the rough, broken edge. I'd been waiting awhile, and I could feel the ache in my muscles, urging me to get up, get moving, get running.

I stretched again and peered over the edge. The perfect launch-pad. Elena would lead Cain along the path and, with one leap, I'd have my workout. The chase, the hunt, the takedown—all more satisfying than the actual fight.

A low whine cut through the still night. I lifted my head, ears swiveling as they tracked the sound to a brown wolf a hundred feet away. Cain, whining for Elena, probably worried she'd given up and taken off.

After a moment, she appeared, a pale wraith sliding silently from the shadows. Cain let out a sharper whine and danced in place like a domestic dog seeing his master come home.

Elena continued toward him, taking her time, tail down, head high. She stopped about six feet away, making him come to her, gaze straight ahead, a queen granting her subject permission to approach.

Cain paced, keeping his distance. Her body language was per-fectly clear—she was establishing hierarchy—but he didn't know what to make of it, and kept pacing.

When he didn't accept the invitation to approach and sniff her, Elena started turning away. Again, clear wolf behavior, not snub-bing him, just coquettishly saying, "Well, if you aren't interested . . ."

Cain went still. As she presented him with her flank, his head lowered, hackles rising. I leapt to my feet, nails scrabbling against the rock, a warning bark in my throat, but before it could escape, he sprang.

Cain grabbed Elena's shoulder, his teeth sinking in as he whipped her off her feet. I raced down the slope as he threw her in the air. She hit the ground, spun, and dove at him, her snarls slicing through the night. Cain let out a yelp of surprise and pain as she ripped into him.

I stood there, ears forward, eyes straining, sight now the most critical sense as I watched and evaluated.

They continued to fight, a rolling ball of growls and fur and blood. I could smell that blood, his and hers, the latter making a whimper shudder up from my gut. I shook it off and locked my legs, standing my ground.

Finally, Elena backed away, snarling, her head down, hackles up. Cain scrambled to his feet, shaking his head, blood splattering. As he recovered, Elena glanced in my direction.

My muscles coiled and uncoiled as I danced in place, my gaze fixed on him, twice her size, too much for her to handle if she didn't have to, praying she made the safe choice. Of course she did. With Elena, common sense always wins over ego. With one final, lip-curling snarl, she ran toward my perch.

She'd covered half the distance when she swerved, circling an oak tree and going back the other way. I caught the scents, dog and human, and saw a man walking a terrier, heading this way.

Elena looped back, darting a weaving path around every obstacle she could find, trying to buy time. I glanced at the dog walker. An elderly man and an old dog, creeping along, oblivious and unhurried.

As Elena circled a small outbuilding, she dipped, her paw probably catching a rodent hole, not enough to make her stumble but slowing her down. Cain lunged. He only caught a mouthful of tail hair. As his snarl of frustration reverberated through the park, the old dog lifted his muzzle in a lazy sniff, then went back to dawdling along beside his master.

Elena disappeared behind the building. A yelp, loud enough to make even the man look up. Elena's yelp. She shot from behind the building, a pale streak, low to the ground, running full-out now, Cain on her heels.

A third shape shot from behind the building, larger than the first two. *That* was Cain—I could make out the odd drop of his jaw. My gaze swung to Elena and the new mutt behind her. Cain had brought backup. Oh, shit!

I crouched, ready to leap from the rock. The man and dog rounded the corner, bringing them right into my path below. I looked over my shoulder, at the long route, then at Elena, now tearing across the park, heading for the river, getting farther from me with each stride.

A split second of hesitation, and then I leapt, sailing over the man and dog and hitting the ground hard on the other side. The little dog started yelping, a high pitched *aii-aii-aii*. The old man wheezed and sputtered, his gasps echoing the pound of my paws as I raced away.

I started closing in on Cain. But he wasn't the one I was worried about. I recognized the other mutt's scent now. Brian McKay. Elena and I had rousted him last year when he killed a hooker. He might be smaller and older than Cain, but he was a hell of a lot more dangerous, and he was right on Elena's tail, the gap between us only getting larger.

Come on, circle around! Bring him back to me!

She finally began to veer, but east, toward the river, heading up an embankment to a set of train tracks. At the top, she started to run back down, then sheered again, staying the course. McKay bought the fake-out, turning to race down the hill, probably hoping to cut her off in descent. When he saw her swerve back, he tried to stop himself but spun too sharp, losing his footing and tumbling down the embankment.

I adjusted my course, heading straight for McKay. He saw me bearing down on him and flew to his feet, bruises forgotten as he bolted after Elena.

The clatter of nails on wood told me she was on the train tracks. As we crested the embankment, I saw her tearing along the railroad bridge with Cain a half-dozen strides behind.

I caught up with McKay at the bridge's edge. He faltered, one of his legs probably complaining from his fall. I launched myself and landed on him. As he went down, his head shot back, throat exposed. I chomped down, eyes shut against the spray of hot blood as I whipped him off his feet. He went wild, all four legs kicking and scratching, body twisting.

I bit harder, then slammed him into a bridge girder. His throat ripped on impact, a huge chunk of flesh coming free, my mouth filling with blood. I dropped him. He fell, shuddering, dying. I bit the back of his neck, swung him up again, and pitched him into the river below.

A quick kill, but during those few minutes the blood pounding in my ears had blocked everything else, and it was only as McKay's body splashed into the water that I finally heard Elena's snarls. I started running. Halfway across the bridge, she'd stopped and was facing off with Cain, her head down, ears back, fur on end.

At first, the mutt seemed uncertain, prancing forward then back, like a boxer bouncing on his heels waiting for the signal. As I rocketed down the tracks, paws pounding the railroad ties, he stopped dancing and dropped into fighting position, as if hearing the sound he'd been waiting for: the arrival of his backup.

I slowed, rolling my paws, footfalls going silent. Then, right behind him, I hunkered down and let out a low growl. He turned, and had he been in human form, he would have fallen over backward. On four legs, he did an odd little stumble, his paws scrabbling against the gravel.

I snarled, teeth flashing, blood flecks spraying as I shook my head. He glanced over my shoulder. Seeing no sign of McKay, he realized what had happened, and swerved back, in flight before he'd finished his turn. He made it two strides, then saw Elena in his path, snapping and snarling.

I backed up two steps and sat. He looked from Elena to me—the challenger and the roadblock. Confused, he kept glancing back as if to say, "You're going to jump me, aren't you?"

Elena gave up and rushed him. She caught him in the chest, knocking him backward. They went down fighting.

It didn't last long. Cain was spooked and distracted, knowing his buddy was dead and the killer sat five feet away, waiting to do the same to him. He managed to do little more than rip out tufts of fur while Elena sank her teeth into his flank, his shoulder, his belly.

Finally, when one bite got too close to his throat, his cowardice kicked in. He threw himself from her and tried to make a run for it. Elena flew onto his back. She grabbed his ear between her teeth, chomped down hard enough to make him yelp, then yanked, leaving tatters. He howled and bucked. She leapt off the other side, putting him between us again.

He flipped around and took a few running strides my way. I growled. He looked from Elena to me, hesitated only a moment, then flung himself between the girders and plummeted into the river.

As Elena leaned through the metal bars to watch him, I circled her, inventorying her injuries. A nasty gash on her side was the worst of it. After a lick to wipe away the dirt, I moved up beside her. Cain flailed in the water below.

She glanced at me. "Good enough?" her eyes asked.

I studied him for a moment, then grunted, not quite willing to commit yet. An answering chuff and she loped off across the bridge. I went the other way.

We toyed with Cain for a while, running along the banks, lunging at him every time he tried to make it to shore. When he finally showed signs of exhaustion, Elena gave the signal and we left him there.

A lesson learned? Probably not. Give him a year or two and he'd be back, but in the meantime he'd have to return to his buddies with a shredded ear and without McKay, and no matter what slant he put on the story, the meaning would be clear: situation normal. I wasn't suffering from a debilitating injury or settling into comfortable retirement with my family. I'd bought myself a little more time.

Elena lifted her head, peering into the bushes that surrounded us.

"Don't worry," I said. "No one can see."

"Something I really should have checked about ten minutes ago."

She pushed up from my chest, skin shimmering in the dark. She sampled the air for any sign of Cain.

"All clear." A slow stretch as she snarled a yawn. "One of these days, we're actually going to *complete* an escape before we have sex."

"Why?"

She laughed. "Why, indeed."

She started to slide off me, but I held her still, hands around her waist.

"Not yet."

"Hmm." Another stretch, her toes tickling my legs. "So when are you going to blast me?"

"For taking off and running down alleys at midnight?"

"Unless you slipped something past me in the wedding vows, I think I'm still entitled to go where I want, when I want. But do you really think I'd go traipsing down dark alleys in a strange city for a bottle of water? Why not just stick a flashing 'mug me' sign on my back?"

"Well, you did seem a bit bored . . ."

"Please. That mutt's been following us since this morning. I was trying to get rid of him."

"What?"

"Yes, I know, I should have warned you. I realized that later, but you'd worked so hard to plan our honeymoon, and I didn't want this mutt ruining it. I thought I'd give him a good scare and send him packing before you noticed him sniffing around."

"Huh."

I tried to sound surprised. Tried to look surprised. But her gaze swung to mine, eyes narrowing.

"You knew he was following us."

I shrugged, hoping for noncommittal.

She smacked my arm. "You were just going to let me take the blame and keep your mouth shut, weren't you?"

"Hell, yeah."

Another smack. "That's what you were doing at dinner, wasn't it? Breaking his jaw. I thought it looked off, and I could swear I smelled blood when we were walking back from the restaurant." She shook her head. "Communication. We should try it sometime."

I shifted, putting my arm under my head. "How about now? About this trip. You're bored." When she opened her mouth to protest, I put my hand over it. "You're tired of St. Louis. There's not a damned thing to do except hole up in our hotel room, run in the forest, and hunt mutts—which, while fun, we could do anywhere. So I'm thinking, maybe it's time to consider a second honeymoon."

"Already?"

"I think we're due for one. So how's this? We pack, head home, see the kids for a couple of days, then take off again. Someplace where we can hole up, run in the forest, and *not* have to worry about tripping over mutts. Maybe a cabin in Algonquin?"

She leaned over me, her hair fanning a curtain around us. "Wasn't that where I suggested we go when you first asked?"

"I thought you were just trying to make it easy on me. We can rent a cabin anytime. I wanted this to be different, special."

"It was special. I was stalked, chased, attacked . . . and I got to beat the crap out of a mutt twice my size." She bent further, lips brushing mine. "A truly unique honeymoon from a truly unique husband."

She put her arms around my neck, rolled over, and pulled me on top of her.

CHIVALROUS

*F*riday-night college parties were the reward for a week of hard work. Time to cut loose. Get wasted. Get laid. All of which was hard to do when your mother kept texting you.

As Trevor handed him another beer, Reese texted back, saying he needed to study and he'd call her in the morning.

Am I cramping yr style? Can't party while talking 2 yr mom.

He choked on his beer, then replied with *Partying? I wish.*

ROTFLMAO. Go on. Party. Just be safe. And don't forget to run this wknd.

Trevor glanced over Reese's shoulder and read the last text before Reese closed his phone.

"Run?" he said.

"Beer run. Promised my study mates I'd pick up a slab tomorrow."

Trevor slapped Reese's back. "I thought maybe you'd joined the track team. Decided footy was getting too rough for you. Don't want to mess up that pretty face." Trevor looked around the room, his gaze pausing on every girl along the way. "Speaking of which, have you made your choice yet? I know to let you pick first or my ego's going to take a beating."

Reese's gaze slid to the dark-haired girl in the corner. She'd been shooting glances at him all night. Shy glances, her pale cheeks flushing when he'd caught her looking, her grip tightening on her wineglass as her gaze ducked away.

She was small and pretty, and looked very sweet. The kind of girl he could take home to Mom, which meant she wasn't the girl for tonight.

He needed a run. Already, the restlessness pulled every tendon as tight as a piano wire. But the kind of run he needed meant driving out of Melbourne, suffering through the torturous Change into a wolf, and spending hours hunting and working it off. Not something he was eager to do any sooner than necessary.

At home, on his parents' farm, Reese enjoyed his runs. Sure, the transformation was hell, but he'd spent years looking forward to his first Change, the way other kids can't wait to reach driving age. At school, though, Changing was a major pain in the ass, so he postponed it for as long as it was safely possible. One advantage to letting that restlessness build? Really great sex.

He knew enough not to let it go too far. A werewolf couldn't risk losing control with a lover. He knew, too, that he had to find the right girl, someone who wanted exactly what he wanted—sex straight-up, no guilt chaser when he didn't stick around until morning. The sweet little dark-haired girl wouldn't do.

He scanned the room. Despite what Trevor said, Reese didn't have his pick of any girl. He just did better than Trevor, who was the rugby team's enforcer and looked like he used his face to do the enforcing. But Reese's dark blond hair, pleasant face, and athletic build usually got him what he wanted, and it only took him one good scan of the party to decide what he wanted tonight.

She was a redhead. Not naturally, he was sure, but he'd find that out soon enough, if the looks she was giving him were any indication. She stood by the makeshift bar with her arm around a blond friend's waist, hand in her friend's pocket, a fake lesbian show that *wasn't* designed to scare guys off.

When she saw Reese watching, she leaned over and nuzzled her friend's neck, fingers kneading her ass, and Reese felt himself harden at the thought of a threesome. Wishful thinking, he knew, but he could always hope.

✢

Twenty minutes later, he was leaving with the redhead. The blonde had stayed behind—the threesome hint had only been bait. Which was fine. Pleasing two girls would take time and patience, and all he wanted was release. Hard and fast release.

When he'd suggested they step outside, the girl—Mandy—was on her feet before he was. They'd made it as far as the back of the building, and he'd put her up against the wall, just for an appetizer, but she seemed quite content to stay there through the main course. He did check, though, asking if she wanted to go to his flat or hers.

She pressed against him, her open shirt falling to her waist, bare breasts pale in the moonlight. "I don't think you'd make it that far," she said as she rubbed his crotch. "In fact, I don't think you're going to make it through the next five minutes."

"Can't help myself." He kissed her hard, and she groaned and pressed against him. "Is that a problem?"

It wasn't. Girls were usually flattered by his eagerness. Flattered and excited, his passion contagious, and when zippers were being yanked down a minute later, it wasn't Reese doing the yanking. That was normal, too. He let the girls set the pace, even if they didn't quite realize they were taking the lead. He always had to be sure he wasn't pushing them into something they didn't want.

But Mandy definitely wanted it. Reese was ripping open a condom when a distant crash stopped him. As he looked around, a girl screamed.

"Sounds like someone else is enjoying herself," Mandy said.

It didn't. Werewolf hearing meant he caught the notes of fear in that shriek. Then he heard the girl protesting, telling the guy to stop. Reese waited. Mistakes happened. Guys go to a party, get drunk, get a little pushy. A good firm "No" usually smacked their brain out of their pants.

Not for this guy. The protests kept coming, growing panicked. Reese zipped his pants and stepped back. When Mandy grabbed for him, he moved out of her reach.

"That girl's in trouble," he said.

"And who are you, Bruce Wayne?"

When he started walking away, she caught the back of his shirt. "Forget her. I'm sure she wants what's coming. She just doesn't realize it yet."

Reese spun, knocking her hand from his shirt and giving her a glare that had her stumbling back.

"Go home," he said, then took off in the direction of the voices.

The girl was a street over, behind another building. She'd gone quiet now. Reese picked up speed, hoping she'd escaped, fearing she hadn't. As he drew closer, he heard muffled protests and a guy telling her to shut up. Then another male voice chimed in.

Shit.

Slowing, Reese carefully edged around the building. The first thing he smelled was booze. The air reeked of it, and he could see a smashed bottle lying in a pool of liquid. That booze was all he *could* smell, so he couldn't tell if it was two guys or more. Werewolf strength meant he could manage two. More? It depended on what kind of shape they were in.

He took a look and realized he didn't need to worry. It was only two thirtyish guys, and they were so drunk they could barely stand upright. One had the girl from behind, his hand over her mouth as she kicked and writhed and punched.

The girl's foot connected with the crotch of the guy in front of her. When he fell back, howling, Reese caught a glimpse of the girl, seeing dark hair and a pale green shirt. It was the shy girl from the party.

Reese crept forward. The men were too intent on the girl to notice him. He grabbed the guy holding her. He yanked him away from the girl, threw him aside, then went after the other one.

After Reese blocked a few wobbly swings and sent them flying with ones of his own, the men realized they were outclassed and took off. He'd chased them for a block, hoping to catch one and hold him for the cops. But those few blows seemed to have knocked the booze from their heads. They made it to the main road just ahead of him, darted through traffic, and hopped into a taxi.

Reese found the girl still behind the building, tugging absently at her torn shirt as she stared down at her cell phone.

"Did you call it in?" he said.

She jumped, skittering back, then saw it was him. "I was waiting to see if you'd catch them."

"I didn't."

Her expression wavered between disappointment and relief. She pocketed the phone.

"You really should call—" he began.

"I know."

She looked around, then retrieved a shoe that had fallen off in the struggle. Her fingers trembled as she tried to get it on.

"Here." Reese bent and put it on her.

"I feel like Cinderella," she said, trying for a smile. "Does it fit?"

He managed to return the smile. "It does. About those guys—"

"I should report it. I know that. But my parents—" She rubbed the back of her neck. "They don't like me going to school here. Big city and all that. If they hear I was jumped by a couple of drunks, they'll cut me off, make me come home. Maybe they wouldn't have to find out, but . . ." She looked up at him. "I really don't want to take that chance. Not when nothing happened."

"Something did happen. You got attacked."

"I know." She shoved her hands into her pockets. "But I'm okay. Can you—can you just walk me to the road? Wait while I hail a taxi?"

He didn't offer to escort her home. That might have seemed like the chivalrous thing to do, but he doubted a girl who'd narrowly escaped rape wanted a stranger near her flat, so he got her into a taxi, and realized only as the car pulled off that he hadn't asked her name.

When Reese got back to his place, it was empty. Not surprising. Niles wasn't around much, which made him the perfect flatmate.

He kicked off his runners, sat on the couch, and picked up the remote. He didn't turn on the TV. Just sat there, staring at his reflection in the blank screen. Then he pulled out his cell phone and hit speed dial.

His mother answered, yawning, on the fourth ring. "What's wrong, baby?"

"Nothing. I just—" He glanced at the clock on the DVD player and winced. "Sorry, I didn't realize how late it was. I'll call you in the morning."

He heard his mother get out of bed. His dad mumbled something in the background.

"He's fine," his mother murmured to his dad.

"I am," Reese said. "Go back to bed. I'm sorry. I just—" *I helped this girl tonight, saved her from a couple guys, and it made me think of you.*

Of course, he couldn't say that, wouldn't jog those memories. He shouldn't have called.

"One too many beers," he said finally. "I totally lost track of time. I'll call in the morning."

"You sound like you want to talk."

He forced a chuckle. "No, I sound drunk, and when I'm drunk, I like to talk. I'll wake up Niles and make him suffer through it. Payback for eating my leftovers last week."

She didn't let it go that easily. Eventually, though, she accepted the excuse, along with his promise to call in the morning.

Reese hung up, but stayed on the couch, staring at the blank television screen. Twenty years ago, his mother had been the college girl leaving a party, the one who'd bumped into the wrong guys. An American, she'd told everyone she just wanted to study abroad and had picked the University of Sydney on a lark. Not true. She'd picked it because she didn't know anyone in Australia, and it was as far as she could get from a bad family situation.

She'd been at an out-of-town party with her boyfriend. Driving back, they'd fought—she couldn't remember over what. He'd kicked her out of the car ten kilometers from town. A long walk on an empty road. She'd ducked out of sight whenever a car passed. Then came the one that didn't pass. They'd had their windows down. Smelled her. Three young werewolves. She hadn't stood a chance.

Raping her wasn't enough. They decided to hunt her. Kill her. Feed on her. Let the police chalk it up to dingoes. Thinking she was unconscious, they'd gone to Change in the bushes. She snuck the keys from the leader's jacket, then took off in their truck.

When she got to the authorities, she had quite a story to tell, about three men who'd raped her, changed into wolves, and chased the truck as she'd sped off. Clearly the girl was in shock after her ordeal. She needed psychiatric help, not the ridicule that would come by making her allegations public. So the police tried to cover it up, but the story hit a few small papers without the scruples to ignore it.

The Australian Pack had found out and sent a delegation to kill the trio of man-eaters. Then they sent another of their own—Wes Robinson—to take care of the girl. That didn't mean protecting her. Their interest was in protecting the Pack, and the girl posed an exposure threat. She had to die.

Wes didn't carry out his orders. He met the girl, fell in love, and ran away with her. All terribly romantic. Unfortunately, the Pack didn't see it that way.

Most Packs forbade long-term relationships. The Australian one, though, operated more like a wolf pack. The Alpha—and only the Alpha—could take a mate. When Reese's parents ran off together,

Wes Robinson wasn't just disobeying a direct order; he'd unwittingly issued a challenge to the Alpha that could not be ignored. So Reese's parents had spent the last twenty years hiding in the outback, farming and raising their son.

He'd been born nine months after his parents met. Also nine months after his mother had been attacked. They hadn't told him that, of course. He'd figured it out when he'd looked up his mother's story and seen the date.

Born nine months after a brutal gang rape. He was pretty sure he knew what that meant. He'd confronted his father about it once. His dad had said, "You're my son." That's all he'd say. Wes Robinson was his father in every way that counted.

If his parents didn't care, Reese shouldn't. In most ways, he didn't. But he still had his hang-ups, like making absolutely sure sex was consensual. And there were things that would remind him, pull him down into his thoughts and fears. The attack on the dark-haired girl had done that. He'd deal, but this would be a long, sleepless night.

Reese had a rugby game the next afternoon. The Pack discouraged their young sons from playing organized sports, knowing that when they came into their powers, they could get into trouble, being too strong, too aggressive. But Reese had been homeschooled, so his parents had decided he needed all the social interaction he could get. They'd made the two-hour round-trip into town twice a week so he could try out different sports at the community center. Rugby was the one he'd stuck with.

When he'd started coming into his strength, his parents had watched closely for any sign that Reese might need to restrict himself to skirmishes with his father. But they'd taught him well. He avoided fights and relied on speed and agility instead.

Now, of course, his parents weren't there to watch him. But that afternoon, someone else was: the dark-haired girl.

He didn't see her until near the end of the game, glimpsing her behind a group of middle-aged men. She seemed to be sitting alone. Was her boyfriend on the team? He felt a flicker of disappointment.

It didn't matter. You couldn't save a girl from rape then ask her on a date. That was all kinds of wrong.

After the game, when he saw her standing beside the benches, he waved. It was the polite thing to do. She walked over. Also the polite thing to do.

"How're you doing?" he asked.

"Fine." She made a face. "Well, not really, but I'm holding up. I just . . . I didn't get a chance to say thank-you last night. Not a proper thank-you, anyway. If you hadn't come along . . . Well, I'm glad you did."

"You're welcome, but honestly, I think you could have handled it. They were pretty far gone, and you put up a good fight. A damned good fight."

She blushed. "Maybe. I wanted to come by and say thanks, though. A friend from the party didn't know your name but said you played on this team."

"It's Reese."

She blinked, confused.

"My name," he said. "Reese Wilson."

Her cheeks flushed deeper. "Right. Sorry." She put out her hand. "Daniella DuMaurier."

One of Reese's teammates shouted that they were heading to the pub.

"Going out for a beer after the game?" Daniella asked.

He'd planned to. And this would be an easy way to ask her out without really asking her out, just casually invite her to come along. But he had a feeling a rowdy victory party with strangers wouldn't be her idea of a good time.

"Nah. Essay due tomorrow. I'm just going to grab a bite to eat. Do you know any decent places around here?"

"No, but I'm sure we could find one." Another blush. "I mean, if you want. Buying you an early dinner is the least I can do."

Over the meal, he smoothly led the conversation, searching for a subtle way to ask her out. He knew he was being overly cautious. She'd wanted to have dinner with him, and by the time they'd found a restaurant she'd been laughing and chatting, completely relaxed, giving all the signs that said, "I'm interested."

Still, he was careful. When he steered the conversation into recent movie releases, though, she admitted there was one she really wanted to see and, wouldn't you know it, so did he. Or so he said. He suggested they go together. She said yes. And that was that.

Reese hadn't had a girlfriend since high school. There wasn't any reason to, not when plenty of college girls were happy to hook up for a night. If he could get sex without the dangers of a romantic relationship, then he would. Because romantic relationships were, indeed, dangerous for a werewolf. Too many secrets to keep.

After three dates with Daniella, though, he'd decided he could make an exception. Sex was still off the menu—he wasn't pressuring a girl who'd nearly been raped—but that didn't stop him from wanting to see her as often as he could, which was as sure a sign as any that this was different.

Daniella was different, too. When he'd first met her, he'd thought she was sweet and shy. He liked that in a girl—or his werewolf instincts did. Someone gentle and delicate, someone he could take care of and protect. And she *was* sweet and shy, but as he'd seen the night of the attack, there also was strength there. An iron will hid behind her delicate exterior. Passion, too. When they kissed, she always started slow and tentative, but it didn't take long to get her motor running.

Delicate and innocent on the outside, tough and hot-blooded on the inside. That fascinated him. Excited the hell out of him, too. Wherever this relationship was going, he planned to follow.

They'd been dating for a month when a long weekend meant trips home for both of them. Daniella's family lived near Sydney, so he saw her off on the plane Thursday night, then made the drive home himself right after his Friday morning class.

Before Daniella left, she'd told him how much she'd miss him, how much she wished she could stay. He'd felt kind of guilty at that. Though he'd miss her, too, he was looking forward to going home.

Home was the outback. Home was endless, empty expanses of red desert and scrub brush. Home was the smell of diesel and wet sheep, the whoosh of the windmill and the whine of the wind. It was his dogs, racing up the dirt road when they heard his truck coming. It was his mother, waiting on the porch with a cold beer and a hot meat pie. It was his dad, ambling in from the barn, his weathered face lit up in a smile. For the next two days they wouldn't do much of anything, just hang out together, talking, then he and his father going for runs at night, his mother coming along, staying in the truck with picnic baskets of food for an American-style tailgate party afterward.

His home life was damned near perfect. A helluva lot better than Daniella's, as he realized during their calls that weekend. By Saturday night her parents were driving her nuts. More than that, she seemed depressed, which worried him. He told himself she just wanted to get back to school—and maybe back to him—but he couldn't help wondering if there was more to it.

His werewolf streak of possessiveness kept nudging him toward one conclusion: she had a guy back home, a boyfriend she'd broken up with to go to college, and now she was reconsidering that decision. He told himself he was overreacting, but when her plane landed, he was there waiting for her with a single red rose.

When she came out, she walked with her gaze down, letting the other passengers elbow and jostle past her, not even seeming to notice. Her hair was pulled back in a tidy ponytail, but it didn't gleam the way it usually did. Her oversized campus sweatshirt seemed to envelop her tiny frame, weighing her down as she trudged along.

"Daniella!" he called as she started heading the other way.

When she saw him, her face lit up. As she took the rose, her cheeks turned as red as the petals. She murmured a thank-you. Then she noticed what he held in his other hand: a wrapped hamburger.

"That's the romantic gesture," he said, pointing at the rose. "This is the practical one. It's late and you're probably hungry."

She gave a tiny laugh and then threw her arms around his neck. "My hero." She hugged him as she said it, but he didn't miss the catch in her voice and the way she clung to him, as if composing herself before pulling back.

"What's wrong?" he whispered as he took her laptop bag.

"It's noth—" She stopped. Pulled herself up straight. "No, it *is* something. I need to talk to you."

"Okay," he said carefully. "Let's get out to my truck, and we'll drive someplace and—"

"No." She grasped his arm. "Now. If I wait, I'll change my mind. I can't change my mind."

Actually, he had a feeling he'd be fine with skipping whatever conversation she had planned, but he let her lead him to an empty section of seats. She walked to the far corner and sat with her hands folded on her lap.

He knew what she was going to say. *There's this guy . . . We broke up when I came to Melbourne, but I saw him when I went home and . . . I'm sorry, Reese . . .*

He steeled himself against the words. He'd fight for her. If there was any hope at all, he'd fight.

"My father is Gavin Wright," she said finally.

He jumped at the name, then tried to cover the reaction by shifting and coughing. He'd misheard. He must have misheard.

"You know who that is," Daniella said. "I know you do."

He forced a laugh. "Maybe I'm showing my ignorance, but no, I don't. Is he a politician? A CEO? Local celebrity? Someone who isn't very happy about his daughter dating a kid from the outback? Is that it?"

Temper flashed in her eyes. "Don't play dumb, Reese."

"Maybe I'm not playing."

She got up and walked to the window. For a moment, she just stared out. Then she wheeled.

"Gavin Wright is the Alpha of the Australian Pack," she said. "And if you pretend you don't know what a Pack is, I'm . . ." She trailed off and lifted her hands. They were shaking. "Do you see that? Don't play games with me, Reese. Please. This is hard enough already."

He said nothing. He couldn't, and if she really was Wright's daughter, she should know that. He could not let on that he had any idea what she was talking about until she proved who she was and confirmed that she knew what he was.

She sat down again, two chairs away, twisted toward him. "Gavin Wright has two daughters. No sons. My older sister is engaged to the Alpha-elect. That's how it works. Only the Alpha can marry. One of his daughters is mated with his successor. The others . . ." She shrugged. "Aren't."

Any other daughters were expected to devote their lives to the Pack—cooking, cleaning, and taking care of the men. A life of celibate servitude. Reese knew that from his father's stories.

Daniella continued. "I wanted to go to college, but my father laughed at the idea. Then a lone wolf who was in trouble with the Pack gave them a tip. He'd smelled a young werewolf on campus here. My dad knew Wes Robinson had a college-aged son. So he decided I could go to Melbourne University. To find you."

Reese realized he was gripping the seat. He let go. "Mission accomplished."

"But I didn't *want* to find you. I hoped I could string my father along until I got a degree. Then, with an education, I could . . ." She glanced away. "Escape."

"Only he expected results, so you had to produce them. You saw me at the party—"

"And figured out who you were. Yes. I could smell you. I'm not a werewolf, obviously, but I have a good sense of smell and I can recognize a werewolf's scent. That's how my dad expected me to find you. Once I was sure who you were, I left the party. But I was so distracted that I walked right into those guys."

She went quiet for a moment, then said, her voice soft, "That would have been ironic, wouldn't it? Your mom gets raped. My dad's trying to kill her because of it, and the same thing happens to his daughter. Poetic justice."

"Don't say that."

"I know I'm not my father, but I still feel guilty about what he did. And now I feel even more guilty because I ended up doing exactly what he wanted. I should have stayed away from you. I tried. That's why I took off so fast that night. But I couldn't stay away."

"So you told him I'm here. He's coming for me."

"No. Never," she said vehemently. "I didn't say anything. I just—I had to tell you the truth. I know this means it's over, but I won't put your life in danger."

"And staying with you means it is in danger?"

She nodded.

"What if I disagree?"

"Then you'd be wrong. Your death is my father's idea of the perfect revenge. But you don't need to run. He won't let any of the Pack come here, for fear you'll scent them. So you're safe at school. Just not with me. I'm going to drop out. I'll tell my father I couldn't find you and I'm homesick and—"

"No."

"I have to. As long as I'm here—"

"—your dad and the Pack are almost a thousand kilometers away. I'm safe from them. You're safe from them. And that's just as important."

He kissed her. It took a moment for her to kiss him back, unsure at first, then heating up until she was in his lap, kissing him deeply and desperately, and when she finally pulled back and whispered, "Will you come to my place tonight?" he got the feeling she meant it as a good-bye. He'd make sure it wasn't.

If sex was her good-bye gift, it turned out to be a bigger offering than he'd expected. She was a virgin. They'd been taking things slow, but he'd attributed that to her rape scare. When he'd figured it out, he tried to stop. But Daniella hadn't wanted to stop. Really, *really* hadn't wanted to stop. While he'd have loved to credit that to his sexual prowess, he suspected she'd been so determined because it was, for her, the point of no return.

After they made love, there was no more talk of Daniella going back to Sydney. She'd made her choice, and she'd picked him over the Pack. He understood the magnitude of that decision.

He understood what it meant for him, too. He'd slept with the Pack Alpha's daughter. His father's crime paled beside that.

It wasn't until his mother's next call that Reese realized how much trouble he was in. He didn't tell his mother about Daniella. He'd already had that conversation with Daniella, and even the suggestion had terrified her. His parents could help, but he needed to convince her that his father wasn't like the Pack werewolves. To convince Daniella that she'd be safe with them. The problem, as he now realized, was that they wouldn't be safe with her.

How *was* he going to tell his parents that his girlfriend was Gavin Wright's daughter? They'd understand her situation, of course.

They'd protect her, help her get away from the Pack. But taking her in meant Wright would redouble his efforts, and wouldn't rest until he got Daniella back and wiped out Reese's family.

So, when Daniella begged him not to tell his parents, he was relieved. That gave him time to figure out how he was going to handle this. In the meantime, he was too caught up in the relationship to think much about the repercussions.

If he thought he'd liked Daniella before, it was nothing compared with how he felt now. For the first time, he could really be himself with a girl. He hadn't realized how much he'd longed for that, how much he'd envied that bond between his parents.

As deeply in love as his parents were, it had been hard for them at first, as his mother had learned to handle all the things that made her husband different, all the things he had to hide from the world. Now Reese had a lover who not only knew his secret but considered it normal. She brought him food when he was dashing between classes. She made sure he got lots of exercise—in and out of bed. She indulged his protective streak and gave him no cause for jealousy. She prodded him to Change, even going with him, staying with him. She figured out his penchant for delaying his run, and taking the edge off with sex, and she accommodated that, too—enthusiastically.

They were in class, three weeks later, when she texted him to remind him it was getting "close to his time," and asking if he was "feeling it" yet. When he'd said he was, she told him to meet her in a nook behind one of the campus buildings.

As he headed there, knowing what was coming, his blood ran so hot that when he smelled a werewolf, he thought, for one confused moment, that it was her. Luckily, his brain kicked in and stopped him. That and the sound of Daniella's voice.

"I *am* looking for him," she was saying. "But it's a big campus and I have classes—"

"We aren't sending you here to go to classes, Daniella," a man answered.

Reese peered around the corner and saw a dark-haired man. He looked about thirty, which meant, with a werewolf's slow aging, he was probably a decade older. Daniella's father? He was acting like it, towering over her, speaking in a growl that made her press back against the wall, books clutched to her chest.

There was nothing in his scent that suggested they were related, though. And the man's stance was a little too familiar to be familial. He was leaning over Daniella, his body a hairbreadth from hers. When Reese saw that, his hands clenched and he stepped out.

Daniella sensed him and glanced over. She looked away fast, but he saw the panic in her eyes. She inched to the side, making the werewolf turn his back to Reese. Then she discreetly waved Reese back.

It took him a minute to obey. He knew he should. If he went after the guy and didn't kill him, this man would expose their relationship. Protecting Daniella meant backing down, as cowardly as it felt.

He didn't leave, though, only moved out of sight, where he could keep listening. They argued for a few minutes, then she led the man away, in the opposite direction, so he wouldn't cross Reese's scent trail. At the road, Daniella escaped by joining a couple of girls she knew and telling the guy she'd "call him later."

Reese followed the werewolf to a visitors' lot, where he climbed into a brand-new SUV and roared off.

Two hours later, Reese met Daniella at an off-campus pub. After the encounter, she'd gone straight to a gift store, where she'd bought a bagful of scented candles. Then to her flat, to light them, change the bedding, and get rid of any sign—and scent—of Reese.

Now they were alone in the back of the noisy pub, clutching beers they had no intention of drinking.

"His name is Keith Tynes," she said. "He's—"

"The Alpha-elect. I know the name. My father . . . talked about him."

"Nothing good, I'm sure. My dad isn't the nicest guy, but Keith?" She shivered. "I feel sorry for my sister. The Alpha's mate is treated like a queen, but it's not worth it. Not with Keith."

"Is he sticking around to hunt for me?"

She shook her head. "He wasn't even supposed to be on campus. I can't believe he disobeyed my dad like that. He's starting to throw his weight around, see how far he can push it, but usually he knows not to push it too far. One call to my dad and he'll get the usual punishment. Dad will make him wait another six months before he gets my sister." A faint sparkle lit her eyes. "Keith was supposed to get her when she turned eighteen, almost two years ago, and he's really getting anxious."

"Horny."

She laughed. "Yes, horny. Speaking of which . . ." Her fingers crept up his leg.

He put his hand on hers. "So Keith will leave?"

"He will."

"And if he doesn't?"

She leaned over and kissed him, whispering, "He will."

Keith did leave. But the close call was a wake-up for Reese. This situation wasn't going to resolve itself. Daniella needed to get away from the Pack and he needed to get away from Melbourne. That meant dropping out and going home, and as much as that would hurt his parents, it would hurt a lot more if the Pack killed their only child.

Step one, though, was getting Daniella to agree to meet his parents. The day after her encounter with Keith, he began a concentrated campaign to convince her they wouldn't murder her in her sleep and send her severed head back to her father.

He started taking every opportunity to talk about his family. Before rugby, he'd tell her about skirmishes with his dad. After a run, he'd talk about their tailgate parties. At dinner, he'd tell tales of his mother's disastrous attempts to cook new dishes. Before long, Daniella was the one encouraging the stories. There was a wistfulness in her eyes when he talked about his family, and he could tell her own childhood hadn't been nearly so happy.

Within a week, she was ready to meet them. That's when Reese started having second thoughts.

Was it really wise to take Daniella to his parents, when they'd spent half their lives hiding from her father? He trusted her completely, but he had to think about his parents' safety. Most important, was there any *reason* to take Daniella to them? He was an adult. He had enough money to get them to America or England. Maybe he should just do that. Leave and tell his parents after he was gone, as much as that would hurt.

Daniella seemed a little disappointed, but she agreed with his logic. They'd go to England. Then he'd call and break the news.

Two days later, he was heading to class, thinking it was kind of silly to keep attending. But he supposed there was still part of him that hoped he wouldn't have to leave, that the situation would miraculously resolve itself. Immature, he knew. Daniella wasn't stalling. She was out emptying her bank account and following up on his lead to get a fake passport.

He was debating skipping class when his phone rang.

"Got it!" Daniella sang when he answered.

"You're a criminal now, you know. Buying fake ID is a criminal offense."

She laughed. "Then I've been a criminal from birth."

True. All her ID was fake, common among werewolves.

"So who am I taking to England?" he asked.

"Gabriella. She's much sexier than Daniella. You'll love—Oh God."

"Daniella?"

"Keith," she said, her voice going distant, as if she'd yanked the phone down.

"Who are you talking to?" Keith called.

"A friend." A rustle, like she was stuffing the phone into her pocket. "What are you—?"

"Didn't sound like a friend." Keith's voice came closer. "Do you think I'm stupid, Dani? That I don't know what you're up to? That I don't know who that was?"

Oh shit. Oh, shit! Where was she? Reese looked around, but he had no idea if she was even on campus.

Come on, Daniella. I'm still on the line. Give me a hint, a clue, and I'm on my way.

"I don't know what you—" Daniella began.

"Cut the crap, Dani. He's your boyfriend, isn't he?"

"Wh-what? Who? That was a friend."

"Bullshit." The voice came closer still and Reese swore he could hear Daniella shaking. "What would your father say if he found out? A human boyfriend?"

"H-hum—" She stopped. Reese could hear the relief in her voice when she continued. "It's not like that. Just a guy I . . . kind of like. We went out a few times, and—"

"You'd better be telling the truth, because you're mine, Dani."

An edge of steel slid into Daniella's voice. "No, Rose is yours. I'm going to be your sister-in-law. I've warned you already—if you ever touch me again, I'll tell my father and he'll—"

"He'll do nothing. I'm tired of waiting. I've got half the Pack on my side, plus your sister. It's our turn, and if your parents don't step down gracefully, you're going to be an orphan."

"Rose would never—"

"No? It's her idea. She's sick of waiting. Sick of serving your mother. Sick of watching me serve your father." He chuckled. "And sick of getting her wedding night postponed. Now I'm bringing you home, and if your father complains, that'll give me just the excuse I need. So call your boyfriend and say good-bye, and I hope all you gave him was kisses, because if I find out otherwise . . . ?" His voice lowered to a growl. "I owe my Pack brothers for their support. If you're damaged goods, you'll be their reward."

"You're hurting me."

"Oh, believe me, I'm going to hurt you a lot more—"

Reese didn't catch the rest of the threat. He started running, phone gripped to his ear, having no idea where he was going, just running, praying she'd remember he was still on the line and tell him where she was.

Even when he slowed and strained to listen, though, he could barely hear anything. Their voices were muffled now. But he could catch the panic in Daniella's and hear the faint sounds of struggle. Then Keith said, "Maybe I'll save myself the disappointment and just check those goods now."

Daniella let out a shriek. Reese ran faster, shouting, "Daniella!" into the phone.

A smack. Then a gasp of pain. Daniella's gasp. He called her again, louder, but the fight got louder, too. Then a *whoomph* and a hiss of pain from Keith.

Footsteps pounded.

"You bitch," Keith wheezed, his voice getting distant. "You'd better run. When I catch you . . ."

He didn't finish the threat. Didn't catch her, either.

An hour later, Reese and Daniella were in his truck, roaring out of Melbourne. He'd screwed up—again. He hadn't wanted to leave, so he'd come up with excuses. *Oh, you need ID. And we need to empty our bank accounts. And figure out where we're going to stay . . .*

Bullshit. He'd been stalling. After Daniella escaped from Keith the first time, they should have packed their bags and grabbed the first boat to Indonesia.

Now they were doing exactly what he'd tried to avoid: taking her to his parents. They had no choice. All her ID—new and old—had been in her purse, which Keith had grabbed as she'd run away. They needed a place to hide and they needed help.

He'd called first. His dad had answered, and Reese said he was coming home for the weekend. His father didn't question it, just figured Reese was homesick.

At midnight, Reese called again to tell them not to wait up. He was exhausted and grabbing a motel room for the night. His mom agreed he shouldn't drive while he was tired, but said, "Is something wrong, Reese?"

"Kind of."

Daniella glanced over sharply. They'd agreed not to tell his parents the truth until they got there. She was worried they might tell him to get the hell away from her as fast as he could. Too little experience trusting anyone, especially werewolves.

"I'm okay for now," he said. "I'll explain when I get home."

A pause. A long one. Then, "All right. Call me when you leave the motel, and I'll have breakfast ready when you get here."

He hung up, and Daniella said, "It's only a couple more hours' drive."

He didn't answer, just checked the mirrors for the thousandth time since they'd left Melbourne.

"Keith isn't following us, Reese." She studied his face. "But you're still worried, and I guess I can't blame you. You don't want to risk leading him to your parents."

"I can't."

"I know."

They started looking for a motel.

⚜

Ten minutes later, they were in a room, but it was an hour before they got to sleep. As Daniella joked, it would be a while before they'd get time alone together. That's what cheap motels were for, he'd said. So they'd taken advantage of it, burning off the stress and anxiety of the day.

Afterward, he'd gone into the bathroom to brush his teeth. When he came out, she lay naked on the bed, examining a tourist map from the desk.

"Trying to figure out where the hell we are?" he asked.

She laughed. "Yes. I found the last town we passed. Now I'm trying to guess where we're going." She pointed at a stretch of land marked with sheep. "I know it's not here. It's the right distance, but it's ranch country. No way werewolves would be farming livestock."

When he didn't answer, she looked up and caught his smile.

"Seriously?" she said. "How'd you manage that?"

He shrugged. "Buy them while they're lambs, and they get used to our smell. A sheep farm is the last place the Pack would look for us."

She let the map slide to the floor. "Smart. Do you have dogs to herd them?" She grinned. "Or just Change and do it yourselves?"

He laughed and stretched out on top of her. "We have dogs."

"Lucky. I always wanted dogs. Pets of any kind, actually." She put her arms around his neck. "I think I'm going to like it out here. Even if it is a million miles from anywhere."

"That's part of its charm," he said, and kissed her.

He awoke alone. The spot beside him had cooled, but the faint smell of shampoo wafted from the bathroom. He stretched and flipped over to check the time—

Shit! It was after nine. He'd set it for six—

No, Daniella set it. Had she done it wrong? Damned motel clocks. No two ever worked the same.

He rolled out of bed and padded to the bathroom. The door was ajar. He pushed it open.

"Hey, we're running late, so—"

The bathroom was empty. He yanked the shower curtain back. The walls were dry. Only a damp film of soapy water still coated the floor.

He hurried back into the room and looked around. There was a note by the door.

Shit. Oh, shit. Please tell me she didn't get spooked and run.

He snatched it up.

Getting coffee, it said. *Be right back!*

Reese grabbed his jeans and was still zipping them up as he strode out, bare-chested and barefooted, his heart pumping so hard he didn't feel the morning's chill. Didn't notice the sour looks of the elderly couple in the motel restaurant, either.

Yes, the server had seen Daniella. She'd ordered coffee, toast, and sausage and taken the food back to her room. When? Oh, at least a couple of hours ago.

Reese tore out of the restaurant. His truck was still in the lot, but he noticed that the interior light was on. He ran over to find the driver's door open. The smell of werewolf hit him. Keith Tynes and at least two others. They'd sniffed inside his truck. Smelling him.

The croak of a raven made him jump. He turned to see two fighting over a piece of toast. Two coffee cups lay beside the take-away box, brown liquid swirling around the battling birds.

Keith had taken Daniella. She'd dropped the tray, maybe tried to run, but there was no place to run, not out here.

But why take her and let him live? Wasn't he their target?

Unless they didn't know who he was. If Reese wasn't Wes Robinson's biological son, these Pack wolves wouldn't smell the connection. Daniella was smart. She'd claim she'd been snatched by another werewolf, looking to strike at the Pack. They'd get her out of harm's way. Then they'd come back for him. Or, better yet, wait for him to drive off into the outback, where there'd be no witnesses.

He had to call his parents. Warn them, just in case.

He ran into the motel room and grabbed his cell phone. His home number rang through to the answering machine. He tried his mother's cell. Same thing.

Reese's hands shook so hard it took him a moment to realize his phone had vibrated. He had two text messages. Both were from his mother.

Don't come home. Run, baby. Just run. Please.

The second had been sent a minute later. Three words.

We love you.

Reese took off.

He went home. There was no way in hell he wouldn't, no matter what his mother's message said.

Any hope that nothing was wrong vanished when he saw their sheep milling about the road. Wandering, confused and lost, some dead, run off the road or just run over. The dogs were dead, too. Matt and Tam. *His* dogs or so his father had said, bringing the balls of black and white fluff into his bedroom one Christmas morning—

Reese inhaled sharply, tore his gaze away from his dogs, and hit the gas, honking and weaving around the sheep.

As he approached the homestead, he could see his father's truck parked in the front yard. Driven right through his mother's garden, the driver's door still open.

Reese smelled the blood first. Then he saw it, a trail leading from the truck to the front door. Bloody drag marks on the porch. Bloody handprints on the door.

He teetered then lunged forward, and ran in, calling, "Mom! Dad!" He followed the bloody trail into his parents' bedroom. There was his father, face down. Dead.

His mother sat on the floor beside him. In one hand she clenched his father's fingers. In the other she held a pistol. Her blond hair fell forward. Dried blood tracks ran down her cheek. More blood pooled on the floor around her, mingling with his father's.

The werewolves must have found his father out with the sheep. He'd gotten away, managing to stay alive until he'd made it back to warn her. She'd known she couldn't escape. Known they wouldn't kill her quickly. She couldn't—wouldn't—go through that again. She'd sent him the messages. And then . . .

Reese dropped to his knees beside them. A sob caught in his chest, lodged there, stopping his breath, and he didn't try to let it out, didn't try to breathe, didn't want to breathe. Didn't deserve to breathe.

"It's my fault," he whispered. "My fault."

"Yep, boy, it is."

He grabbed for the gun, but Keith easily wrenched it from his shock-numbed fingers. Reese scrambled to his feet. He saw the gun barrel pointed at him, and he didn't care, just dove at the man, praying he could do some damage before the bullet killed him.

No bullet came. The gun whacked Reese's forehead. He fell back. When he tried to rise, Keith hit him again and again, until he couldn't get up, just crouched on all fours, retching.

He heard a voice and lifted his head. His eyes wouldn't focus, but he still recognized the slight figure in the door.

"Daniella," he croaked.

Flanking her were two big brutes. Werewolves. He could smell that. There was something else about their scent, too. Something familiar. As his head stopped spinning and he saw their faces, he knew where he'd seen them before.

The night Daniella was attacked. These were the men who'd attacked her. That's why that alley had reeked of booze. Splashed around to make their scent so faint that Daniella wouldn't recognize them as werewolves. Outside werewolves Keith had hired to hurt her.

When Daniella stepped forward, the two men did nothing to stop her. There was no sign that she'd struggled against her captors. No sign that she was the least bit concerned for her safety. He saw that and he knew he was wrong. They hadn't splashed around the rum to disguise their scent from *her*.

"No," he whispered. "Daniella . . ."

Keith put his arm around her neck, one hand toying with her hair. "She's something, isn't she? A worthy mate to the Alpha."

Reese puked, emptying his stomach onto the floor as the werewolves laughed.

When he looked up again, he searched her face for some sign that she was just playing along. But she was clear-eyed, calm, and resolute. He remembered how he'd marveled at the dichotomy in her, sweet and gentle on the outside, hot-blooded and passionate on the inside.

Dichotomy? No. The sweet and gentle side had been an act to lure in a young werewolf eager to be chivalrous, needing only a damsel in distress to protect.

When her gaze fell on his parents' bodies, he felt a blaze of hate so strong a growl vibrated through him. How many hours had they spent talking about his parents? All the stories he'd told, bringing them to life, showing her what amazing people they were. And now she surveyed their corpses without a spark of emotion.

"It was her idea, you know," Keith said. "Her father wants me to marry her sister. Rose is the sweet one, like her mother. Dani takes after her daddy, and Gavin thinks an Alpha needs a submissive, supportive wife. I was open to the idea of a stronger partner, though. I just needed some convincing."

Reese could figure out the rest. The Pack had heard he was at Melbourne University. Daniella had volunteered to get him. She'd set up that rape scenario in the alley, knowing it would echo his mother's past and draw him to her. Then she'd confessed to being the Alpha's daughter. Make her the victim. Put him in the role of protector. Get him to talk about his parents in hopes he'd give away their location. When that failed, she'd forced his hand. Made him take her to them. Only he'd stopped at the motel. Impatient and fearing he'd change his mind, she'd gotten enough information for the Pack to find his parents. Kill them. Wait for him.

"She'll make a fine Alpha female, won't she?" Keith said. "Willing to do anything for her Pack, however unpleasant."

As the others laughed, Reese looked up at Daniella. "Oh, I wouldn't say it was all unpleasant. She sure seemed to be having a good time."

Keith tensed. Daniella opened her mouth, but Reese kept going.

"Gotta hand it to you," he said to Keith. "You're not the knuckle-dragger my dad said you were. It takes a damned fine leader to put the Pack's interests in front of his own, and a damned big man to let another guy screw his bride before he gets the chance."

Daniella sneered. "Right. Like I'd let you touch me—"

"Oh, I did a lot more than touch. But I don't blame you. You want to be Alpha female, but to do that you need to marry this old guy. Had to get your fun while you could, then you can fake the wedding night, trust he's dumb enough and horny enough not to notice." He turned to Keith. "Don't worry, though. I was the first. And I broke her in real good."

Daniella lunged at him. Keith caught her by the back of the shirt.

"Tell me he's full of shit, Dani."

"Of course he is. He's just trying—"

"If I'm lying, tell me this," Reese said. "Why'd she shower before she met up with you guys? You could smell the soap on her. What did she need to wash off so badly that she'd risk waking me up to do it?"

Daniella lunged again. This time Keith whipped her right off her feet, snarling, "He'd better be bullshitting, Dani, or—"

Reese leapt for the gun dangling from Keith's free hand. Keith recovered too fast for him to grab it, but Reese managed to smack it out of his hand. It hit the floor and skidded between the two other werewolves. Reese dove and got it.

One of the werewolves grabbed for him. Reese kicked him in the jaw, then leapt to his feet and raced into his bedroom. He slapped the lock shut and then grabbed his desk chair and jammed it under the handle.

The hinges groaned as a werewolf threw himself at the door. Reese aimed the gun and waited.

Keith's muffled voice said, "You break that door down and he's going to shoot you."

Not as dumb as he looked. As they conferred, Reese checked the chamber, making sure he had at least four—

There was one bullet left.

No way. No fucking way.

He took a deep breath. One bullet. He burned to use it on Daniella, but he knew he'd never manage it before the others got him. And even if he did, did killing her truly avenge his parents?

There was only one way to do this, as much as his gut twisted at the thought.

He lifted the gun, took a deep breath, yelled, "You want me dead? Here you go." And he pulled the trigger.

The gun fired. As Reese's body hit the floor, the werewolves went silent.

Then, "Shit."

"Should I break the door—"

"No. We need them to disappear. No signs of forced entry. Find the key."

As Reese slowly rose, he rubbed the hip that had taken the brunt of his fall. He glanced at his bed. The bullet had gone into the mattress, silencing the impact.

Reese took a pocketknife from his dresser and snuck to the window. He climbed out and crept around to the barn. Keith's SUV was hidden behind it. He slashed the tires, then, crawling, got to his dad's truck and did the same. He was just getting into his own truck when he heard Keith inside, saying, "He's got something jamming the door shut."

When they heard his truck roar down the lane, they raced out. Reese forced himself not to look in the rearview mirror. Forced himself not to think of going back and facing them. Not to feel like a coward for running. He still did the last. But his mother had told him to run, and she'd been right.

Run until he was ready to go back. Until he was ready to take revenge. One day, he would be. No matter what it took, one day, he'd be ready.

Lucifer's Daughter

*N*othing gets my blood pumping like a museum. Millennia of murder and mayhem gathered under one roof. A delicious banquet of guilt-free chaos custom-made for an Expisco half-demon.

I climbed from the car as my boyfriend handed the keys to the valet. Then I saw it.

"No," I whispered. "It's just a vision, right? A horrible vision."

Karl walked over and slid an arm around me. "Actually, I think she's beautiful."

We were staring up at a banner announcing tonight's event—the opening of a new exhibition sponsored by my grandmother. She'd said it was a display of World War Two memorabilia, in memory of my grandfather. It wasn't.

Smiling down from the banner was a face that horrified me as no vision of death and destruction ever could: my byline photo under the *True News* masthead.

"*The Hope Adams Exhibit of the Inexplicable*," Karl read. "Sounds . . . intriguing."

"I cannot believe Gran would do this."

"No? Isn't this the same woman who used to take you to churches with brown-skinned icons to prove that God loves you, even if you aren't white? Of course, that was easier than finding horned icons, to prove God loves you even if you are the devil's spawn."

I glared at him. Of course, my grandmother—like everyone in my family—had no idea I was a half-demon. But I suspect if she did learn the truth, she'd find a way to convince me *that* was okay, too.

I loved my grandmother. Sure, she could be a bigoted old battle-ax, but it couldn't have been easy when her son—one of Phila-delphian high society's most eligible bachelors—announced he planned to marry an exchange student from India. Gran had accepted his choice, though, and accepted all of her grandchildren, including the one born after the marriage broke down: me. She was determined to prove her love, even if it meant sponsoring an exhibition to say, "My granddaughter investigates Bigfoot stories for a supermarket tabloid and, damn it, I'm so proud of her."

Karl's attention had wandered to another sign. A photograph of a huge sapphire-encrusted pendant announced a traveling exhibit featuring the Amulet of Marduk.

I sighed. "Reminder to self: never bring a jewel thief to a museum. You know the rule. No stealing at any event where we are invited guests."

He walked over to the sign.

"Karl . . . We had a deal . . ."

"I believe the deal is that I may not steal jewels from *guests* at events to which we are invited."

"Okay, but then taking the amulet would break your deal with Clayton, which says—"

"That I can't steal artifacts of historical significance. The Amulet of Marduk is an Egyptian reproduction. Bling. Very old . . ." He looked at the sign again, and his blue eyes gleamed, the wolf in him spotting prey he liked far more than rabbits. "Very valuable bling."

"No."

"If I'm not breaking the rules . . ."

"Sure you are. Remember the one that says, 'Thou shalt not steal'?"

A faint eye roll at such a bourgeois notion.

"Fine," I said. "You sneak in the back and do your thing, while I hang out at the party with Nelson Graves. Remember Nelson?"

Karl gave a rumbling grunt that sounded suspiciously like a growl.

"Gran says he asked if I was coming tonight and if I was still with you. He told her he'd see what he could do about that." I pursed my lips. "It's tempting. He's attractive, under thirty, rich, and, best of all, has a job that's unlikely to land me in a prison visitor's room anytime soon."

Karl put his hands on my hips. "Start that and you won't get to your party anytime soon."

"I mention another guy, and you feel the need to assert your property rights? A little medieval, don't you think?" I stepped away. "But if that puts you in the mood, think how much better it'll be after I spend a whole evening with Nelson. Provided, of course, that you don't steal anything."

He arched a brow. "Threatening to withhold sex if I misbehave? A little medieval, don't you think?"

Before I could answer, a town car pulled up to the curb with my mother in the passenger seat. Karl strode over to open the door. I couldn't see the driver, and tried to remember whether she was coming with the Democratic congressman or the Republican one. I could never tell them apart, and it was so embarrassing when I got it wrong.

As the congressman talked to the valet, my mother pointed to the banner. "For the record, I had no idea she was doing this."

"I know."

"She's just trying to be supportive."

"I know. I just wish she'd find a less"—I looked up at the banner and cringed—"public way to show it."

She hugged me. "I know."

As we climbed the steps, Mom asked me how my work was going. She never asked about Karl's. I think she knew he wasn't really in the import-export business. She didn't care. As she'd said even when we were just friends, "He's good for you, Hope," and to her, that was all that mattered. For Karl's part, even when he saw her wearing her most valuable jewels, that gleam never entered his eyes, which in him was a sign of unparalleled respect.

The congressman—Democrat, Karl mouthed—was waylaid on the steps, and Mom waved for us to go on inside while she waited for him.

I stepped through the doors to find myself face-to-face with . . . myself. A giant banner hung from floor to ceiling, just in case anyone had missed the one outside.

"Oh God," I said. "I don't think I can do this."

"I don't blame you." Karl pointed to a service door. "I do believe that will take us into the rear of the museum, near the display for the amulet. And with those banners all over the building, no one will wonder who you are if we're caught wandering about."

"Nice try. We—"

The hall went dark. Voices rose in a chant. I heard a scream. Felt a splatter of warm liquid. Licked my lips and tasted blood.

The chanting grew louder, but the screams drowned them out. I strained to see deeper into the vision, hoping to catch a glimpse of whatever was responsible for the delicious chaos washing over me.

The screams faded, and I felt Karl's hands rubbing my arms. I blinked and looked around. He'd tugged me into a corner.

"Trouble?" he said.

I shook my head. "Just a vision of past ritual torture or human sacrifice. You know museums. Full of dull, dry hist—"

The hair on my neck rose as a voiceless whisper called to me, promising more sweet chaos . . .

"Hope?"

"Museums," I said, shaking my head, and motioned him into the foyer.

"Ironically appropriate, don't you think?" Karl whispered.

We stood before a display dedicated to human–demon hybrids in myth and popular culture, including Hell Spawn—*True News*'s answer to *Weekly World News*'s Bat Boy.

The whole exhibit was like that—linking my articles to supernatural legends. Fascinating, actually. And, yes, flattering, once I got past the cringe factor.

Tour guides led partygoers through the displays. We were in the first group, with my mother, the congressman, and Gran.

"I wish your father could have been here," Gran said. "He's so proud of you, dear."

"I'm sure he is," Karl murmured in my ear. "But it's a long way to travel."

I glowered at him. My *father* might be Lucifer, but my *dad* was still Will Adams. He was on business in Indonesia and had sent a gift with Gran—a silver armband engraved with mystical symbols. Ugly as hell, but it was his way of showing his support, and a lot more welcome than sponsoring a museum exhibit in my name.

When Karl took off to use the restroom, I watched him weave past scaffolding. The museum was in the final stages of renovations—which were actually Karl's fault. We'd first met here four years ago when I'd tried to stop him from stealing something—surprise, surprise—and nearly got the place burned down running from someone *else* on his tail. Thousand-year-old papyrus scrolls and fire half-demons really don't mix.

Karl hadn't commented on the renovations. Nor had he commented on our return to the scene of our first meeting. I'm sure he remembered—kind of hard to forget—but Karl wasn't the sentimental type. Also, he hadn't made the best first impression. It'd been two years before I'd go out with him, which I'm sure, for the sake of his ego, he considers a failure best forgotten.

Gran was pointing out the new plasterwork when the director arrived. "The guest of honor," he said, pumping my hand. "Isn't your exhibit marvelous?"

"It is."

He lowered his voice. "Some board members were opposed to the show, saying it would be pandering to the basest segment of society."

"Understandable. It's—"

"And I said, that's the *point*. Entice them with the lurid and the ludicrous and maybe they'll get lost on the way to the restrooms and actually see something edifying. In tough times, we all need to do what we can. However distasteful." He nudged me. "You know all about that."

Gran pushed between us. "Actually, my granddaughter likes her work. And I like it, too. Mythology is an important part of any culture, and—"

—a lesson you won't soon forget, a voice boomed.

I jumped. Mom put a hand against my back. The lights flickered, but no one else seemed to notice. As Gran continued lecturing the director, a tendril of chaos wrapped around me, tugging me deeper into the museum.

Oh, hell, where was Karl? And what was he getting into?

I excused myself and hurried into the back hall.

No sign of Karl. I closed my eyes and concentrated. I could pick up blips of chaos from the party. Anger. Jealousy. Envy. When I tuned that out, I got a jolt of the real stuff, coming from the jewelry exhibit.

Oh, hell.

I jogged along the dark corridor.

Thrall of Lucifer, heed my words!

I spun, nearly tripping. The hall was empty.

You have rained down chaos and destruction for long enough. May you spend eternity suffering the torment you have visited on so many.

Something wrapped around me, tight as a mummy's bindings. I struggled to get free, shrieked, and shouted curses in languages I didn't recognize—

"Hope!"

I snapped out of the vision to find myself on the floor, lying across Karl's lap.

I scrambled to my feet. "You took it, didn't you?"

"What?"

"The Amulet of Marduk. Damn you, Karl, I asked—"

"I didn't take anything."

I grabbed his tuxedo lapel and reached inside the jacket for the hidden pocket.

He caught my hands. "If you want to undress me, there are better places to do it. In fact, I saw a suitably dark—"

"What did you steal?" I asked.

"Nothing. Yes, I was in the room with the amulet. Yes, I have every intention of taking it. But not tonight. I wouldn't do that when—"

Something small and furry scampered past a doorway.

"Rat?" I said.

He inhaled and frowned. "No, it smells like . . ."

Chattering erupted. Then the sound of tiny nails skittering across the floor. The creature darted out of a dark adjoining room and launched itself at me. That's when I smelled the thing—an awful stink of formaldehyde and badly stored fur. The beast thumped onto me, claws clutching the front of my dress. A tiny spider monkey face turned up to mine.

A tiny *dead* spider monkey.

Its eyes were beads and half its teeth were missing. At every joint, the fur and skin had ripped open. Sawdust spilled out. Through the openings, I could see bone and the wire that had held the monkey in a pose—until it'd been reanimated and no longer cared to be in that pose.

Karl grabbed the monkey by the scruff of the neck and whipped it away from me. It hit the wall and exploded. Sawdust and fur flew everywhere, including into my mouth. I spat and clawed it out, gagging.

Again, the sounds of tiny scrabbling nails filled the hallway. I looked up. One arm and one leg were still attached to the monkey's torso as it pulled itself toward me.

Karl strode forward.

"You can't kill a reanimated corpse," I said.

"I can try."

He stomped on it. The arm and leg launched from the torso like rockets.

I winced. "Better hope the SPCA doesn't catch you doing that."

He snorted and kicked the bits into a storage room.

I stared at the tufts of fur and curls of sawdust left behind on the polished floor. A top-notch necromancer can reanimate long-dead corpses, but what was the chance that one was practicing his craft during a museum charity event? At the same time that Karl was poking around ancient artifacts?

"Show me where you were," I said. "And what you did."

He'd been in the traveling jewelry exhibit, checking out security so he could return another day to steal the amulet. It was still there, though, and he swore he hadn't even touched its glass box. What he *had* handled was a display in an identical case. As a test run, he'd opened it and closed it again.

"And that's all?" I said.

"I picked up that," he said, pointing to a small jewel-covered box inside the case. "The sign says it's bronze with semiprecious stones. It's wrong. The stones aren't valuable, but the box itself is gold. I considered pocketing it, but . . ." He shrugged. "Not while we're invited guests."

"And not when it's an object of historical significance."

He said, "Hmm," which meant that was open to interpretation and he'd interpret it for himself when he came back for the amulet.

I bent to read the plaque. As I did, I saw the pattern on the box he'd picked up—symbols that told me this was not, as the museum claimed, a fifteenth-century noblewoman's keepsake box. It *was* meant for keeping something, though.

"You opened it?" I said.

"Not intentionally. It seemed sealed, but when I was examining the jewels, the lid popped open. I closed it."

"Not fast enough." I straightened. "It's a soul box for demons. Used by witches and sorcerers powerful enough to bind one."

Shoes squeaked outside the door.

"I've found you," a breathless voice said.

Nelson strode across the room, gaze fixed on me as if he didn't even see Karl.

"Uh, sorry, we were just looking for the ladies' room. I need to, uh, freshen up."

"Why?" Nelson stopped in front of me. "You are already the most beautiful thing I have ever laid eyes on."

"Umm, thanks . . ."

Behind me, Karl growled.

Nelson dropped to one knee. "I am yours, mistress. I live to serve you. To worship you."

"Guess that demon soul isn't in the monkey anymore," Karl murmured.

"You don't think I'm worthy of worship?" I said. "Maybe—"

Demon Nelson started licking my shins.

Karl turned to me. "You were saying?"

"Never mind. You're going to need to disable him. Just don't—"

Karl grabbed Demon Nelson by the back of his jacket and started swinging him toward the nearest display.

"—do that," I said. "Don't break any displays. And don't break him."

Karl paused, as if considering whether he'd heard me.

Demon Nelson squirmed and shrieked. "Defiler! You are not fit to speak to my master's daughter. You will pay for your—"

Karl dropped him headfirst onto the floor. Then he pinned him under one Italian loafer. I walked closer, staying out of licking distance.

"Who are you?" I asked.

He didn't pause. "Nybbas, mistress."

He went on, giving his demon equivalent of rank and serial number. He was a demi-demon under Lucifer. He'd gone AWOL a few thousand years ago and had himself a rollicking unauthorized shore leave in ancient Sumer, leaving death and destruction in his wake, until—as I'd seen in my vision—he'd ended up trapped in that box.

Now he was out and very, very grateful. He recognized me as Lucifer's daughter and presumed I was the one who'd set him free. It didn't seem wise to argue.

"I will repay your kindness, mistress," he said, tongue extending, unsuccessfully, toward my shoes. "I will be your humble slave until my debt is paid, and then you shall tell your lord father how useful I have been, and he will take me back."

I've never met my father. Never wanted to. Again, though, I didn't set him straight.

"That's very sweet," I said. "I'm sure you'd make a wonderful demon slave, but it's the twenty-first century and there are laws against that sort of thing. So how about I just let you go back to hell, where I'm sure Lucifer will be happy—"

"Nooo!" he howled.

He leapt to his feet, catching Karl off guard, and darted out of his reach.

"I must prove myself first," he said as he dodged Karl's lunge. "If I please you, my master will be pleased."

"Fine, then. Clean my condo for a few days and we'll call it even."

"I must show my respect properly. I will prepare a feast in your honor. A feast of chaos. The sacrifice of a hundred souls—"

"No! No sacrifices. I command—"

"Hope?" A quavering voice called from the hall. "Is that you, dear?"

Nybbas stopped and smiled. "The first offering."

"No!" I said. Then to Karl, "Catch—"

Karl dove at Nybbas and knocked him to the floor. I raced into the hall. Outside the exhibit room, I slowed and tried to look sheepish.

"Hey, Gran," I said. "Caught us doing a little unauthorized touring. Karl wanted to see the Amulet of Marduk. He read about it in the paper."

"Is that what he said?"

She smiled as her gaze traveled over my dress and hair, which was in even more disarray than usual. She tried to peer into the room. When I blocked her view, she chuckled.

"Not in a state to be seen, is he?" she said.

"Uh, no, he's just—"

"Karl is a very attractive man, Hope. Very powerful. Very . . . virile." Her eyes shone with something that looked frighteningly close to lust and she tried, again, to peer around me. "It's not easy to keep a man like that happy. It takes a lot of time and effort." That sparkle again as she smiled. "But you seem to be doing a fine job of it. A fine job."

"Er, thanks . . ."

She patted my arm. "I'll cover for you two. Just don't be too long."

I returned to the exhibit to find Karl kneeling on the struggling demon.

"She's old," the demon whined. "Let me sacrifice her, so she may do some good in her final days."

"That woman is my grandmother," I said as I walked over.

The demon stopped writhing. "She gave birth to his lordship's chosen vessel?"

It took me a second to figure out that he thought Gran was my mother's mother. Though two weeks in Nassau had given my grandmother a nice tan, no one was likely to mistake her for

Indo-American. But if this demon had racial identification issues, I wasn't setting him straight.

Nybbas lay still for a moment, then he bucked, knocking Karl off. He leapt up and danced back out of Karl's reach.

"*This* one would make a suitable sacrifice," Nybbas said. "A werewolf is a base creature, unsuited to be consort to a demon princess. Your father would be pleased if I rid you of this embarrassment."

"You want to kill me?" Karl bared his teeth. "You need to come a little closer first."

He grabbed for the demon, who backpedaled then feinted and dove at Karl, managing to snag his leg and send him crashing to the floor.

"Enough!" I said, jumping between them. "He's not my consort. He's my bodyguard." I turned to Karl. "Stop playing with your prey and catch him. I command it."

Karl arched an eyebrow, but charged. This time he foresaw the demon's feint and threw him down, then pinned him on his stomach again.

Nybbas glanced over his shoulder. "I suppose, as a bodyguard, he is suitable. Sacrifices must be made, though. I will begin with my host."

Karl hesitated and looked down at Nelson's body beneath him. Then he backed off, just a little. I glowered. He sighed, then leaned on the demon again.

"The princess says you may not sacrifice your host," he said. "Sadly."

Nybbas nodded. "And the princess must be obeyed."

"She must?" I said. "I mean, yes. She must. The princess commands that you are not to kill that host or my bodyguard. In fact, the princess asks that there are to be no sacrifices made on her behalf. She commands you to leave that body and begin your journey home."

"As you wish."

Nelson's eyes glowed yellow, then faded to their normal brown as a warm wind circled the room and his body collapsed, motionless, under Karl.

"He's gone," I said.

"Hmm." Karl rose.

"Too easy?" I asked.

"I'd say so."

"Damn."

I grabbed the soul box before we left the exhibit. When I caught up with Karl, he glanced at it and nodded.

"Good idea. It's more valuable than the amulet. Particularly given its purpose. It could fetch a small fortune on the supernatural black market."

"Very funny. I'm borrowing it, then returning it to the exhibit as it was before you tampered with it—demon soul and all." I tried to hand it to him as we walked down the back hall. "You open it; I'll turn on my chaos detector."

"Open it?"

"That's how the soul got out. Just do whatever you did before. And quickly."

I pressed the box into his hands.

"I think this demon princess business is going to your head," he said.

"Open it."

He took the box and examined it, grumbling that he didn't know how he'd done it the first time so he could hardly be expected to do it again. I concentrated on picking up tendrils of chaos.

I caught a blip of fear. I was homing in on it when a wave of chaos hit. I stumbled back. Karl caught me.

"I think—"

Darkness enveloped me. Voices chanted. A scream drowned them out. The rich coppery smell of blood filled the air. Hot droplets spattered my face. Someone intoned an incantation. The shrieks continued. The screams of a demon about to be cut from his mortal form and shoved into a very tiny box for a very long time.

I yanked free of the vision. Karl was holding me. I was still standing this time, which was always a plus.

"Did you find him?" Karl asked.

I shook my head. "Just another flashback of him being stuffed in that box. Maybe we should split up while you try to open it."

"And if I can't open it?"

"Just keep—"

A shriek cut me off. Karl spun toward the noise. A real scream, then, not a chaos playback. Some days it was tough to tell.

We took off in the direction of the scream. Everything had gone silent now, but I could feel undercurrents of chaos throbbing through the air. Karl headed straight for them, following voices I could barely detect.

We turned the corner to see a beefy security guard with a party-goer pinned against the wall. Beside him, a red-haired woman bounced, doing absolutely nothing to help her date, just whimpering and jabbering.

"We were looking for the ladies' room," she was telling the guard. "The other one was full. We didn't know this part of the museum was off-limits."

"You broke my fucking nose," her date mumbled, trying to talk with his face mashed against the bloodied wall. "Call 911 before this psycho kills me, Tara."

"You don't need to yell at me, Rick," she whined.

I recognized the voice and the names. Tara Dunlop. During our debutante year we'd approached something like friendship, ending when she caught Rick with me in a back hall a lot like this one. The fact that he'd been pinning *me* to a wall at the time hadn't mattered. I was the little slut who'd tempted her boyfriend. When I'd had a breakdown as my powers hit, she'd made sure every one of our acquaintances knew why Hope Adams missed her high school prom: because the psych ward didn't grant day passes.

Karl peered down the hall. "Isn't that . . . ?"

"Uh-huh."

I'd told him the story after Tara tried luring *him* into a back room at a New Year's ball.

"Perhaps allowing a sacrifice or two isn't such a bad thing," he said. "Seeing that I can't open the soul box, this might be our only way to get that demon back to hell."

"Tempting," I muttered as I began walking toward them. "Very tempting."

"Oh, oh!" Tara chirped. "Someone's coming. It's—" She leaned around the security guard and saw me. "Oh."

The guard turned my way, Rick still dangling from his arm. The guard's eyes flashed yellow. "You are early, my princess. The sacrifice is not yet complete."

"Princess?" Tara said.

"*Sacrifice?*" Rick yelped.

"Is this a friend of yours, Hope?" Tara said. "Figures. Bet you met a lot of them in the loony bin. Is that where you met him, too?" She gestured at Karl. "I heard it was a dating service. Gold-Diggers-R-Us."

"Last chance," Karl whispered to me.

"There will be no sacrifices," I said, walking over to Nybbas. "I thought I made that clear."

"No, princess. You asked that no sacrifices be made on your behalf. That means you do not wish the deaths to weigh on your conscience. A human failing, but I understand. I will make the sacrifices for you and—"

"And no." I stepped so close I could smell the guard's cheap cologne. "I do *not* want the sacrifices. I command—"

The guard's body collapsed at my feet.

"We need to get that box open," I said as we strode down the hall, having ensured the guard was only unconscious and left Tara and Rick making a beeline for the back exit. "Are you sure you don't remember how you did it?"

"Yes, I remember. I'm just pretending otherwise to liven up a dull evening."

"Okay. Sorry. We need a backup plan, then. Paige and Lucas have a dispossession spell that might work, but we'd have to get them here from Portland. Meanwhile, this bastard has free run of a building filled with potential victims. We need to get everyone out so we can—"

The vision flashed again. I pushed it aside faster now, recovering after only a split-second blackout. When I came to, though, I found myself staring at a red box on the wall.

I glanced over at Karl. He plucked a glove from his pocket and pulled the fire alarm.

As plans went, it was far from foolproof. For one thing, as the partygoers streamed toward the exits, their chaos washed over me . . . and washed away any chaos being caused by Nybbas himself. Then someone shouted, "Where's the tour group? Has anyone seen them yet?" and I looked over to see the closed doors to the new exhibit.

I yanked on the door. It didn't budge. Karl grabbed it and heaved, tendons in his neck bulging. Then, with a crack, the door flew open and we raced through.

Inside, it was pitch-black and silent. Chaos thrummed through the room. Then a whimper, followed by a harsh whisper, someone urging silence.

"I can smell you," a woman's voice sang. "I don't need lights to find dirty, stinking humans."

When the fire alarm sounded, the lights must have gone off. Now they were trapped as Nybbas hunted them.

"I'll stop him," Karl whispered. "You stay here." He pressed the box into my hands. "Work on this."

"I can't—" I began, but he was gone.

I held the box, my fingers running over the jewels. He was right—opening it had been a fluke the first time. All we could do was catch whatever body he'd jumped into and get these people to safety before he grabbed a new one. With a room filled with fresh bodies to possess, though . . .

Shit.

I turned the box over in my hands, touching the jewels randomly, frantically, as I strained to hear Karl.

"Is that a wolf I smell?" the singsong voice said.

A grunt, then the thud of a body hitting the floor. A woman started to scream. Karl apologized and laughter rang out—in a man's voice now.

"You may be a fast wolf," Nybbas said from his new body. "But you aren't nearly fast enough."

A scream made me jump, and I nearly dropped the box before I realized it was just the vision again. I squeezed my eyes shut and forced it away.

Then a woman shrieked, "Get him off me. Get him off me!" and footsteps thundered across the room. A thump, as Karl grabbed the demon off his new victim. A laugh as the demon jumped bodies. Only this time I recognized that deep chuckle. Recognized it very well. Nybbas had leapt into Karl.

"Get out of him!" I said. "I commanded you—"

"—not to kill your wolf." Nybbas giggled. "I won't. I promise."

"I command you—"

"I can't hear you!" Nybbas said. "Can't hear anything. I will find my sacrifices and then I will return to my master and tell him what I have done, and he will be pleased."

I tried ordering him again, but he just kept getting louder, drowning me out.

The vision threatened again. I pushed it back.

Nybbas inhaled deeply. "Better sense of smell. Better night vision. Better hearing. This makes it almost too easy."

I turned the box over. I just had to hold this damned chaos vision at bay long enough to concentrate—

I stopped. Chaos vision. Of Nybbas's incarceration.

"There you are," Nybbas said. "Come here, human. Let me taste—"

An *oomph* and a hiss as whoever Nybbas caught escaped. Then a clatter and a howl of rage as he tripped over something.

I squeezed my eyes shut, wrapped my hands around the box, and cleared my mind. The vision hit like a left hook to the temple. I struck the floor, and everything went dark.

I heard the demon's screams. Then chanting. Then a man's voice reciting the incantation. I blinked hard, and the vision came clear.

I stood in a temple. At the altar, a bearded man held the soul box aloft. Women in red robes ringed him, chanting. At his feet, a bound man struggled.

The sorcerer pressed the jewels on the box. The lid flew open.

One of the women took a knife from her robe, raised it, and stabbed the bound man while the sorcerer continued the incantation. As the last word left his mouth, the demon was ripped—shrieking—from his still-living host, a yellow pulsing light being dragged toward the box. When it disappeared inside, the sorcerer smacked it shut.

I snapped from the vision, but the screams continued. A woman's screams now, her nails scratching the floor as Nybbas dragged her. I quickly hit the jewels in sequence as I recited the incantation.

As I hit the last jewel, the box popped open. I squeezed my eyes shut, and finished the last words.

"No!" Nybbas shrieked. "Mistress, no! I will obey you. I will—"

Yellow light flashed, then a glowing ball streaked toward me. When it disappeared inside the box, I slapped it shut. The box rocked and jumped. Then it went still.

I won't say Karl was shaken up by the demonic possession. More like pissed off, mostly at himself, as if getting possessed were a personal failure of will. We'd discuss it later. For now, we didn't trust that Nybbas was gone. After escorting everyone out of the exhibit, I assured my mother and grandmother that we were fine. Then, as the fire trucks arrived, we snuck back inside and canvassed the museum. It was empty. No humans. No demons. Just us, staying two steps ahead of the fire crews.

We replaced the soul box in the display. Keeping it would only alert the museum to the theft. Better to return later with magical help to seal the box forever.

We were heading for the exit when Karl whisked me into a closet.

"Someone's coming," he whispered.

"I don't hear anything."

He lifted me onto a crate. As he pressed against me, I felt a bulge . . . in his tux jacket. I slid my hands inside the coat.

"You did steal something!" I yanked out a box from the hidden pocket. "Damn you, Karl—"

"Shhh. You don't want us to get caught roaming the museum. Particularly if I did steal something."

"Bastard," I hissed.

I pushed him away. It was a jewelry box, one he must have brought so if he got caught, he might convince a naive guard it held only a gift for his girlfriend.

I opened the box to see . . . a diamond solitaire ring.

"*Not* stolen," Karl said.

On each side of the diamond, there was an engraved symbol for eternity, matching the charm Karl had bought for me last year. The writing inside matched my charm, too. Three words. *No matter what.*

"I haven't gotten any more poetic. No more romantic, either." He gestured around the closet. "In my defense, I did try. It seemed perfect—returning to the place we first met. It didn't quite work out the way I planned, though."

I lifted the ring. "So is this . . . ? I mean, is it what it looks like?"

"Ah, sorry. I'm making a mess of this, aren't I? Let's try that again." He took the ring and the box from me. "I know this isn't what you want right now. That's fine. I'll wait. But someday, when you're ready . . ." He held out the box, the ring back in place. "Will you marry me?"

"Um, you saw what you'd be getting yourself into, right?"

"Let's see . . . High-society in-laws on one side. The Prince of Darkness on the other. A demon princess for a wife. A lifetime of chaos and general anarchy. Is that what I want?" He met my gaze. "Absolutely."

He lifted the box. I took the ring, looked up at him, and put it on my finger.

HIDDEN

PROLOGUE

"There's a wolf in the forest."

Peyton's big sister, Piper, looked up from her homework. "What?"

Peyton pointed at the window. "A wolf. Out there. He was watching me." She tugged one pigtail. "He watches me a lot. I think he's lonely."

Piper scrambled off her chair, put her hand to the glass, and cupped it to peer into the darkness.

"He's kinda hard to see," Peyton said. "Because he's black. But he has blue eyes. I can always see his eyes."

Their brother, Pearce, walked in, sneering. "Yeah, a blue-eyed black wolf. She saw a dog, Pipe."

"No, I saw a wolf. He's right—" Peyton pressed her nose to the glass. "He's gone. But it was a wolf. He was really big."

"How big?" Piper asked.

Peyton lifted her hand to the top of her head.

"Uh-huh." Pearce turned to Piper. "Dog. Wolves are smaller than Mrs. Lee's German shepherd. And they're gray with brown eyes. She's a baby, Pipe. She imagines things."

"I'm not a baby! I'm almost five and I go to school."

Piper headed for the door. "I'm going out to take a look."

⚜

Piper hadn't found any sign of what her sister had seen outside, but it still worried her. Mom didn't pay nearly enough attention to Peyton these days, and she was liable to let her wander into the forest looking for her "wolf." They lived near Algonquin Park. There *were* wolves in their woods—plus bears, porcupines, and lynx. Piper tried to watch her little sister, but she was in high school now and couldn't be with her all the time.

She went in to tell Mom what Peyton had seen, but Mom was on the phone with Roy, Peyton's dad. They'd split up six months ago. Things had been better with Roy around. A lot better. Kids always whined about their stepdads, but Roy had been great. Now he was gone, and Mom was on the phone with him, fighting as usual. He wanted custody of Peyton; Mom wouldn't even let him see her.

Piper had overheard Aunt Nancy saying Mom was doing it to punish Roy. Piper hoped her mom would wake up soon and decide he'd been punished enough. That she'd realize a four-year-old was more than she could handle when she had two jobs and friends and boyfriends. Piper hated being disloyal to her mother, but she secretly hoped that someday Roy would just come and take Peyton. It would be better for everyone. Especially Peyton.

That night, after everyone was asleep, Peyton stood at her bedroom window and watched the wolf. She had asked her teacher yesterday if wolves could be black, and they'd looked it up on the computer and found pictures of black ones. Pearce wasn't so smart, even if he was almost twelve.

After that, Peyton dug out the camera Daddy had given her for Christmas. Mommy had gotten mad, saying Peyton was too young for one, but Daddy said he got a good deal on it, and Peyton loved taking pictures. Or she used to, when they'd go into the forest together and find butterflies and hummingbirds. But then Daddy left and Peyton put the camera away. Now she was going to use it to get a photo of the wolf and show Pearce.

She couldn't take pictures through the window. Daddy had taught her that. So she tiptoed past Piper's room and slipped into the back hall. Then she put on her coat and boots and went outside.

The wolf was still at the edge of the forest. When she came out, he didn't move, just looked at her. She lifted the camera. The wolf backed into the darkness.

Peyton took a few careful steps, until she saw the glow of his blue eyes. She lifted the camera. The wolf moved back. She moved forward. He moved back.

"I just want to take your picture," she said.

He tilted his head, as if listening to her. She raised the camera. He stretched out his front paws and lowered his head, tail wagging. Then he let out a little yelp, like Mrs. Lee's dog, Baxter, when he wanted to play. As she pushed the shutter button, he raced off.

Peyton checked the shot, like Daddy showed her. All it showed was the forest and the tip of a black tail.

She sighed. Hearing another yip, she glanced up to see the wolf again. He opened his mouth, tongue hanging out, like he was smiling. When she tried to snap a picture, he dropped and rolled on the ground, so all she got was a blur.

"That's not funny," she said.

He raced around her in a big circle. Then he stopped, right in front of her. That's when she realized she'd walked all the way into the forest.

She tensed to run back to the house, but he just stood there. He lowered his head and flicked his ears. Then he inched closer, his head still down, and as big as he was, he didn't seem scary at all. She reached out and patted him. His hair was so thick and soft it was like the coat Aunt Nancy had, with the fur collar, and Peyton only meant to pat his head, but soon she was scratching him behind the ears and burying her fingers in the fur around his neck.

Then he ducked away and danced back. She stepped forward. He stepped back. She laughed. He ran a little ways and she thought she'd scared him off, but he stopped, as if waiting for her.

She glanced over her shoulder at the house. He yipped, and he sounded so lonely and looked so hopeful that she couldn't resist.

"Okay," she said. "Let's play."

He yipped, as if he understood. Then they played together, her chasing, him hiding then jumping out and running. At first she kept looking back, making sure she could see the lights of the house. But then she forgot as she kept chasing him, going farther and farther into the forest.

They'd been playing for a while when he took off. She called for him to come back, but he didn't. The game was over. He'd gone home. So should she.

She turned around and peered into the darkness. There were no lights anywhere.

Peyton took a step. Dead leaves crackled under her boots. A moan whispered through the trees and she went still, her heart pounding. It was just branches moving in the wind, that's what Daddy told her. But it had sounded different when he'd been with her. Now all she could hear was the wind, making the branches moan and creak, rustling the leaves as it whined through the tree-tops. Then came a shriek, right beside her head.

She started to run and tripped. She hit the ground hard. Something jabbed her cheek. She wiped at it and felt blood. Biting back a whim-per, she tried to get up, but her foot hurt and she fell again.

She kept trying, but it hurt too much. Her foot throbbed and her cheek bled. And it was cold. So cold and dark and spooky and she was lost and no one would ever find her. That's when she started to cry.

She'd been huddled on the ground for a while when she heard a voice.

"Hello?" a man called.

She tried to stand, but her foot still wouldn't let her, so she got up on her knees and called back, "I'm here."

Footsteps came toward her. "I thought I heard crying."

"I-I'm lost."

"I see that." The man walked over and the first thing she noticed about him was his blue eyes. They looked just like the wolf's, and she blinked. The man smiled and crouched beside her, and she realized he just had regular blue eyes, like Mommy and a lot of other people.

"My name is Peyton James," she said. "I live at 228 Oak Lane."

"Ah. You must be Roy James's little girl."

She nodded.

"I played poker with your daddy. He used to talk about you all the time. Come on, then. My place is right over there. I'll get you cleaned up and warmed up and back home to your mommy."

"I can't stand. I hurt my foot."

He bent and looked at it. "Seems like your ankle's twisted. We'll take a better look at it over at my place. I'll carry you there. All right?"

Peyton nodded. He lifted her and she curled up against him, so nice and warm, and let him carry her through the forest.

ONE

When I pulled into the lane of our rented Christmas cottage, I was disappointed to see it empty. Clay wasn't there yet. Not that he'd expected to beat us, but the kids and I had hoped he might. He'd hoped so, too. What he'd *really* hoped was to make the drive with us, but he'd been in Montreal at a conference at McGill and when a winter storm hit, it made more sense for him to head straight across to Ontario rather than loop down to New York State and pick us up.

Kate was out of the car before I even had it in park. Leaving the door open, she raced into the front yard.

"There's more snow here!" she squealed.

Her twin brother, Logan, pulled on his hat and mitts before following. "No there isn't. It's the same amount."

"How much is at home?"

"Twenty-seven inches. But we're in Canada now, so it's centimeters. About seventy centimeters."

Kate pointed at a pile beside the drive. "That's more than seventy cent-er-meters."

Logan rolled his eyes at me as I grabbed bags from the back.

"Because it's a drift," he said.

"What's that in it?"

He walked over as she bent to point at something. As soon as he was close enough, she grabbed his jacket and pitched him headfirst into the drift.

"Should have seen that one coming, baby," I said as I walked to the door.

I put down the bags to fumble with the lockbox. Behind me, Logan sat on the drift, grumbling, until Kate made the mistake of thinking he might be seriously upset, went to apologize, and found herself lying in the snow beside him.

She should have seen that coming, too. She probably had, same as he did. But if you don't go along with the prank, you lose the right to retaliate.

I left the kids roughhousing in the snow but didn't close the inside door, so I could hear them. I opened the living room curtains, so I could keep an eye on them, too.

I've read articles about bubble-wrapping your children, and sometimes I think I'm guilty of that. Granted, the twins are only four, but I hadn't been much older than them when I was trekking down to the corner store alone. Of course, in my case that was because no one in my foster homes much cared what I did, and most times whatever danger I encountered on the streets wasn't as ugly as what waited for me inside those homes.

But I do hover too much with the twins. I chalk it up to instinct. Not just maternal, but wolf—as a werewolf, I'm naturally protective.

Finally, when Kate ventured too close to the forest's edge, I stepped onto the porch.

"Paths, Mommy," she said, grinning. "There's lots of paths."

"I know. We'll go exploring as soon as I've unpacked. Just come back into the yard."

Logan gave me that look that has me convinced he's a fourteen-year-old trapped in a four-year-old's body. "We know not to go in the woods, Momma. Kate's just looking. I'm watching her. It seems . . ." He gazed wistfully into the forest's dark depths. "Nice."

Is Logan a werewolf, like Clay and me? He should be—it's passed through the male line. Except Clay and I are both bitten werewolves. Either way, it *shouldn't* pass on to Kate. Yet seeing their expressions as they gazed into the forest made me wonder, as I'd been wondering for the past couple of years. Both showed secondary characteristics as well—keen hearing, excellent reflexes, increased strength. But even with hereditary werewolves, that shouldn't happen so young. I told myself it didn't matter. Whatever would be, would be. That was Clay's attitude. I worried a little more. Okay, a lot more.

"See that stump?" I said, pointing. "You can go in that far."

"Thanks, Momma," Logan said. The books say children don't develop the ability to display sarcasm until they're about six, but they also say kids shouldn't be reading fluently—let alone devouring reference books—before first grade, meaning whoever wrote them has never met my son.

I stuck out my tongue at him—proving that he doesn't inherit his maturity from me—and went back inside.

I let myself wander past the front room, out of sight of the kids, but kept my ears attuned for the first squeal of trouble.

The chalet was gorgeous. Jeremy had picked it out, so I'd expect no less. I didn't want to imagine how much a two-week rental cost. We could afford it, but I still stress over things like that.

Clay and I live with Jeremy. Clay always has—or he has since Jeremy found him as a child werewolf in Louisiana. He brought Clay home and raised him, and when I came into the picture, the household expanded to three.

Well, not exactly. There was a decade in the middle where I'd come and gone, Clay and I locked in an endless war of resentment and betrayal and love.

Clay was the one who'd bitten me, in a panic when he thought Jeremy would separate us. Maybe that sounds like something to be forgiven, but it's not, and for ten years the anger and the hurt and the hate came very easily. The love was tougher to deal with. That's what kept me running until, finally, he changed and I changed, and we resolved to try again. It still wasn't the most serene relationship, but in that way our children do take after us—they'll bicker and they'll battle, but the only time they're truly miserable is when they're apart.

Occasionally, though, the bickering and battling—and even just the good-natured rambunctious roughhousing—does become a bit much for the other member of our household. So when Jeremy mentioned a chalet for Christmas, Clay suggested we go up a week early, and let Jeremy and the rest of the Pack join us on the twenty-sixth.

It would be our first Christmas with just the four of us. As much as I love Jeremy, I kind of liked the idea.

I decided there was really no need to unpack as soon as we arrived. So I tossed the bags in the bedroom and carted in the groceries we'd bought in town. Perishables in the fridge, the rest left in the bags, granola bars and juice boxes stuffed into a knapsack, and then back outside I went.

A white Christmas is never a given. Not at home—just outside Syracuse—and not even here, near Algonquin Park. But it was December 21 and we'd had snow for almost a week now, with no sign of a sudden rise in temperature before the holiday.

The twins are still at that age where the first snow of winter is like their first ever. While I'm sure they remembered snow, it seemed to be more of a sensory memory—the chill of flakes on their skin, the crunch of the crust under their boots, the sweet, clean smell of it. When it started to fall a week ago, they raced outside, and I'd barely been able to get them in since.

Now, as I tramped along, they ignored the paths and zoomed through the brush and trees, as if every unbroken expanse was new territory to be conquered.

They zipped out of sight a few times, but I could still hear the swish of their snow pants, so I didn't call them back. Then they disappeared and everything went silent. When I couldn't catch their scent on the wind, I knew it only meant they were downwind, but my heart started to thump.

"Logan? Kate?"

A purple mitten appeared over a bush. I trekked over to find them crouched, their hats off, ears to the snow. They motioned me to silence as I approached.

"Mice," Kate whispered.

I knelt. Even before I put my ear down, I could hear the *skritch-skritch* of mice tunneling under the snow.

"Can you catch one?" Kate asked.

I lifted my brows. "Catch one?"

"Dad can catch them," Logan said.

His eyes glinted with a look I knew well from his father. Challenge. I laughed under my breath.

"Oh, he can, can he?"

I took off one glove. The twins giggled and hunkered down. I put my ear to the snow, listening and waiting. Then—

My hand came up empty. The twins covered their mouths to stifle laughter as I mock-glared at them.

"Dad can't always do it the first time, either," Logan said.

"Thank you."

I cleared my throat and made a production of getting into position again. I listened for the patter, then scooped up a squirming mouse. I held it firmly, keeping its teeth away from my bare skin. Those oversized incisors only flashed a couple of times before it got a whiff of my wolf scent and froze.

"Can I hold him?" Kate said.

"Dad lets us if we keep our mitts on and our hand flat."

I put the mouse on Kate's outstretched palm. It cowered there as she lifted it to her face and petted its tiny head.

"It's okay," she crooned. "I'm not going to eat you."

"I wonder what it would taste like?" Logan said.

"Crunchy," Kate said, and they both started giggling.

Which, actually, is true. As wolves, Clay and I chomp them down like popcorn. Sounds completely revolting when I'm in human form, but that won't stop me from doing it next time we Change.

Logan reached over to touch the mouse, and they talked to it and patted it as if they hadn't just been discussing what it would taste like. I could chalk their comment up to innocent childish curiosity. After all, they certainly didn't see us eating mice. They didn't know we were werewolves.

Kate dug a hole in the snow and carefully lowered the mouse in. As she did, the breeze changed and I caught a scent that had me tensing and lifting my head.

"What do you smell, Mommy?" Kate asked.

"See," Logan said. "What does she *see*."

They exchanged a glance, and for a second I felt like the child, watching the adults passing a look that said they were humoring me. About a year ago they'd started noticing when we smelled things. Maybe it was the involuntary flare of our nostrils. Sometimes I admitted it—if it was something that could be reasonably smelled by anyone. The rest of the time I'd say no, that I'd just heard or seen something.

This was the first time they'd called me on it with that shared look. Clay would say it's a sign that we should tell them. I said hell no. They were still much too young to be burdened with that secret. We just had to be more careful.

"Was it Dad?" Logan asked.

"Hmm?"

"Did you . . . see Dad?"

Kate shook her head. "No, if it was Daddy, she'd be happy." She slid onto my knee, her arm going around my neck. "She's worried."

I tried not to look startled. I shouldn't be. Our quiet son may be the intellectual prodigy, but our wild daughter is the genius when it comes to reading emotions.

I hugged her, burying my face against her blond curls. "I thought I heard a strange noise, but it's gone now. Nothing to worry about."

She studied my expression and nodded. It was true. I had no idea what I'd smelled—it'd been too faint. Just a whiff of something that said danger, gone before I could seize and decipher it. As I stood, lifting Kate in my arms, I looked around, listening and sniffing. Nothing.

I resisted the urge to herd the kids back inside and we continued exploring the forest. A few minutes later, I caught a scent that I did recognize.

"Daddy!" Kate squealed when she caught me smiling.

She raced to her brother and hit him hard enough to send him flying. Then she grabbed his hand and yanked him to his feet.

"Daddy's here! Let's sneak up on him."

Logan glanced at me. "Momma?"

"Go on."

The kids raced back in the direction of the cabin. I caught a distant movement to the left. So did they, Kate screeching then Logan shushing her as they slipped off in that direction.

I found a stump to sit on and listened. I heard the swish of snow pants as they tried to sneak up on Clay. Then his laugh when they failed. Their shouts as they tried to catch him. Yelps of frustration when they lost him. Finally, the nearly silent crunch of careful footfalls behind me.

I waited until the footfalls stopped, then I dodged to the side as Clay tackled air.

"Getting old," I said. "Losing your touch."

"You're losing yours if you didn't take advantage of the chance to knock me into the snow."

"Only because you'd have pulled me down and then we'd have ended up in a place we don't have time to visit, unless you led the kids a lot farther away than I think."

He stepped toward me. "Nah, but there is a nice thicket over there. We could probably hide for a few minutes before they found us."

"But then I'd have to be quiet. It's been a week. It won't be quiet."

He grinned and caught me up in a rib-crushing kiss, one that reminded me that these occasional weeks apart were not necessarily a bad thing.

"Think I can wear them out enough for a nap?" he asked.

"Not their first day here. They're wired."

"Mmm."

He kissed me again. At some point, I thought the ground disappeared from under my feet, but I wasn't really sure until I felt a tree against my back, then his hands on my rear, lifting me up to straddle him. As he pushed against me, I gasped.

"Very nice," I said. "But probably not a good idea considering we have about two minutes before they find us."

He tilted his head, blue eyes glinting. "It's been a week. Two minutes is probably—"

I slapped a hand over his mouth. "No. It's not. I want at least five."

He laughed and pulled my hand away, then kissed me again, letting me stay on the ground this time, which helped a bit, but not much. Just the smell of him—the heady scent that had already faded from our bed—was enough to make me think that thicket didn't seem so bad. I could be quiet. Quiet enough, anyway.

"You sure about that nap?" Clay said. "I passed a drugstore in town. Gotta be something there to help them sleep."

I chuckled. "If I honestly believed you'd give your kids cough medicine to make them sleep, I might be tempted. But I think it's going to have to be a shower."

"That'll do." He cocked his head again, and I picked up the faint whisper of snow pants. He gave me one last smack of a kiss.

"Now you need to go work up a sweat to justify it."

He grinned. "That won't be hard. I think we're about to be—"

Kate let out a war whoop as she launched herself from the bushes and flew onto Clay's back. He spun around and grabbed Logan as he rushed out. Kate dropped from her perch and grabbed his leg. Clay went down, managing to twist just in time to avoid landing on Logan. The twins piled on as they tried to pin him. There was a flurry of snow and a tangle of arms and legs. Then Kate sailed into a drift, her brother following, and Clay leapt to his feet and ran.

Kate squealed and gave chase. Logan glanced at me. I motioned that we'd slip through the woods and try to cut them off. A blaze of a grin lit up his face. His father's grin. I planted a kiss on top of his head.

"Do you think we can catch them?" Logan whispered.

"I'm sure we can. And if we can't . . ." I hefted the knapsack. "Food. We can lay a trap."

Another grin. Then we set out.

TWO

We caught Clay and Kate without resorting to traps. A snowball fight ensued, which started as Logan and me versus them, somehow switched to guys versus girls, and ended up as parents versus kids. We lost. I could say we let them win, but they've been taking archery lessons from Jeremy and their accuracy has much improved. Also, they've learned that we're fast on the ground but if they launch an aerial attack from the trees, we're in trouble.

The food came out next. Clay and I didn't get much—the kids declared that first pick went to the victors, which is a Pack-ingrained logic we can't argue with.

As we ate, Kate gave Clay the rundown on our schedule for the next few days. They'd planned it with military precision. Logan even wrote out lists, which made me suspect he'd been spending too much time with Lucas.

Bonfires, tobogganing, hiking, board games, gift wrapping, Christmas baking . . . they were going to keep us busy. Also, unbeknownst to me, they'd noticed a place in town that rented snowshoes and cross-country skis, so they'd added those activities to the schedule, withholding that information until Daddy arrived because while Mommy would probably say yes, it was a sure bet that Daddy would.

While they chattered, I felt the hair on the back of my neck prickle. I peered into the woods, then got up and paced around, trying not to be too obvious about it, but I couldn't find any scent on the breeze. When Clay caught my gaze, he arched his brows. My slow look around told him something was making me anxious, and he excused himself for a "bathroom break" to do a wider search but came back with nothing.

"Sorry," I murmured when he returned. "New territory."

"Alpha instincts kicking in," he said. "Can't complain about that."

In a Pack, the Alpha is responsible for the safety of the group. If he's around, everyone else can relax. A couple of years ago, if you'd asked me whether I did that when Jeremy was there, I'd have rolled my eyes and said no. I wasn't like the others. I wasn't raised a werewolf. I didn't share their Pack mentality.

Then Jeremy named me Alpha-elect. Which I could say is an incredible honor, but the truth is that if Clay didn't want the job, there was really no one else—and Clay decidedly did not want the job. He was the ideal Beta—second-in-command, Pack enforcer, Alpha's bodyguard. The best fighter around and happy to keep that as his defining role, leaving the boring politics of leadership to someone else. Namely me.

Only after I became Alpha-elect did I realize how much I *did* relax when Jeremy was around. I'd assimilated the mindset without realizing it.

Now, suddenly, every new scrap of "territory" had to be scouted for danger. I knew Clay would do that—it was his job, and I suspected he'd done a full circle before meeting up with us. But I'd become hyper-alert, too, and something out here bothered me. Maybe it was because the kids were with us. Maybe it really was that Alpha instinct kicking in, as Clay said—a little too new and a little too raw, sensing danger where none existed. Whatever it was, I breathed easier when we finally headed inside.

⚜

Next on the kids' agenda was quiet time, when we were all supposed to enjoy private pursuits. So we set them up in the family room with their hobby bags—books, games, and other activities—and announced that we were taking a shower. Together.

Kate sighed. "Are there water problems here, too?"

"We aren't sure yet," I said. "But we are on a well system, just like at home, and you know what happens there. Sometimes it gets a little low."

"But it never runs out," Kate said.

"That's because we conserve it," Clay said.

"We should get ours fixed," Logan said, not looking up from his book.

"Uh-uh," Kate said. "No strangers in the house. Mommy and Daddy can just keep sharing showers when it's low."

"That we can." Clay picked her up and tossed her onto the sofa. "Just for you."

There was a bathroom in the master suite upstairs, but that was too far away from the kids. After pushing open three hall doors and finding a closet and two bedrooms, I think Clay was ready to say screw it and try our luck with a bed instead. The next door was a bath. He propelled me inside and managed to kick the door closed, lock it, and get me on the counter all seemingly in one motion. Then he set the alarm on his watch for ten minutes—about as much time as we could count on interruption-free.

Clothing came off in a flurry of deep kisses and sharp tugs, laughs and curses when something didn't quite peel as fast as we'd like. Ripping would have been easier. But we're kinder to our attire when the kids are around—one too many times having to explain that Mommy's shirt got caught on a branch during her walk with Daddy. And so did his jeans. And the socks? Well, they kind of fell off. Somewhere. Clothing destruction was now reserved for kid-free trips.

I was still shucking my jeans as Clay pulled me from the counter, kicked open the shower door, and swung me inside. My back hit the wall hard enough to leave me wincing at the bang.

"Loud pipes," he murmured.

"Uh-huh. You just better hope they don't come running to investigate."

"That's okay. I'll be done before they get here."

I laughed and wrapped my fingers in his curls, pulling him in for a deep, hungry kiss that served for ten seconds of foreplay before he was inside me. I wasn't complaining. It felt so damned good. Like he'd been gone two months instead of two weeks. The feel of him. The smell of him. The sound of his harsh growls as he thrust.

Clay could joke about being fast, but I'm no better. Foreplay has its place, but not now, not when we'd been separated. It wasn't long before I arched, hissing, biting my lip to keep from crying out. His hands slid up to the back of my head and pulled me down in a kiss, stifling his growls and my gasps as we climaxed.

We stayed there, me still straddling him, panting, our noses buried against each other's shoulders. I closed my eyes and inhaled his scent and felt him shudder and sigh, and whisper in my ear, telling me how much he missed me, how much he loved me.

Then his watch beeped. He smacked it off with a soft growl. His hands moved to my hair, entwining his fingers in it as he leaned against my ear again, hot breath tickling.

"They're being quiet. I think we have a few more—"

A rattle at the door. A knock. Kate's voice. "Mommy? Daddy?"

Another growl, this one harsher, swallowed as he rubbed his face, looking abashed.

"Ditto," I murmured as I grabbed the towels we'd draped over the shower door.

A clatter and scrape at the door as Kate poked something into the lock.

"We really need to teach her not to do that," I said.

Another abashed look. Jeremy says Clay had every bathroom lock broken at Stonehaven within a month of living there. The concept of privacy is a human one. As a bitten child, Clay had been more wolf than human, and the process never seemed to revert. When he got older, he stayed out of bathrooms if the door was closed—usually—but only because he understood that's what we wanted, even if he thought it was a little silly.

We'd taught the twins to knock and wait before entering. It worked with Logan. Kate interpreted it as "knock and wait three seconds before entering" and nothing we could say changed her interpretation.

At least the knock gave us time to get the towels on before she popped the lock.

"Good, you're done." She scrabbled onto the vanity and started chattering about her book.

As usual, Logan was right behind her. He'd never break into the bathroom, but he never stops her, either. Let Kate risk getting in trouble and then slip in innocently behind her.

"It's almost dark," he said. "We need to eat dinner so we can have the bonfire."

Clay scooped up his clothes. "Just let me get dressed, bud. I'll make dinner if you'll help."

Logan nodded, then looked from Clay to me.

"You're not wet," he said.

"Hmm?" I glanced in the mirror to see my hair, still combed and perfectly dry.

We'd forgotten to turn on the shower. Clay and I both whispered a curse at the same time.

"We, uh . . ." he began.

"Couldn't figure it out," I said, backing into the shower. "The controls are different and . . ." I fussed and got a trickle of water. "There. You need to turn this part."

"Oh. Huh." Clay stepped back into the bathroom. "We should have that shower, then, darling. Just give us ten more minutes, guys—"

"Hurry," Kate said. "I'll wait here."

"Me, too." Logan parked himself on the closed toilet lid.

I looked at Clay. "The shower can wait. We'll need one even more after the bonfire. All that smoke."

"Good idea."

THREE

*I*n the summer, the kids expect weekly bonfires, which can be tough when it isn't dark until ten and you really look forward to some adult time before bed. It's much easier in the winter. Colder, too, but I'm the only one bothered by that. Like her father, Kate doesn't seem to feel the chill. If Logan does, he never mentions it, just bundles up and snuggles in beside me.

With bonfires comes food. Oh, hell, pretty much every tradition in a werewolf family comes with food. For fires, it's hot dogs and sausages, marshmallows and s'mores. We settle in with our roasting sticks and talk. If it's the whole Pack, the kids stay quiet, as if hoping to convince everyone they're asleep, so they'll hear something they otherwise wouldn't. This time, they were the ones who did the talking.

The topic was school. They'd started prekindergarten this past fall, after months of debate. Kindergarten wasn't mandatory in New York State, so Clay had been content to let the kids stay home. I thought they could use the social interaction. Logan wanted to go. Kate did not. The solution would seem to be to send Logan by himself, but even broaching the possibility brought howls from both sides.

Jeremy sided with me on the social interaction issue. We already had the kids in swimming lessons and gymnastics. They went to craft classes, too, which Kate loved. But, really, they needed more.

I'd tried mommy-tot playdates, but . . . I struggled with the mommy part. Hearing the other women's stories of their children always made me feel I was screwing up, disciplining too much or not enough, scarring my kids for life because we didn't have pets or stick to a regular bedtime. So I stopped the playdates and settled for playground visits. With no other kids in the Pack, that meant the twins spent most of their time in the company of adults. More peer interaction was a must. Even Clay reluctantly agreed it would be wise.

Eventually, Jeremy was the one who'd persuaded Kate to go, by stressing kindergarten's emphasis on crafts and music. After the first few days, she'd declared this school stuff wasn't so bad. I think, too, that she enjoyed the academic part. At home, Logan was leaps and bounds ahead of her. Although we praised her, it wasn't until she got to school and compared herself with the other kids that she finally felt smart.

The problem, as it turned out, was Logan, and his experience was resurrecting bad memories for Clay. After Jeremy had rescued Clay, he'd been put in kindergarten—at seven years old. He still remembers the horror of being expected to hold hands and sing songs when he thought he'd be studying science and history and math. That was what it was like for Logan. Hearing him at the bonfire—struggling to add to his sister's enthusiastic retellings of classroom adventures—broke my heart.

I leaned against him as he pulled a marshmallow from his stick. "Did I tell you Jeremy and I are going to check out that new school? It's the same one your dad went to. It's a private school, so they can give you special lessons. Harder ones."

"Isn't that the one Dad got kicked out of?"

Clay choked on a s'more.

"Where did you hear that?" I asked.

"Uncle Nick. He was talking to Reese. He said Daddy got kicked out of kindergarten."

"For cutting up the guinea pig!" Kate said, giggling from Clay's lap.

"Dissecting." Logan gave her a stern look. "That's different. It was already dead."

"Exactly my point," Clay said. "But your mom and Jeremy say the school has changed from when I went, which was a while ago."

I grinned. "A long, long, long—"

A handful of snow hit my cheek.

"A while ago," Clay said. "But I've seen the curriculum, and it's much better. They'll put you in the right classes. I'll make sure of it."

"And me?" Kate said.

"Extra music lessons," I said. "They have voice coaches, too."

She squealed and jumped on her brother and they went down, rolling like puppies in the snow, until they got a little too close to the fire and we both leapt up to pull them back.

In the commotion, we didn't notice someone approaching. It wasn't until a whiff of scent wafted past that I stiffened and shushed the kids. Clay caught the smell, too, and got to his feet.

"What's wrong, Dad?" Logan said.

"Someone's coming." Kate tilted her head and frowned. "It's one of us."

The hair on my neck bristled. It *was* "one of us." Not a Pack member. Nor anyone we knew. But a werewolf. His scent told me that. What did Kate mean, though?

The mutt was coming through the woods. We could hear the crunch of snow under his boots, his shape still hidden by the leaping flames. Clay stood between us and the forest. I resisted the urge to stand at his side and stayed sitting with Kate on my lap and Logan by my shoulder. I put my arm around Logan but tried to keep it casual. If I look like I'm cowering behind Clay, it sends the message that I'd be easy prey without him—a message most mutts are already looking for.

I used to say I was the only living female werewolf. I might be. But I've seen enough in the last ten years to be wary of making such a definitive statement. I'll only say I'm the only one we know about.

As I said, the gene passes through the male line, meaning a female werewolf must be bitten. If a mutt bites a human, even by accident, he usually makes sure it's fatal. Otherwise, it's an exposure risk. Even if the human escapes, his or her chances of surviving the transformation are slim. A woman who survives finds herself a target of every male who's dreamed of a mate. Refuse, and she'll be killed. Accept, and his rivals won't let them be happy for long.

Such is the life of a female werewolf. Unless she's lucky enough to be taken in by an Alpha who'll help her through the Change, then be adopted by the Pack and mated to the most feared werewolf on the continent. All that made my life easier, but I'm still hyperaware of my body language around outside werewolves. While I'd much rather face this mutt on my feet, ready to fight, that would confuse the twins even more.

The man stepped into the firelight. He looked mid-thirties, which meant—with our slow aging—he'd be a decade older. Dark hair, husky build, his thick beard crystallized with snow. He was dressed in a parka, the hood pulled up, his blue eyes the only spark of color.

"You think this is a good idea?" Clay said, his voice a growl.

The man was a few inches taller than Clay, and with that puffy jacket he seemed twice as wide, but he flinched at the growl, gaze dropping, instinctively submissive.

"I, uh, went to the front door. Then I smelled the fire and heard voices."

"And you figured you'd just invite yourself to a bonfire with my *family*."

The emphasis on the last word had the man's gaze skittering to us, but he glanced away quickly.

"I, uh, saw your wife or, uh, I guess she's your ma—"

"Wife."

"Right. I saw her in town with the little ones. I wanted to introduce myself, so you didn't cross my scent—"

A cough from me drowned out the last word. Kate twisted to glare at me for interrupting the drama.

"I wanted you to know I was here," he said. "That's the right thing to do, isn't it? I mean, I've never actually, uh, met another—"

"Clay?" I cut in. "I'm going to take the kids inside."

He nodded, his gaze never leaving the man. Logan protested as I took his arm. Oddly, Kate stayed silent, and gave her brother a look that quieted him better than my shushing, as we went in.

FOUR

When we got inside, Logan said, "Why did we have to come in? He was just saying hello."

"Mommy and Daddy don't like him," Kate said. "They don't want him here." She looked up at me as I unwound her scarf. "Is he a bad man?"

"I don't know, baby. He's a stranger. Everyone has to be careful of strangers."

"Even if they're like us?"

Especially if they're like us. I couldn't say that, of course. I couldn't even acknowledge her question because I wasn't sure what she meant or how to deal with it. I had to talk to Clay first. So I finished getting them undressed as I listened to the voices through the door.

"I'm real sorry about that," the man said. "I didn't mean to spook the little ones."

"You didn't. I'd just like you to be very careful what you say around them."

"Oh. Right. Sorry."

"So, let me see if I understand this. You saw Elena with the kids at the store and smelled what she is."

"Yeah. I was in shock at first, thinking I was mistaken. I mean, I didn't think there were any women. Like I said, I don't know a lot about us. Just what my father told me and my brother."

"So you saw her, all alone with her kids, and you thought you'd pay a visit after dark. See if she needed any company."

"No, I—"

A thump and a gasp. I pushed back the sidelight drape and glanced out. Clay had the mutt by the collar. The guy lifted his hands in surrender, making no move to fight. I squelched an instinctive twinge of disgust. The wolf in me might see cowardice, but my human side knew the mutt was being smart, not giving Clay any reason to pummel him into the nearest tree. Odd behavior for a werewolf, though. Faced with a challenger, bravado usually overrules brains, at least until the pummeling begins.

"You know who I am, right?" Clay said, pulling the mutt's face down to his.

"N-no, I—"

"Bullshit."

"No. Honestly, I don't. Like I said, it's just me and my brother. I don't know who you are. I'm sorry if I should."

"He's lying," Kate said.

I looked down to see them both peering out the bottom of the window. I yanked them back fast.

"He's lying, Mommy. He knows who Daddy is."

Damn it, I wasn't the only one who could hear through that window.

"All right, then," I heard Clay say. "Let's pretend you don't know and I'll tell you who I am and what I do to—"

I grabbed both kids, one under each arm, and hightailed it deeper into the chalet. Only when I couldn't hear Clay's voice did I put them down.

"How does he know Daddy?" Kate asked, as if our conversation hadn't been interrupted.

"Maybe he's run into him before. At a college or a conference."

"Then why's the man lying?" she asked.

"I don't know, baby. How about we get a snack, since our bonfire was interrupted."

She let me steer them into the kitchen but wasn't distracted. "He's scared."

"Of Daddy? No. They're just having a . . . disagreement."

"He *should* be scared of Daddy." Her tone was almost defensive. "But he was scared before he even saw him."

"Nervous," Logan said. "He was stuttering. 'Nervous' is the word you want."

She wheeled on him. "I know what 'nervous' means, smartypants. People talk like that when they're scared, too, and he was scared. I can tell."

He nodded, a quiet apology. Kate turned to me.

"It's because he's one of us, isn't it?"

"I don't know what you mean by that, baby," I said.

I regretted the words as soon as I said them. She could tell I was lying and the hurt in her eyes cut like a dagger.

"I'm sorry," I said, reaching for her.

She backed out of my grasp. "You do know what I mean."

"Okay." I hunkered down in front of her. "What?"

"You *know*."

"I'm not sure I do. Tell me."

She glowered, jaw working as if she was trying to find words. Then she stamped her foot and howled, "You know! You know!" and I realized *she* didn't know. Somehow she understood that the man had a connection to us. Maybe she caught the werewolf notes in his scent. But because she didn't know what we were, she couldn't put words to it.

Watching her face redden in frustration, I felt as if I was betraying her. There are two values a Pack wolf places above all others: loyalty and trust. We tried to teach our children that they could trust us in every way.

Except one. This secret we were keeping.

It was the right thing to do. It was too much for them to process at their age. Too big a burden of secrecy for them to bear. Yet, looking at Kate's fury and frustration, I imagined what it would be like when we finally did tell her. Would she look back on all the

times we'd evaded her questions—or outright lied—and hate us
for it?

"I'm sorry," I said. "I know you're angry, Kate, and I'm really,
really sorry."

A scowl. That was all I got. Then she spun and strode to the
counter, where I'd set out a bowl of fruit. She grabbed an apple.
Logan silently appeared beside her with a juice box. She took it
with a grunt of thanks, vented her frustration with a huge chomp
on the apple, then stalked to the hall. As she swung out, she col-
lided with her father.

"Hey," he said. "What's wrong?"

She shot another scowl my way. "Nothing," she said, then circled past him and continued down the hall.

I was still crouching where she'd left me. Logan walked over,
gave me a hug, and murmured, "She'll be all right, Momma," then
followed his sister.

When they were gone, Clay closed the door.

"She said the guy outside is 'one of us,'" I whispered. "But she
doesn't know what that means. She just . . . smells it or senses it. I
don't know. She wanted me to explain."

"Ah."

He walked over and took an apple.

"They're too young," I said. "Everyone agrees." A pause as he
bit into the apple. "Everyone except you."

"Yep."

"They're four, Clayton," I said, struggling to keep my voice
down. "*Four.* I could barely deal with it at twenty-one."

"That was different." He put the apple down and came over,
arms going around me, as he realized I was shaking. "We're not
going to fight about this. If you want to seriously discuss it, okay.
But if you just want to convince me that you're right? This is our
special Christmas, Elena. We can fight about this anytime. Let's
not do it now."

I slumped against him. "I'm sorry. I . . . She was just so angry and confused, and I felt so . . . bad."

"You're doing what you think is right. Hell, I'm not sure it isn't. Jeremy agrees with you." He squeezed me. "We can talk about it later. At home. Where the kids won't be left alone to fend for themselves if we kill each other."

I laughed against his shoulder, then took a deep breath and stepped back. "Okay, so what happened outside?"

Clay picked up his apple again and circled to the door. A deep sniff to reassure himself that the kids weren't poised on the other side. He said, his voice low, "He stuck to his story. He saw you and the kids in town. He didn't want to spook you, so he got out of your way. Then he found out where you were staying and decided to introduce himself, so you'd know there was another werewolf here."

"And you don't buy that."

"No, darling, I don't. He could have followed you to the truck and said a quick hello. Finding out where you're staying? Coming after dark? Damned stupid move if he knows who I am, which makes me think he doesn't."

"He does," I said. "Kate accidentally overheard. She says he's lying. He knows who you are."

"Huh." He didn't question Kate's intuition. "Okay, then he's a fucking idiot."

True. Anyone who knew who Clay was—and it was pretty much a given that every werewolf on the continent did—knew that coming after me wouldn't mean a quick, painless death. To protect Jeremy on his ascension to Alpha, Clay had once cut up a trespassing mutt, kept him alive as long as possible, then made sure a second mutt saw the result and distributed the tale, along with Polaroid pictures. Clay had been seventeen. That's the story. The truth is a little more complicated. But . . . let's just say Clay really hopes those photos have faded to blank frames before our kids are old enough to stumble on one.

Clay did what he thought he had to do. Together with the occasional reminder killing, it has meant that the Pack hasn't had to worry about trespassing mutts for thirty years. It means, too, that when we're away from home, most still steer clear. So why hadn't this guy?

"He knew you were here," I said. "There's a second car in the driveway. Your scent is all over the place. Even if he missed that, he'd have smelled you when he came around the house. Plenty of time to realize his mistake. So why go through with it?"

"He wasn't looking for a challenge, that's for sure. Guy was so nervous I thought he was going to piss his pants."

"Not just nervous. Kate said he was scared. Did he say anything else?"

"Small talk. Did we know anyone around here? Were we up for the holidays? Babbling. I shut him down and sent him on his way."

"Getting answers. Finding out why we're here. If he knows who we are, then he knows one damned good reason why we might be in his hometown."

"Hunting a man-eater."

I nodded. "I'll check the local news archives. See if this place is known for folks walking into the forest and not walking out again."

FIVE

I took my laptop and we settled into the living room with the kids. Kate was still annoyed with me. Not angry—no more glowers—but she wasn't bouncing over to snuggle on the couch, either. They were both reading on the floor, Logan on his back, deep into the first Harry Potter book, Kate on her stomach, flipping through her illustrated children's encyclopedia of myths and legends.

When I saw what she was reading, I'll admit to a dart of panic—thinking she might be looking up werewolves—but she was just working her way through Norse myths. The book fascinated her, and I could say that was because she felt a subconscious recognition that her own family belonged in those pages. But there's a more prosaic explanation for her interest—namely, a father who's an anthropologist specializing in ancient religions, legends, and folklore. She'd heard stories of skin-walkers and Egyptian gods before "Goldilocks and the Three Bears."

Clay started the fire. I pulled out blankets from a box and laid them over the kids. Logan thanked me. Kate acknowledged hers with a nod, but didn't look up from her book. Clay had brought a stack of anthropology journals he hadn't gotten to yet. With one in hand, he nudged me from my corner of the sofa and plunked down, so I was sitting with my back against him instead. I opened my laptop and set to work researching.

These days, it's easy to find news on the Internet, but I have access to better sources. I'm a freelance journalist. Being a Canadian living in the States, I've made that my specialty—covering Canadian issues for American publications. I usually stick to small markets. Such magazines and news outlets don't pay a lot, but they let me get away with writing pieces based mostly on research, phone calls, and e-mail.

In a place this small—the nearest town was barely a thousand people—you'd think it'd be easy to search for local missing persons. But that's the problem. It's *too* easy, meaning any man-eater living here would drive three hours south to Toronto to hunt. Yet if he's a true man-eater, he'd have a hard time controlling himself—if he stumbled across someone in his own woods while he was in wolf form. That's usually how we catch them.

I found five regional cases of missing persons in the past two years. One was a twenty-year-old hiker, found three days later in Algonquin, cold and hungry. Two were seniors who'd wandered away from their caretakers. One was found alive. The second wasn't, but he'd died from exposure, no signs of animal attack. The last two were children.

My heart picked up speed as I read those reports, though I told myself they almost certainly had nothing to do with our resident werewolf. Man-eaters know a missing child raises too many alarms.

The first was a seven-year-old boy who'd wandered off from a campground. Like the hiker, he'd been found, cold and hungry. The second was a four-year-old girl who'd disappeared from her home at night. She hadn't been reported missing for almost twenty-four hours, because the girl's mother woke up late, found the child's room empty, and presumed her older daughter had taken her to the sitter. The sitter had been happy to have a day off and never called to check. It was dinnertime when the mother realized her little girl was gone. The police didn't even have the time to launch a search before the girl's father called to say she was with him and the case was written off as a custody dispute.

"Is that work?"

I looked up to see Kate standing in front of me. I shut the browser.

"Just a little research," I said.

"You're not supposed to be working. It's family time."

"Huh." Clay folded his journal. "Well, then I guess we're both in trouble, because I'm working, too. You're reading. We're reading. I don't think it matters *what* we're reading."

"Yes, it does. You aren't supposed to work on a vacation. You're *always* working."

Clay laughed and elbowed me. "She's got a point, darling. We work at least fifteen hours a week."

Kate nodded. "Too much."

"He's teasing you, Kate," Logan said as he sat up. "Most people work a lot more."

"Forty hours a week is normal," I said.

"Uh-uh," Kate said. "That'd be crazy."

"You know Emily and Sarah at school?" Logan said. "That's their babysitter who comes to pick them up, because their parents work all day."

"Their parents just say that," Kate said. "If I was their mommy, I'd make them go to a sitter, too. *All* the time."

"I bet half the kids in your class have daycare in the afternoon," I said. "Your parents are just very, very lucky that they can do most of their work at home. When Uncle Nick and Uncle Antonio come, ask how much they work. Uncle Nick works about forty hours a week. Uncle Antonio runs his own business, so he probably does sixty."

"That's crazy!" Kate said.

Clay leaned over and mock-whispered, "I agree."

"When we have quiet time, your dad and I might do a little work. We like our jobs. But we'll only do it when you're busy. Okay?"

She nodded. I started to reopen my browser.

"I'm done reading," she said. "Can we play a game now?"

Clay glanced at me. I wasn't finished—I needed to go further back with missing-persons reports. But Kate was standing there, her expression wary, having not quite forgiven me. As much as I wanted to reassure myself that we didn't have a local man-eater, this *was* our vacation.

I closed the laptop and walked to the shelf of board games.

"Can we play—?" Logan began.

"Not Scrabble," Kate said. "You always win. I want—"

"Not Sorry. You don't even try to win. You just like sending other people back to the start."

Kate smiled.

"How about card games?" I said, pulling a few off the shelf. "We have Uno, Pit—"

"Spoons!" they yelled in unison, and grabbed for the regular deck of cards.

"All right, but you know the rule."

Clay slid down to the floor. "Game over at first blood."

"That's right," I said. "Now go grab some spoons."

Two hours and a dozen card games later, the kids were sound asleep in front of the fire, wearing hot chocolate mustaches, with shortbread cookie crumbs scattered like halos around their heads. We knew better than to move them. So I settled back on the couch with Clay and opened my laptop again.

"You know, you work *all the time*," he said.

I laughed. "The worst of it? When she says something like that, I actually have two seconds of guilt before I slap myself upside the head. I think we *should* work forty-hour weeks for a while, so they see how good they have it."

"Forty hours? That's crazy."

I laughed again and leaned back against him. Yes, we were both in the extremely lucky position of not needing to work. Living with Jeremy meant pooling our resources, and the lion's share came from him—early years of very good investments, followed by a career as an artist whose work now commanded obscene sums of money.

In those dark years after the bite, when I'd been eager to see the worst in Clay, I'd been quick to accuse him of wasting his genius and an expensive PhD, dabbling in his field like an academic dilettante. The truth is that if we needed to work full-time, we'd be screwed. The Pack was our real job. Clay couldn't hold down a tenured position and I couldn't work in an office when we both might have to leave at any moment to investigate a potential man-killer or exposure threat. Between our two "jobs," we still probably didn't put in full-time hours, but it was like being a firefighter—we had to be ready to mobilize at a moment's notice.

This particular fire—the mutt—seemed more smoke than flame. I searched missing persons. I searched murders. Nothing. Now I'd need to investigate him and his brother to write up a dossier for our files. Then later, if I noticed a rash of missing persons in Toronto, I'd know whose door to knock on. A minor inconvenience on our Christmas getaway, but it was a job I couldn't take a vacation from.

I was about to tell Clay it'd be a research case when I did one last search. "Death by misadventure." That's when I found it.

Once I finished reading, I motioned Clay out of the room. I didn't speak until we were in the kitchen with the door closed.

"There was a death here two weeks ago," I said. "College student home for the holidays. He got drunk at a party, wandered into the woods, and fell down a ravine. Guy walking his dog found the body the next day."

"Let me guess. The corpse wasn't all there."

I nodded. "Scavenged by canines. Dogs, they think. Or wolves. We're close enough to Algonquin for wolves. It wasn't a missing-person case because his parents figured he'd crashed at a friend's place. It wasn't a murder case because the police presumed he died in the fall."

"Autopsy prove that?"

"I don't think they did one. Small-town tragedy just before the holidays. No one's looking too closely."

"It'd explain why our mutt's scared shitless. Chows down on a local kid and two weeks later we show up."

"Do you think he'll bolt?"

Clay shrugged. "Kinda hoping he does. Let us enjoy our holidays and then we can come back next month to take care of it."

I paced across the kitchen. "Either way, we need to investigate. And we can't do that with the kids here. Goddamn it!"

Clay came up behind me and touched my waist. "We're not going to send the kids away, darling. This is our Christmas together. Just the four of us. Like you wanted."

I turned. "I never said—"

"You don't need to. Most times, you're good with the extended-family thing. But Christmas . . ." He shrugged. "Christmas is different. You think I don't realize that?"

He did. He had from the start, that my first Christmas with him, someone who might give me what I'd lost when I was five. A family.

The Pack hadn't really celebrated Christmas before I came along. They did get together and feast and exchange gifts. Sometimes there was even a tree. But there were no gingerbread cookies or mistletoe or stockings by the fire.

When Clay realized I wanted a real Christmas, he'd done what he always did when faced with a human custom he didn't fully understand: He researched it. Then he'd given me a perfect holiday.

"This is our Christmas," he said. "Just the four of us. I know you want that and I know you'd never ask for it. So I set one up, and I'm not going to let some mutt spoil it."

"But the kids—"

"—will be fine, because I'm calling Nick and getting him up here with Reese. We have three days left. They'll babysit. We'll investigate. It'll be wrapped up by the twenty-fourth, and if it isn't, the investigation can wait. The guys will go home and come back with Antonio and Noah on the twenty-sixth."

I shook my head. "We can't make them leave for two days. They'll stay. We can do this another year—"

"No, we're doing it this year. They'll go home or find a hotel."

"That's not very nice."

"Nick's used to it. I'll call him."

One of the requirements for our Christmas getaway cottage had been a large master bedroom suite with a king-sized bed. Because, despite the fact that the place had five bedrooms, part of a perfect vacation for the twins meant sharing the parental bed, something that was strongly discouraged at home.

So, when I woke up to feel Clay's fingers slide between my legs, I bolted upright.

"No kids," he murmured, tugging me back down.

"What? Where—?"

"Do you really think I'd let them wander around a strange house alone, darling? Especially when we've got a mutt nearby?"

I blinked back sleep. "Right. Sorry. So . . ." More blinking. "Nick."

"Mmm-hmm. A storm was rolling their way, so they decided to outrun it. Just got in." He wrapped his fingers around my leg. "It's not quite eight. So you can either go down with them or get a little more sleep."

"Are those my only options?"

"They are."

I smiled. "Sleep it is, then."

"Good."

He started tugging me down again. I resisted.

"Is—?"

"The door is locked."

I smiled, and sank back down onto the bed and let him get back to work.

SIX

*W*e showered. Together. Which is always more fun, particularly when you don't need to set an alarm. Then I dressed and went downstairs while Clay shaved. That's a chore I'm sure he'd hoped to skip for a few days, but if we were investigating, he couldn't look as if he'd just stumbled out of the bush. To be honest, Clay could probably stumble out of the bush after a week without even showering and still get his questions answered by most of the female population, but shaving never hurts.

Our kitchen had been commandeered by a young man dressed in baggy sweatpants and a tight Columbia University tee, his feet bare, dark blond hair tousled as if he'd just rolled out of bed himself. Or slept six hours in a car while Nick drove.

"Kids put you to work already?" I asked as Reese came around the center island for a hug.

"They did. Barely got my shoes off before they handed me the pancake recipe."

Reese is one of two young werewolves the Sorrentinos adopted after our Alaskan adventure. I suppose, given that Reese is twenty-one, "adopted" isn't quite the right word. I'd tracked the young Australian to Alaska, trying to warn him that a couple of mutts were after him. Before I could get to him, he'd bumped into two other mutts. I'd sent Reese to Nick and Antonio to recover from his injuries. They'd persuaded him to stay, working for Antonio and going back to university.

For years, Jeremy and I had tried to bolster the Pack's depleted ranks by recruiting seasoned mutts. An exercise in futility. They were true lone wolves, uninterested in the social advantages of a Pack. If they did want to join, it was because they were in trouble and needed protection. With Reese, I realized we'd overlooked the best recruiting option—young wolves, those still feeling a pack animal's need for brotherhood.

Reese was an all-around good kid. He'd grown up on a sheep farm in the outback, raised by a werewolf father and a mother who'd known what her husband and son were, which is extremely rare. Great parents, judging by their son. Both dead now, and Reese blamed himself for that. So he came with some serious baggage, but he was coping. He is a smart and loyal team player, which makes him ideal Pack material. And he knows how to cook.

When I offered to help, he refused.

"You guys take a break this morning," he said. "If I need help, I'll enlist him."

He pointed a wooden spoon and I turned to see another young man in the doorway. This one was seventeen, but looks a couple of years younger. Two inches shorter than my five-ten. Slight build, light brown hair hanging into dark eyes that didn't meet mine, as if unsure of his welcome.

"Noah!" I said as I walked over to hug him.

As always, he hesitated before returning the embrace. At first I'd thought he wasn't comfortable with typically exuberant Pack greetings. But when it finally came, his return hug was never tentative, and I'd come to realize that no matter how many times he got an enthusiastic greeting, he was surprised by it. Like not meeting my eyes at first. He always seemed braced for us to decide he wasn't worth the trouble and kick him out.

"I'm done with school for the Christmas break, so Nick asked if I wanted to come. I thought he should call first, but he said you'd be asleep."

"He knows he didn't need to ask. We just didn't think you'd want to waste your holidays playing babysitter."

"It's okay." He looked out the window at the backwoods. "Seems like a nice place."

"It is. And the kids will keep you busy. You wouldn't happen to know how to snowshoe, would you?"

A half smile. "Sure. Dennis and I did it all the time." Dennis was a former Pack member and Noah's grandfather, who'd been murdered before we arrived in Alaska. "I can teach them if you want."

"I want. Speaking of the kiddies . . ." I looked around. "They're with Nick, I presume?"

Noah nodded. "In the living room."

I peeked in, spotted Nick and the twins, and got my phone. I snapped a couple of photos and sent them off. Then Kate saw me and shrieked. Logan zoomed past, his sister at his heels, both giggling as they raced from the room. I stepped into it and took some more pictures.

Nick Sorrentino. Forty-seven—a year older than Clay. Being a werewolf, he looks more like thirty-five. Despite a night of driving, he was sleek and impeccably dressed, his casual pants and sweater probably worth more than my best cocktail gown. Even the dark stubble on his face seemed a deliberate part of the look—the *GQ* magazine version of a guy roughing it in the wilderness. All he needed was his usual killer smile, which was absent this morning, possibly because he was tied to a chair.

"That's got to bring back memories," I said.

It was, indeed, a familiar look for Nick. Or so I've heard. As a child werewolf, Clay had loved to practice stalking and his favorite target had been his best friend. To make it a proper challenge, though, Clay had to give Nick an incentive to run and hide. Which meant that when Nick lost, he'd find himself tied to a tree and left in the forest, sometimes forgotten.

"I'm humoring them," Nick said. "They heard us arrive, and apparently your husband suggested they ambush me."

"I didn't tell them to tie you up, though," Clay drawled as he walked in. "You get a picture for Antonio and Jeremy, darling?"

"Snapped and sent."

"They'll be very amused," Nick said. "Now I'll get out of this before I lose feeling in my wrists. You need to talk to Kate about how tight she ties her ropes."

He lifted his hands behind the chair and his biceps flexed to snap the rope. It didn't break.

"Spending more time in the spa than the weight room again?" I said.

"Ha-ha. The rope is just a little stronger—" He tried again, neck muscles bulging.

The rope stayed intact.

"Not gonna work," Clay said. "My kids aren't stupid. They tied your hands back-to-back. You can't get the leverage to break it."

He crouched behind Nick and fussed with the knots.

Nick sighed and looked at me. "So, how's your vacation going?"

"Okay," I said. "But no one's tied me up yet."

"Trip's still young, darling," Clay said as he stood. "Looks like I'll need to work on knots with the kids. They used a reef, which isn't a bad choice, but a constrictor would have been better." He lifted his head and sniffed. "Is that ham?"

"Ham and blueberry pancakes. Reese is cooking."

"Huh. Better get some before the kids eat it all."

Clay headed for the kitchen. Nick shook his hands, as if expecting the rope to fall off.

"Do you really think he untied you?" I said. "He was just checking his kids' handiwork."

"Figures. Can you please—? Elena? Elena?"

By the time Nick got himself free, the food was gone. He helped himself to mine. I could have pointed out that I wasn't the only one who'd abandoned him, but he knew better than to steal from Clay's plate.

The chalet had a lovely dining room with a table for ten and huge windows overlooking a patch of birdfeeders. Had we been in there, I'm sure we'd have enjoyed the sight of bright red cardinals or blue jays. But we never made it out of the kitchen. We ate leaning against the counters, kids perched on the island, everyone talking, the chatter and laughter loud enough to scare any birds from those distant feeders.

"Thank you, Reese," I said as I helped the kids load their plates into the dishwasher. "That was great."

"I see you got a menu all worked out, so I'll cook while I'm here."

"How come you don't offer to do that at home?" Nick said.

"Because you guys can afford to hire someone." Reese took the menu from the fridge. "Oooh, Christmas cookies." He turned to the kids. "Are we going to bake cookies this afternoon, guys?"

"Yes!" Kate said.

Clay caught my eye and started opening his mouth to tell Reese no. The four of us baking cookies was one of my favorite traditions. I cut Clay off with a shake of my head.

"Except we can't do the gingerbread," Logan said.

Kate nodded. "Gingerbread is Mommy and Daddy's favorite. They have to make those with us."

It took Reese a moment to figure out what Kate had said. As with many four-year-olds, while her parents could understand her easily, others had to decipher her speech.

"Ah," he said. "So, gingerbread is Mom and Dad's domain?"

She nodded. "We can do sugar cookies. They're in special shapes, too. We have reindeer and Santa Claus and snowmen."

"But no wombats or Tasmanian devils or kangaroos," I said.

"Kangaroos?" Reese snorted. "Who wants a cookie in the shape of a giant rat?"

"It's a marsupial, not a rodent," Logan said. "I looked it up the last time you said that."

"Well, books aren't always right, mate. They're giant rats. Smart ones that learned to hop on their back legs to convince us they're cute and harmless. Now, Tasmanian devils we could do. Just cut out cookies to look like Kate—"

Kate squawked and her brother laughed.

"Okay, guys, we're off," I said. "We'll call."

Clay and I tried to slip out. We made it as far as the door before Kate took a flying leap from the counter and zoomed into our path.

"Where're you going?"

"Mom got a call," Logan said as he walked over. "She needs to check out a story here. That's why Uncle Nick came, remember?"

"Right," I said. "So, we'll see you—"

"When?" Now it was Logan.

"We'll be home by dinner."

"Dinner!" Kate said. "You're working all day?"

"No," Clay said. "It's almost lunchtime now. We'll be back before dinner and we'll be here all evening."

Nick walked into the hall and scooped up a child under each arm. "I think I heard someone mention a bonfire and moonlight skiing. We need to pick up skis in town so we'll be all set."

"Snowshoes, too," Noah said as he walked in. "I'm going to teach everyone snowshoeing tonight."

"Then you kids need to rest up, don't you?" Nick said. "Lots of naps."

Normally, they'd have screeched at that, but they kept glowering at us.

"We'll be as quick as we can," I said.

Nick jerked his chin toward the door, telling us to just leave. He turned, a child still under each arm, and headed toward the kitchen.

"I bet you haven't asked Reese how he lost his fingers yet," Nick said. "I think he's going to tell you the real story this time."

"He never tells the real story," Kate said.

"Then I guess you don't want to hear the latest one?"

A pause, as if they were struggling not to give in, then Logan said, "Was it a kangaroo? With big rat teeth?"

Kate started giggling.

Reese had lost part of the last two fingers on his right hand during his run-in with the mutts in Alaska. That'd been their way of saying hello. When the twins met him, they'd barely gotten past the introductions before Kate asked what happened to his fingers. Jeremy had tried to shush her, but Reese answered with a long, elaborate story involving two grizzly bears and a fish. Ever since, each time they asked, he'd make up a new story.

Now, as Nick carried them into the kitchen, I heard Reese saying, "A golden eagle. Apparently, he thought they were worms. Bit them right off."

"How did he think they were worms?" Logan asked.

"Well, that was probably my fault. I was out . . ."

I was putting on my boots at the front door when I realized Noah had followed us.

"So, when you guys check out this stuff, it's like a murder investigation? Detective work?"

"Part detective," I said. "Part . . ."

"Thug," Clay finished.

"I was going to say enforcer."

"My role is mostly thug work," Clay said. "Elena questions the guy. I encourage him to answer in the only language most mutts understand. But that's just part of the process. The rest is investigating the murder. Talking to folks in town, trying to get answers from the police, the coroner . . ."

"Cool. Maybe someday I can come along. Learn the ropes. That's part of being Pack, right? Knowing how to handle this stuff?"

"It is."

I put on my jacket. Clay nudged me. I followed his gaze to Noah, who was still standing there. Another nudge and meaningful look before I understood. Noah wanted to come along *this* time.

Clay could just invite Noah himself. That's what we would have done before. But now I was Alpha-elect and Clay had decided I should take charge in the field, which meant I had to invite Noah on my own.

Of all the things that annoyed me when I joined the Pack, this topped the list. Sure, Jeremy was the leader, but he had a smart Pack of loyal wolves who'd never try to undermine him. So why couldn't they make suggestions? Give advice?

Because that's not how a wolf-brain works. Werewolves want an absolute leader. Jeremy will occasionally open a matter up for discussion, but the final word is his and no one questions it.

Now I'm ready to be that leader . . . in all cases but one. Clay is my husband. My mate. My partner in every aspect of my life. An imbalance of power there makes me very uncomfortable. I don't want to rule him any more than I'd want to be ruled by him. So we've come to an agreement: in the field, I'm in charge but he's free to nudge, like he was doing with Noah.

I was also free to ignore him. Part of me balked at the thought of taking a seventeen-year-old boy on an investigation. We might do things that I'd rather Noah didn't see. But he was nearly an adult and had already seen more than any kid should. This *was* part of Pack life, and as Alpha, it'd be my job to integrate Noah and to teach him, even if it involved things I wished he'd never needed to learn.

"Do you want to come along?" I asked.

"Can I?" No smile, but his eyes lit up.

"For part of it. We might ask you to stay in the truck for a while."

"That's okay. I'll go tell Nick."

SEVEN

*O*ur mutt's name was Douglas Eaton. He'd offered it to Clay the night before, which was good, because Clay couldn't ask without seeming to take a friendly interest. Pack werewolves can't take a friendly interest in mutts. Another of those harsh wolf realities that seemed draconian to me, until I spent some time around mutts and realized civility was interpreted as weakness. A friendly werewolf is a naive werewolf. A naive werewolf is an easy mark.

We didn't have an address for Eaton, but it was easy enough to get. I just took Noah with me into the post office and asked, saying we needed to drop off a present.

The middle-aged clerk dismissed Noah with a glance. She took slightly longer with me. Trying to tell if I looked like I was from "around here" or the city. It makes a difference in small towns. I'm forty-one, though I look more like early thirties. Five foot ten. Slender, Jeremy would say. Skinny, I'd say, though having the twins had helped me develop some semblance of curves. An athletic build, I suppose. I was dressed in worn jeans, a ski jacket, and hiking boots. No makeup. White-blond hair tied in a ponytail.

It didn't take long for me to pass her "not a city girl" test. Just a woman and a teenage boy, maybe a nephew or stepson. Neither remotely intimidating. She gave us the address and directions. Even sketched a map on an envelope and wished us a Merry Christmas.

⚜

It took a while to get to Eaton's place. As the postal clerk said, his house was "out with the cottages." In other words, in the woods.

The region up here can be divided into cottage country and non-cottage country. There are plenty of cottages *in* non-cottage country, of course, but they're the kind of places owned by average folks, passed down through the generations. Places you lend to your buddies and their families, and get a bottle of rye whiskey in return. In other words, not the million-dollar summer homes surrounding every lake. There were no lakes in this area, not good ones anyway. Just cottages in the woods. And these cottages weren't winterized, meaning the roads to them had big signs warning NOT MAINTAINED IN WINTER.

Luckily, we'd brought the 4x4. Jeremy's truck. It's an SUV, but Clay and I call it "the truck." We're not really minivan/SUV people. Jeremy isn't, either, but we live in a northern climate and since two-thirds of our household is too damned stubborn to drive anything but a car, the job of being a responsible adult falls to Jeremy.

Contrary to what some 4x4 owners think—as evidenced by the sheer number of them in the ditch after every snowstorm—they aren't invincible winter tanks. It was slow going to Eaton's place. We had to follow twin rutted tracks through three feet of snow. More than once it looked like we'd need to get out and push.

"Are Nick and Antonio getting you out for much winter driving practice?" Clay asked as he maneuvered through another drift. "I know you weren't driving when you lived in Alaska."

"We've done some, but there isn't snow like this at their place."

"I'll take you out when you come back after Christmas."

I twisted in the front seat. "If you want a real challenge, have him take you in *his* car."

Noah's smile said he wouldn't mind that at all. Clay drives a BMW M3. Convertible, no less. Jeremy learned decades ago that cars are the one indulgence he can lavish on Clay without objections. Pre-kids, Clay's tastes leaned toward Porsches, but with the children he needs a four-seater, and he started paying attention to things like safety ratings.

Clay spent the rest of the trip passing on winter-driving tips. If Noah had heard them already, he gave no sign of it, just leaned forward, nodding and asking questions. When he had Clay's attention, he liked to keep it. Fortunately, it wasn't hard to get—Clay's a natural teacher.

"That it?" Clay pointed at a blue metal flag poking from the snow. A six-digit numeral gave the lot's "911 number." Out here, the mail was general delivery, so you needed that number—along with the street name—to give to 911 in the event of an emergency.

"That's it."

It was a short driveway, shoveled nearly down to the dirt, and empty. At the end stood a small cottage. All the windows were dark.

"Doesn't look like anyone's home," Noah said. "What do you do now?"

"Break in," Clay said.

I looked over the seat at Noah. "We'll search for basic information on Eaton, for both the investigation and my dossiers."

"Right, because you wouldn't find any evidence of man-eating inside," Noah said. "The guy's not going to leave body parts in the freezer."

I was going to agree and leave it at that, but Clay beat me to a reply. "We've never found any in the freezer. With man-eaters, it's not about developing a taste for eating people. There are two ways a werewolf ends up chowing down on humans. One, he's young, like you. New to the Changes. Lets himself get too close to people. Maybe he's hungry. Maybe he's feverish. Maybe he just sees someone running and instinct takes over, and that instinct doesn't distinguish between humans and deer. It's all prey."

"Which is why I only Change on the buddy system."

"Right. In a year or so, we'll start having you Change in places where you can smell humans. Then in places where there *are* humans.

You'll learn control. Even then, if you let yourself Change when you're hungry and you stumble on someone who runs? Takes a helluva lot of willpower to keep from chasing him. Even experienced werewolves have been known to screw up."

"And if that happens with a mutt? What do you guys do about it?"

"Same thing we'd do if it was a new kid. Beat the crap out of him. Let him know we're watching. That's usually enough. Mutts are going to mess up. Their support system isn't good enough. It's the second kind of man-eater we're worried about—the ones who don't bother learning control because they like the chase. That's what drives them. They eat their prey because they catch it. But they don't chase to eat. They chase for fun. That's not wolf. That's human. They're nothing more than killers."

"Serial killers."

"Right. So they don't leave parts in the freezer, but we do find stuff lying around. Sometimes trophies. Sometimes whole bodies. Sometimes only—"

"Time to knock on the door," I said. "If he's home, he's probably seen us sitting out here and bolted."

"Nah. He bolts, we can track. He'd know better. He's not here."

Clay was right. Eaton wasn't home.

"Now, the thing about breaking into a mutt's place is, he's going to know you were there," Clay said to Noah as I peered through the windows.

"Because we'll leave scent."

Clay nodded. "So if you don't want him knowing, you can't go in. Most times, though, you go in because you're okay with him knowing. Trespassing on his turf is a challenge. In fact, sometimes even if we don't want to search the place, we'll break in. Otherwise, he'll smell us at the door and think we didn't enter because we're afraid of him."

"All clear inside," I said. "We'll—"

A howl cut me short. Noah's head jerked up, following the sound. Another howl joined in. Then a third.

"Shit," Noah whispered. "How many are there?"

"Probably about a dozen," I said.

His eyes rounded.

"It's a sled-dog team," I said. "We passed a sign advertising excursions. Sounds like wolves, though, doesn't it?"

"The pitch is different," Clay said. "The rhythm is different, too, because they're howling for a different reason. Loneliness. Boredom. If you hear one in the woods, howling for others, it'll sound more like us, so you have to be careful."

Noah nodded.

"Now, back to the break-in. We could search for a key. Could even pick the lock. If we *break* the lock, he has to fix it." Clay opened the screen door and gave the knob a hard twist. It snapped. "Extra inconvenience for the mutt. Shows we're not messing around."

"But knowing how to use picks is a bonus," I said. "Sometimes brute strength just doesn't cut it. Karl will teach you how to pick locks and work with alarm systems."

A hint of a smile. "And you're okay with me learning that when I've got a juvie record?"

"Sure," Clay said as he opened the cottage door. "You ever get into that shit again? Lotta trees behind Stonehaven. I'll string you up from one."

"And let the crows peck at my corpse?"

"Nah. Doesn't hurt if you're already dead."

Noah only laughed. He didn't doubt the punishment would be severe, but he seemed almost relieved with Clay's honesty. With the absolutes. None of that wishy-washy "If you screw up, we might get kinda upset." You screw up, you're in shit. It's language wolves understand.

We stepped into the cottage.

"So," Noah said. "How come *Karl* isn't hanging by his thumbs from a tree somewhere? He's a thief."

"Karl's special," I said.

Clay muttered under his breath about exactly how *special* Karl was. That was the problem with recruiting experienced mutts— you take them as they are. Karl was a jewel thief. He was also a damned good addition to the Pack. A top-notch fighter, and a guy who came with a very valuable set of special skills. I'd known Karl for almost twenty years, long before he joined the Pack. He wasn't the easiest member to deal with, but I could handle him.

"Karl knows what he's doing," I said. "He gets his own set of rules. Which means he's allowed to steal, but if he ever gets caught . . . ?"

"Tree time," Clay said.

"Which you would enjoy *way* too much."

"Only with Karl. Because he's special."

I shook my head and walked farther into the cabin. It was a decent size. Winterized, obviously. Well kept on the outside and surprisingly nice on the inside, looking more like an urban professional's condo than a wilderness cabin. Two bedrooms, one with a bed, the other used as an office, with a large maple desk with a Mac laptop and neat stacks of paper. The bookcases held actual books. Leather sofa set. Big-screen TV. Well-equipped kitchen. Food in the fridge, none of it human body parts.

"If his scent wasn't all over this place, I'd think we had the wrong address," I said. "This is nice."

After a quick tour to get the layout, we gave the place a closer inspection. Clay sniffed for "leftovers," checking closets and looking for basement or attic hatches. I went into the office. I thought I'd caught a whiff of someone else in there.

There was a futon across from the desk. When I sniffed it, I picked up the second scent and knew why it'd been tough to separate.

"A relative," I said to Noah, who'd been following me. "A

werewolf relative, which means the scent is similar to his. Eaton mentioned a brother. Smells like he slept here, but not last night."

I waved Noah over to sniff for himself while I looked for signs that the brother was more than a casual visitor. I found it in the closet—clothing too small for Eaton. Not a lot, though.

"Is he living here?" I mused aloud for Noah's benefit. "Or just leaving a few things for when he visits? Let's check the bathroom. If he's a semi-permanent resident, we'll find his things in there."

We didn't. Not even a spare toothbrush. There was one of everything, all of it belonging to Eaton.

"So his brother only visits," Noah said. "That could still make him the man-eater, right? Comes to see Douglas and kills that college guy while he's here."

"Could be. They're both suspects now, meaning we need to dig up everything we can on both of them. We're looking for two things in particular. First, the brother's name and where he lives, so we can search for man-eating cases there. Second, whether Douglas Eaton has business elsewhere or seems to take a lot of trips, anything that might indicate where he could get away with indulging a man-eating habit."

EIGHT

I sent Noah to search the bedroom. Clay had the living area. I was taking the most likely source of information—Eaton's office.

I figured out his occupation first. There was a shelf of medical books, mostly pharmaceutical. Pens and notepaper advertised the local drugstore. And, to confirm my hunch, a stack of business cards in a drawer said Eaton was the local pharmacist. Probably at work today, which was good to know. We'd need to talk to him, but it was better if we gathered everything we could first.

It was an odd occupation for a mutt. They're a transient bunch. That's our fault mostly. Traditionally, only Pack wolves can hold territory. Even Jeremy admits it's an archaic system, and it had led to serious trouble years ago, when Karl decided he was tired of asking us for territory and joined a revolt against the Pack. I've argued it would be easier to track troublemakers if we *didn't* keep them on the move. The problem is, like anything else, if you relax the rules, they don't see a kinder, gentler Pack—they see a weak one. So we've been working on ways to grant temporary territory to mutts who've proven themselves worthy.

Historically, the Pack only concerns itself with mutts south of the border. There are just a handful in Canada, with no Pack of their own. I've been monitoring my country, though, so we do enforce our "no snacking on the humans" law in Canada. Not the territory one, though. Too much territory, too few mutts.

But it was a law we could call upon, if it suited our needs. Here, it could be leverage to throw Eaton off balance when we interrogated him.

I checked Eaton's laptop. It was password protected, which could mean something but probably didn't. I've never met a mutt yet who blogged about his adventures in man-eating or exchanged support-group e-mails with others who had a taste for human flesh. Being a pharmacist, he probably had confidential patient information on it.

A search through his filing cabinet gave me a lot more. The guy was a meticulous record keeper. A high school diploma showed he was originally from North Bay, about three hours north of here. There was something in the dossiers about a werewolf living up there with two sons. Probably Eaton's family. I'd have to get Jeremy to take a look.

Eaton had gone to college in Toronto. After that, he moved around, judging by his Records of Employment. I wrote down all the towns, so I could check for bodies, but if I found any, they'd be old. The deed to his cottage was dated twelve years ago. He'd settled here and seemed to be staying. He'd paid off his mortgage years ago and had bought several surrounding properties when the land went up for sale. Expanding his privacy buffer. Smart move.

He drove a 2007 Dodge Ram. Bought used this year, paid cash. I made a note of the vehicle and the license plate number.

"I found something on the brother," Noah said.

I looked up from the desk.

He walked over and put down an open photo album. "This was in the closet."

He'd opened it to one of the last pages. It was dated five years ago, likely when Eaton—like many people—switched to digital. There were a few pictures of him and a guy who had to be his brother. They looked similar, except for size—his brother was a couple of inches shorter and maybe fifty pounds lighter. Noah took the photo from the page and flipped it over. On the back was written "Me and Mark. Trout Lake. July 2004."

"We have a name, then. Excellent. Thanks." I put the photo in my jacket pocket. "For the dossiers, since I doubt he'll willingly supply a more recent shot."

Clay appeared in the doorway.

"Find anything?" I asked.

"Nah. Got a cubbyhole under the floor, but the hatch is in plain view and it seems to be all camping stuff inside. No attic. No smells of decomp anywhere. Even searched the couch. Only found a fishing lure."

He put it on the desk. I picked up the hook. From the other end dangled a couple of squares of hammered metal and a small blue feather.

"That's an earring," I said.

He frowned at it. "You sure?"

"Yes."

"Looks like a lure to me, too," Noah said. "Bet it'd work with fish." He stopped smiling. "Wait. An earring? That could be a trophy, right?"

"Possibly," I said. "But a trophy should be kept someplace safe. This was between the sofa cushions, which sounds more like one of the brothers had company." I pocketed the earring. "If it was a local, she might be a good source of information. I think we're done here. Time to head to town."

"Elena Michaels," I said as I shook the hand of the local physician, Dr. Woolcott, who also served as coroner. "I'm a freelance journalist working on a series of articles on wolf encroachment into human territory. Have you heard of the North American Society for Lupine Relocation?"

The gray-haired man shook his head. Not surprising, since the "society" didn't exist. At least, not as far as I knew.

I continued. "They advocate a clearer delineation between humans and wolves. Namely, forced relocation of wolves living too close to human settlements. They claim that wolf attacks are on the rise and that, contrary to popular belief, wolves do kill people but the attacks are mislabeled as scavenging. I'm putting together a series to investigate that claim, by looking into cases of canine scavenging near known wolf populations."

He nodded. "The Mitchell boy. Tragic. Very tragic."

He walked to the filing cabinet and pulled out a folder. When he returned to the desk, he hesitated. I prepared to rattle off some of the publications I'd worked for, even provide references if necessary. I had my ID in hand. All very legit, except for the part about writing the story, but that's the beauty of being a freelancer—if I haven't presold the series, the only person "assigning" me the job is myself.

He looked at Noah. "And this is . . . ?"

"Noah. He's interning with me on his school holiday."

"Ah." A grandfatherly smile. "Are you enjoying yourself, son?"

"I am."

"Well, you may not enjoy these photos. They're a little . . ." He leaned over to me and lowered his voice. "Graphic."

"I won't look," Noah said.

Woolcott thumped him on the back. "Good boy. I know kids these days have probably seen worse in horror movies, but this isn't special effects. Real death can be hard to take, first time you see it."

Nine months ago, Noah had watched his grandfather be tortured and murdered. I doubted anything in those photos would be new to him, but his expression was perfectly solemn when he nodded. Then he retreated to the patient's chair across the room.

Woolcott showed me the photos. Dillon Mitchell had been found at the bottom of a ravine, only a few hundred feet from the house of a friend, where he'd partied the night before. He was discovered by a neighbor taking his dog for an early morning run. Investigation revealed that Dillon had left the party at one-thirty in the morning. Woolcott guessed he'd fallen over the edge of the ravine and died.

"There was trauma to the back of the head. Whether that was the cause of death or . . ." He glanced at Noah. "Son?"

"I'll step out."

When Noah was gone, Woolcott said, "He may have just been knocked unconscious. There was a lot of bleeding—the scalp was sliced open, and if you've ever cut your head, you know what that's like. It's possible that whatever . . . ate him smelled the blood."

"And the scavenging actually killed him."

He nodded. "I didn't tell the parents that. I was even hoping to spare them the scavenging part, but they insisted on seeing the body. If you do write your article . . ."

"I won't mention the possibility that he wasn't dead yet."

"He may very well have been. The blow seemed strong enough."

"Did you recover the rock he struck?"

Woolcott shook his head. "He'd been dragged a ways by the scavengers. We found where he'd fallen, from the blood. Lots of rocks. Some had blood on them."

I leafed through the photographs. The boy had definitely been eaten by something. Damage to the stomach—the usual starting point. It hadn't gone much beyond that, which was consistent with a werewolf. Wild animals will eat as much as they can. Whatever ate Dillon Mitchell took only a few bites.

I picked up another photo. Paw prints in the snow.

"Canine," I said.

"Yep."

I flipped through the file. It wasn't just the coroner's report. The police had apparently given him all the scavenging evidence as well.

"I don't see a size for the paw prints," I said.

"Oh, he was big. Over a hundred pounds, I reckon."

In other words, no one had measured the prints. Guessing at the size was extremely unhelpful. There are two kinds of wolves in the Algonquin Park area: gray wolves and the smaller Eastern Canadian wolves. The latter averages about seventy pounds. The grays are closer to a hundred. Dogs and hybrids can be much bigger. Werewolves are larger still, because we retain our mass when we Change. Without a measurement, I had no idea if this could be one of the Eatons.

"Any hairs found?" I asked.

"Nothing obvious." In other words, if there'd been a tuft caught in a tree, they'd have grabbed it, but otherwise they hadn't looked.

"Only one set of tracks?"

"Hard to tell. The snow was pretty trampled by the time the officers arrived. Some was from the man who found Dillon, and his dog."

Right. The dog. "Any possibility the dog found the body sooner . . . ?"

He shook his head. "She's a Lab. The prints were bigger. I know there's not much there to help you, but we really weren't interested in what ate him. Bad enough something did. As for whether it could have been wolves, I've got a theory of my own, and I don't know whether it supports the direction you're leaning."

"I'm not leaning either way. Just collecting data."

"Good, because I think what ate him looks like a wolf but isn't."

"Sled dogs."

His brows lifted. "Very good."

"I saw that someone around here owns a team."

"That's right. Bobby Walters. Runs his team professionally, and makes extra cash with the tourists when he isn't racing. Bobby's a great guy. Really good with his dogs. But they get away from him every now and them. Damned canine Houdinis, those huskies. And when they get free, they go looking for food. When they're in training, the best way to get them to obey is to hold back on dinner until they've done the work. Meaning if they get loose . . ."

"They're hungry."

"And they aren't pets. Chow's cheaper, but whenever Bobby can give them meat, he does. Hunters around here shoot more than they want to dress? They take the extra to Bobby. Same with road-kill. He pays them, hauls the carcass out back. Dogs do their thing."

Meaning they might have done it with Dillon Mitchell.

Noah and I were heading out when Woolcott's nurse stopped us.

"You're investigating the Mitchell boy's death?" she whispered.

I nodded. Didn't clarify the exact nature of my story. Just nodded.

"I have information," she said, leaning forward, gaze tripping around, like she was about to turn in a Mafia kingpin. "Can I speak to you outside?"

"Sure."

"Go around back," she whispered. "I'll come out the rear door."

NINE

Whether you're playing journalist or private eye, there are two common types you encounter: the steely eyed "I ain't tellin' you nuthin'" ones and those who can't tell you their story fast enough. Sadly, neither type usually knows anything useful. They just think they do.

I waved to Clay in the truck, giving him the two-minute sign. He nodded.

The nurse was already at the back door. She didn't come out, just opened it and talked, which made me wonder why the hell we couldn't step inside. I suppose this way felt more clandestine. To me, it just felt cold. I pulled my jacket collar up and hunkered down, trying not to stamp my slowly freezing feet with impatience as she gave us Dillon Mitchell's life story. It could be summed up as "he was a good kid." Which is pretty much the same story you'd get in every case like this.

"I think he was murdered," she said finally. "Everyone's saying it was an accident, but I don't believe it. He only had a beer or two, I heard. Not enough to fall off a cliff."

Actually, according to the coroner's report, his blood level had been 0.11, meaning he wasn't plastered but he'd had more than a couple of beers. Of course, his friends at the party were going to claim otherwise—no one wanted to be responsible for letting him leave drunk.

"I think it was that Romero girl. They'd been fighting something awful since he came back from college. She'd been seeing that other guy, and apparently didn't bother to tell Dillon."

"This is Dillon's girlfriend?"

The nurse nodded. "She's doing a victory lap at high school. Grades weren't good enough for college. Poor Dillon comes home and hears she's been spotted with this new guy. She says they're just friends, but I don't think so."

"Who's the new guy?"

"He's not a local. His brother is, and he's bunking down with him while he looks for work."

This sounded familiar. "Do you know his name?"

"Mike, I think. Or maybe Mark. Doug Eaton's his brother. Works at the pharmacy. Such a nice guy. His brother seems like a sweetheart, too. Just got mixed up with the wrong girl."

I called Clay and told him we were going to hike over to the coffee shop. It was a two-block walk through the center of town, which was busy with holiday shoppers. There was some advantage to Noah and me being seen, as I was sure the nurse wasn't going to keep news of this "murder investigation" to herself. If we were spotted around town, more witnesses might come forward.

As we walked, I used my phone to search the Internet for "the Romero girl." Lori was her first name, according to the nurse.

"Got a Facebook hit," I said. "Matches for name, town, and school."

"Sweet." Noah took the phone as I held it out. He flipped through tagged photos of the girl. "Makes it easy to find someone, huh? That's why I figured you guys wouldn't want me having one. A Facebook profile, I mean."

"Is that a problem? We could figure something out if you really wanted one."

"Nah." He gave me back the phone. "I just tell my friends I don't have time for that shit. Sure, they bitch, but the alternative . . ." He shrugged and shoved his hands into his pockets. "I don't want to be found. It's not just the probation thing. I'd finish that if I could. I just . . . I don't want to be found."

When we'd taken Noah from Alaska, there'd been no easy way to do it. We didn't have a custody claim, and he was still on probation. So we just took him. He'd called his mother from Vancouver and said he was with his dad and wasn't coming back. She didn't care. It just gave her something to tell the police.

We'd gotten him new ID—the Pack has centuries of experience with that. We were claiming he was Antonio's nephew, so Noah had decided to take the Sorrentino name. A few weeks ago, he'd bought a Christmas card for his mother and we'd had Lucas and Paige mail it from Portland. I'd thought he *wanted* to send that card, that he missed his mother. But I realized he only wanted to make sure she knew he was safe and happy, in case any maternal twinges made her consider looking for him.

"Whatever happens, you don't ever have to go back," I said softly as we turned the corner.

He nodded, his gaze fixed on the snow being kicked up by his boots. We passed a middle-aged couple and exchanged Merry Christmases.

"You like being a journalist?" Noah asked.

"I do."

"It seems cool. I'd like the investigating part, but then you have to write the stories, and I'm not good at that. I've been thinking . . ." More snow kicked. "I might like law enforcement. As a career. But I suppose I can't, with the fake ID and all."

"You'd be surprised," I said. "I'm sure we could back up the paper trail enough, if that's what you wanted."

He shrugged. "I dunno. Everyone says you need to be at least five foot ten, and I don't think I'm ever going to get there."

"You've still got time. Besides, there isn't a height restriction in most places these days."

"If I want to investigate, though, I need to be a detective. That means I should have a degree. I don't think I can get one. Hell, it'd be a miracle if I got into college."

"Nick says you're getting good grades."

He looked over at me. "And what kind of grades did Nick get?"

"Um, good enough."

"Which is what I'm getting. I'm passing. For me, that's an improvement. Holding me back a year was a good idea, but it only means I get Cs instead of Ds. I just . . . I don't do well in school. I understand stuff if I'm doing it, but remembering terms and lists and equations?" He shook his head. "They just don't stick."

When we gave Noah new ID, we'd made him a year younger—sixteen instead of seventeen. We said it was because all the trouble in Alaska had put him behind. In truth, he was young for his age, in every way. His father said his mom drank while she was pregnant and Noah had FAE—fetal alcohol effects, which is a less severe form of fetal alcohol syndrome.

I'm not fond of labels. I feel like, when you stick one on, it glosses over the underlying issue. In my case, I avoid movies or novels about abused kids, because it brings back nightmares. Does it help to call it post-traumatic stress disorder? Not really. I have issues that I'm still working through and I'm going to keep working through, and that's what matters.

What matters with Noah is helping him cope with his problems. He's easily frustrated and has difficulty concentrating, which really doesn't help in school, but Antonio, Nick, and Reese are all working with him, and I'd say that C grades were a marked improvement for a kid who'd been failing.

I could tell him that. Be supportive and encouraging. But I'd seen Clay with him and I'd seen what worked.

"Do you want to go to college?" I said.

"I don't know."

"Well, that's up to you. If you want it, you're going to need to work for it. You're right. Becoming a cop wouldn't be easy. We'd have to fix your background to withstand security checks. You're a little small, so you'd need to really bump up your workouts with Antonio. He's not a big guy, either, but he's the only one in the Pack who can take on Clay."

"But Antonio's build is different. I'm skinny—"

"And if you don't put in the effort, then you'll stay skinny."

He squared his shoulders. "I can put in the effort."

"Then do that. Same as school. No one expects you to be as strong as Antonio. No one expects you to be as smart as Clay. Just make the effort. That's the only way you're going to find out if you can get what you want."

A few more steps. Then, "You're right."

"Whew."

He smiled over at me. We walked in silence until I pointed out the coffee shop across the road. As we crossed, he said, "I was thinking of asking Antonio if I could do part-time security at the office. I hate to ask, because I'm not really qualified, so he'd just be giving me a job because I'm his . . ." He struggled for a word. "Ward. Honorary nephew. Whatever."

"And as his honorary nephew, you're entitled to a job in the family business. It's called networking. You take advantage of every 'in' you have. Ask him. He'll set you up."

"Okay."

We stepped into the coffee shop. It was a Tim Hortons—the chain that seemed to have found its way into every town big enough to support one. Clay sat in the corner by the side exit. That door wasn't shutting properly, and I could feel the draft ten feet away. That explained why Clay had chosen it—it was an unpopular spot. But the corner was no longer as empty as it had probably been when he sat down. A group of young women had taken the table beside his. They were talking loudly, overdoing their excited chatter and laughs, casting glances his way.

"Oh, look," I said as we walked in. "Clay's making friends already. He's such a sociable guy."

Noah grinned. "Does he really not notice those girls? Or is he just pretending he doesn't?"

"He might not be pretending. He used to get nasty about attention, but he's learned that can backfire. Lots of women like a bad boy. Since they're not about to stop noticing him anytime soon, he's just stopped noticing them noticing."

"Rough life."

I could have said it *was* rough. Clay would be much happier blending into the woodwork. But no awkward teenage boy wants to hear about the hardships of a middle-aged guy who has twenty-year-old girls drooling over him.

This time, though, I think Clay did notice. Sidelong glances are easy to ignore. A table of giggling girls is not. The second I got inside, his head shot up. He waved us over to where two coffees waited, one beside him and one across the table. I started for the one across the table, but he tugged me to his side and gave me a kiss.

"Public displays of affection?" I murmured. "Those girls must really be getting on your nerves."

"They started off talking about how hot older guys are, then moved on to discussions of their favorite sex positions."

"Ooh. Learn anything?"

He growled under his breath and moved me into the seat between him and the girls. I smiled at them. They gave me a once-over, with sniffs that said I wasn't worthy.

I took a sip of my coffee, then told Clay what we'd learned. I kept my voice low. That's an advantage to werewolf hearing—we can discuss things in public that we don't want overheard. Noah had to lean forward to listen in, but he could follow the conversation. Or he did until he got distracted by a girl passing the window.

"Uh, Elena?" Noah said.

He nodded toward the door. The girl was coming into the coffee shop now. She wore a cropped leather jacket, boots with three-inch heels, and a miniskirt. At least she had on tights to keep her legs warm. I couldn't blame Noah for getting distracted. She was pretty, with long blond hair and—

"Shit," I murmured. It was Lori Romero. Noah had recognized her from her Facebook photo.

"Makes it easy, huh?" Noah said.

It would have, if she hadn't plunked herself down with the girls beside us.

"Great," I muttered. "No way they're chatting with me."

"I'd give it a shot, but I'm a little young for them," Noah said, then looked at Clay.

"No," Clay said.

Noah grinned. "Oh, come on. Take one for the team."

"The team will survive."

"But if she's dating Mark Eaton, then we know she likes older guys."

Clay started to growl a response, but I cut him off.

"She *is* dating Mark Eaton," I said. "Check the earrings."

"Fishing lures," Noah said.

"Which is not absolute proof," I said. "But she's the only girl there that favors dangling, sparkly earrings, and we know she's rumored to be seeing Mark. Now we need to talk to her."

"Get Reese to do it," Noah said. When I hesitated, he continued, "He won't be thrilled, but it might be good for him. Whatever happened in Australia, he's got to get over it and start dating again. Nick says it isn't healthy."

Clay snorted. "He would. Just leave Reese alone. He'll come around." He shot a quick look at the table of girls. "But, yeah, maybe we should bring him to talk to—"

My cell phone ring cut him short. It was Nick.

"Hey," he said. "Just thought you should know, your local mutt stopped by."

"What?"

Clay's head shot up. I pulled the phone from my ear so he could listen in.

"He was playing good neighbor," Nick said. "See how you guys were making out, if you needed directions to local services, suggestions for good hiking spots, recommendations on local attractions . . ."

"Bastard."

Nick chuckled. "Yeah, I felt like a jerk telling him to get lost. He really did seem like he was being friendly. But over-friendly, if you know what I mean. Kate says he's still scared."

"Kate was there?"

"He brought gifts for the kids. They heard and came running in before Reese could catch them. The guy wanted to talk to them. Kate was willing to chat, and she isn't too happy with me for sending him packing." A pause. "She said . . . She said he's one of us. That we should be nicer to him. I'm . . . not sure if she overheard you guys talking . . ."

"She didn't. She said that as soon as he came around last night."

"Huh."

"Did she elaborate?"

"Nope. Want me to ask her what she means?"

"Better not. I tried, and it did not go well. I'll explain later."

"Well, this mutt's not making it easy, either. You know what he brought them for gifts?"

"What?"

"Stuffed wolf pups."

TEN

We pulled over a hundred feet from Eaton's cottage. Through the trees, we could see his pickup in the drive.

I looked back at Noah. "Remember that part where you need to stay in the truck? This is it."

"I know Clay's going to work the guy over."

"But you don't need to witness it."

His jaw set. "I've seen worse."

I glanced at Clay. His expression was impassive, but I knew what he wanted.

"Can we have a second?" I asked Clay.

He got out of the truck and walked into the woods, circling the cottage, as if scouting.

I turned back to Noah. "You may be okay with seeing what Clay does. But he's not okay with you seeing him do it."

"Oh." A pause, as confusion flickered over his face. Then understanding. "Oh."

I lowered my voice more, in case Clay could hear. "What he does works. It keeps the Pack safe. Doesn't mean he likes doing it. No one should like doing that."

"Right. Of course. I didn't mean—"

"I know."

Noah nodded. "Okay. I'm sorry. Tell him—"

I reached back to squeeze his hand. "I don't need to tell him anything. Just stay in the truck. Please. No matter what. Okay?"

"Okay."

✠

I rapped on the door. I could hear Eaton inside. Probably considering his chances of escaping out a window. I was about to knock again when he opened the door. Clay charged, slamming Eaton across the room. The guy was on the floor—Clay on his chest—before he could blink. I stepped in and closed the door behind me.

"What the fuck did you think you were doing?" Clay snarled. "If you've got a death wish, mutt, just take a goddamn gun and blow your brains out in the woods, because I do not have time for this shit."

"I-I—"

Clay cut him short with a left hook to the jaw that sent blood spraying. "I told you last night to stay the hell away from my family, and what do you do? Come strolling by today like you're the fucking Welcome Wagon. And you come when I'm not at home—"

"I didn't realize that. Your car was there. The truck was gone, but I knew your wife—" His gaze started to dart toward me, then he stopped himself. "I knew she drove the SUV. So I figured it was okay."

"After I *told* you—"

"I wanted to apologize for spooking you."

"You didn't spook—"

"Alarm, I mean. Or, um, catch you off balance. Coming by your place last night was stupid. An invasion of territory. I get that now. Like I said, I don't know any other werewolves, so I don't understand all the rules."

Clay hauled him up and threw him into an armchair. Eaton stayed down. He kept his gaze lowered. Cowardice? Faking submission? Or smart enough to know he didn't want to give Clay an excuse?

Clay glanced at me for orders. I walked between them, letting Eaton know I wasn't hiding behind my mate.

"You gave our children wolves," I said. "Toy wolves."

"What? No. They're huskies. Dogs. Check the tags. A friend of mine runs a team of sled dogs and I was inviting them—I mean, you two and them—out for a visit. These ones have been raised with me around, so they're fine with the werewolf scent, and I thought that might be a treat for your kids. I know, when I was growing up, I always found that tough, not being able to get near animals."

When we didn't reply, he said, "Ask your friend at the house. I gave him a pamphlet."

"And you still don't think that was going to piss us off?" Clay asked. "I told you last night that our kids don't know, and you give them toys that look like wolves?"

Eaton protested that the toys had blue eyes and didn't really look like wolves. I said nothing because the truth is that our kids *do* have toy wolves. When they were babies, it'd been something of a joke with our friends—Pack and other supernaturals. We all thought it was cute. But now, coming from Eaton, it seemed like a threat. *Leave or I'll tell your kids your secret.*

"What do you want to tell us about Dillon Mitchell?" I said.

He hesitated, frowning, as if trying to make the mental shift. Then he went still.

"Yes, we know about the boy," I said. "I saw the autopsy reports. Saw the photos. Saw the paw prints. So a young man dies in the forest, eaten by an oversized canine, and there's a werewolf in town. One who's very nervous having us around."

"N-no. I mean, yes, I'm nervous. I told you, I've never met other werewolves. But I've heard the stories. I know, if I bump into one, he's not going to shake my hand and invite me out for a beer. There's one of me and at least four of you. So, yes, that makes me nervous. But I had nothing to do with that boy dying or being eaten. That was scavengers. I'm no man-eater."

"And your brother?"

His head shot up. "Mark? N-no. He's not even here. He lives in North Bay."

"But he was here when Dillon Mitchell died. We know that. He was seeing Dillon's girlfriend."

Eaton tried to hide a surge of fear, but it was so strong I could smell it.

"No. Our dad raised us right. We don't kill people. We sure as hell don't eat them. I know how this must look, and yes, I knew about Dillon and I was afraid that's why you were here, but it's a complete coincidence. The night Dillon died, I was with my girlfriend, in the next town over. I can give you her name. It's only fifteen kilometers away, so sure, I could have come back and killed Dillon, but that wouldn't make sense. My girlfriend doesn't know what I am, obviously, so I'm not going to come back here, Change for a run, kill a guy, then go back and crawl into bed with her."

That would be true if Dillon had just been a guy he'd bumped into on a run. But if it was murder—if Eaton killed him intentionally—this would provide a decent alibi. Which would make more sense if this Eaton, not Mark, had been the one dating Dillon's girlfriend.

"So you were at your girlfriend's, and your brother was here alone?" I said.

A pause.

"We know he was here that night," I said. "You say you weren't. Ergo, he was here alone."

"He might have been with Lori. That's—"

"Dillon's girlfriend. So they were a couple?"

This would seem a simple-enough question. Far simpler than being asked about murder and cannibalism. But he hesitated, his jaw working, chewing over a response.

"Yes," he said finally. Tentative agreement. Uncertain. He followed with a firmer, "Yes. They are. I'd rather he was dating someone closer to his own age, but it doesn't seem to be serious. I'm sure they were together that night. Maybe even at the party." A pause. Then, firmer again, "Yes, they would have been at the party. Which means Mark didn't do it."

"I thought you *knew* he didn't do it," I said. "Because he's not a man-eater."

"Of course. But *you* don't know that, so I'm pointing out that it wouldn't make sense for Mark to be at a party with a girl, then sneak out to Change and hunt down her ex-boyfriend."

His logic was flawed. Before the party, Dillon hadn't realized he *was* Lori's ex-boyfriend. That could have led to a fight. If Mark wanted him out of the picture, he could kill him as a wolf, which presumably couldn't be traced back to him.

"I want to speak to Mark," I said.

"He went home to North Bay, like I said."

"Okay. Give me his cell phone number."

"He doesn't have one. Can't afford it."

"His landline, then."

No answer.

"E-mail address?"

"He's . . . in the bush. I know that sounds bad, but he does it all the time. Just packs a bag and heads off for a week or so."

"In the middle of winter?" I said.

"Sure. Camping's fine if you have the right equipment."

"And where is he camping?"

"Somewhere outside North Bay. He doesn't have set spots."

"Of course he doesn't."

I stepped back. Clay shot forward. Eaton tried to scramble up, but he was too slow. Clay grabbed him by the shirtfront and slammed him into the wall.

"You say you don't know who we are, but you're full of shit. We can *smell* the lies. No matter how isolated you are, you have some contact with other werewolves. Every mutt does. It's a matter of survival. There's exactly one female werewolf out there. Not hard to figure out who she is, which means you know who I am, too."

"I-I wasn't sure . . ."

"Bullshit. Who am I?"

Eaton didn't answer. Clay plowed his fist into Eaton's stomach. Eaton gasped, eyes rolling.

"Try again. Who am I?"

"Clayton Danvers."

"And who's she?"

"Elena Michaels. I mean, Dan—"

"Michaels," Clay said. "So you know who we are. Now tell me what we do. Who does Elena speak for?"

"The Alpha. She speaks for the Alpha. You two enforce the will of the Alpha. You keep the Laws of the Pack. You hunt man-eaters."

"And what do we do when we find them?"

He swallowed. "You kill them."

"No." I stepped forward. "For a first-time offender, we remind him of the Law. We show him why it's not wise to break the Law. It's a painful lesson, but there's no permanent damage until the second lesson. There is no third lesson. By that point, it's clear the problem isn't one the werewolf wishes to resolve."

Was that standard procedure in every instance? No. Every case was different. But those were the basic stages we followed.

I took another step, close enough to see sweat beading on Eaton's broad forehead. "If your brother confesses to accidentally killing and eating Dillon Mitchell, he'll get the first lesson. However, if he refuses to come forward, I'll need to dig deeper to find him, which may turn up more cases and make us decide that he's passed the point of warnings."

"I don't know where he is."

"Yes, you do. You have twenty-four hours to get him and call us. Understood?"

Eaton nodded.

We returned to Noah and moved the truck to an empty cottage a half-kilometer away. Then Noah and I hiked back. I was certain

Eaton knew where his brother was, and pretty sure he was the one hiding him. So we hoped to catch him going to check on him. But he didn't. We waited for an hour—swapping spots halfway so I could warm up—then Nick called to say Reese was almost done cooking and the kids were simmering themselves, watching the clock. We headed back.

We found dinner on the table. Everyone was just settling in. When Kate and Logan didn't greet us at the door, I told myself they were just hungry. Parents can't compete with food. When we walked into the dining room and neither looked up, I knew trouble was brewing.

"That man came over today," Logan said before I could sit down. "He brought us a present."

"So I heard," I said.

Logan pulled his toy from his lap and set it on the table. "It's a Siberian husky."

"No," Kate said. "It's a wolf."

Logan shook his head. "The tag says they're huskies. And they have blue eyes." He pointed at the bright blue beads. "Wolves can't have blue eyes."

"They can if they're babies."

"Your sister's right," Clay said. "Wolves can have blue eyes when they're first born. But Logan is correct, too. Those are huskies."

"Logan's is a husky. Mine's a wolf."

I smiled and bent to stroke her curls as I passed. "All right. Yours is a wolf. Do you have a name for her yet?"

She looked up. Her gaze met mine. I could feel that gaze searching, and I struggled to hold it, to keep smiling.

"Why are we being mean to the man, Mommy?" she asked.

"We aren't—"

"Uncle Nick was mean to him. Uncle Nick's never mean to anybody."

I glanced across the table. Nick looked at me helplessly.

"I don't think he meant to be mean," I said carefully. "But the man is a stranger, and we don't like strangers giving gifts to our children. You know the rule. We don't take anything from strangers."

"But he's one of us."

"She has a point," Reese said from down the table. "You really should be nicer to a fellow Canadian, Elena. Aren't you guys supposed to be nice all the time?"

I made a face at him.

He leaned toward Kate and mock-whispered, "I think your mom's been down in the States too long. She's getting rude, like your dad. Then she comes up here, and another Canadian is just being friendly and she gets all suspicious, because in the States no one is friendly."

"Uncle Nick is."

"Uncle Nick's weird."

Nick shot back and they continued on, the others joining in, successfully distracting the twins. At least for now.

ELEVEN

*A*fter dinner, everyone cleaned up for Reese, then left him prepping pancake batter for the morning while they went outside. I stayed with Reese.

"Thanks for rescuing me," I said.

"No worries. They're smart little guys. That's good in some ways." He took down the flour. "And a pain in the arse in others."

"No kidding." I walked to the fridge, poured myself a glass of water, and handed him a bottle of beer.

He checked the label and let out a sigh of relief. "Not American. Thank you."

He popped the top and chugged half the bottle.

"I was wondering something," I said. "How old were you when you found out you were a werewolf? If you don't mind talking about it."

I knew what had happened in Australia. I was the only one Reese had told. Clay realized he'd told me—we don't keep secrets—but he'd never ask me for the details. He was just glad that someone knew.

Reese's parents had been killed by the Australian Pack. It was an old grudge. Every Pack is different and it seems the Australian one fit into the "gang of thugs" category. His parents had been hiding since before he was born, and when they were found, it was through Reese. Not his fault. But he blamed himself. So I raised the subject of his youth—and, by extension, his parents—as little as possible.

"It's getting easier," he said. "Never going to be easy, but if I won't talk about them?" He shrugged. "Doesn't seem right. Not what they'd want."

"No, I'm sure it isn't."

He took another long draw on the bottle, then measured the baking powder before continuing.

"I don't remember them telling me. Maybe I always knew, or maybe I was so little that I don't remember finding out. It was just part of who we were. Dad could Change into a wolf. Which meant he could hear me if I snuck out of bed at night or smell my scent all over the kitchen if I'd raided the refrigerator, so there was no use lying about it. That was normal life for me."

That's what Clay had wanted. Don't make a big production out of it. Just let them grow up with it as part of their lives. I couldn't believe he'd suggest such a thing. Let *toddlers* know their parents Changed into wolves? We'd have to police every encounter with non-supernaturals until they were old enough to understand why it was a secret.

"And you never let something slip? To the kids next door or down the street?"

He lifted his brows. "Remember where I grew up?"

"Right. Sheep farm. The outback. No kids next door."

"Sure there were. If by 'next door' you mean the farm ten kilometers over. By the time I was old enough to visit on my own, I was practically old enough to Change. Sure, I had playtime with other kids. My parents made sure I didn't grow up a completely anti-social little heathen. They'd drive me to town twice a week for footy from the time I was old enough to kick a ball. Dad was always there, in case I stuffed up."

"Which you never did."

"Uh, not exactly. When I was three, Mom took me to the zoo and I was watching the wolves and informed a lady that my dad could turn into one of those. She called the cops. They sent scientists to kidnap and study him . . ." He grinned over at me.

"Let me guess—she patted you on the head and told your mother you had a vivid imagination."

"Nah, she gave Mom shit for letting me watch horror movies. Then, when I was five, I was watching cartoons at a family friend's place. There was a wolfman, and I said that wasn't a proper werewolf and tried to tell the other kids what a proper werewolf was."

"And your dad stopped you?"

"Nope. He let me finish, then explained the difference between folklore werewolves and movie werewolves. Both times, though, I caught hell when I got home. Got a long lecture plus a double helping of chores around the farm. I learned my lesson."

He finished his beer, then covered the dry pancake mix with plastic wrap. "You thinking of telling the twins?"

"I . . . don't know. They're so young."

"Yep. You don't live on the outback. And your kids are in school already, which my parents never had to worry about, with me being homeschooled. Tough choice. I wouldn't want to make it." He grabbed another beer from the fridge. "You coming outside?"

I nodded.

"Good. I told the kids we were going to sabotage Nick's snow-shoes. We'll need you to distract him while we work."

Snowshoe lessons from Noah. A hike through the woods with the kids, Reese and I keeping our snowshoes on, Nick abandoning his halfway through after landing in one too many snowdrifts, Clay doing the same . . . possibly because Nick wasn't the only victim of snowshoe sabotage.

Nick didn't figure it out. Clay did. I landed in a snowbank of my own. Kids piled on. Snowball fight ensued. Bonfire back at the cottage. No interruptions. No unanswerable questions. Kate snuggled up on my lap at the fire while Logan sat with his dad and Reese, deep in a discussion I was too sleepy to follow.

The kids' good mood continued to bedtime. We let them stay up with the adults, then put them down after midnight. The twins brought their toy dogs, and as they settled in, Kate put hers on her chest, staring at it. I tensed and glanced at Clay. He shook his head in answer to my unasked question. Don't try to distract her. Just wait and deal with whatever was coming.

"The man said his friend has sled dogs," Logan said. "He invited us to come see them. Kate said dogs don't like us, but he said these ones like all kids."

"They won't bite or run away," Kate said. "He promised."

"That's a hard thing to promise," Clay said.

"But we could try, couldn't we?" Logan asked. "He says they're close by. We can play with the dogs and, if we want, we can take a sled ride."

Kate looked at me and asked, "Can we?" with none of her usual imperiousness. She feared what the answer would be. Sensed it, I think.

"We'll see," Clay said.

She nodded. Admittedly, a "We'll see" from me was often Mom-speak for "Probably not, but I don't want to disappoint you and I'm hoping if I delay an answer you'll forget the question." From Clay, it really did mean we'd consider it.

"I'm not sure it will work out," Clay said. "But if Mr. Eaton's offer still stands after Christmas, we'll take you over."

An honest response. Both children nodded. And that was it. No anger. No more questions. They curled up between us with their stuffed dogs and fell asleep.

Which should have been a relief. They were already abandoning the fight. If I kept up this course of action—avoid questions, distract when I could, maneuver out when I couldn't—they'd forget.

Would Kate really forget, though? Or just give up?

When they finally did learn the truth, would she remember this?

Of course she would. She wasn't a baby. She'd remember and she'd be furious, rightfully so.

Clay would back me up and pretend it was a mutual decision. Present a united front—that was our tenet of parenting. He'd take a share of Kate's resentment and anger, which wasn't fair, meaning I'd have to admit that he'd wanted them to know all along.

So yes, Kate would be angry, and probably Logan, too, but how deep a betrayal was it? We can pretend we're honest with our kids, but we aren't. Not really. We tell them stories about Santa Claus, and we know they'll be upset when they learn the truth, but we hope they'll look back and see the magic we added to their childhood.

Clay and I had never considered forgoing the Santa myth. He'd never had it himself. When he was bitten, there'd been no place for jolly gift-bringing elves in his new reality. There hadn't been much Santa in my life, either—my first Christmas in a foster home, an older foster brother told me the truth. Yet we'd never considered not perpetuating the legend with our own children.

So we did lie. We lied to bring magic to their lives and we lied to protect them. When we finally told Logan and Kate the truth about what we were, would they understand my reasons? Or would they only understand that I'd lied? That Kate had trusted me . . . and I'd failed?

I could fix this. I could tell them the truth. Yet at the very thought of it, my gut twisted and my brain shrieked. Our children were too young for the truth. I just had to weather this storm.

And yet . . .

I couldn't sleep. I lay there long after the kids had drifted off and Clay had joined them. Then I eased out of bed and opened the door.

I could hear Reese and Noah, still down in the family room, talking in front of the fire. Only one place to go. I pulled on a sweater and the thick woolen socks Clay had discarded. Then I slipped out onto the master-suite balcony overlooking the back woods.

TWELVE

I stood there, torn between wanting to make a decision and not wanting to rush and make the wrong one, not when I was distracted by other problems. This was so damned important.

The more I thought about it, the further I got from a decision, which infuriated the hell out of me. Any day now, Jeremy could say, "I'm stepping down. You're Alpha." What kind of Alpha would I make if I was freezing my ass off at 2 a.m., unable to reach a conclusion on a parenting issue? An Alpha had to be decisive, to say, "This is my choice," in a way that convinced every Pack wolf that there was no other option.

So what the hell was Jeremy even thinking naming me Alpha? I *always* had doubts. There was no black and white in my world. There were a thousand shades of gray, a thousand permutations for every decision, a thousand possibilities for every choice. You want someone who can make an absolute decision and stand by it, damn the consequences? You want Clay. And if Clay has other qualities not befitting an Alpha, then you make it a joint position. I'd suggested it. Jeremy said no. Clay said no. One wolf to rule them all. That's how it'd always been and how it always would be.

When a warm body pressed against my back, I jumped. Clay's arms tightened around me as he pulled me against him.

"You're freezing, darling. *I'm* the one who doesn't feel the cold, remember? Come back inside."

"Soon."

A soft sigh. The heat vanished as Clay stepped away and I had to fight the urge to back against him again, tell him to stay. He retreated inside. A moment later, he returned, and moved up behind me again, pulling a comforter around us, his body so blissfully warm that I closed my eyes, everything else sliding away.

"Hear the wolves?" he murmured.

I lifted my head and picked up the distant howling of a wolf pack, miles away.

"If you didn't hear that, you really are thinking hard."

"Worrying," I said.

"Thinking."

I smiled and leaned against him.

"She'll be all right," he said. "They both will. We'll fix this mutt problem, the kids will move on, and we'll return to our regularly scheduled Christmas getaway."

I turned in his arms. "I'm starting to wonder if you were right."

He paused. "I'd say I must be dreaming, but you don't seem in the mood for jokes."

"I think we should have told them from the start. Made it part of their lives. We should have discussed it more. I should have listened more."

"We talked plenty. You listened. Honestly? I wasn't completely convinced that my view was right. If I was, I'd have fought for it."

"You did."

He lifted his brows. "If I really thought it was the absolute best thing for our kids, you'd have had a battle on your hands. That was just debate."

"With chair throwing."

"Heated debate. Chair throwing is just getting your attention. Fights involve chair breaking."

"Ah."

He pulled me closer. "There's no right answer. I was working from the basis that assimilation into a culture is easier if it's introduced from birth. But the kids *have* been assimilated from birth.

They're treated like werewolves. They live like werewolves. They just don't understand the rationale behind it. It's like . . ." He paused. "Like growing up in a society with ancestor worship, and you do all the rituals and celebrate the holidays, but the 'why' isn't explained until you're old enough to really understand it."

"And you're okay with that?"

"I'm not thrilled with waiting, but it isn't as if you and Jeremy said we had to pretend to be a normal human family for them. Then I'd have fought like hell. If they'd known we were werewolves from the start, the only real advantage is that you wouldn't be on this balcony, freezing your ass off, wondering when is the right time to tell them. The disadvantage is that it's an exposure risk."

"Which is minimal, when you really think about it. No one's going to believe four-year-olds who claim their parents turn into wolves. The real exposure risk comes when they're old enough to Change. I mean, *if* they . . ."

I trailed off.

"That's the real problem, isn't it?" Clay said.

I looked up at him.

"You're right about the exposure risk," he said. "Hell, I think you just parroted my own words back to me. The true risk comes when a werewolf begins his Changes. When he can throw a classmate into a wall and kill him. When he can start shape-shifting in the middle of a party. By then, they *have* to know. The real reason you don't want to tell them? Because we don't know if they're ever going to Change. You've heard Nick and Reese talk about what it's like, hitting their teens, the excitement, the anticipation. It's like waiting to be old enough to drive or to drink, multiplied by ten. Everyone warns you it'll be painful as hell, but you don't care. You're finally going to be able to turn into a wolf. You're finally going to join the Pack."

He paused. I turned to listen to the wild wolves and felt tears prickle.

Clay lowered his voice. "For our kids, that might not happen. That's what you're afraid of. Bringing them up in a life they might never fully share."

"I think . . ." I paused, gathered my thoughts. "They smell like werewolves. They seem to be showing secondary powers years before they should. But that's . . ."

"Different."

I nodded. "I want to see that as proof that they'll be able to Change. Which, in some ways, is crazy. Life would be easier if they couldn't. Take the secondary powers. Leave the pain of the Change. Leave the constant struggle for control. Leave the risk that some-day you're going to lose that battle and look down to see a person, a dead human being—"

I choked. Clay hugged me so tight I couldn't breathe. I squeezed my eyes shut and tried not to remember those days in Toronto, when I'd run from Jeremy, when the Change was still a fever-blind blackout. When I'd woken up to see what I'd done.

"I don't *ever* want our children to go through that," I said. "So I should be happy if they don't Change. But I'm not, because I know how important it will be to them. I know that, in spite of the risks, I'd never give up . . ."

I couldn't finish that. I've reached peace with what Clay did, but that further admission is too much. Too exculpatory.

"You wouldn't give up being a werewolf," he murmured. "You just wish it'd happened another way."

I nodded.

Another bone-cracking squeeze. "So do I, darling. More than anything."

I rested my cheek against his chest. The wolves had gone silent now, so I listened to the thump of his heart.

After a moment, he said, "It should have gone the way I planned. Let you know what I was. If, at some point, you wanted to join that part of my life . . ."

I would have. I know that now. It wouldn't have been a quick decision, but the time would have come when I'd have wanted to share that with him, wanted to experience it for myself. When I'd have realized it would complete me. That's exactly what I was afraid of with our children. That they would realize this was what they needed to complete their lives, and that they'd never be happy without it.

"I think . . ." I cleared my throat, moved back, started again. "I think Logan will be all right. I think he'll Change. It's Kate I'm worried about. What if she doesn't? If he does and she doesn't?" I shook my head. "Maybe I'm being silly. She's only four. She won't be the same person when she's old enough to realize it won't happen. Maybe she'd be okay with it."

He said nothing.

I met his gaze. "She won't, will she?"

He still said nothing, as if even he couldn't put a voice to that fear, that our daughter would not be okay with it.

"She'd want to be bitten," I said. "She'd want us to . . ." I couldn't finish. After a minute, I said, "Yes, that's what I'm afraid of. That's why I don't want to tell her any sooner than I have to. We can tell her it won't happen for her and hope it will be a surprise if it does, but that won't matter. She'll think it will happen and when it doesn't, she'll want it. She'll come to us and she'll ask, and if we say no . . ." I forced myself to meet his eyes. "I'm afraid we'd lose her."

A pause. Then, "That's a lot of ifs."

I let out a short laugh. "Worrying about worst scenarios? That's not like me at all, is it?"

His turn to laugh. "Okay, so let's work it through. Worst scenario. Kate grows up expecting to Change into a wolf. Logan does Change. She doesn't. She asks us to bite her. We say no—it's too dangerous. She hates us forever because we're standing between her and happiness." He stopped. Looked me squarely in the eye. "Only that's not true, is it? If we say no . . ."

"She can go to someone else," I whispered. "A mutt."

"I can hope our daughter would be smart enough not to let some random mutt bite her. But could she con a mutt into it? Maybe even a Pack member? Reese, Noah . . . her brother? We could say no all we want, Elena. That wouldn't stop it from happening. And it won't matter if we tell her now or in a few years. She's still going to want it. All we can hope is that it won't be an issue—she *will* Change. And if she doesn't? We're going to need a game plan . . . in sixteen years, when we're certain it's not going to happen on its own."

"So there's no sense stressing about it now."

"Right."

I exhaled. "Which brings back the original question. When do we tell them?"

"I'm okay with telling them now. I'm okay with telling them in a year, two, three, even four. Longer than that? I have a problem. So, you have four years. When you're ready, we'll figure out how we're going to do it. And any time you want to talk about it?"

"I know where to find you."

"You got it."

I put my arms around his neck. "Thank you."

He arched his brows. "For making myself available to discuss a parenting issue with the mother of my children?"

"No. For knowing what was really worrying me, even when I wasn't sure myself."

I kissed him. His hands slid under my T-shirt, fingers hot against my skin. He hoisted me onto the railing.

"Feel sturdy enough?" he said.

"It's not a long fall."

He laughed and reached to shake the railing. When it didn't budge, he murmured, "Good," and pulled the comforter around us again.

As we kissed, a shadow moved against the balcony doors. "I think we have company," I murmured.

He turned as Logan cupped his hands against the glass and peered out. I hopped off the railing. Clay opened the door and whispered, "Hey, bud, you want to come out?"

Logan nodded. Clay picked him up and shut the door quietly, then swiped snow off a chair. He sat, Logan on his knee, tugged me onto his other knee, and wrapped the comforter around us.

"Warm enough?" he asked.

Logan nodded.

Clay leaned over to his ear and whispered, "Listen. Do you hear that?"

Logan cocked his head. His eyes widened. "Wolves?"

Clay nodded.

Logan stared out at the sky, listening intently, with this wistful look on his face, and I could tell myself I was imagining it, but I knew I wasn't. He might not understand what he felt, but when he listened to those wolves, he felt something.

Everyone said Kate was so obviously her father's daughter. Our friends teased Jeremy that it must be like having Clay all over again. Jeremy would smile and nod, but he'd told me that Clay had been more like Logan, serious and quiet, even when he was cutting up the classroom guinea pig and tying Nick to trees. The boisterous energy came later, but there was still that quiet side of Clay, and I could see it now, as he rested his chin on his son's head, looking out into the night, listening to the wolves.

I twisted sideways, rested my cheek against Clay's shoulder, and watched them until I drifted off to sleep.

THIRTEEN

When I opened my eyes, Kate was crouched on the bed, her face a few inches from mine, staring as if she could will me to wake.

I blinked and yawned.

"Uncle Nick and Reese are up," she whispered.

I glanced at Logan, sitting beside her. Behind him, Clay was sound asleep.

I nodded. "Go on."

Once they'd left, I padded to the door and locked it. Then I reached under the bed to retrieve something I'd stowed there the day before. The next maneuver was tricky, but Clay was so soundly asleep that I managed it with barely a hitch in his breathing.

When I was done, I tugged back the covers. He didn't notice the sudden draft and kept sleeping.

He'd worn sweatpants to bed, for the sake of the kids, but his chest was bare and he was lying on his back, arms over his head. It was a very nice image. Being Pack enforcer means Clay is in amazing shape. He has to be—he doesn't have the natural advantage of size, like some werewolves. Average height, average build. Above-average body. Perfectly toned biceps, muscled back and chest, flat stomach.

When we'd take the twins to parent–tot swimming lessons, Clay would walk out of the changing room and mothers who'd gawked at him clothed would almost fall into the pool. But when they took a closer look, the frowns would come, then the confusion and concern, and the questions. Is your husband a war vet? Was he in an accident? Because, as perfect as Clay's body appeared, on a closer look, you saw the scars. Decades-old white ones. Pinkish newer ones. Pits and divots, from chunks ripped out in wolf fights. And on his right arm, the ruts of missing tissue, cut out after an infection that left the limb forever weakened.

The overall damage isn't disfiguring, but on an otherwise jaw-dropping guy, it's discomfiting. Women look at that map of scars and they're horrified. I look at it and I see his life story. I can trace every scar with my eyes closed. I know where each one came from. A few are even from me. Some friendly fire, some not.

I have scars, too. Not nearly as many, but enough that I used to be uncomfortable in a bathing suit. I've gotten over it. They're part of my life story, too. Who I am. Who I've chosen to be.

I leaned over Clay now, the tips of my hair tickling his chest, my fingers running across a few of those old scars, remembering. But that wasn't what I was here for, so I pushed the memories aside and settled for admiring then touching him, tasting him, testing exactly how soundly asleep he was. When I flicked my tongue over his nipples, he groaned softly but didn't wake. Very soundly asleep. Good.

I carefully tugged down his sweatpants and boxers. Then I set about waking him up. It took a few minutes. The soft groans slowly deepened to a delicious growl, a sound more felt than heard, vibrating through him. Finally, a gasp. His eyes opened. He chuckled. He tried to reach for me. Then he grunted in surprise.

I lifted my head. He was arching back to look at the rope binding his wrists to the headboard. He gave an experimental tug. Then his fingers slid to the knots.

"Do they pass muster?" I said. "I used a constrictor knot, like you suggested."

He looked down at me, lips curving in a sleepy grin. He flexed his fingers, motioning for me to come up.

I shook my head. "I'm good. And since you're stuck, I can do what I want. And what I want to do"—I lowered my head—"is finish what I started. Acceptable?"

"Don't have much say in the matter, do I?"

"Tragic."

"It is." He grinned, thumped back on the pillows, and let me continue.

We spent the morning with the kids. I did cheat a bit, skipping a walk to "do a few things around the house." Clay bustled the twins off before they could protest. I did tidy up, but spent most of the time on my laptop. Research on the Eatons and on disappearances in North Bay, nothing much turning up on either.

I called Jeremy. He shared my opinion of the situation. There was definitely something going on with the Eaton brothers. Likely Mark was the culprit and his big brother was hiding him.

Jeremy shared my risk assessment, too. Minimal. Eaton knew there were at least three adult werewolves here. He wouldn't risk a strike against us. If Mark was a man-eater, the chances he'd kill again soon were small.

Given all that, Jeremy also seemed to share Clay's hope—that the Eatons would bolt and we could relax, enjoy our Christmas, and take care of them in the New Year. Jeremy couldn't say that, of course. Man-eating was a serious offense that we had to pursue with full vigor. But he made it clear that if the Eatons ran, chasing them would be a waste of time until we had more information.

He also agreed that taking the morning off was fine. I'd seeded my journalist story. We could relax, let that spread, and see what came of it. Honestly? I didn't expect anything, and I don't think Jeremy did, either, but he let me have the excuse.

We talked about the kids, and about Kate's questions, too. Jeremy listened and said little. Part of that was transitioning me to

Alphahood, when he'd still be there to give advice when asked but wouldn't offer it. And part of it was just his general approach to the rearing of our children. He played a huge role in their lives, but Clay and I were their parents. We made those decisions.

Instead, I posed questions about children in the Pack, the process of telling them, and the Pack's history with it. What had gone wrong? How had the Pack dealt with it? I didn't ask for his opinion or advice. I'd gotten that when the twins were born. Now it was up to me.

We left after lunch. As planned, we swapped Noah for Reese. Telling Reese he was being taken along as bait had been my job and not one I'd enjoyed.

It seemed simple enough. I was asking him to flirt with girls, not brawl with a biker gang. For Reese, though, I think the brawl would have been less painful.

Like I said, Reese comes with baggage. The issue that caused Nick the most consternation, though, was his complete disinterest in dating. When we sent Reese and Noah to the Sorrentinos, Antonio had decided to step back and let Nick take on the role of guardian. It'd been the right move. When I was pregnant, Nick admitted he'd started thinking about a child of his own. Once the twins came along, he realized single fatherhood was not for him. Taking in Noah and Reese had eventually satisfied that parenting instinct. But at first, the only thing Nick felt confident helping them with was girls.

I tease Nick about being a player. He isn't. No woman who dates him is ever under the illusion that she has him to herself. He's had exclusive relationships, but they're definitely the exception. If a woman hopes to change that, then chances are she won't even get into his bed, because by his age he's developed a razor-sharp sixth sense for women who say they're good with sex and friendship when they're really hoping for a wedding ring—or at least a set of house keys.

When Reese first went to live with them, Nick had gone through his little black book, looking for a woman with younger sisters, nieces, et cetera. Because, really, what better way to welcome a young guy and take his mind off his maimed hand? There were parties and double dates in those early days, when Reese wasn't comfortable refusing. But Nick figured out fast that the dates weren't leading to hookups or even second dates. I knew why— his parents had died because Reese fell in love with the wrong girl. Nick didn't know that, but I'd convinced him to respect Reese's decision and be patient with him, even if he did worry that prolonged celibacy really couldn't be good for the young werewolf's health.

So asking Reese to flirt with girls was not as easy as it sounded. But I did it because part of being an Alpha is giving orders you know your Pack won't like. While you can respect their issues, and help them work past them, you can't let those issues get in the way of their Pack responsibilities.

FOURTEEN

$\mathcal{F}$ inding Lori was less of a problem than we expected. She was at the Tim Hortons with her friends again. I sent Reese in ahead of us. Clay and I circled the block, then followed. We weren't averse to her knowing Reese was with us, but we didn't want to advertise it, either.

When we got into the coffee shop, Reese was standing beside the girls' table. He'd bought a coffee and stopped to ask them something—recommendations for a bar, it sounded like. He was playing it cool, takeout coffee in hand, looking ready to leave once the conversation ended, but I could already tell they had no intention of letting him get away that quickly. They'd known every guy in town from birth, and now here was a cute Aussie. By the time we'd bought our coffee, they'd persuaded him to take a seat.

We took a table across the shop. The noise level—lots of patrons chattering and calling out holiday wishes—meant we couldn't hear Reese, but that was intentional. If I could listen in, I would, and they might figure out we were eavesdropping. Better to trust Reese.

We'd barely taken our seats when I noticed a girl watching us. Watching *me*, not Clay, which was good, because she looked about fourteen. All it took from me was a smile and she zipped over.

"Are you the reporter?" she asked. "The one writing about the wolves?"

"I am." I gestured to the empty seat beside me.

She didn't sit, just stood there, clutching a hot chocolate.

I waited a beat, then said, "Are you interested in wolves?" It was a decent bet. She was too young to have been at the party. Well, no—that's the mother in me, who'd like to think fourteen-year-olds wouldn't party with college-aged kids. But this one didn't look like the type.

She sat quickly and blurted, "I think it was wolves. That killed and . . ." She swallowed. "Everyone says the wolves don't come down here, but my little sister saw one in the woods behind our house."

"A wolf?"

She nodded. "A black one."

That had Clay's head snapping up. "Black?"

"There is such a thing," she said, her chin lifting. "I looked it up. Eastern wolves are never black, but gray wolves can be." She hesitated, then added, "It might not have been a full wolf, though. She said it had blue eyes, and it was really big."

Shit.

"When did this happen?" I asked.

"In September. Before my stepdad came for Peyton—that's my sister."

Peyton. The little girl who'd gone missing. And she'd seen what seemed to be one of the Eatons in wolf form shortly before she disappeared?

"Your sister," I said. "Have you heard from her?"

"Oh, sure. Her and my stepdad call every week. They're hoping to come up for Christmas, maybe New Year's. My mom and my stepdad are still working out custody stuff, but I think Mom's okay with Peyton staying with him."

The girl was definitely with her father, then. I exhaled in relief. Yet if the Eatons were getting that close to children while in wolf form, that was a problem. A big one.

I talked to the girl and made notes, so I'd seem like I was really a reporter. While we chatted, I noticed someone waiting his turn to speak to me. A bearded man in a plaid jacket. I smiled and nodded, acknowledging him. I didn't rush the girl, but I didn't prolong the conversation, either. When she was ready to go, I thanked her for her information and gave her my e-mail address.

She'd barely vacated her chair before the bearded man slid into it. He nodded to Clay first.

"I'm Bobby Walters," he said. "I hear Doc Woolcott talked to you about the Mitchell boy."

The man's name sounded familiar, but I wasn't sure why until he said, "My dogs didn't eat that boy. I know the doc thinks they did, and I'm sure that's what he told you, but they didn't."

"Okay."

He leaned forward, as if waiting for me to challenge him. When I didn't, he pulled back and ran his tongue over his wind-chapped lips.

"They didn't," he said. "When I went out that morning, they were all in the pen. They were all hungry. None of them had got out. I'm real careful about that, because they did escape a few times after I built the new kennel. There's bear in these woods and damned fool city hunters who don't know a wolf from a husky. I gotta look after my dogs. I can't let them get out. I've taken care of that."

"Okay."

"You don't believe me."

I looked at him. "I'm not from the SPCA. I'm not from an animal rights group. I'm not trying to blame anyone for what happened. I'm just gathering data for an article that covers over a dozen incidents like this. If I find that wolves seemed responsible, that's okay. If it seems to be dogs, that's okay, too. It's all just data. Even if you told me your dogs did it, I wouldn't report that to anyone. It's not my concern."

"They didn't do it."

"Okay."

"They were in the kennel all night."

"Okay."

He stayed for another minute, and I realized he wanted me to argue, because he wanted the chance to defend himself and his dogs. Not to me, but to everyone sitting around us, listening in. People blamed them, and he knew it. When I wouldn't argue—and Clay didn't say a word—there was nothing he could do but leave.

As Walters was leaving, Reese got my attention, motioning that he was done. I nodded, and gestured discreetly to let us leave first.

We got out the door, and saw a familiar face heading our way— Douglas Eaton, his shoulders hunched against the cold, no coat on, walking fast, Tim Hortons debit card in his hand.

When he saw us, I expected him to decide he really didn't need that caffeine hit after all. He did glance behind him, but only to look at Walters, who was climbing into his truck. Walters waved and shouted something about poker. Eaton replied. Once Walters had driven off, Eaton sped up again until he reached us.

"Morning." He managed a smile for me. "Getting your Timmy's?"

"I was."

"You're Canadian, right? I mean, I'd heard that." A spark of panic, his gaze shooting to Clay. "Not that I was prying—"

"It isn't a secret," I said. "I grew up in southwestern Ontario. Went to U of T. So, yes"—I lifted my almost empty cup—"getting my Timmy's. Not a double-double, though."

A nod and a more genuine smile at that, but still cautious. "I, uh, see Bobby was in there. He's the guy I mentioned to your friend. With the sled dogs." He glanced over his shoulder, making sure no one was close enough to overhear, then lowered his voice. "He was telling you his dogs didn't eat that boy, wasn't he?"

"He was."

Eaton shifted his weight. "Well . . . I'm not sure I'd pay much attention to that. They do get out. Yes, I know you think I'm going to say that since you suspect my brother or I did it, but I'd appreciate it if you'd take a hard look at Bobby's dogs. Check the police reports and Woolcott's report, maybe talk to the guys at the scene."

"We will."

"Okay. Thanks. I—"

"Doug?" The voice called out from behind us.

We turned to see Reese striding toward us with a pained look on his face. It wasn't him who'd hailed Eaton, though. That would be the person who was likely the cause of Reese's expression. Lori Romero, hurrying along beside him faster than her high-heeled boots should have allowed on the icy sidewalk.

"Did you get my message?" Lori said to Eaton as they reached us.

"Yeah, sorry, Lori. Things have just been busy. I'm sorry Mark isn't calling you back, but . . ." He shrugged. "I'm just his brother."

She nodded and seemed ready to hurry after her prey, only to realize Reese had stopped, too. Eaton and Reese hadn't met yesterday at the chalet, so Eaton extended a hand. "Doug Eaton." Then he turned back to Lori. "About Mark. I'm real sorry, hon, but if he's not returning your calls, you might want to forget him. He's got a girlfriend in North Bay. I know they've been having trouble, and he probably didn't mention her, but I think they're back together."

"Oh." Her eyes widened, gaze shooting to Reese, mortified. "Mark and I weren't— We're just friends. I was worried because he said he'd drive me to Toronto tomorrow for last-minute Christmas shopping."

"Well, he must have forgotten, because he's gone back to North Bay and—"

He was interrupted as a snow-covered minivan slowed beside us. A middle-aged woman in the passenger seat called out, "Lori?"

"Hey, Mom," Lori said. "I'm sorry. I was just heading home. I got caught up talking to the girls at Tim's."

Her mother's gaze shot to Reese, and she said dryly, "I see."

"Mommy!" shouted a voice from the backseat. "I saw Santa, Mommy!"

The man in the driver's seat put down the rear window, and I saw a little girl about Kate's age bouncing in her booster seat, her lips cherry red from the candy cane clutched in her hand.

"I saw Santa, Mommy!"

I realized she was talking to Lori. The young woman stepped to the window and leaned in to kiss her, then pretended to bite the candy cane. The girl shrieked and pulled it back.

Lori turned to Reese. "This is my daughter, Patsy."

There was a note of defiance in her voice.

I said hi, and asked the little girl about her Santa visit. After she'd chattered at me for a minute, her grandmother said, "We'd better let the nice people go, Patsy. Poor Mr. Eaton is freezing. Where's your jacket, Doug?"

She chided him when he admitted he'd left it in the drugstore. The little girl waved at him and said something about candy canes. Eaton promised her one next time she came by, but he stayed on the sidewalk—he hadn't joined us at the minivan window.

"Lori?" her dad said. "Can we give you a ride home? Your mom has her optometrist appointment at three and—"

"You need to drive her because of the eye drops. I know. Sorry." She turned to Reese and whispered, "Text me," then opened the minivan door and climbed in.

When they were gone, Eaton said, "I should leave, too. Just one more thing I meant to mention. I don't know how far you guys run, but you should steer clear of the bog to the northeast. It looks frozen, but it's not. Nearly fell in a sinkhole out there a week ago."

"Steer clear of the bog," I said.

"Right."

He said his good-byes and we parted. When we were back at the truck, I said, "If Eaton is hiding his brother, I think we have a pretty good idea where he is."

"Northeast of our chalet," Clay said, and climbed into the driver's seat. "Near the bog."

FIFTEEN

*T*he events of the last couple of hours had only reinforced what I'd already suspected. Mark Eaton killed Dillon Mitchell. His brother knew. When we arrived in town, Eaton thought we'd come for Mark and squirreled him away. Now he was madly trying to cover his tracks. Convince us his brother had gone on a walkabout in the woods and couldn't be reached. Blame local sled dogs for the scavenging. Suggest to his brother's girlfriend that his lack of contact only meant he was no longer interested.

Mark Eaton *had* been at the party. When Reese was talking to the girls, he'd mentioned the tragedy and Lori's friends had filled him in. Lori had tried to convince Reese she was not a grief-stricken girlfriend by admitting she and Dillon had already broken up and she'd been at the party with a "male friend" to convince Dillon that the relationship was over. The friend, Reese confirmed, was Mark Eaton.

Lori's friends thought Reese looked like a sweet hookup, too, and the bonds of friendship only stretch so far. So they'd hinted Mark was more than a friend and mentioned a fight between the two guys.

As for what happened after that, the general consensus seemed to be that Mark and Lori had taken off and spent the night at his brother's place. Lori hotly denied it. She said they'd stayed at the party after Dillon left and then Mark drove her home.

Did Mark follow Dillon out and kill him? Did he drive Lori home and come back to hide his crime by scavenging the remains?

Or did Lori *and* Mark follow Dillon out? Did he die accidentally, and Mark returned to cover it up?

I wasn't happy with any of those scenarios. There was a piece missing here, but we weren't finding it until we found Mark Eaton.

Locating the bog took some effort. After consulting maps and the Internet and finding nothing conclusive, I had Clay ask at a gas station. Turned out the kid manning the pumps was an avid snowmobiler. He knew exactly what we were looking for. When we said we'd been warned to avoid it, he seemed perplexed.

"It's frozen," he said. "If I can ride my sled there, it's safe for you guys to walk on, and it's a great place if you're looking for wildlife. Some folks around here get funny about visitors. Act like the forest belongs to them. It's public land. You want to hike, go ahead. Just be careful. Cell phones don't work out there. You get lost, you'll be walking awhile before you pick up a signal."

"When did you last Change?" I asked Reese as we tramped into the woods.

"Three nights ago." He kicked aside a length of vine before we tripped over it. "You're going to Change to track this guy, right?"

"We are."

"So will I, if you need me—"

"If Elena needs you to Change, you will," Clay cut in. "Doesn't matter if you did it a week ago or ten minutes ago."

"I know that. I just meant . . ." He caught Clay's look and gave a soft growl of frustration. They held each other's gazes until Reese dropped his first.

It probably seemed like a small thing to Reese. A matter of semantics. But when the Pack is so small and so tight-knit, it's easy to let lines blur in the field.

"Let me rephrase that," Reese finally said. "If you were going to give me the option of a pass, Elena, I don't need it."

"Maybe, but if you aren't due for a Change, it'll take you longer. You can follow on foot. We'll howl when we find Mark Eaton. You can make sure he doesn't bolt while we're Changing back."

"And you can carry our clothing," Clay added.

Clay found us thick pockets of bush that allowed privacy. Werewolves rarely Change communally. It's like going to the bathroom: you don't want anyone watching you do it. Clay, of course, doesn't see the hang-up, but this is one case where Jeremy has insisted he learn to respect our idiosyncrasies. A werewolf that's uncomfortable is a werewolf that can't Change.

Speaking of uncomfortable . . .

At Stonehaven, we have a special spot for winter Changes, sheltered from the wind, with a raised platform and cubbies for our clothing. No such luxury here. My clothing hung from bushes, rings and watch zipped in a coat pocket, as I knelt naked in the snow and tried to convince my body, once again, that it's possible to completely change its structure. Even after twenty years, my body declares that skepticism with a kind of pain not known to anyone who hasn't given drug-free birth to twins.

As usual, Clay was finished first. My excuse is that he has an extra twenty years' experience. I tell myself that means it hurts him less, meaning it'll hurt less for me one day, too, but I suspect that's not true. He's just less of a wuss about the "Oh God, kill me now" agony.

He was out and circling my thicket while I still lay, belly down in the snow, panting. Once he was sure I was at the recovery stage—and therefore unlikely to add to his scar tissue if he interrupted—he stuck his muzzle in and prodded my flank. I growled, fangs bared, a warning against impatience. When I found the energy, I opened my eyes.

He stood in front of me, a huge golden wolf with bright blue eyes. Our hair color translates into fur color and our eyes stay the same, as does our mass. Otherwise, we're all wolf.

Clay lowered his nose and touched it to mine. A gentle, loving gesture to his exhausted mate. Promptly followed by chomping the nape of my neck and swinging me out of the thicket into a snow-drift, then dancing away before I could retaliate.

I did retaliate, of course. I just had to catch him first. We play-wrestled for a few minutes. My last two Changes had been alone at Stonehaven while Clay was gone. Changing alone is like dining out alone: it satisfies the physical hunger, but it's awkward and lonely and otherwise completely unsatisfying. Clay and I had reunited as humans two days ago. This was our wolf reunion, and it was just as important.

It was only when we finished that Reese came to collect our clothing. He'd been less than fifty feet away, sitting on a log, guard-ing us. I'm sure he'd seen us goofing around, but he stayed where he was until Clay ran over. I hung back. There's something uncom-fortable about being in wolf form around a Pack mate who's still human. I'm fine if it's Clay, but even that took years. My issue. I'll get over it someday. Or I won't.

I'd told Reese he could follow us, but the key word there was "could." He could attempt it and he had my permission to do so. Physically being able to follow, though, was an impossibility. We took off, loping over the snow, moving fast enough that our paws didn't break the crust, leaving him to trudge along, falling far-ther behind.

As we ran, Clay kept his nose up, sampling the air, searching for human scents. We'd Changed south of the bog and the wind was coming from the north, which put us in perfect position to catch a scent. But we had a better plan than that. If Doug Eaton was keep-ing Mark out here, he had to visit him. That meant driving, park-ing, and walking. There might be a road to the north of the bog, but that would be a longer drive along difficult roads. If he parked, it made sense he'd do it on the road we'd come in on, so we were running roughly parallel to that road as I kept my nose down and searched the ground for Eaton's trail. I could pick up hints of scent, but they were old hiker and hunter trails buried by snow.

We were all the way to the other side of the bog before I finally hit Doug Eaton's scent. He was right on top of the snow—big boot marks where he'd tramped through in the past day.

After that, following him was easy. He made no attempt to cover his tracks. Probably figured, in all these miles of wilderness, we'd never find his path. Besides, he'd warned us away from the bog.

Yet the fact that he'd warned us off meant we *didn't* race pell-mell down the trail. In fact, we slowed so much that Reese caught up. I motioned for him to scan the surrounding woods as we walked. Why? Because we could be stepping into a trap.

Still, I doubted it. He and his brother would be facing at least three Pack wolves. That was exactly the kind of arrogant, macho, brain-dead move I'd expect from a lot of mutts, but Eaton did not seem arrogant or macho or brain-dead. What he did seem to be was naive. Living up here, away from other werewolves, he had no experience covering crimes. He'd come up with what probably seemed a perfectly plausible excuse to keep us away from the bog.

As I expected, no one leapt out at us. Eventually, we found the cabin. More of a shack, really—a weathered wood building meant for shelter and nothing more.

There were no windows on this side and the wind was coming toward us, but we still kept our distance as we scouted in a wide semicircle. Turned out there were no windows at all. When the wind hit, though, it went right through the old shack and carried a fresh scent out to us. One scent. Mark Eaton.

Reese motioned that he'd circle again. I nodded, then nudged Clay toward a patch of brush to begin his Change. Less than ten minutes passed. Then he stepped, naked, from the thicket.

"Any sign of—?" he began.

A blast of bitter subzero wind whipped past.

"Holy shit! Okay, *that's* cold."

I gave a growling chuckle and nudged him back into the thicket. He grabbed handfuls of my fur, yanked me close, and huddled against me.

When I grumbled, he said, "You make me Change, you gotta keep me warm."

I chuffed and gave him a look.

"Yeah, you're Alpha-elect, so you're the one giving the orders, but as the commander, it's your job to keep the lowly foot soldiers from freezing to death."

He pulled me onto his lap, then buried his face in the fur around my neck. For Clay, there is no disparity between forms. Two halves of the whole. He could huddle here with me and talk to me as if I were in human form. It's me, either way. Of course, there is one area of our lives where he does mark a distinction between the wolf me and the human me, and never the twain shall be confused, for which I am very grateful. I can adjust to a lot, but that would take unification of form a step—hell, a few miles—too far.

Moments later, I caught Reese's scent. He should be able to smell us downwind when he got closer, but with a young werewolf it's never a guarantee. When I tried leaving the thicket to guide him, Clay tightened his grip and kept me firmly on his lap.

Reese stopped outside the brush and tried blindly pushing clothing in.

"I'm decent," Clay said. "And even if I wasn't, it's nothing you haven't seen before."

"Right. I just thought Elena might be—"

"She's not."

Reese stuck his head in. "Ah. She made you Change back while she keeps her fur coat. Smart."

"Sadistic," Clay said.

He took his clothing and finally let me get up. I went out and waited. A minute later, Clay followed.

I told them to leave my clothing and go on to the cabin. Actually, "told them" is a bit of an exaggeration. Giving orders in wolf form is a test of any Alpha's communication abilities. I suppose we could learn some more sophisticated form, but if I ever suggested we develop a code, I'd be laughed out of the Pack. Like wolves, werewolves have gotten by just fine without speech for millennia.

My Change back wasn't faster, but when I finished, it was too damned cold to lie down and give myself time to recover. I yanked on my clothes and headed out.

The guys were at the cabin. Clay understood that waiting was a given. While Jeremy rarely joined us in the field, I wanted in on everything.

Clay waited for my signal, then threw his shoulder against the door. The door flew clear off its hinges, and he charged inside. We followed, flanking his rear.

SIXTEEN

*I*nside, we found a mattress on the floor, and Mark Eaton on the mattress, sound asleep. Clay grabbed him by the back of his jacket and yanked him into the air. Only then did he wake, all four limbs shooting out.

"Wh-what—?"

He stopped. He went still. He twisted to look back at Clay and his nostrils flared.

"You're—"

Clay threw him onto the mattress. He scrambled up, blinking madly, shaking his head as if to clear it.

"You— I—" More blinking as he swallowed. He made a face. Drugged. So he wasn't hiding here willingly. Eaton must have decided drugs were safer than ropes. Or more humane.

"Do you know who we are?" I asked.

He jumped at the sound of my voice. I stepped forward. He stared at me. Openly gawked. Not an uncommon reaction. From werewolves, that is. I would be the first female of his species Mark had ever seen. More important, the first he'd ever smelled. Apparently there's some scent I give off, some combination of pheromones that makes the guys—or at least their bodies—say "hot damn."

Most handle it badly. We're talking about men accustomed to letting their bodies take charge and their brains trail behind. Some settle for flirting. Some attempt displays of male braggadocio rarely seen outside bars in New Jersey. Some launch straight into caveman "jump me" mode, only to learn that, while I may be female, I'm still a werewolf.

Smart ones act like Reese had when he first met me—after that first shock of physical reaction, he couldn't put enough distance between us. The other night, when Eaton stopped by, he'd made damn sure he stayed back and didn't look my way, not with Clay standing right there. Again, smart.

The feeling would pass as they got used to me. It was only those first encounters that were troublesome.

So when Mark Eaton gaped at me, I thought we were going to have a problem. But he only gawked, the way you might if you saw a zebra strolling in downtown Toronto.

"She asked a question," Clay said. "You'll answer her. Now."

"Right. I know who you are and what you're doing here. You're investigating the death of Dillon Mitchell, and my brother has convinced you I did it."

"Convinced us?"

Mark waved at the shack. "He knows that by holding me here, he's convincing you that either I've bolted or he's hiding me from you. He's pulling his submissive routine, isn't he?"

We said nothing.

"I'm sure he is. Acting all nervous. Going out of his way to persuade you it wasn't me, while nailing the holes in my coffin with . . ."

He blinked more, as if still struggling to focus.

"Are you saying your brother killed Dillon Mitchell?" I asked.

"No, Doug isn't a man-eater. I don't know how that boy died, but it wasn't Doug. Not unless Dillon knew something and Doug killed him for that. I don't think he'd eat him, but—" A lip curl of distaste. "I guess he might, if he was trying to cover it up. That might be it. Doug kills Dillon, trying to make it look natural. Except that it brings you guys running, so he has another reason to lock me up."

"*Another* reason?"

"He wants—" His head shot up. He looked from me to Clay to Reese. "If you guys are here, where are your kids?"

"What?"

"Your kids. Your little girl. Who's looking after her?"

"Why?"

"That's what he's after. That's why he locked me up here. So I couldn't warn you. He saw your little girl and—"

I wheeled on Clay. Before he could speak, I had the keys from his pocket and was running for the door, pushing Reese in front of me, calling for Clay to bring Mark.

Mark didn't need to finish. I knew exactly what Doug Eaton had seen when he looked at my Kate. The same thing foster fathers and brothers had seen when they looked at me, all those years ago.

Prey.

As much as I wanted to drive, this was one time where the chain of command didn't apply. When I tried getting into the driver's seat, Clay picked me up and dumped me on the passenger's side. He was right. My heart was thumping so hard I could barely breathe.

I called Nick's cell again. My fingers shook so much that if I'd had to do more than hit Redial, I doubt I'd have managed it. But, like the half-dozen times I'd tried while we were racing to the truck, there was no signal.

In the backseat, Reese was doing the same, trying Noah's number. Mark sat beside him, silent.

"Still out of range," Reese said. "But they're okay. Nick's with them and he—"

"She knows," Clay said.

Reese just wanted to reassure me that the twins were safe with Nick, but right now I probably wouldn't relax if the entire Pack was with them.

I turned to Mark. "Tell us about your brother."

I hoped to hear something to convince me that I'd misunderstood or he'd misinterpreted. But Mark's story was exactly what I expected.

Growing up, Douglas Eaton had always been awkward around girls his own age. He'd dated but seemed to be performing a duty. Mark had decided his older brother was gay. He knew their father wouldn't be able to handle it, so he went along with Eaton's charade and didn't push him toward women.

Then came the night, a few months ago, when Mark showed up unexpectedly and found his brother home with little Peyton James.

"He'd lured her into the woods in wolf form," he said. "He got her lost, then Changed back and 'rescued' her. When I got there, he hadn't done anything yet. He was just . . . staring at her. I took one look at his face and I knew I'd made a huge mistake about my brother. If I hadn't shown up that night . . . Maybe he wouldn't have done anything. Maybe he was still working up to it. Or maybe he'd been working up to it for years, with other girls, and if I hadn't come by . . ."

He went on to explain that he'd persuaded Eaton to relinquish the girl. Except they couldn't just let her leave. Mark didn't trust his brother not to do the same thing again. He had to remove temptation. Eaton knew Peyton's father and knew he wanted custody, so Mark persuaded him to call and say he'd found Peyton wandering the woods and he thought her dad needed to take her before her mother's neglect led to tragedy.

Things had seemed to improve after that. There'd been no more incidents, and when Mark suggested moving in, Eaton acted happy. He even introduced Mark to Lori Romero.

"Who just happens to have a little girl," I said.

Mark nodded. "I didn't know at first. She's only twenty, so I never suspected that. Then I found out. I broke it off with Lori the night of the party. Doug didn't like that. We've been arguing ever since. Then we were in town the other day and smelled you. Doug saw your daughter and . . . and I knew we were in trouble. Big trouble. Maybe he could control himself with human girls. But a werewolf's daughter?" He shook his head.

Mark had tried to sneak over and warn us. His brother caught him. They fought. An argument turned to blows. Mark ended up with cracked ribs, a possible concussion, and a sprained ankle— we'd had to help him into the truck. He'd woken to find himself drugged and dumped in the cabin. He'd tried to escape yesterday, but only made it a few hundred feet on his injured foot before collapsing. His brother had found him. He'd told him we were on the trail of a man-eater and suspected him. If Mark tried to escape again, Eaton would tell us where to find him.

"Got a signal!" Reese said. "And Noah's phone's ringing. It's . . . going to voice mail."

"Leave a message," I said as I dialed Nick's phone. It blipped out the first time, but worked the second. It rang. Rang. Rang.

"You're reached the voice mail of Nick Sorr—"

I hung up and tried again.

I left a message for Nick. There was nothing else to do.

Nick wasn't the best fighter in the Pack. He wasn't the smartest guy in the Pack. But he was the most loyal. If we asked him to look after our kids, that's what he'd do and that's all he'd do until we returned. If Eaton struck, then it wouldn't matter that Nick wasn't the strongest Pack member. That would be like saying a second-string major league player wasn't good at baseball—he was still head and shoulders above any amateur.

The real issue? I was furious with myself. Eaton was a pedophile. I was a sexual-abuse survivor. How the hell hadn't I figured it out? I'd seen him around Kate. I'd seen him around Lori Romero's little girl. In both cases, he'd seemed anxious. I'd noticed that, but somehow it hadn't pinged my radar. Maybe I had no radar at all, and I'd been fooling myself that I did, and I'd let my daughter slip into the sphere of a predator because of it.

SEVENTEEN

I was out of the truck as soon as it slowed. Reese was, too, and he beat me to the front door. The first tug told me it was locked, but before I could push him out of the way, he slammed his shoulder into it and the door flew open. Then he stepped aside and let me through.

The house was empty. I ran to the back door and found all the coats and boots missing.

"They've gone out for a walk," I said as Clay brought Mark through.

"You have to find them," Mark said. "Doug's been watching the house, waiting for you to take her out so he can lure her off, like he did with the James girl."

Before he finished, I was out the back door. Reese and I took off at a run, and I made it to the forest's edge before I realized Clay wasn't with us. I looked back. He had Mark, arm around him to keep him upright as he limped along.

I knew babysitting a wounded mutt was not what Clay wanted to do right now. He said nothing, though. Sticking to his assignment until I said otherwise.

I glanced at Reese. I could tell him to watch Mark, but that meant one less person hunting.

"Leave him," I said to Clay.

"No, I can help." Mark pushed off from Clay's support. A few faltering steps, then he stumbled.

"Stay there," I said and we took off.

⚜

Mark was right. His brother was in the forest. I picked up his scent on the wind right away.

I'd screwed up. It wasn't just that I hadn't recognized what Eaton was. I'd left my children vulnerable in another way—by not telling them what *we* were.

I'd left them unprepared to deal with a werewolf threat. It didn't need to be a pedophile—any mutt could have targeted them. If they knew that, then we could have taught them—what to expect from a werewolf. Simply telling them to avoid strangers wasn't enough.

Eaton had lured Peyton James away from her house using his wolf form. Could he do that with Kate? Of course he could. Because, then, he wasn't a strange man—he was a wolf, a creature that fascinated her, even if she didn't understand why, and if she saw one, she'd follow, because I hadn't prepared her to do otherwise.

"Can you smell him?" I asked Clay as we ran along the path from the chalet.

"Eaton?" He lifted his nose to the wind and inhaled. He nodded grimly.

"Reese? Can you?"

He was trying, but finally he said, "No. Sorry. But I can smell Nick, Noah, and the kids on this path. I can follow if you two want to go after—"

"No. Clay?"

"On it."

He veered northwest. My cell phone rang. As I fumbled it from my pocket, Clay didn't stop, just looked back, anxiety flashing in his eyes. I waved for him to wait.

"Just got your message," Nick said in greeting. "Damned jacket's so thick I didn't hear it ring. The message was garbled, too. Something about Eaton and Kate?"

"Where are the kids?"

"Right here. We're playing hide-and-seek."

"Hide—?" My voice squeaked with panic.

"Um, yes. I can hear them and find them by scent, Elena. Not exactly a fair game, but it's safe."

"Right. Sorry. Could you please—?"

"Noah?" he called. "Find the kids." Then, to me, "We'll round them up and take them back to the cottage. Trouble, I'm guessing?"

"Eaton's out here. Possibly in wolf form. He's after Kate."

"Kate? Why—?" Only a brief pause. Then he swore. In some things, he catches on faster than anyone else. He understands things better, too, and I didn't have to say another word. He knew exactly how freaked out I'd be. He signed off with an abrupt promise that he'd find Kate and get her to safety.

Clay took off after Eaton. Reese and I raced to where I could now hear Noah's voice.

"Kate!" he called. Then, "She was right there. I could hear—"

Nick's whisper, shushing him before Eaton overheard. I ran full out, branches lashing me, heart pounding. I could hear Reese behind me, whispering, "It's okay. Nick's got them. It's okay," and part of me wanted to whip around and tell him to shut up, just shut up, it wasn't okay. But I heard the anxiety in his voice and felt him, right there on my heels, and I knew we were lucky to have him, damned lucky, and I had to hold it together, be the kind of Alpha he expected. The kind they all expected.

A figure moved in the trees. Downwind, so I couldn't catch the scent, and the forest was so thick that all I saw was a flash of a parka and dark hair.

Eaton.

I held up my hand, stopping Reese before he plowed into me. Eaton was just standing there, almost hidden in the trees. Looking east. Watching something. I eased in that direction and saw Kate in her purple snowsuit, doing a very poor job of hiding as she crouched behind a log. Her hat was askew, blond curls tumbling out, her cheeks rosy from the cold, her blue eyes dancing. My beautiful little girl. And Eaton stood, less than fifty feet away—

He shifted, and I sucked in breath so fast I nearly choked.

It wasn't Douglas Eaton watching Kate. It was Mark.

"Damn it," Reese whispered, relieved. "Moron couldn't stay put." He started forward.

I grabbed Reese's arm as I stared, transfixed, at Mark Eaton. I saw him watching my daughter, and the look in his eye hit me like a fist to the gut, and I knew what had been missing when Douglas Eaton was around Kate and Lori Romero's daughter. This look. The one that brought a thousand memories spilling back, and a whimper bubbling up in my gut, silenced by a wave of fury. I launched myself at Mark, barely hearing Reese's exclamation of surprise.

Mark *did* hear Reese and he turned, saw me, and ran toward Kate, his ankle obviously fine. He was closer, but I was running as fast as I could and—

My foot caught on a vine. I stumbled. Reese grabbed me and I recovered fast, but it was enough to give Mark the advantage he needed.

"Kate!" I shouted.

She looked up and grinned. Then she saw my face and turned, as if sensing Mark. Seeing him, she jumped up. She started to run to me, but he was almost to her and—

A shape dropped from the trees and landed on Mark's back, knocking him down. Mark reared up. He grabbed Logan and wrenched him off, arm swinging to throw him. I hurled myself at him. Kate did, too. She caught his arm and sank her teeth into his hand. He screamed and dropped Logan. I grabbed Logan and tossed him to Reese, then caught Kate and pulled her off Mark. She didn't let go, and when I pulled her away, she took a chunk of his hand with her. Blood spattered the snow as Mark yowled.

He charged us. I wrapped my arms around Kate and backed away, stumbling and tripping, but I couldn't put her down, not even to fight him, couldn't let her go. He pounced. I kicked and hit his shin and he fell back, but he only snarled and shook himself off and came at us again. Reese hesitated, Logan in his arms, looking to me for direction. I shook my head, telling him not to let go of Logan.

A shout from the east. Nick racing at us, Noah right behind. Mark ignored them and charged again. I dove, shielding Kate. As I fell, a blur shot from the trees to the west. Clay barreled into Mark's side and sent him flying. Then he fell on him. Mark hit him with everything he had, fists and feet and even teeth, snapping and snarling as if he were in wolf form, instinct taking over.

Clay glanced at me. I nodded. Then I hoisted Kate up, her face pressed against my chest, and motioned for Nick to take Logan from Reese. We hustled the children away from the fight. Reese stayed, and when I glanced back, he was circling with Noah, waiting for Mark to make a run for it. He wouldn't try. Clay wasn't fighting hard. Not yet. Just keeping things going until we got the kids far enough away. When we did, I heard an unmistakable snap as Clay broke Mark Eaton's neck.

A bush crackled to my left. I looked over to see Douglas Eaton, in human form, jogging through the woods. He saw me and stopped. I tensed, but he kept his distance. He looked at me, then at Nick, each of us clutching a child to our chest. His gaze swung behind us and I glanced over my shoulder to see what he did—Clay standing over Mark, the boys at his back.

"He came after our daughter," I said.

Eaton's head dipped, his gaze unable to meet mine. "I'm sorry. I tried . . . I didn't know what to do."

I nodded, hugged Kate tighter, and headed back for the house as Eaton walked to where his brother lay dead in the snow.

EIGHTEEN

*T*he kids were fine. At first, I wasn't sure how much they understood, but as I cleaned Mark Eaton's blood from Kate's face, she said, "That man wanted to hurt me."

I hesitated, and the mother in me wanted to say, "No, everything is fine, it was just a mistake." The Alpha in me knew I couldn't. Whether my children were werewolves or not, they were part of the Pack and they needed to understand the dangers.

"Yes," I said. "He did."

"Logan saved me."

She looked at her brother, standing beside the sink, watching with quiet concern, and she smiled. He mumbled something and dropped his gaze, but his eyes glowed.

"He did," I said.

"You and Daddy helped," she added. "I did a little, too. But it was mostly Logan."

"It was." I bent and picked him up in a hug so tight he squirmed until I put him down again.

"It was just lucky," Logan said. "We were trying to trick Uncle Nick and Noah. Kate was only pretending to hide. They'd find her and I'd jump out of the tree. Only it wasn't them that found her, so it was an even better plan than we thought."

"It was."

I looked at them, and I thought of what had almost happened and—

"I'm okay, Mommy," Kate said, putting out her arms for a hug.

I kissed her and blinked back tears, and wet the cloth again.

⚜

When I'd finished, Nick was waiting outside the door. Clay had brought Eaton to the house to speak to me. When I turned the twins over to Nick, he put an arm around my shoulders and whispered, "We'll talk later."

When it came to my past, I'd learned that Nick made a better confidant. By talking to Clay about it, I was saying, *These people hurt me and I forbid you to do anything about it.* He tried to hide his frustration, but I'd come to realize it wasn't fair, and turned instead to the guy who'd just listen and offer me all the support and sympathy I needed—and the kick in the ass when I needed that, too.

I found Clay out back with Reese, Noah, and Douglas Eaton. I sent the boys inside to help Nick with the twins and then took Eaton farther from the house, where we could talk.

Clay had him repeat his explanation to me. The short version was this: take the story Mark had given and reverse the brothers in it.

Growing up, Mark Eaton hadn't taken much interest in girls. Douglas hadn't noticed at first—he was five years older, and off to college before his brother entered high school. When he realized it, he'd suspected his brother was gay and tried to help him deal with that. Mark had gone along with the ruse.

Soon, though, Eaton noticed his brother's interest in little girls. He saw the way he looked at them, the work and volunteerism he chose to bring him in contact with children. When a girl in their father's neighborhood went missing, Eaton asked Mark if he'd known her. Mark figured out what he was saying. They had a blow-out fight, Mark took off, and the girl turned up with her mother, who'd lost custody.

Eaton had apologized and the brothers made up. Then came the night Eaton returned unexpectedly from his girlfriend's place and discovered Mark had gone for a run. He decided to surprise him . . .

and found him at that decrepit cabin with Peyton James. Nothing had happened, but Eaton realized she posed too great a temptation and called her father.

After that, Mark confessed. Lots of sobbing. Lots of self-recrimination. Promises to get help. Vows to stay away from children. Barely two months later, he started dating Lori Romero, who had a little girl. Eaton insisted he break it off. The next morning, Dillon Mitchell was dead after what could have been a werewolf attack, and Mark began a subtle campaign of blackmail: either Douglas backed off about Lori and her daughter or Mark would frame him as a man-eater. When we showed up, Douglas thought that was exactly what his brother had done. Hence his fear. And when he realized we had a young daughter? Fear had escalated to outright panic.

Did Mark fight with Dillon and kill him? Did he eat him? Douglas suspected the death had been accidental and Mark had taken a couple of Bobby Walters's dogs out to eat the body. But I think, in spite of everything, he just couldn't bring himself to think his brother was capable of murder and cannibalism.

To keep Mark away from Kate, Eaton had drugged him and put him in the same cabin where he'd brought Peyton. Then he'd kept coming around us, trying to figure out what to do next. I think he knew something had to be done, that Mark wasn't going to stop, that the next little girl he targeted wouldn't be as lucky as Peyton. Was that why he tipped his hand about the bog?

Mark's foot hadn't been injured, as he claimed. And apparently Mark had found a way to skip his last dose or two of sedative, leaving himself clear-minded enough to trick us. He'd caught our scent as we'd circled outside. Then he'd called Eaton on the walkie-talkie his brother had left him and whispered that we'd come for him and he was in the backseat of our truck heading to our chalet. Eaton had to get over there right away and save him. Eaton fell for it and everything played out as Mark intended—us racing back to the cabin, smelling Eaton in the woods, focusing on him, and letting Mark get to Kate.

In an ideal world, Eaton would have told us everything from the start. But the reputation of the Pack has endured for centuries, and that reputation says we would have saved ourselves the bother of an investigation and just killed him and his brother. That changed under Jeremy, but it will take more than a generation or two before we can reasonably expect the average mutt to trust us to make a judicious decision.

Eaton had whisked his brother away before he could go after Kate. He'd tried to get to know us better, maybe decide if we could be trusted. If that was truly his goal—and I think it was—then we had failed. Normally, I'd have listened, but having the twins there had made me anxious and defensive. An unfortunate collision of circumstances.

Later, I would talk to Jeremy about what I could have done differently. Maybe nothing.

For now, I sent Reese and Nick to help Douglas Eaton bury his brother in the frozen earth and then we left him alone with his grief.

Nick, Reese, and Noah left the next day. Jeremy had found them a place in Toronto where Antonio would join them, while Jeremy spent Christmas with his girlfriend, Jaime. Karl and his wife, Hope, would meet the Pack in Toronto, and they'd all come up as planned on Boxing Day.

Yes, I felt bad about kicking the guys out after all their help. But they insisted and Clay insisted, and the next day, when I took the kids to town, we came back to find them gone and our own Christmas began.

And begin it did, at warp speed. Less than twenty-four hours after being attacked by Mark Eaton, the kids were making gingerbread cookies and chattering about Santa and panicking when Clay pretended we'd left their stockings at home. There were no questions about the Eatons or what happened in the forest. Everyone was safe. Christmas was coming. Life moved on.

We crammed Christmas Eve full of everything on the kids' list. By the time the stockings were hung by the chimney with care, Kate and Logan were nestled all snug in front of the fireplace, having literally done that final task and then dropped onto the rug and fallen asleep. We carried them up to bed.

I got the fire going again—the kids had insisted we put it out earlier, so Santa wouldn't get immolated. Clay took off to do something, and I was sitting in front of the blazing fire, munching a cookie left for Santa, when he came into the family room, hair dusted with snow.

"You were outside?" I said.

"Making reindeer tracks."

I lifted my brows.

"Did you hear the kids earlier, talking about reindeer?" he asked.

I had. Kate had been concerned that the chalet roof was too steep for the reindeer to touch down on, and Logan insisted they didn't *really* fly.

"That would be magic," Logan had said. "There's no such thing as magic except in books, like *Harry Potter.* Reindeer can't fly. It's scientifically impossible."

One could argue it is just as impossible for a man to visit every house in the world in one night. Our son may be scary smart, but he's still four. His logic isn't perfect. Still, he was certain there was no such thing as flying reindeer.

"So you made reindeer tracks?" I said.

"I did. Not on the roof, of course. That wouldn't work. But they landed in the middle of the yard, then walked over to the house. I figured that should do the trick. I considered adding deer droppings, but Logan would figure out the size differential, so I settled for tracks. Plus a few tufts of deer hair caught in the bushes."

"You gave our kids flying reindeer."

"I did."

I put my arms around his neck, and wrapped my hands in his damp hair and kissed him. "God, I love you."

He kissed me back, then said, "If I'd known how many brownie points this daddy stuff could win me, I'd have talked you into kids years ago. Would have saved me a lot of trouble."

"It would have."

"Problem is, they're going to grow up." He paused. "We may need to have more."

"We may." I wrapped my hand in his shirtfront and pulled him down in front of the fire.

We lay in front of the fire, naked, legs entwined as we ate ginger-bread cookies and drank hot chocolate from the thermos I'd brought in earlier.

"This feels familiar," he said.

I smiled. "It does."

"Twenty years."

I bit back a sleepy yawn. "Hmm?"

"Twenty years since our first Christmas."

"Twenty? No, it can't be . . ." I calculated. "Shit. It is."

Twenty years since our first Christmas together. Twenty years since we'd been curled up together on another rug, in another place, munching on gingerbread cookies and sipping hot chocolate.

"The cookies are better," he said. "They actually look like ginger-bread men now."

"Because we remembered to buy cookie cutters."

He laughed and we lay there, lost in memories. Then he glanced under the tree.

"I think I see a gift under there for you."

I laughed. "No, you're not going to make me open one early this time."

"One won't hurt." He nudged a small present off a pile with his foot. "There. It fell. Don't make me put it back."

Still grinning, I reached down and scooped it up. It was small and flat, oddly shaped.

"Please don't tell me it's another spare set of keys," I said.

"Mmm, maybe."

I unwrapped it. Inside, I found a silver tree ornament. A circle surrounding a cutout of two wolves on a snowy hill. He'd had it engraved with the years of our first Christmas and this one.

"We're starting a collection," he said. "You'll get one every twenty years. I figure we have three or four more to go. Which could mean a lot of kids, to keep me in your good graces."

"You don't need kids for that," I murmured.

I ran my fingers over the wolves. Part of our lives. Such a huge part of our lives. A part that we were keeping from our children.

That, I realized, was the real issue. When our children are old enough to understand, they'd look back on a childhood where they'd been raised as normal kids, believing their parents were normal people, and they wouldn't see a harmless fantasy, like reindeer tracks in the snow. They'd look back on every part of their lives—on their relationships with the rest of the Pack, on all the times I'd done "research," all the times Clay and I had to leave on "a trip," even on things as small as why they couldn't have pets—and they'd see lies permeating every aspect of their lives. Every person in their lives telling them lies. Every person they'd trusted to tell them the truth.

We gave them the fantasy of a normal family because that's what I wanted. That's what I'd dreamed of, and as much as I loved my life, there was still part of me that thought "normal" was what my children deserved. But it wasn't. They deserved us—their parents and their extended family—as we really were. They deserved *our* normal.

"I want to tell them," I said.

He didn't ask what I meant, didn't need to, just nodded and said, "Okay."

"Can we talk about that?" I said. "Now? I know it's not the time, but—"

"Now is fine."

NINETEEN

*C*hristmas morning. Awake at dawn, the kids tumbling down the stairs, Logan tripping over Kate and sprawling to the floor, Kate helping him up, making sure he was okay before the race resumed. Presents. Not a lot, because, let's face it, for our kids, Christmas came year-round, endless toys and books and games from friends and family and, yes, indulgent parents.

Santa gifts first. Then stockings. Then breakfast—pancakes and ham and cookies. Then gifts to each other, still in pajamas, curled up in front of the blazing fire. Later, some talk of going outside, but for once the forest didn't call to anyone, and we were all quite happy to laze about and play board games.

We missed lunch. Hardly shocking, considering breakfast never really ended. At two, the kids realized they'd skipped a meal and insisted on going through the motions of making lunch, even if no one was particularly hungry.

Afterward, they fell asleep by the fire. When they began to stir from their naps, Clay took off. Once the twins were fully awake, they asked where he was.

"He just stepped out," I said, gazing at the window. "He'll be back soon."

"What are you looking for, Mommy?" Kate asked as she climbed onto my lap.

I was about to say, "Nothing," and slide her back to the floor, then I stopped. *Was I ready for this? Really ready?*

I took a deep breath, then settled her on my lap and leaned down to her ear.

"Watch," I whispered.

Logan glanced up from the floor, still sleepy. It took a moment for him to figure out something was going on. When he did, he walked to the window and gazed out.

"What are we looking for?" he asked.

"Just wait."

It only took another minute. Then Clay stepped from the forest in wolf form and my heart jammed into my throat.

I'd wanted to explain it first, sit them down, tell them everything. This had been his idea. What the hell had possessed me to go along with it? How were they supposed to process this? What were they thinking? What was I even going to say?

Clay walked toward the chalet, slowly, his blue eyes fixed on the window. Waiting for me to appear and change my mind, madly wave him away. I wanted to, but I was frozen there, watching him.

He stopped, lowered his head, and chuffed, breath streaming from his nostrils. Kate slid from my arms. She walked to the window, pressed her hands to it, her nose to it. Her head tilted one way then the other as she studied him. Then she turned to me with a blazing grin.

"It's Daddy, isn't it?"

I hesitated, certain I'd misheard. Worry clouded her eyes.

"Mommy? It is, isn't it?"

I nodded. Forced the words out. "It is."

She turned and slugged her brother in the arm. "Told you." She looked at me. "I told him. I saw the werewolves in my book and I said they're real, and he said they weren't."

"You didn't say you thought Dad was . . ." Logan stared out the window.

Kate took off, shouting that she was going outside, and I didn't think to stop her. I just watched Logan. He didn't step closer to the window. Didn't press against it. There was no smile on his face. He just stared.

I slid from the chair and crouched beside him. "I know this is a big shock, baby."

He kept gazing out the window as Kate now raced over to Clay, plowing through the snow in her slippers, no coat on.

"Is it magic?" Logan asked.

"Yes."

He turned to me. "Can you do that, too? Turn into a wolf?"

I nodded.

"And Jeremy and Uncle Nick and everyone?"

I nodded.

"And me?"

He watched me, his face still expressionless. When I didn't answer, he said, "When I'm older, will I be able to do that?"

"I . . . we don't know. Maybe."

He grinned then, a grin as bright as his sister's, so sudden it made my breath catch.

"Cool," he said.

He threw his arms around my neck, gave me a quick hug, then raced to the door. Before he ran out, he turned around.

"Can I go—?" he began.

I smiled. "You can."

A second later, the door banged shut. Another second and he was out there, no coat, no boots, wading through the snow to where his sister stood beside Clay, running her hands over his fur. Clay turned. Logan stopped. Clay stepped forward, and looked him in the eyes. Then, slowly, Logan reached out and patted Clay's head and Clay licked his face.

Logan giggled, so loud I could hear him. He wiped his face. Kate pounced on Clay from the back. Logan jumped him, too, and they went down, shrieking and giggling, rolling in the snow.

I'd done the right thing. Maybe I should have done it sooner. I don't know. Didn't matter. But it was done now and everything was fine.

Kate waved at me through the window. Logan beckoned me out. I smiled, lifted a finger to say I was coming, then headed for the back door to grab their coats and boots and join them.

FROM RUSSIA, WITH LOVE

I was dreaming of the ravines in Toronto, racing through them, feeling . . . lonely. Crushing loneliness—and frustration and self-loathing because I shouldn't have been feeling lonely, damn it. I'd chosen that life. I'd chosen that man. Good choices, both of them. And yet . . . not for me. That's what it came down to, in the end. Something can be good and decent and worthy, and still not make you happy because it doesn't fill that pit inside you. And you won't be happy until it is filled, however hard that will be. So that's what I remember. The loneliness, and venting my frustration on the coyotes, and racing through the forest when what I was really running from was the man who'd bitten me, the man I'd still loved . . . and hated . . . and loved.

"Elena." A voice whispered in my ear as my paws ripped up the soft earth. "We're here."

A hand shook my shoulder. I growled and tried to shrug it off. Then I felt it, the warmth of his touch.

"Clay . . ."

I opened my eyes. He was right there, his blue eyes inches from mine. I inhaled the rich scent of him, and for a second I was back in that forest, back in that time, and I felt my insides crumple, as if I were still only dreaming of him, and hating myself for it.

Then he pulled back and I saw his face, the faint lines around his mouth and his eyes, and I catapulted through time, back to now, back to here. Here. Now. On a plane. Going to see our children.

For a moment, that, too, seemed like a dream, and I felt a prickle of anger for letting myself imagine it.

"Elena?"

I blinked and looked out the window, into the darkness, at the city lights below. I could see my reflection. Not the young woman in the forest. Not anymore. I lifted my hand to the glass and saw the ring on my finger, the same ring he'd given me twenty years ago, before it all went to hell. The ring I'd thrown back at him again and again until, finally, I put it back on.

"Till death do us part," I whispered.

"Hmm, that sounds ominous," Clay said. "You planning something I should know about?"

I smiled and leaned against his shoulder as the plane descended into St. Petersburg.

I travel a lot, both as a freelance journalist and as the Pack's mediator, but I can count on one hand the number of times I've left North America. Landing in a country where I don't know the language is disconcerting. I feel lost, and I hate that. So I was quiet as we disembarked and went through customs, anxiously scanning the signs for international travel icons and trying to remember my very few words of Russian.

"Baggage," I murmured. "Baggage . . ."

Clay steered me through the crowd. He knew even less Russian than I did, but being in a non-English-speaking country doesn't bother him, because he has no interest in communicating with anyone anyway. I let his sixth sense for escape routes guide us as I gawked about, taking it all in.

"We'll come back to St. Petersburg next week," he said as he prodded me along. "Bring the kids. Check out the museums."

As we walked, Clay rolled his shoulders, stretching.

"How's the arm?" I whispered.

If anyone else had asked, they'd get an abrupt "Fine." A festering zombie scratch five years ago nearly cost Clay his arm and he's been dealing with the fallout ever since. After the week of hard fighting we'd just been through, he'd been feeling it again, but after a moment's hesitation he said, "Not more than a twinge or two since yesterday. Guess I've finally learned to compensate."

"I'm sure any of those guys you put down would agree."

He smiled and waved me toward the baggage claim.

In the arrivals area, I caught sight of Nick Sorrentino almost immediately. He was easy to spot. Most of the people around him looked as if they'd slept in the terminal. Nick was as bright-eyed, clean-shaven, and impeccably dressed as if it were midday, not midnight. The young man beside him didn't look nearly so chipper. Nineteen-year-old Noah—Nick's ward—was chugging Coke to stay awake. Though they'd been in Russia for a week, he hadn't quite adjusted to the time difference.

As I scanned the crowd around them, Clay whispered, "You better not be looking for the kids."

"Of course not. I—"

"—told Nick not to bring them."

"Right."

"You weren't just saying it because you thought you should, while secretly hoping Nick would bring them anyway."

"Er, no. Not really . . ."

He gave me a look. "If you want the kids, you can't tell him not to bring them. You're Alpha-elect. He'd consider that an order."

"Damn." I sighed. "Do you think I should have said he could bring them?"

He shrugged. "Tough call. Worrying that they'll get grabbed in the airport is a bit paranoid. On the other hand, we did just finish stopping a crazy supernatural cult from unleashing a killer virus. And that cult *was* after our kids. So I'd say a little paranoia is warranted."

That's why the kids were here in the first place, under the added protection of the Russian Pack. That cult had been gathering supernatural rarities because its leader had proclaimed them signs of the coming supernatural revolution. Twins born to two bitten werewolves was an extreme rarity, so Kate and Logan had been high on Gilles de Rais's shopping list.

When we made it over to Nick, he swooped me up in a feet-off-the-ground hug and kiss that earned us a few stares from onlookers. There was a time when I would have squirmed away, worrying what people might think. I've learned not to care. Nick is my Pack brother and my friend. So I hugged him back and kissed him and he told me the twins were fine, sound asleep when he left. He knew that's the first thing I'd want to know, so he told me without being asked, which is the real mark of a friend.

Noah didn't hang back like he used to, as if uncertain he'd get a hug too. But with the instincts of a hereditary werewolf, he knew his place in the Pack, and he waited until I was done with Nick before stepping forward.

"Is Hope okay?" he asked as I hugged him. "How's the baby? Karl isn't being an ass, is he? He'd better not be, after everything she's been through."

I tried not to smile. Noah had developed a bit of a crush on Hope over the last few years, which meant he had no love for Hope's husband. Which also helped endear him to Clay.

"Mother and child are fine," I said as we headed through the terminal exit doors. "Which is a miracle, all things considered. Karl's doing well. Recuperating himself and taking care of them. Behaving himself."

"He damned well better," Clay said. "He's in shit and he knows it. He ignored a direct order from Elena. He's on probation now."

"Probation?" Noah jogged to catch up as we crossed the road. "What if he leaves the Pack?"

"He won't," I said. "Having a baby means he needs us more than ever."

"He's definitely off the fence now," Clay said. "Tripping over himself to make sure he doesn't get kicked out." He smiled, relishing the memory.

"He'll be here for the Meet," I said. "Jeremy told him he could skip it, but he's coming, with Hope and the baby."

Noah nodded. "Good."

There was no fight over who'd drive the rental car. Nick gave Clay the keys as soon as we drew near. There wasn't a fight over the passenger seat, either. Nick just opened the door for me. Like Noah, he's a hereditary werewolf and innately understands hierarchy. He may be a year older than Clay, but he falls below us on the ladder, and he's fine with that. A higher position means more responsibility. As far as Nick is concerned, he has the better end of the deal.

He does have his responsibilities now, though. Namely, the younger werewolves—Noah, Reese, and Morgan. Noah and Reese lived with both Nick and his father, Antonio, but Antonio has stepped back, leaving "the boys" to his son. Morgan hasn't settled yet—he's still too restless for an apartment in the city—but when he's on Pack territory, he stays with the Sorrentinos, which puts him, too, under Nick's jurisdiction. It's a responsibility that suits Nick. It fulfills his wolf's instinct to teach a younger generation, while letting him skip the often chaotic and mystifying baby and child stages.

As Clay drove, we talked about what had happened back in the States, and what was happening here. They'd spent the past week with the Russian Pack, Morgan joining them when we'd finally made contact with him. Now, with the danger passed, our Pack had moved to a rented cottage, where we'd relax and recuperate for a few days before Jeremy showed up for the Meet, to discuss any fallout from the mess back home.

Clay and I knew of some fallout that *wouldn't* be discussed. Fighting our way out of Nast headquarters, with Savannah and Adam, we'd just discovered that Jeremy's father, Malcolm, was not nearly as dead as everyone thought. Jeremy didn't know. If we had our way, he never would. Malcolm was a brutal, murderous bastard, who'd vented his worst on Jeremy.

Right now, Malcolm was still in Nast custody. We'd leave him there until we could negotiate with Sean Nast and get him back. Then we'd kill him. If that was my first act as Alpha, I'd be satisfied, though there was a time when the thought would have horrified me. Perhaps it still should. Politically, I do oppose the death penalty. Does that make me a hypocrite? Maybe. But I oppose it not because it seems unnecessarily cruel, but because I think life in prison is a more fitting punishment. And there's always the risk of executing an innocent man. When Clay and I carry out the Pack's death sentence on a man-killing mutt, I know damned well he's guilty, because Jeremy would never order it unless my investigation left no doubt. Obviously, locking up the perpetrator isn't an option for us. With Malcolm, he was already locked up and would presumably stay there for the rest of his life, but as long as there was a chance he could escape and come after Jeremy, I'd rather see him dead. It was that simple. If that makes me a bad human being, so be it. It makes me a good Pack wolf, and that's what matters.

The cabin we'd rented was a little over an hour outside St. Petersburg. We were on a highway for almost that long before Nick told Clay to turn off onto a regional road. After about five minutes, Clay took a sudden right.

"Um," Nick said. "If you heard me say to turn, your ears are still plugged from that flight—"

Clay turned left sharply and hit the gas, zooming a little ways down a forested road before slamming on the brakes and turning off the engine.

"Piss break?" Noah said.

"We've got a tail."

"What?" I said, craning around to peer behind us into the night.

"A car followed us off the highway. It was hanging back. Lights off."

As I watched, the moonlight illuminated a dark car passing the end of the road. It paused, as if the driver was peering down our track. Then it continued on.

"How far are we from the cabin?" I asked.

"About five miles," Nick said. "But . . . Okay, you know how I said the kids were sleeping when I left? They weren't. There's no way we were getting them to bed when they knew you guys were coming. We told them Antonio would drive them out to meet you."

"What?"

"You only said not to bring them to the *airport*. I texted Antonio about ten minutes ago to say we were on our way. They were going to meet us on that road back there. As a surprise."

"That's them following us, then?" I said.

He shook his head. "We rented a VW van."

Meaning we had someone following us . . . while our kids were on the way to meet us.

"I'm calling Antonio now," Nick said before I could ask.

"I'm calling Reese," Noah added.

Noah couldn't get a signal. Nick could, but there was no reply, suggesting the others were out of range. I cursed under my breath as he tried again. We spend so much time off the grid that you'd think we'd wise up and invest in really good two-way radios.

As Nick kept trying, the car reappeared on the road behind us. It stopped and idled there.

"What's he doing?" Clay asked, squinting.

"Just watching us."

We could turn around and go after our pursuer. But that was risky, with Antonio and the kids so close by.

I thought fast. Then I told Clay my plan.

As I made my way through the dark forest, I reflected that a Russian forest did not look, feel, or smell that much different from the woods at home. I also reflected that I shouldn't forget that I *wasn't* at home, because I had no idea what was out here in the way of deadly fauna. So far I'd only picked up the familiar scents of squirrel and rabbit. Nothing too worrisome. Not that it mattered. A grizzly could lumber into my path right now and I wouldn't let it deter me. My children were on the other side of these woods.

As I walked, I kept hitting speed dial, cycling through Antonio, Reese, and Morgan. There wasn't really any point in leaving a message every time it rang through to voice mail, and I was probably racking up a four-digit phone bill, but the calls made me feel better. Every few rounds, I'd ring Nick, too. That was a little more productive, as he reassured Clay that I hadn't yet been devoured by rabid Russian squirrels.

I'd climbed out of the car and slipped off into the forest after our pursuer had carefully backed up, getting all but the nose of his car out of sight. Once I made it to the kids, Clay would go after whoever was in that car.

When I emerged onto the main road, I could see the van parked ahead of me. I kicked it into high gear, jogging along the ditch.

I expected the door to fly open, Reese or Morgan to come tumbling out, wondering what the hell I was doing. But the van remained silent and still. I drew close enough to see through the darkened windshield. The front seats were vacant. I broke into a run, and yanked open the side door to find a pair of empty child seats.

I could smell them all in the van—Antonio, Reese, Morgan, and the twins. There was no scent of blood. No scuff marks in the roadside dirt suggesting a struggle. I peered into the dark night, my heart hammering.

Maybe one of the twins had to go to the bathroom.

So they all went traipsing into the forest? Not likely.

What, then?

I dropped to a crouch and picked up a trail immediately. Reese had climbed from the passenger's seat and gotten the twins out. Then Antonio and Morgan joined them from the driver's side and . . .

I followed the trail around the van, in a complete circle.

What the hell?

It went into the forest about twenty feet, then just . . . ended.

That wasn't possible. I hunkered down for a better sniff. As I did, I thought I caught a stifled giggle. I straightened fast and inhaled, but there were no scents on the breeze. A tree branch creaked. The wind sighed through new leaves.

I bent again. And something dropped from above, hitting me squarely on the back and knocking me facedown to the dirt. Arms went around my neck. Small arms, smelling faintly of soap and candy.

"Mommy!"

Kate somersaulted over my head, landing on her back and wrapping her arms around my neck again as I rose. I hugged her tight and lifted her. Then I looked up. A face peered down from the branches above, teeth glinting in a Cheshire cat grin. Before I could say a word, Logan dropped from the tree, nearly taking us both down with him.

"Hey, Momma," he said as he hugged me.

I gave him a one-armed bear hug back. I didn't get "Momma" very often these days. That's what he used to call me, until he decided he was too old for it.

I kissed their cheeks and boosted them up, one arm under each. That was still easy to do, at least for a werewolf. They were both small for their age, and had lost their baby fat. Kate still had her round cheeks, which, along with her blond curls, made her look deceptively angelic. Logan's face had already thinned out, the shape starting to look more like mine, his hair somewhere between the gold of his father and sister and my silver-blond.

"Did we surprise you?" Kate asked.

"Yes. Scared me a little, too."

"Why? We're with Antonio."

"Still, finding an empty van is going to worry your mom." Morgan's voice rang out with his footsteps. "As I tried to tell these guys . . ."

Even before they stepped from the shadows of the forest, it was easy to tell who was who. Morgan was in the lead, the tallest and leanest of the three. Nick's father, Antonio, right behind him, was the shortest in the Pack and the heftiest even now, as he passed sixty. Last came Reese, between the two in height and size, bringing up the rear.

"Sorry if we worried you," Antonio said. He kissed my cheek. "The kids just wanted to have some fun."

"Where's Daddy?" Kate said, squirming.

I lowered them to the ground. "He's coming. Reese? Can you take them back to the van? I need to talk to Antonio for a minute. Morgan? Bring up the rear, please."

Reese hung back with the kids as I started out with Antonio.

"We were followed," I murmured.

I thought we were far enough from the kids. Unfortunately, I have a tendency to underestimate their hearing, and I barely got the words out before Kate said, "By who?"

I winced. "I don't know. Someone in a car might have been following us, so your dad just wanted to be super-careful. The cell phones didn't work, so I came to warn you. It's okay, though. Dad has it under control."

"'Course he does," Kate said.

Logan jogged up beside me. "Is it really okay, Mom?"

"She's a little worried," Kate said to her brother.

I have no idea where Kate gets her emotion-reading skills from. Certainly not her father. And not me, either. She already has a knack for reading body language or facial expressions or vocal tone that borders on preternatural.

Before we stepped from the forest, I caught the distant sound of a car engine. I waved for them to stay back as I leaned out. A car was coming up the road. With its lights off.

Had our pursuer slipped away without Clay noticing? I found that hard to believe. Clay can handle a car like no one I know. If that vehicle had budged, he'd have whipped around and cut it off before it got anywhere near us.

I squinted into the darkness.

It wasn't the same car. The one following us had been boxier and lighter in color.

The car stopped. It idled there, as if it had just noticed the van. Then it reversed down the road and backed into a laneway, out of sight.

"Antonio," I said as calmly as I could, "I want you and Morgan to get in the van. Head down the road as if you just pulled over for a pit stop. Then block that car in the laneway and see what we've got."

"Unless that little car is stuffed with werewolves, we could handle it more directly," Antonio said.

I hesitated. After Noah, Morgan was the Pack's weakest fighter. He was training, but he was a long way from being ready to undertake potential combat missions. Although he was a hereditary werewolf, his family had believed in lying low and staying out of trouble, and they'd isolated themselves in the wilds of Newfoundland for generations. Reese, on the other hand, had been raised by a father on the run from the Australian Pack. While he favored flight over fight, he had come to us battle-ready, and had taken on the role of sparring partner to help train Morgan.

Yet whoever didn't go with Antonio stayed with me, protecting the twins. I couldn't take Morgan for that. It wasn't just a matter of his fighting ability—the kids didn't know him well, and wouldn't stay with him if I needed to go scouting.

So I had to rely on Antonio for this one. Even at his age, he was as good a fighter as Clay. He also had the experience to know when and if he could face a challenge . . . and when he should hold tight and wait for backup.

"Okay," I said. "If you two can handle it, go ahead. Otherwise, just block him in."

Antonio nodded, and he and Morgan headed out.

Reese and I retreated into the woods with the kids. We'd gone a couple of hundred feet when we reached an old hunting cabin, long abandoned. It listed, but a shove on the walls didn't set any boards creaking ominously. The windows were shuttered, leaving a single point of entry at the door. Easily defensible.

"We're going to hide in there?" Kate said as I came back out after scoping out the interior.

"It'll be fine," Reese said. "The spiders here aren't any bigger than house cats. Or so I've heard."

She gave him a look.

"At least they aren't poisonous," he said. "If it was Australia, they'd be poisonous."

"Everything's poisonous in Australia," Logan said.

We tried prodding them inside, but Kate dug in her heels.

"Why do we have to hide?" she said. "You're werewolves."

"The guys following us might be, too," I said.

"Or they might have guns," Reese said. "I can catch bullets in my teeth, but you guys need more practice. And your mom?" He leaned over them and whispered, "Hopeless."

"They're right," Logan said to his sister. "I don't like hiding, but

Dad can take care of this. He needs to know we're safe, so he doesn't get distracted worrying about us."

My son. Some days, I think he's already more qualified to be Alpha than I am. I kissed the top of his head and gave them both a nudge. They went inside.

Before I followed them in, I turned to Reese. "Stand guard by the door. It's the only way in."

"Got it."

I wouldn't be surprised if there *were* cat-sized spiders in that cabin. Or at least cat-sized rats. I could certainly smell droppings, though nothing scurried away from us.

The cabin was a single room, maybe fifteen feet square. It stunk of rotting wood as well as small animals. I led the twins to the back corner.

There was no cell phone signal in here, either. I'd have to wait it out until I heard Clay or one of the others looking for us. In the meantime—

A figure appeared in front of me. Just appeared, materializing from nothing. The kids lunged, but I was faster, and pounced on the intruder. Kate shouted for Reese. As I pinned the figure to the wall, a vaguely familiar scent almost pierced the stink of the cabin.

"Don't shoot!" he said. "Or, er, bite, claw, punch . . ."

I knew that voice. I grabbed the guy by the shirtfront and slammed him against the wall again. He was about my age, completely nondescript, except for a thin, curving scar from his temple to his nose.

"Xavier," I said.

"You know him?" Reese said as he ran in.

"Unfortunately."

I first met Xavier nine years ago, when he was playing mercenary. "Playing" being the key word, complete with gun, camo, and tough-guy sneer. But the word "mercenary" really only suits him as an adjective. He's a con artist. He can be anything, do anything, say anything if he sees a way to a fast buck.

Reese strode over, glowering at him. "How'd you get past me?"

Xavier glanced at the twins. "Uh, I, well, you see, I'm wearing really dark clothing, so I snuck—"

"You must be a teleporting half-demon," Logan said. "Tripudio, Evanidus, or Abeo?"

"Evanidus," I said.

Kate sniffed. "No wonder he isn't very good at it."

"Clayton's progeny, I presume?" Xavier said. He'd met Clay just before the kids were born. It hadn't gone well.

"Reese?" I said. "Take the kids outside."

"Oh, there's really no need for that," Xavier said. "I'm unarmed. They're perfectly safe."

"That's not why she wants us gone," Kate said. "She doesn't want us watching if she needs to hit you." She lowered her voice. "It's okay, Mom. He deserves it."

"Definitely Clayton's progeny." Xavier looked at me. "Elena, I'm sorry if I surprised you. I was—"

"You followed us from the airport. You and a friend."

"Not really a friend. More of an associate. And I've already backed him off. I come in peace. I just wanted to talk to you, and a contact who works for the Cortezes gave me your flight info."

That was one employee who wouldn't be working for the Cortezes much longer.

Xavier must have caught the look on my face, and hurried on. "The plan was to speak to you as soon as you got out of town. Just drive up alongside, say hi, find a place to grab a coffee. But I got caught in a traffic snarl, and I didn't want my associate handling this, so he followed you while I caught up."

"So you want to talk?" I said.

"Please. If you'd just let me down—"

I hoisted him higher. The kids giggled. Since Xavier could just teleport out of my grasp, he must really want something.

"You weren't nearly so keen to chat with me last week," I said. "When I called to ask if you had any information on Gilles de Rais."

"Because I didn't have any. And I couldn't ask around because I was in Europe. Do you know what overseas cell phone rates are like?"

"You should have invested in a calling card, because a little assistance last week would have bought you a lot of goodwill right now."

"Er, right. I didn't understand the extent of the threat, see? I'd been in Europe for months. Totally cut off. Then I go home and some guys try to jump me. Seems someone gave this de Rais dude my name. Told him I was well connected—which I am, of course—so I might be useful."

"Uh-huh. So now that it affects you in particular—"

"Sure, but that's not why I'm here. Not entirely. With this virus I heard about, the supernatural world is in serious danger. So I came to help you." He paused. "In return for protection."

"Little late," Reese said. "The threat—"

I stopped him with a look, then turned back to Xavier. "You followed me from St. Petersburg—and cornered me with my kids—because you want to team up? You've got a strange way of trying to recruit an ally."

He tugged at his collar. "And you've got a strange way of greeting an old colleague. Been spending too much time with your crazy-assed . . ." He glanced at the kids. "Refreshingly eccentric mate."

I wrapped my fist tighter in his shirtfront, making him cough.

"But it looks good on you," he managed. "I've always said I like a woman who can take care of herself. You could before, too, but you were a little wobbly on the self-confidence when I met you in Winslow's playroom. You remember that? When we were prisoners together, watching each other's back?"

"I was his prisoner. You were his employee."

"But I still helped you, didn't I?"

"For a chit, which I repaid. Do you remember *that*? You made me steal the From Hell letter while I was six months pregnant."

"But it all worked out. You have two beautiful, smiling . . ." He looked at the twins. Both were staring at him stone-faced, Logan coldly appraising the situation, Kate tensed to pounce.

"It all worked out," he insisted, his voice a little less certain.

"Did it? Have you forgotten that letter released zombies? One of them gave Clay a really nasty scratch."

"But he's fine now, right?"

"After a very long, very grueling rehabilitation. You should ask him about it sometime."

Xavier looked like he'd rather swallow thumbtacks.

"Point is," I continued, "you haven't won any friendship points with the Pack. Clearly what you're angling for here is protection. But if we're going to protect you from whatever is scaring the crap out of you, we'll need more than a few tidbits of gossip in return. And this friend of yours, the one who followed us from the airport . . ."

"Not really a friend."

"Associate. A supernatural you owe a favor?"

"Something like that."

"And to repay him, you offered to cut him in on this deal. A two-for-one protection plan."

Xavier looked at the kids. "Your mom is one smart lady. You guys are really lucky—"

"Attention on *me*," I said, giving him a shake. "So I'm right. You want protection from this threat for you and your associate. That's going to cost you. I want three chits. Redeemable at any time."

"Three? No. I don't do multiples. How about one? For anything—"

"Three."

"Like a genie," Kate said with a smile. "You'll grant her three wishes."

"They're called djinn in the real supernatural world," Logan said. "They do grant wishes. Usually only one, though." He looked up at Xavier. "But you aren't a djinn. So you'll give our mom three. One for you. One for your friend. And one for sneaking up on us like this. If you don't, she'll make you wait and talk to our dad about his arm." He paused. "He really doesn't like talking about his arm."

"Whoa. You kids are . . ." He looked at me. "Adorable. Absolutely adorable."

"Just wait until they grow up," Reese said with a chuckle.

"So what's it going to be?" I asked Xavier. "Three chits? Or wait for Clay?"

I got my chits. In return, I promised that Xavier and his "associate" would be under Pack protection until Gilles de Rais was dead and his virus was contained. I didn't tell him both things had already happened. Apparently, whoever gave him our flight information hadn't shared that information.

When Antonio and Morgan came back for us, they told us they'd found Xavier's rental car empty and had tried to track him. His teleporting skills made that tricky, and they'd finally given up and come to make sure we were okay. Clay had followed Xavier's associate when he'd backed off. I explained the situation. Clay was fine with it. The "threat" was over.

I awoke the morning of the Meet to hear the kids whispering and giggling. They'd been sharing our bed, an indulgence we didn't feel right denying them after we'd abandoned them for a week. When I opened my eyes, they were sneaking out the door. I played possum until I heard their footsteps pounding down the hall.

"Sounds like Jeremy's here," I said as I rolled over. He and Jaime had flown in the night before, along with Karl and Hope and the new baby. "We could go greet him. Or we can take advantage of a few minutes of privacy—"

I was talking to myself. The bed was empty.

I rose on my elbows. "Clay?"

He wasn't in the room. His side of the bed was already cool, as if he'd left a while ago. I frowned and checked the clock. Just past seven. Clay wasn't an early riser, and even if he did wake before me, he usually stayed in bed.

I was sitting up, yawning, when the door opened.

"I figured the kids woke you," Clay said as he slipped in. "Sorry about that."

I slid down under the covers, and pulled back the sheets for him.

"Damn," he said, giving me a look that sent heat coursing through me. "I would love to take you up on that, darling, but I need to ask for a rain check. Jeremy wants to speak to you."

"Ah. Pre-Meet business."

"Yep." He looked again at the spot I was offering him. "But it could wait a couple of minutes . . ."

"No. I just remembered, there's no lock on that door. We'll get Nick to take the kids for a walk later. Toss me my clothes."

When I left the bedroom, I caught the distinct smell of pancakes and ham. My favorite breakfast. I smiled and picked up my pace. The others were already in the dining room. I thought they were eating, but when I got there, they were just hanging around the table, with no food in sight.

I glanced toward the kitchen. "I know I smell breakfast."

"We ate it all," Kate said.

There were none of the usual "good mornings" or hugs from the rest. Just grins. A lot of grins.

"Okay, what's up?" I said.

No one answered. Jeremy was at the table with his back to me, and turned as I came over.

"Where's Jaime?" I asked, as I bent to give him a quick hug.

"I dropped her off at a spa for a much-needed rest. She'll come out tonight."

"And there's supposed to be a baby. I know there is . . ."

I looked around and saw Karl, on the far side of the table. He looked exhausted, partly from the new baby, I was sure, but also because he was obviously still recuperating, having been shot and nearly killed in Miami. He stood with one hand braced on the table for support, despite the fact there was an empty chair right beside him.

"Sit," I said.

When he hesitated, I added a growl to it. "Sit."

He sat, eliciting a few chuckles from the others. Clay was right. As pissed off as I was about Karl's recent disobedience, it did have the added bonus of making him extra obedient now.

"Baby?" I said.

"She's with Hope in the other room."

"Okay, well, I don't know what you guys are up to, but if there's no breakfast on the table, I have a baby to visit . . ."

Clay cut me off. "They're sleeping. It was a long flight."

As if on cue, I heard a distant gurgle. "Then what's that?"

"What's what?"

"I didn't hear anything," Noah piped in. "They're both sound asleep."

"Uh-huh. Okay, so I don't get breakfast. I don't get to see the baby. What exactly do I . . . ?"

I trailed off as Jeremy shifted his chair and Reese stepped away from the table, revealing a game board.

"Chess?" I said.

Jeremy waved to the seat across from him, and the others moved to let me through. "You're going to play a match against me."

"Why?"

A faint, crooked smile. "Because you always say werewolves don't settle their differences over a nice game of chess. I think it's time to rectify that."

"Differences?" I stopped in mid-step. "What's wrong?"

"Sit," he said. My feet instinctively started moving again, but my gaze stayed fixed on him, my heart picking up speed. Clay squeezed my hand as I moved past him, but I pulled away.

"Did I do something wrong?" I asked. "In the field?"

"You were perfect in the field. But we have a tradition to uphold, and I thought you'd prefer this to an actual physical challenge."

"A challenge?" My gaze shot from Jeremy to Clay. "What's going on?"

Clay leaned in to whisper, "Just play along."

I slid into the chair. Logan had slipped around and was standing on my other side. Kate squeezed past her father to get next to me and leaned her elbows on the table.

"You can beat him, Mommy," she whispered. "Ask Logan for help if you get stuck."

"I think your mom will do just fine," Jeremy said.

I looked at the board. "The game's half done."

"Yes, well, everyone's hungry, so we're moving this along," Jeremy said. "Reese and Logan set it up. Apparently, there's the possibility of a quick victory, and several possibilities for an equally quick defeat. So take a few minutes, then make your move."

I took those few minutes, and a couple more. Then I made my move. Jeremy made his. We made two more and . . .

"Checkmate," I said, moving my piece into position.

"That's it, then," Jeremy said. "I've been vanquished, and I will gracefully step aside."

He smiled, his eyes meeting mine, and I swear everyone in the room had stopped breathing. Jeremy got to his feet, grinning now.

"And with that, our first order of Meet business is concluded. Having vanquished her predecessor in a challenge match, Elena Michaels is now Alpha of the North American Pack."

⁜

I passed the morning in shock, leading the Meet as best I could, but a little uncertain, as if I expected Jeremy to take me aside at any moment and tell me it was just a practice run and he was still in charge. He didn't. Jaime, Hope, and baby Nita joined us for a celebration lunch, which lasted well into the afternoon.

We napped after that. It took me a while to drift off, my brain still buzzing, but eventually the big meal did its work and I fell asleep. When I woke, the kids were gone. Clay was still beside me, snoring softly. As I lifted my head, I caught faint shouts and laughter from outside. I slipped from the bed and went to the window to see my Pack out on the lawn playing a game of touch football.

There was no sign of Hope and the baby—it was a little chilly for a newborn. Jaime must have stayed inside with them. So it was just the Pack. Even Karl was there, sitting on the ground off to one side. Normally he'd forgo the fun and games unless Hope insisted. When Kate zoomed past, his hand shot out, as if to grab her leg. She screeched and veered off and he smiled, calling something after her.

Morgan was another who usually stayed on the sidelines. Not by choice, in his case. I could tell he always wanted to join in. He just wasn't yet comfortable enough to be sure of his place, and rarely touched the ball during games. He had it now, though, running as Logan guarded him. He made it halfway to the goal before Reese tackled him, sending him flying, the ball leaping from his hands. Kate grabbed it and ran off, chortling as Reese shot her a thumbs-up. She made it down to her end and scored, throwing her arms in the air and dancing.

Antonio got the ball next, only to lose it to Nick, who handed it off to Noah. As Noah raced down the yard, a figure shot from beyond my sightline and tackled him. For a second, seeing only dark hair, I was confused. It wasn't Nick or Antonio or Karl. So who . . .

The figure grabbed the ball and threw it to Morgan and Logan, and as he did, he twisted and I caught a glimpse of his face.

"Jeremy?" I whispered, then I laughed.

Arms wrapped around my waist, Clay coming up behind me. "Hmmm?"

"Jeremy's playing. That's not a sight we've seen very often."

"He isn't Alpha anymore. Things will change."

"Good. He looks like he's having fun." I leaned back against Clay. "I was just thinking that this reminds me of that time in Alaska, after Jeremy told me he wanted me to succeed him. I was watching everyone playing in the snow when I realized this was going to be my Pack someday."

"And now it is."

"And now it is," I echoed.

"You're ready. You know you are."

"As ready as I'll ever be."

"You're ready." He kissed the side of my neck. "That's your Pack down there, Elena. All yours."

I was turning to hug him when Kate caught sight of us in the window and yelled. Logan motioned for me to open up. I did.

"Are you coming out?" he called.

"Yes!" Kate shouted. "We need you! Dad, you're on my team!"

"Then the *Alpha* is on ours," Logan said, looking over at her. "Which means you're going to lose."

"Am not!"

"Are too."

"We'll be right there," I called.

Clay nudged me aside and yelled, "Give us five minutes." He glanced at me and grinned. "Maybe ten."

He shut the window before they could complain. Then he pulled the curtains, and put his arms around my waist again.

"Does the Alpha have any orders for her Beta?" he asked, smiling.

"I'm sure I can think of a few."

VANISHING ACT

*I*f the world was a fair place, everyone who ever summoned a demon would explode the moment he said the first words. Preferably before he had the chance to pass on his dumbass DNA to anyone else. When does the summoning of the demonic *ever* end well? Well, not unless I'm the one doing it, but I'm a pro. Also, part demon. Which helps.

I peered into a half-finished apartment splattered with what remained of the guy who'd summoned this particular demon. There wasn't a piece left bigger than my fist. While I was tempted to snap photos as a warning to other potential summoners, I had a job to do—namely, find the damned demon before he took a more innocent victim.

My business card says, *Savannah Levine, private investigator.* I'm still working on fulfilling the job title. At twenty-two, there's a learning curve. I've been with the agency since I was sixteen, but until last year I was the receptionist. My guardians—Paige and Lucas—run it. My boyfriend—Adam—is the only other employee. It's a family business, if your definition of family is flexible. Mine is.

My backup was taking a while to arrive. Not surprising, given that Adam was in Chicago, and Paige and Lucas were clear across Portland handling another case. I'd gotten the call about a potential demon-summoning and arrived here to discover that "potential" meant "happening right this moment." That's when I'd called Paige.

So I was slinking through a half-finished apartment complex by myself, trying to capture this demon before it found the exit.

Fortunately, it wasn't very smart. Unfortunately, it knew I was tailing its ass . . . and it liked to talk.

"I just have one thing left to say to you, witch," it yelled, its voice echoing down the hall.

"If only," I muttered.

"Can you guess what it is?"

"'*Stop me before I kill again*'? Happy to oblige."

It snorted. "I'm going to kill again. And again, and again. And do you know why?"

I stopped to zero in on its voice. "Because you're a demon."

"Because you don't want me to. Because for all your tough talk, you're as big a bleeding heart as Lucas Cortez. He ruined you, and now you're just as weak as he is, because all I need to do is threaten to kill a few humans and you'll . . ."

"Does it ever shut up?" a voice whispered in my ear.

A hand clamped over my mouth before I could cast a spell. I recognized the voice. I still clocked him in the chest.

Adam let out a soft *oomph* as I followed the blow with a kiss.

"You're back early," I said.

"Surprise." He pulled back, then whispered, "You okay?"

"Sure. Why?"

"Because I just snuck up on you and didn't catch an energy bolt in the gut."

"Sorry. Yeah." I made a face. "Distracted. Bad day to be on call alone." Before he could ask what was distracting me, I said, "But I'm not alone anymore, so let's put this bastard down and get home, where you can help me clear my head. It's been a long—and lonely— two weeks." I motioned toward the demon's voice, still babbling. "Is there a subtype that kills by boring its victims to death?"

"Nope, I think it's just this one. But at least we always know where it is."

"And it's too busy yapping to know I've got a friend. Let's take advantage."

✣

Adam knows me better than anyone, and he was right that I was seriously distracted. As for what was distracting me . . . ? It didn't have a damn thing to do with demon hunting, so I'd shoved it aside, apparently less successfully than I thought. But now that Adam had called me on it, I would focus, because I sure as hell wasn't letting Adam get hurt while I was angsting over a personal issue.

I sent Adam back outside, to come in another door and help me flank the demon. With us, partner-in-charge is a flexible position. Neither of us is what you'd call a born leader. I blame Paige. She's been my guardian since I was twelve and Adam's friend since they were kids, so both of us grew up letting her give the orders. Then she met Lucas, who's just as alpha as she is. Adam and I eased into support positions, and though we're happy there, one reason we like working together is that, while there's comfort in following a competent leader, there's more satisfaction in standing *beside* an equally competent partner.

So far, the demon had made no move to actually leave the build- ing and make good on its murderous threats. Killing people isn't nearly as much fun in practice as it seems in theory. No matter how creative you are—flaying, disemboweling, bisecting—the screams of the dying lose their appeal after a few millennia. Finding a mortal you can play a challenging game of hide-and-seek with? So much more interesting.

"Tell me again how you're going to kill me," I said as I made my way across a floor joist.

"Slowly."

"Boring."

"I will rip out your fingernails one by—"

"Clichéd."

"I will stake out your body with a thousand cuts and let starving rats feast on you."

"Impractical. Where would you find all these starving rats? Well, you could probably find *one*. Maybe even rabid. That would be better. The rat would die of rabies before it ate enough to kill me, but then I'd be infected and perish in horrible agony and madness."

"You really are Lord Demon Balaam's grandchild, aren't you?"

"No, I'm my mother's daughter." I stepped off the beam and headed for a gap in the wall studs. "And my father's."

"True. Perhaps you aren't such a bleeding heart after all. Perhaps we could even work together."

I ducked through the gap into the room with the demon. "And deprive that poor rabid rat of its last meal?"

The demon froze. I almost did the same, because I didn't see a demon. I saw a kid, maybe sixteen, pale and thin, with torn jeans and matted hair, and I had to remind myself I was looking at a shell. An empty shell, the boy who'd inhabited it already dead before the demon jumped in, his spirit hopefully enjoying an afterlife that made up for all the shit the world had dumped on him.

It still took a split second to "see" a demon. The gore helped. The blood from the guy who'd summoned it dripped from its filthy clothing and dirt-streaked face. Blood and bits of . . . everything else.

I cast a knockback spell. The demon stumbled . . . right into Adam's waiting hands—he'd snuck in while I'd distracted the demon with chatter. Adam grabbed him by the shoulders, his fingers blazing fire. The demon howled. It wrenched free and slammed a fist into Adam's gut.

They fought, a brawl enhanced by demonic strength and demonic fire. I concentrated on expelling the fiend—without letting it slip away into any other convenient hosts. Adam and I were protected by a tea Paige brewed. Foul stuff, but possession is a whole lot fouler.

I dispelled the demon back to the hell dimension without any serious complications. Like I said, I'm a pro. Also? This demon was strictly minor-league, no match for Adam, the son of Lord Demon Asmondai. It helps that, unlike Balaam, Asmondai was somewhat fond of his offspring, particularly this one. Killing Adam would piss off a very powerful demon, and that protected him better than any brew.

So, as fights went, this one was relatively uneventful. I cast; Adam pummeled; the demon went home. And then so did we.

We went to my apartment because it was closer. Only two floors closer, in the same building, but after a two-week separation every extra step counts. We barely made it through the door with our clothes intact. Didn't make it as far as the bed. At least I managed to get the front door closed, which always helps keep a good relationship with the neighbors.

We did get into the bedroom the next time around. Not the actual bed. It was at the far side of the room. Much too far away.

Afterward, we lay on the carpet, catching our breath.

"Missed you," Adam said.

"I could tell."

He laughed and pulled me on top of him. "Next time, you'll take me up on that offer of a plane ticket for a mid-trip visit."

"Mmm, I don't know. I hate having you away, but I really like it when you come back. There's something to be said for two weeks of celibacy."

"Then just come hang with me. We'll get separate hotel rooms."

"And that arrangement would work—"

"—about as well as separate apartments?"

"Yep."

He lifted me up and tossed me into bed. A remarkable feat, given that we're both six feet tall. I admired his form as he did it. At thirty-two, Adam's in the best shape he's ever been, and he's always been in a damn fine one. He jokes that he's upped his workouts to keep up with me, but I worry that last year's battle with Balaam spooked him. He denies it. I don't push. We're all dealing as best we can with the fallout of Gilles de Rais's assault on our world. I spend more time honing my spells; Adam spends more time lifting barbells.

After he threw me into bed, he walked out. He didn't go far. I heard the fridge open and then close. He returned, popping open two beers and handing me one.

"Sublet on this place is coming up soon, isn't it?" he said, putting his beer on the nightstand.

I tensed. Luckily, he didn't notice, his back to me as he plunked onto the bed. He stretched out beside me.

"Next month," I said.

"Any thoughts on that?"

"Not really."

"Kind of a waste having two apartments when we're always together in one or the other."

I'd taken the sublet seven months ago. Yes, I'd moved into Adam's building *after* we started dating. I'd still been living with Paige and Lucas, and Adam and I had decided my first major step toward independence shouldn't be moving into my boyfriend's apartment. The unspoken plan had always been to reconsider that when my sublet ran out. Yet now I said nothing. I watched him sit up, take another slug of his beer, hoping to give me time to say, *Oh, right. Let's talk about that.* I did not.

I lay there, stomach churning, feeling like the biggest bitch in the world. And the biggest coward.

"So . . ." He fidgeted with his beer can. "We have options. Obviously, if you're comfortable with this arrangement, that's totally fine. My lease comes up in the fall. We could reconsider then."

He glanced over. When I didn't answer, he seemed to take that to mean I didn't want to postpone moving in together, and he exhaled in relief, then thumped his can onto the nightstand, resolved now.

"Okay, so options. One, you move into my place. But my apartment isn't any bigger than this one. So I'm kind of thinking . . ." Deep breath. "I'm thinking we could get a place for us."

A sidelong glance my way. I nodded, and his grin ignited. He leaned over and gave me a smack on the lips. "We're on the same page, then. Good."

No, we're not. I mean, we are. I want this. God, how I want this. But . . .

Talk to him, damn it. How hard is that? You two barely shut up when you're together.

I don't know what to say. I need . . . I need to work this out first. On my own.

Adam continued. "Okay, so like I said, we have choices. We can stay at my place while we work them out. I don't want to rush getting a place, because . . . well, options, right? We can get a better apartment, or maybe a townhouse. Or . . ." He picked up the can again, taking a slug, his resolve shaky again. "There are other possibilities. I've, uh, got enough put aside for a down payment if you, uh, wanted a longer-term option."

"It'd have to be fifty-fifty if we went that route."

"Of course. I just didn't want to presume. Is that a yes, then?" His grin hovered there, behind his eyes, ready to ignite again the moment I said the word.

Yes, I want to move in with you. Yes, I want "long term." I want a condo, a house, something that says I plan to be with you for as long as you'll have me. Hopefully forever.

Yes. God, yes.

"Can I think about it?" I asked, and that light in his eyes evaporated.

Still he smiled, and said, "Sure. It's a big step. We've got a few weeks before you need to decide on the sublet."

"I only need a few days."

"No problem." He leaned over and kissed my forehead, and I knew it *was* a problem. That wasn't the response he'd hoped for. Not at all.

"I'm not trying to rush you," he said as he crushed his beer can. "I'm never going to rush you, Savannah."

"You aren't. I just . . . I need to think about that."

"Sure. Absolutely. No problem." More can crushing. "So, uh, we should . . ."

A phone vibrated. We both looked toward the front hall, where we'd left our jeans.

"Bets on whose it is?" he said, pushing out of bed.

"Yours. I can tell by the tone."

"Of the *vibration*?" He laughed, relaxing now as he headed for the door. "Bullshit. Dinner says it's yours—Paige calling to remind us to file a report before we get distracted."

"Too late."

He came back in holding my phone. "Not Paige. Dinner's still on you, though."

"Never agreed."

"Too bad."

I rolled my eyes and took the phone. The name came up blocked. A call forwarded from the office, then. When you run a PI agency for supernaturals, most calls come from blocked and private numbers.

I answered with, "Savannah Levine, Cortez and Winterbourne Investigations."

"Hello." It was a male voice. Age indeterminate because he seemed to be lowering it. Again, not unusual. "We spoke earlier today about Denver Brown."

Denver. Not a name I'd forget, no matter how busy my day had been. And definitely not one I'd forget considering he'd been the *reason* my day was so crazy.

Denver Brown. Approximately my age, maybe a couple of years older. Dark hair. Average height and weight. And that was all I knew about him . . . barring the fact that he was currently spattered over a half-finished apartment.

"Right," I said. "You're the one who gave me the tip. A little late, mind you, but one fewer demon summoner in the world isn't necessarily a bad thing. We managed to send the demon back before it killed anyone who *wasn't* stupid enough to summon it."

Silence stretched out long enough for me to say, "Hello?"

"Denver's dead?"

The voice had changed now. Higher pitched. Younger. Barely able to get the words out. Shit. Oh, shit.

When my tipster had phoned earlier, he'd claimed to know the black market merchant who sold Denver his materials.

They aren't friends of mine, he'd said. *Not the guy selling that shit, and definitely not the dumb kid who plans to use it. I just want the kid stopped before he does something stupid, and if you can put the merchant out of business, all the better.*

A supernatural doing his civic duty. It happened at least once a week, though usually with infractions far less serious than summonings. But this tipster had been very clear that he didn't know Denver Brown. He'd been lying. I replayed my words—my sarcastic, heartless assessment of the situation—and my stomach lurched.

Seeing my reaction, Adam frowned and put his hand out to say, *You want me to take it?* I shook my head.

"There were . . . complications," I said. "Before I arrived." I winced at that. First words out of my mouth? Deny responsibility.

"So he's dead?"

"Yes, I'm afraid—"

"That's fine," he said, deepening his voice, pulling the persona back in place. "Dumb kid. What does he expect, right?"

"I'm—"

"I'll handle it from here. Just tell me where to find . . ." A slight crack covered with a cough. "The body. I'll track down family and make sure they know and that he gets a proper burial."

"We'll handle—"

"You've done enough. Thank you. Where can I find him?"

Sweat trickled down my forehead. "Can we meet? I think we should talk—"

"Not necessary. Just tell me where he is."

"Let's meet. Completely confidential and—"

"And apparently I'm going to have to find him myself. Good day, Ms. Levine."

The caller hung up. I sat there, heart pounding, thinking of that room. That horrible room where the demon got his revenge.

No, it was okay. He couldn't possibly find it.

But someone would, and then this guy would hear what had happened to his friend.

"Savannah?" Adam sat beside me. "What's going on?"

In my mind, I saw that room with the blood and the bits of Denver Brown covering every surface. My mental gaze dropped to a pile of belongings in the corner. Brown's jacket, folded neatly. On top of it, a cell phone.

I jumped to my feet and raced out the bedroom door.

"Tracing a cell phone isn't that easy," Adam said as he drove us across town, zooming along the quiet side streets, taking whatever shortcut he could find, at whatever speed he dared. "Even we have a helluva time doing it, despite our contacts."

"Did you hear what I said?" I whispered.

"No, sorry. I missed it. Damn wind noise." He forced a smile for me. "Another reason to stop buying Jeeps, right?"

"I meant, did you hear what I said to that kid?" I mimicked myself, infusing my voice with extra sarcasm. "'One fewer demon summoner in the world isn't necessarily a bad thing.'" I inhaled a jagged breath. "I was talking to someone who *knew* him, Adam."

"You had no way of realizing—"

"Does it matter? Really? If I want to make fun of demon summoners to you, that's fine. You know I'm just being a smart-ass. But I should damn well have the decency to keep my mouth shut when I'm talking to anyone else, because I don't know *who* I'm talking to. And they don't know me. That kid cared about Denver Brown, and that's how he got the news of his death. One fewer dumbass in the world. Ha-ha."

Adam reached over to squeeze my leg. A quick squeeze, withdrawing quickly because he knew I wasn't looking for comfort. "You made a mistake," he said, because that was the right thing to say, not *Oh, don't be so hard on yourself.* I didn't want that, either.

"It's a lesson for both of us," he said. "I'm just as likely to make a crack like that in front of the wrong person. I've certainly done it before."

"Not as bad as that one."

"Only for lack of opportunity. With each other, it's fine, but we need to pretend the rest of the world is Paige. You know if you said that to her, you'd get a stern look."

"Even if she secretly agrees with the sentiment?"

A snorted laugh. "Yeah. Okay. Bad example. But we'll fix this. Paige and Lucas are meeting us. Everything will be fine."

Adam and I watched Paige zip her Prius into a parking spot a block from the building. She and Lucas were deep in conversation. I walked over to stand beside the car and tapped my watch. Neither noticed. They weren't arguing. I've rarely heard them argue. They were just talking about some matter of discussion or debate, completely wrapped up in it and each other. Nine years together, and they still never seemed happier than when they were in each other's company. That's what I have with Adam, and I want it to last, and I think it can. I really think it can. But the moment I start dreaming of that . . .

I tapped the window. Lucas got out first. Lucas Cortez. Thirty-three. Shockingly, not wearing a suit, but only because we were about to clean up a very messy crime scene. Glasses, short hair, as unassuming a guy as you could want to meet. Also, heir to the most powerful American Cabal—a position he'd gone from outright refusing to grudgingly accepting once he realized that the supernatural world was actually *worse* off if he turned his back on his family business. It was complicated. That's the best that could be said about it.

Paige grabbed her purse and got out. Paige Winterbourne. Thirty-one. Long, curly brown hair. Five foot two with an enviable figure. Ten years ago, she'd rescued me from the people who'd killed my mother. I'd repaid her by being the most ungrateful little bitch imaginable. I'd been twelve and pissed at the world, and I sure as hell hadn't wanted to be in the care of Glinda the goody-two-shoes Coven witch. She still gave up everything she had to fight for me. The tough side of me comes from Mom. But everything that's good in me? That's Paige, and I adore her for it, with a love, an admiration, and a respect I show every chance I get.

"God," I said. "Could you drive any slower? Seriously, Paige. You have got to trade that milk box in for something with balls."

"Like your motorcycle?" She popped the trunk open and handed me an overstuffed duffle. "Notice how, when we actually need to work, someone *else's* bike stays in the shed." She looked at Lucas. "Can't stuff crime-scene cleanup supplies in your saddlebags, can you?"

"She actually did exceed the speed limit," Lucas said to me. "By at least five miles an hour. For almost the entire duration of the trip."

"Please note that he did not ask me to increase my speed, likely because he didn't want to be the one explaining to the nice traffic cop why we have crime-scene cleaning supplies in our trunk." She took out another duffle for Adam. "I also brought a plastic bag to remove the body. Please tell me I only need one."

"Uh . . ." I glanced over at Lucas. He obviously hadn't relayed my description of the corpse in detail. Not surprising. There was a reason I'd told him rather than Paige.

"One will be sufficient," he said. Which was technically true.

We started for the building.

"Do you want to tell me what happened?" Paige said.

She didn't mean with the demon. She meant the phone call afterward. When I didn't reply, she said, "Lucas? Adam?" In other words: *Can you guys walk on ahead?*

"They can stay," I said. Then I told her what happened. No, I told her what I'd done, blurting my confession as if I were still a kid and had set the curtains aflame with an errant fireball. Except, as a kid, I'd have followed that with a dozen reasons why it wasn't really my fault—it was my over-juiced powers plus the fact I'd been interrupted by her phone call, and who makes flammable curtains anyway. Anything to lay the blame elsewhere. Today, I took the fall, fully and completely.

"I was insensitive," I said as I finished. "A big shock, I know."

"Not so much insensitive as failing to consider the possibility that the caller wasn't who he seemed to be," Lucas said.

"Which in our line of work . . ." Paige began.

". . . is pretty much a given," I finished. "Especially with an anonymous tipster. Therefore it is better to keep my mouth shut, because if I say summoners deserve to die horribly, they'll think I actually mean it."

"I doubt the caller believed you'd be so callous," Lucas said. "You were following a tip with no expectation of payment. Risking your life to help a summoner before he got hurt. One would not honestly believe you cheered this man's demise."

"The logical argument," Paige whispered to me.

"I still *said* it," I countered. "Which means I still *sounded* like a callous bitch."

304 · KELLEY ARMSTRONG

"True," Lucas said.

"And considering the caller was young, he might not realize I obviously didn't mean it."

"Also true."

Paige whispered, "The limitations of the logical argument. Rational? Yes. Comforting? Not so much. It's done. You won't do it again. You can't undo it. You can just make sure the problem isn't compounded by the boy finding his friend's body. It was an easy mistake to make, because none of us has a very high opinion of summoners. With good reason. The death of Denver Brown is a tragedy. He did, unfortunately, bring it on himself."

"Just best to not tell his loved ones that," I said.

She squeezed my arm. "Exactly."

We turned the corner.

"Doing this in broad daylight is less than ideal," Lucas said. "Fortunately, when we drove past the building, there was no sign of a police presence, meaning the scene has not yet been discovered, and likely won't be until nightfall, when I presume it's being used by squatters."

"It is," I said. "Looks like they got it half constructed and ran out of money."

"More likely a legal battle." He listed a few potential reasons. Not that it mattered. Lucas likes lists. He's also a lawyer. We humor him on both fronts. "The point being, of course, that as crime-scene locations go, it's not an overly worrisome one. Still, someone will need to stand watch. Paige? If you could do the honors, I would appreciate that. Now, the ideal spot to guard—"

"Do I get a say in the matter?" Paige asked. "Or am I being assigned a task?"

"I'm simply suggesting the best use of our resources—"

"No, you're barreling on as fast as you can, in hopes I won't notice that you failed to give me a say in the matter." She turned to Adam. "How bad is it?"

"Uh . . ." He struggled for a poker face and fell back on ignorance. "How bad is what?"

"And my question is answered. Can I ask what the demon did to Denver Brown?"

"Rather you didn't," I murmured.

"Adam?"

"I, uh, wasn't there."

She gave him a look that said that was no excuse. "Cortez?"

Lucas paused. When they first met, she called him by his last name, partly to say she wasn't forgetting who his family was and partly because she knew he didn't like the reminder. Yes, it hadn't been love at first sight. These days, it's usually "Lucas," but she'll still pull out "Cortez," either to tease him or to warn him. This wasn't teasing.

Lucas cleared his throat. "While I believe science has disproven the notion of spontaneous human combustion—"

"Ah. Okay. Got it." She looked at me. "Messy?"

I nodded.

"And you'd like me to stay outside?"

"Please."

She looked at the other two, who seconded my nods. Then she sighed. "All right."

We didn't just waltz into the building where two corpses lay— figuratively speaking. A solid twenty minutes of scouting preceded our entrance, as Paige, Lucas, and I all cast sensing spells to detect the presence of life. There *was* life, of course. The vermin variety, judging by the strength of the resulting pings. We then snuck in the side door and set supernatural alarms at the various entrances. When we neared the scene, we secured it with trip-wire illusions, which would scare the shit out of anyone sneaking up on us. In other words, we took all precautions.

Paige retreated to her post on the roof, and we headed for the death room.

Adam and I had taken the most direct route out of the building after I'd expelled the demon. In other words, he hadn't lied to Paige—he'd never seen the carnage. No reason for it, and the farther we'd stayed from a potential crime scene, the better.

Now, as I led them to the spot, they both stopped short and stared. I remembered earlier, running down this hall, hearing Denver Brown summoning the demon. I'd caught one glimpse of him. Just a sliver through the half-open door as I ran toward it and he staggered back, and then—boom.

One second I was looking at a guy, not enough to see more than that he seemed to have dark hair. Then he was gone. Burst like . . . well, at the time, I'd thought *like a human piñata*, but seeing the room again, I felt sicker about that than the actual gore within.

There wasn't a big-enough piece of Denver Brown left even to say he'd been human. It looked as if someone grabbed buckets of blood and offal from a slaughterhouse and threw them on the walls.

But it *wasn't* slaughterhouse slop. It had been a man whom someone had cared enough about to try to stop him from doing this. Who'd called us to stop him. I looked around that room, and even if I couldn't see anything recognizably human, it had still been a person.

That's why Paige wasn't here. Not because she couldn't handle gore, but because she'd walk in here and see a life lost, see a victim who died horribly, and she'd wake in the night seeing this room again, imagining what happened to Brown and feeling the horror of his death.

Lucas saw a victim, too. First and foremost. The tragic waste of a life. No nightmares for him, though. That wasn't how he processed things. He saw tragedy, and he imagined solutions. Lucas would handle this with action, going after the black market merchant, reducing the chance it would happen again, at least in our city. He'd mark Brown's passing that way.

Adam's tanned face was pale, brown eyes darker than usual. Seeing the horror of the death scene. Processing it a little slower, taking longer to make the jump to "this was a person." But making it and dipping his chin, a moment to recognize a life lost before squeezing my hand and then unzipping his bag. That was how he dealt with it: get to work.

We didn't sanitize the scene. That's impossible these days, though according to most crime shows we were screwed the moment we stepped into that room, leaving behind some rare clothing fiber that could be traced back to our front door. Which is bullshit, of course. We took basic precautions—gloves, booties, burnable clothing—but we weren't overly worried. Upstairs lay a corpse covered in Denver Brown's blood. The street kid would be blamed for his murder.

Now, as I worked, I thought of that street kid. He would have been dead when Denver found him, probably OD'd, giving Denver a body for his summoning. Whatever had gone wrong in that kid's life, someone still loved him and might spend the rest of his or her life wondering how he could have fallen so low as to murder a man. This is why, most times, I don't mind whatever anti-empathy gene I inherited from my parents. It's so easy to get crushed by those thoughts. When you lead the kind of lives we do, it helps if the mental leap from "corpse" to "victim with family and friends" is a tough one.

We removed the evidence of Brown's death—teeth and bone and tissue. There wasn't as much as there should be. While low-level demons aren't overly powerful once they're in a host, there's a moment during transition when they can use their host as a conduit. That's what the demon had done, decorating a room with its summoner.

The demonic force that exploded him seemed to have inciner-ated or otherwise consumed part of him, too. We picked up what remained, and we left the room spattered with blood. Any attempt to clean it would be useless—the blood would still be visible under ultraviolet.

As we were ready to go, Lucas's cell buzzed with a text.

"Paige spotted someone," he said. "A young man is circling the building. He's decently dressed."

In other words, not another street kid looking for a place to hole up. My caller from earlier, I presumed. He had indeed managed to trace Denver's phone here.

"Should we head him off at the pass?" I said. "Or slip out and let him see . . ." I looked at the red-sprayed walls. Under other circumstances, I'd have voted for slipping out. But after what happened on the phone, I couldn't even finish that sentence.

"I'll handle this," Adam said.

I shook my head. "You can come, but I'll talk to him. My mess; my cleanup."

Lucas hefted the bag. "Paige and I will cover disposal. You deal with the boy."

We followed Paige's directions to the north side of the building. We'd made it to the first floor when she called back.

"Possible trouble," she said. "There's a car."

"Yep," I said. "Big city, lots of them."

She ignored that. "A dark sedan stopped a block away. It seems to be tailing the boy. Now it's turning the corner into a laneway. And . . . the car door is opening. Driver getting out. Passenger, too."

"Dark suits and sunglasses?" I said. "Little metal wands that made you forget what you've just seen."

"Try Portland's finest."

"Shit."

"That's worse?"

"Uh, yeah," I said. "Cops are real. And you haven't finished making us handy memory-wipe sticks for them yet."

She snorted. "I'll get on that. In the meantime . . ." A few murmured words as Lucas must have reached her. "We'll take the police. You focus on the target."

She signed off, and I told Adam what she'd said.

"Cops? Shit."

"My words exactly," I said. "Personally, I'd rather face demons. I can dispel *them*."

We continued toward the side exit. At least the trip-wire illusion hadn't gone off yet. We'd know if it did. The screaming always gave it away.

I calculated our speed on the way to the door and compared it with our target's estimated arrival trajectory. I may have stopped taking math the moment they let me drop it, but summer vacations with a werewolf Pack gave me top-notch hunting skills. So when I cracked open the door, I should have seen our target five to ten feet away, depending on how much he'd slowed once he reached that laneway. Instead, I saw an empty passage.

I swore and backed up. Paige said he'd been heading into the service lane. Even breaking into a run, he wouldn't have made it through the door that fast. Nor could he have run to the other end of the lane by now.

"Changed his mind?" Adam said.

"Must have."

I was halfway down the lane when my phone buzzed. Paige. *Pull back. Something's not right.*

A squeak sounded behind me. Adam wheeled first. A man stepped into the lane. Shades and a suit. *Not* a cop. I hit him with a knockback before he could show me what he really was.

He staggered back. Another man flew around the corner, his hands out to cast a spell. My energy bolt was faster. So was Adam, barreling toward him. He engages; I cover. It's not my natural choice, but anyone who's played an RPG knows that rear line is where a good spell-caster belongs.

Another energy bolt, this one for the first guy, now charging Adam. Then something flickered right beside Adam. I caught a split-second glimpse of a figure—smaller, male, brown hair. I shouted, "Adam!" and he disappeared. *Adam* disappeared. One second he was there, the other figure flickering beside him like a hologram. Then they both vanished.

"Adam!"

The sorcerer recovered from my energy bolt and threw one of his own. I dodged it. Fingers clamped on my shoulder. I spun, spell on my lips, but there wasn't time to cast before the lane disappeared and I landed ass-first on . . .

Linoleum?

I blinked and looked around. I was sitting on the floor of a darkened office. Fingers gripped my arm again, and I yanked free a half second before I recognized the touch.

"Adam?"

"Shhh," he whispered against my ear. "Someone's here."

We both scanned the room. Definitely an office. Unused for a long time, given the stink of dust and the tattered motivational posters. Even before the dust, it would have required some serious motivation to work here. I joke about my office at the agency. It's a closet. No, really—it's our supply closet. Once I graduated from receptionist to investigator, Paige rearranged the supplies to give me a place to work in private. I use it for storage. My real "office" is Adam's, chair pulled up on the other side of his desk. We say it's for convenience, but the truth is we just like it that way. Also, my office is a closet.

This one might not have been an actual closet, but I'm guessing that's what the builders intended. Four desks had been crammed into an area less than six feet square. A dust-crusted phone on each said "telemarketing" to me. So did the fact that two of the phones had been smashed to bits of plastic and wire.

There was clearly no one else in the room. Adam and I barely fit inside without standing on a desk.

"Where—?" I whispered. My phone vibrated before I could finish.

I flicked it on, ready to send a quick *Not cops!* message to Paige and Lucas. Paige had already done so, her text managing it in a single and more useful word: *Cabal.*

I resisted the urge to send back, *Which one?* Obviously not the Cortezes. There were three others. Well, four actually. The Nast Cabal had split in two. My brother Sean runs one half; my uncle the other. If it was my brother's side, they'd never have jumped us. My uncle's? We'd be lucky to have survived. Family feuds. Always interesting. Rarely lethal. Unless you're the Hatfields and McCoys. Or the Nast Cabal.

There was no sense asking Paige which Cabal it was. If she knew, she'd have said.

I popped back a *Yep*, meaning *Already know; already dealing; still alive.* Adam touched my arm, getting my attention. I followed his gaze to the door, but I couldn't hear anything. He gestured. Right, spells. My *job*. I cast a sensing one and, sure enough, it brought back the blip of someone right on the other side of—

The blip stopped. I recast quickly. Before I could even get the final words out, Adam was in flight, vaulting onto the desk and tackling a guy. His target was not quite out of his teens. Slender with short brown hair, and that's all I saw before he started to flicker again. Adam clocked him and he stopped flickering.

"Teleporting half-demon," I said.

Adam's look said, *You think?*

True, it was obvious, except for the part where this kid hadn't been the only one to disappear. There are three levels to most half-demon subtypes, depending on the power of daddy. Adam, and my mother, came from the top tier of their subtypes, the rarest one, fathered by a lord demon. Teleporting half-demons have three levels, too. None of them can take someone with them. This kid had.

"You okay?" Adam said, hunkering down as the kid shivered on the floor. Sweat plastered his hair to his head.

"Um . . ." The kid rubbed the spot on his jaw where Adam had hit him.

"Don't expect an apology," Adam said, straightening. "We've got a Cabal team out there, somewhere, and the only person who can tell us what's going on was trying to teleport out."

"Because you jumped me."

"Because you teleported *in* behind us. Next time, use the door and say hello. I'm guessing you're the one who called Savannah?"

The kid nodded and pushed his sweat-soaked hair back.

"Care to talk about that?" Adam said. "'Cause we'd kinda like an explanation."

The kid's mouth opened then shut, and he looked ready to keel over from exhaustion.

"You're overusing your powers," Adam said. "You can't zip in and out like that. Not at your age."

I nodded. "Like Adam said, doors work just fine. Save the zipping for when you really need it."

"Adam." The kid lifted his gaze to the guy standing over him. "Adam Vasic. Your dad—your stepdad—he's the expert, right? On all this. The demon stuff. He's the guy I wanted to talk to, but Denver . . ." He swallowed. "Denver wouldn't listen. He said it wasn't safe. So he talked to a demon instead." The kid choked on something like a bitter laugh, cracked around the edges. "Stupid jerk. Stupid, stupid—"

I clapped a hand over the kid's mouth, whispering, "Shhh!" as my sensing spells picked up a presence.

A footstep creaked in the hall. I mouthed to the kid, "Which Cabal?" but he only frowned. More footsteps. Meaning more than one operative. I took out my phone, typed *Which Cabal?* and showed the kid, but his expression didn't change. Meaning he had no idea what I was talking about.

The biggest problem with being a half-demon is that it's not the usual kind of hereditary power, where whichever parent passed it

along is there to tell you what's going on. Dad's long gone, leaving
Junior to figure it out. Adam had gotten lucky—when he started
showing a disturbing affinity for fire, his mom wasn't the type to
tell herself he'd outgrow it. She went looking for help and found
Robert Vasic.

To help with the problem of discovery, half-demons have an
intricate network funneling kids and teens to the answers they
need. It's an imperfect system and it seemed as if this kid was only
partway through it. As for why a Cabal was after him . . . ? I had
a pretty good idea about that. What mattered now, though, was
getting him the hell out of their path.

I texted Paige. She replied right away. They were tracking two
members of a Cabal team around the outside of the building. I told
her I was more worried about the ones *inside*.

On it, she replied. *Be ready.*

Fight or flight?

Flight, she answered. *Sorry. You've got baggage.*

In other words, we had a civilian to look after.

The guys in the hall had started opening doors. They seemed to
be locked, which meant it took a few seconds for each. Once we
took cover, I typed another question for the kid.

Can you get us out? Teleport for three? Or two?

When he mouthed, "I can try," Adam shook his head. The kid
was out of juice, and we needed to find another way. Unfortunately,
we were locked in a tiny office, with Cabal goons patrolling the
only exit.

Our door opened.

"Hiding under a desk?" the guy said despite the fact we were
well hidden. "Not quite living up to your reputation, are you, little
witch? Surprise, surprise. Proof you don't have sorcerer blood after
all. Just a cowering witch-mouse."

I started to fly out, but Adam's fingers wrapped around my
wrist. I swallowed the temper flare. Jumping out, spell blazing, was

exactly what the guy expected after that insult. I knew better . . . and I still fell for it. Immaturity or sensitivity? Probably some of both, with a generous helping of ego mixed in.

Adam motioned for the kid to move behind the next desk. When he hesitated, Adam gave him a push.

"Do you think I can't see you moving?" the Cabal agent said. "Casting from behind another desk isn't going to help, little witch. I know where you are."

A heat sensor. That's what the guy was using, not spells. The sensing one is witch magic. Sorcerers can learn it—Lucas had—but most don't bother.

Adam motioned for me to go the other way, behind the next desk. As I did, the guy grunted. Then he said, "Mr. Vasic, I presume. Too bad your powers require physical contact. Not much use against a sorcerer, but from what I hear, you aren't quite bright enough to figure that one out. A charging bull, just like your demon daddy."

The guy didn't know shit about demons. Asmondai preferred to think things through. *My* granddaddy was the charging-bull type. Which I suppose explains why I'd fallen for the taunting and Adam only rolled his eyes.

The guy kept talking. Mocking us. I waited until he got to "yo momma" jokes about mine, signaling he was coming near the end of a very limited repertoire. Then I threw a fireball at the guy behind him.

Yes, there was a guy behind him. If there are two Cabal grunts in a hallway and one finds his target, the other's not going to keep looking. My sensing spell had confirmed that, so I hurled a fireball, which confused the hell out of the sorcerer. A *fireball* coming from the location he thought held Adam? Clearly Asmondai's son had learned a new trick. The sorcerer quickly cast a spell. I dispelled it and slammed him with a knockback as Adam flew from behind his desk and launched himself at the guy.

Cabal dude number two had recovered from the fireball and was leaping at Adam when he got double-whammied. I cast at the same time as someone in the hall—Lucas or Paige. The guy went down. I ran out and pinned him there as Adam dealt with his target, which took all of thirty seconds, because if a sorcerer won't learn witch magic, all you have to do is grab his hands and he can't make the appropriate gestures for sorcerer spells. I had my guy flipped onto his stomach and was checking his pockets when Paige jogged down the hall.

"Did I miss a letter in 'flight'?" Paige asked. "Or did you willfully misread it?"

"Pure defense," I grunted as my target struggled. "We tried hiding. It didn't work. Plus, he made fun of us for it."

She shook her head and handed me a plastic tie from her pocket. I secured my target while she tossed another to Adam.

"Leave them to us," she said. "There are more on the way. Lucas is holding them off."

"Are you sure? We can—"

She pointed into the office, where the kid was peeking from behind a desk.

"Right. Half-demon civilian to worry about. Come on, kid. Let's get you out of here."

We tried to get the kid talking on the drive back, but he was too busy watching for trouble, likely ready to zap out at any provocation—including being forced to talk when he didn't want to.

As we led him into our office, he looked disappointed. The outside is underwhelming. Oh, hell, even inside it's not exactly Cabal executive suites. The first time I came there, when Lucas and Paige bought it, I'm sure I made some less than enthusiastic comments about the dull industrial facade. Truthfully, though, I couldn't have been happier. This was their dream. I'd rolled my eyes at that, too—opening a private investigation firm to help other supernaturals . . . supernaturals who might not always pay their bill . . . who might not even *be* billed. Deluded do-gooders, both of them. But it was what they wanted and, more than that, it had meant that we were staying in Portland. Indefinitely. At that moment, we became a family.

But yes, the building itself wasn't much to look at. You don't run a supernatural detective agency out of a Pearl District office tower.

Lucas and Paige own the whole building. We rent out the lower offices to tenants who are not supernaturals. That might seem dangerous, but, given who Lucas is, any supernatural who applied would almost certainly be a Cabal spy, possibly even a *Cortez* Cabal spy, sent by Benicio to protect his son. We can handle the protecting part just fine. When the kid saw the sheer amount of security needed to get up to our offices, he visibly relaxed.

"That guy said you're a witch," he said as I cast a protective spell.

"Yep."

"He seemed to be casting spells, too."

"Yep."

I led the kid into the meeting room while Adam checked the security system. I could tell the kid wanted to ask more about my powers. The problem with rescuing a civilian from Cabal goons and whisking him to a secret, spell-guarded location? He's going to lose that civilian innocence fast. Under normal circumstances, we don't go around revealing ourselves, but you can't protect a supernatural from other supernaturals without employing means that are, well, supernatural.

"Coffee? Coke?" I said.

"Coke, please. And do you have ice? For my arm. I think Adam burned it when he grabbed me."

"First-degree," I said. "It'll clear up in a day or so. I'll get you some ointment. I buy it by the bucket."

Adam was walking in as I said that. It was for his benefit, and I shot a grin his way. He didn't seem to notice, just walked to the fridge and took out a can of Coke.

"Two more please, garçon," I said.

He shut the fridge door and popped open his can.

"Was it something I said?" I asked as I walked to the fridge.

"Hmm?" He glanced at me, his eyes unfocused, mind elsewhere. When he realized I was taking out two more cans, he mumbled something like an apology and settled into a chair. I tried to catch his eye, but I'd lost him. It'd been a long day—flying halfway across the country and helping me in two fights. Plus the sex, which had been kinda strenuous. I didn't blame him for zoning out now that all was quiet.

I gave the kid his Coke and the ointment. "You have questions; I have questions. Considering we just saved your ass from a team of Cabal goons, how about I go first?"

He hesitated, then slowly nodded. "Sure."

"First, a name. It makes communication much less awkward."

"Keefer."

I waited for more. When it didn't come, I said, "Outside the military and paramilitary worlds, we prefer first names."

"That is my first name."

"Oh. Got it." I paused. "Wasn't there an actor . . . ? In the nineties or something . . . ?"

"Sutherland. Yeah. Mine's spelled different."

"And your last name?"

"Rather not. Sorry."

I glanced at Adam, but he was still zoned out. I popped the top on my can and took a gulp. "Okay, Keefer. I get that you want to play this close to the vest, and I don't blame you, because ninety-nine percent of the time that is the correct move in our world. Probably in any world. But if you expect us to help you, we're going to need to feel like you're on the level. A surname will help."

He fidgeted in his chair. Then he said, "Brown."

"Brown. Okay. So—"

"I'm going to check on Paige and Lucas," Adam said, cutting me short. He pushed to his feet and was gone before I could say a word. I stared after him. Then I looked at the spot he'd vacated, his Coke can abandoned.

Something's wrong.

No, he was tired. Understandably so. I pushed my brain back on track. What had we been talking about? Names. Right. Keefer Brown. *Brown* . . . Oh, shit.

"Denver was your . . ." I almost said "cousin." Hell, distant cousin. *Please let it be a very distant cousin you barely knew at all.* But I looked at Keefer and I flashed to that split-second glimpse of Denver before his death, and instead I said, "He was your brother."

"Yeah." Keefer rubbed his hands briskly against his legs, the *skritch-skritch* of the friction filling the silence. "Which is why I didn't want to give my name. Let's skip that, okay? Just move on."

Skip that. Move on. Words that sounded so callous if you hadn't lost someone close. If you did, you understood. *Nope, don't want to talk about my mom. Nope, nothing to see here. Move on.*

The young man who'd died in that apartment didn't just have a name now. He had a family. A younger brother who was sitting right in front of me. A younger brother who'd learned of his death by me saying "one fewer demon summoner in the world isn't necessarily a bad thing." A younger brother who'd almost walked into that room filled with blood and viscera, his brother's remains, spattered over the walls and floor and ceiling and—

I yanked open the door and looked for Adam. No sign of him. I closed the door and took a seat.

"It was quick," I said finally. "His death, I mean. Really quick. He wouldn't have known what was happening. He wouldn't have felt anything."

"Okay."

"And you don't seem to know a lot about our world, but I can promise you he went someplace good. My parents . . . Well, they're gone, but I know where they are and they're happy, and they ended up in a decent place even if they didn't quite deserve it." I forced a smile. "So your brother will be someplace good. Which I know doesn't really help a lot, because he's not here and . . ." I cleared my throat. "Sorry. Babbling."

"It's okay. Thanks."

"Move on?"

"Please."

I chugged the rest of my Coke and tossed the can. It clanged as it circled the rim of the trash, then fell in.

"Two points," Keefer said, passing me a weak smile. *Moving right along . . .*

"Yep, and that's the best I can do, despite every effort to get me on the girls' basketball team in school."

"No one ever tried getting me on our team, as you might guess. Mine was track, because I was fast. Mostly just running away from other kids, though."

"Now you don't need to run. Just disappear. Then pop out behind and clock them."

"Yeah, I guess so."

"When did it start? The teleporting?"

"Two years ago, when I was fifteen. Denver and I . . . we're on our own. Mom died when I was twelve and our dad took off a few months later. I do pretty well in school, so I had a scholarship to a good one, but not the money to look like I belonged there. I got hassled. That day, it was three guys. If it'd been just one, I could take him. Denver taught me some decent moves and, like I said, I'm fast. But three? Running like hell was the only option. So I did, and then—*poof*, I ended up clear across the school yard in one stride."

"Cool," I said. "Also, shit-your-pants scary if you don't know what's going on."

"I totally freaked out. I kept trying to come up with rational explanations. The best I could manage was that I blanked. That I was running and had some kind of adrenaline surge and my brain shorted out. Which didn't explain the fact that those three guys were as freaked out as I was, swearing they'd seen me vanish. Of course, they were potheads, so I blamed that. But then it kept happening."

He continued his story. It wasn't a short one. These things never are—you don't wake up one morning able to teleport and find answers by evening. It took Adam's mom a long time to get from "my kid's a budding pyromaniac" to Robert Vasic's door. So it was with Keefer, except instead of a mother who wouldn't accept easy answers, it had been his brother.

The first year had been fumbling in the dark. They started with the most rational explanation—that he was blacking out when he ran. They spent more money than they could afford before learning there was nothing physically wrong with Keefer, and if he persisted in this delusion, the doctors suggested he was in need of psychiatric help. By then, Denver and Keefer knew it wasn't a medical or psychological problem, because Denver had borne witness to the fact that his brother could teleport. There was no answer to that in the natural world. So Denver started searching outside it.

Searching "outside" the natural world is a complete crapshoot for humans. Their most obvious resource—the Internet—is 99.99 percent bullshit. Unless you know what you're looking for, you'll never find that .01 percent of truth. But you can set off some alarms with your searches, and that's what Denver had done.

Six months ago, they'd received an invitation from a private clinic. This clinic had learned of Keefer's condition and would not only examine him for free—with the best equipment and best experts available—but pay him generously for his time. Yeah, Denver didn't fall for that one. It's as transparent as the Nigerian prince who wants to give you $1,453,234.23 after stumbling over your Internet profile and thinking you seem like a nice person. Sadly, though, there's a reason those scams persist. Because some people are idiots. And greedy as hell.

Cabals know this. They also know that people suddenly displaying weird powers don't normally run around exercising them and having a grand old time, as they do in the movies. They worry and they fret, and the smart ones seek answers. If the half-demon community had gotten wind of Keefer, their approach would have been more subtle. Cabals say screw subtle. You want answers? We'll not only give them free, we'll throw in a bag of cash and a pony.

Denver had refused. Which is the right move when a Nigerian prince e-mails you. When a Cabal makes you an offer, though? It's not only one you can't refuse; it's one you really, really shouldn't. They'd gone after Keefer, discreetly at first, which suggests it may have actually been the Cortezes.

Whichever Cabal it was, when their invitation failed, they seem to have backed off. As a potential high-level teleporting half-demon, they'd keep an eye on him, but he was just a kid and his brother was skittish, so best to step away and monitor the situation intermittently.

The problem with that? Another Cabal had taken notice. And the minute the Cortezes backed off, they pounced. Sort of. An actual "pounce" would involve kidnapping. This Cabal went further than the Cortezes only by making direct contact with Keefer. They told him they were a team of medical researchers and that someone had brought Keefer's case to their attention because they were investigating another incidence of "temporal displacement" that might be related to his. Was he willing to talk? Nothing intrusive. Just a few questions and then, if his case did indeed fit their research parameters, they would offer their expertise and any required examinations, free of charge, of course, with a small stipend for any inconvenience, as was usually offered to those participating in medical research.

This would have been the St. Cloud Cabal. The most scientific. The least aggressive. Keefer had nibbled the bait, but Denver wouldn't bite. Then Keefer learned he could teleport others with him and, not surprisingly, the St. Clouds really did pounce, attempting to take him captive. They failed, and Denver took his little brother on the run.

They'd managed to dodge the St. Clouds for a while. But then their luck ran out. Their pursuers became even more aggressive and impossible to shake. Because it was another Cabal. I was certain of that, just as I was certain which one it was. They all have their trademarks. Ferreting Keefer out first, assessing, and withdrawing until he reached adulthood? Cortezes. Playing the scientific angle and then failing on the follow-through attack? St. Clouds. Swooping in for the kill and pursuing like the hounds of hell? Oh, yeah. That was my dad's side of the family. The Nasts.

Keefer knew none of this. He'd never heard the word "Cabal," apparently—not in this context, anyway. To him and Denver, there'd been a single group of shady and dangerous individuals stalking and hunting them the whole time. Denver had thought it was the government, maybe the military. Yeah, it's amazing how many conspiracy charges leveled at the American government are actually the result of Cabal actions.

As for what happened next, it was a bit of a muddle because Denver had stopped sharing his findings with his brother. I suspect that happened right around the time Denver's digging unearthed the word "demon." He didn't want to scare Keefer. Nor, I'm sure, did he want his little brother thinking he'd lost his mind. But someone had set Denver on that trail. Someone had also set him on our trail, because it was no coincidence he'd wound up in Portland. And no coincidence Keefer contacted me to help.

After they'd arrived in Portland, Keefer had found our business card in Denver's wallet with a note on the back: "These guys can help. *Call them*." Denver brought Keefer here, then followed his brother when he went to meet the guy who sold him the demon-summoning supplies. Denver asked the black market merchant about us and, not surprisingly, the guy told him we were all kinds of trouble and that the demon was Denver's best bet. Summon and hold it and get answers. That's when Keefer called me. And that's when his brother went to that empty building, summoned a demon, and learned, too late, why you don't trust a guy who sells black market rituals in a back alley.

"That's my story," Keefer said. "Your turn. What am I and what the hell is going on?"

"I can tell you what you are, but I'm really not the expert." I walked to the door and opened it. "Hey, Adam?"

No answer. I looked down the empty and silent hall. There was no way anyone could break in. Not without setting off a shitload of alarms. Still, my heart beat a little quicker when he didn't reply.

I motioned for Keefer to wait and hurried down to Adam's office. He was there, lying on the couch in the near dark, lights off. Sleeping, I thought. But when I stepped in, I saw his eyes were open. Staring at the ceiling.

"Hey," I said.

I got a grunt in return.

"I know you're tired," I said. "But this kid needs some answers, and you're the demonology expert."

Another grunt.

"Adam?"

"In a minute." He pushed up and strode past me without a glance my way. I watched him walk into the hall . . . and then into the bathroom, the door shutting behind him with a hard click.

Something's wrong.

How? What could have happened in the couple of minutes between arriving here—when he'd been joking with Keefer—and joining us in the meeting room? Nothing, other than exhaustion setting in.

Or maybe he'd checked his e-mail and something there annoyed him, and he was tired enough that it spun his mood on a one-eighty. Adam is the most easygoing guy I know. But his dad *is* the lord demon of fire. Adam has a temper. Something had set that off, and he was waiting for it to settle. Being exhausted only made that tougher.

I rapped on the bathroom door as I passed. "I'll give him the basics, okay? No rush. Like I said, I know you're tired."

He didn't answer. I returned to the meeting room.

"Have you ever heard the term 'half-demon'?" I said.

Keefer's look answered with an emphatic no. So I explained. I finished by saying, "That's what Adam is. It's where he gets his fire power from—literally. My mom was one, too, with visual powers. I don't get any of that. It's not hereditary past the first generation. I have demon blood, and it adds a turbo boost to my spell-casting, but that's it. And the demon part doesn't mean what people might think it does. It doesn't *make* you demonic. It just gives you power, and it's up to you to decide how you want to use it. For trouble or for good, like Adam does."

"Okay . . ."

"Actual demons, though? That's another story. Definitely demonic."

"Yeah, kinda figured that out."

"Right. Sorry." I'd been pacing as I talked. Now I lowered myself into a chair and cast another glance at the door, hoping for Adam. He was so much better at the empathetic stuff. And the demon stuff. I said as much—about the demon part—to Keefer, suggesting he save questions for Adam.

"How about Cabals, then?" he said.

"Yes!" I said, with perhaps a little too much enthusiasm. "I can definitely explain about Cabals. In three words: supernatural corporate mafia."

"Supernatural . . ."

"Basically, they're huge corporations, and they do the usual corporate stuff—sell products and services on a multinational level. If I gave you names, you wouldn't recognize them unless you subscribe to *Fortune* or *Businessweek*, but if I started naming their product lines, you would. They hire supernaturals almost exclusively. Our powers give them a massive advantage in the business world. Supernaturals get good-paying jobs where they don't need to hide what they are, and they get medical benefits and a lot of other stuff that can be tough for us to find otherwise. In return, the Cabal owns your soul. Well, not literally, but pretty damned close. It's not exactly an ethical business model. Hence the mafia part of the description."

"Uh-huh."

"They were coming after you for recruitment." I considered telling him I suspected he'd been targeted by three Cabals, but that just got confusing. And, possibly, terrifying. "The one we just encountered is almost certainly the Nasts. Half of it, at least. They split and . . . Never mind. The point is that they're the, well, nastiest of the bunch. Their idea of recruitment is more like conscription, at least for someone like you."

"Why?"

"Because you've got some wonky powers. Even an Abeo can't teleport someone with him."

"Abeo?"

"Top-level teleporting half-demon. Fathered by . . . I forget which lord demon. Adam knows. He'll explain the levels and test your powers, just as soon as he . . ." I glanced toward the hall. "As soon as he's done whatever he's doing. In the meantime, I'm going to make a call. See if I can get a handle on what's going on here, maybe put some pressure on the Nasts to pull their dogs. I've got an in with one of the CEOs."

I told him to grab another Coke if he wanted it and make himself comfortable. Then I called Sean. He answered on the third ring with, "Hey, what's up?"

"Got a situation that I think involves Uncle Josef, and if it does, I'm looking for some familial intervention."

Sean snorted, possibly at my use of "uncle"—Josef tends to blow a gasket when I call him that—or possibly at the suggestion that Sean was in any position to intervene with the opposing half of the family business.

"What have you got?" he asked.

"Teleporting half-demon kid with wonky powers."

Silence. Then, "Kid?"

"I use the term colloquially. For those of us with an Ivy League education, he is what you would refer to as an adolescent. Seventeen years of age, which means, according to intra-Cabal regulations, too young to be recruited. Not that anyone really gives a shit about the intra-Cabal regulations. Still, it seems the Cortezes backed off after they assessed him. I'll tell Lucas to pass on a thanks to his dad for that show of restraint. The St. Clouds went after him next but lost him. As inept as ever. Uncle Joe's bunch, though? They're hot on his tail. Here. In Portland. Going after me in the process, which I believe is also a violation of intra-Cabal regulations." I paused. "No, wait. That only applies to the protection of inner-family members from rival Cabals. Doesn't count if it's your own family going after you, right? Except Josef doesn't consider me family, so then it does count because you do and therefore, as your sister, I fall under your protection. Damn, that's complicated."

Silence.

"Lost you, didn't I?"

He chuckled, but it was a little off, a little forced.

"Sean?" I said.

"Sorry, I was waiting to see if you were done talking."

"Ha-ha. Yes, I am. So this kid . . ."

"Does he have a name?"

"Everyone does."

"And you're not giving it to me."

"Client confidentiality. I love you dearly and trust you completely—in personal matters. In business? Fifty percent."

"Thanks."

"Hey, with Benicio, it's twenty-five percent in business, fifty in personal, and he's the closest thing I've got to a granddaddy. Love him. Don't trust him as far as I can throw him. You win that contest."

"Knowing Benicio Cortez, that sets the bar a little lower than I like. All right, though. Point taken. I'm a Cabal CEO now. A high-powered teleporting half-demon a year from official recruitment age is ripe pickings. I won't deny it. So keep whatever details you can and I'll see what my associates in Josef's camp say."

"Calling in the spy network, huh?"

"Just for you. Because I love you dearly and trust you ninety percent. Even if you are a pain in the ass."

"That's what little sisters are for."

He promised to call back as soon as he had results. I pocketed my phone and looked over to see Keefer staring at me.

"That was your brother?" he said.

"Mmm-hmm."

"He runs one of these Cabals?"

"Right, but . . . it's complicated. I didn't give him details on you because, yes, that'd be a little too tempting. Sean's a good guy, but he's also head of a Cabal. The one that's after you, though, is the other Nast Cabal. And, yes, they need to come up with team names, because otherwise it's really confusing."

"Your *uncle* runs the other half? The one that's trying to kidnap me? And Lucas, the guy in charge of this place, did I hear you say his dad runs a Cabal?"

"Lucas and Paige are *both* in charge of this place. Best to remember that if you want to stay on their good side. But otherwise? Right on all counts. It's complicated, like I said. The point is that you're perfectly safe here."

"Uh-huh."

I glanced toward the door. "Let me go grab Adam. He can talk more on the demon stuff while we wait for Paige and Lucas."

I found Adam back on the couch. "Hey, did you forget something?"

He didn't answer.

"Look, if you're tired, we can put this off, but I keep telling the kid you're coming to talk to him, and . . ."

As I walked over, I saw two sheets on the otherwise empty table. My gut twisted. I took another slow step, gaze fixed on them, telling myself I was mistaken, that they couldn't be what I thought. But of course they were.

"If you want to keep something from me?" He spoke with his gaze still on the ceiling. "Don't leave it lying on your desk. Not when the security panel I need to access is right above it."

"I . . ."

His gaze swung my way. "When were you going to tell me, Savannah?"

"I was—"

"Were you going to actually break up with me before you left? Or just pull a vanishing act? Move across the country and hope I got the message?"

"No! I—"

He sat up. "I didn't even know you'd applied to college out of state, and maybe that's irrelevant right now, but that's what I keep thinking. I never even knew you'd applied, and I can't figure out why not, because I made it damned clear that if you wanted to go to college, I'd never hold you back, no matter where you went. Hell, I offered to go with you. Set up a satellite office for a few years. That was the problem, wasn't it? Me making plans. *Hey, you want to go to school out of state? I'll go with you.*" He looked up at me. "You could have just said no."

"That's not—"

"*No, Adam. You're moving too fast, Adam. I need my space, Adam.* I tried . . ." His fists clenched, and I caught a whiff of smoke. "I tried so damned hard to play it cool, even if you've never given me any indication that you want that."

"Because I—"

"I'm so damned careful, Savannah. A year of being so careful, because I know you're . . ." He swallowed back the rest. "A year of taking every step with care, to be sure you're okay with it. Do you really want to live in the same building as me? Okay. Are you really okay with sharing an apartment most of the time? Okay. Do you seem like you want me to back off? Like this is more togetherness than you expected? Like I'm moving too fast? No. You've never once even hinted at that. And now this." He picked up the college admission offers. "I don't get it. I just don't."

"It's not like—"

His gaze lifted to mine and I saw the pain there, roiling tamped-down fire behind his eyes. "I would have let you go, Savannah. One word and I would have let you go. Friends first. That's what we said. Friends don't pull this shit." That fire flared, his temper rising as he got to his feet. "Friends have a little more respect for each other than this. They don't make the other person feel like a goddamn loser for missing some sign that I'm sure as hell you never gave."

"Savannah?" It was Paige, out in the hall. "Adam?"

"It's not like that," I said quickly, before she reached us. "I can explain."

"Oh, I'm sure you can. Just as I'm damned sure it comes down to the same thing. That this relationship isn't what you wanted. That it's not what you expected. That I'm not what you expected. And it's not enough to dump me—you have to run across the country to get away from me."

"Adam?" Paige appeared in the doorway. "What's going on?"

"Personal," he grunted.

"I can tell that, but where—?"

"Can we have a few minutes?" I said. "We'll take this outside. Keefer's in the next room."

"Which room?"

"The meeting room."

"No," Lucas said, walking up behind her. "He isn't."

Keefer was gone. He wasn't in the bathroom or poking around the office. And the security system hadn't caught him leaving because he'd teleported through the wall.

"It's my fault," I said. "I was talking to Sean, and he got a little freaked by the fact that my uncle is in charge of the Cabal chasing him. And that my brother is in charge of another Cabal. And that Lucas's father . . ." I exhaled. "Shit. I'm sorry. I thought I'd explained it well enough, and he didn't *seem* too worried, but what makes perfect sense to me is going to seem scary as hell to some kid who didn't even know what a Cabal *was*." I looked at Paige and Lucas. "I screwed up. I didn't think it through. I'm sorry."

"It's my fault, too," Adam said. "Savannah was trying to get me to help her out with the kid, and I was AWOL on personal stuff. Which is unacceptable."

I glanced over, interpreting his jumping to my defense as a sign that he wasn't as hurt and angry as he'd seemed, but he didn't look my way, and I knew he was just being fair, because that's who he is. Always. That stung all the more because *I* hadn't been fair. I'd been a coward. Just not for the reason he thought.

"Well, Keefer's not here," Paige said. "And taking the blame doesn't help to find him. The farther he gets, the harder it'll be to track him. Can you two still work together?"

"I'll go with Lucas," Adam said. "We'll take my Jeep. You and Savannah stick close to the office and search with your spells."

He pulled out his keys and headed for the door without another word.

Paige and I started by scouring the building, separating as we cast our sensing spells. There was no sign of Keefer within a block radius, and beyond that, it was impossible to track him—too many directions to go and too many other people setting off our spells. Paige called Lucas, and they divided driving territory while we headed for the Prius.

When we drove from the parking lot, I said, "I screwed up."

"We aren't talking about Keefer, are we."

"No, sorry. Later, right?"

"You can look while you talk. Go on."

"You know I applied to Portland State for criminology and Pacific Northwest for art."

"Yes . . ."

"I didn't get in."

She looked over sharply. "When—?"

"A few weeks ago. I didn't say anything because, well, no big shock, right? All I cared about in high school was getting out, and my grades reflected that. As for my art, I've barely drawn in years. I applied just to see, but I knew you and Lucas were right—I'd need extra work to get into either. I got two other acceptances, though. On the opposite side of the country."

"Oh? I didn't know you'd applied anywhere else."

"No one did. You suggested I cast a broader net, so I did. Anyway, I got the acceptance letters this week, and Adam found them on my desk. I hadn't told him."

"About getting accepted?"

I went quiet, staring out the open window.

After a moment, she said, "When you say *no one* knew you'd applied, that doesn't include . . ."

I stayed quiet.

"Oh," she said. Then she sighed.

She turned the corner before speaking, carefully. "If you thought Adam would have a problem with you going out of state, Savannah . . ."

"He wouldn't. We'd discussed it. If I wanted to go on my own, that was fine. Or we could both go and maybe open a temporary satellite office for the agency. Now he thinks I got spooked when he suggested coming with me, because I wanted to get some distance, and that's why I didn't tell him."

"Which isn't the reason at all, is it?"

I glanced over. Paige slowed to peer down a side street at a kid walking the other way.

"Keefer doesn't have a jacket," I said. "And he's shorter."

Paige nodded and sped up. "Back to Adam. I know you don't want distance. I know you're happy. Crazy-in-love happy. Both of you. If he thinks for one second that you're making plans to bolt? He's overreacting, I have a good idea why, but first, you. Why didn't you tell him?"

I stared out the window for another quarter mile. "Because I don't want to go. And, yes, I know how stupid that sounds. Why did I apply if I don't want to go?"

Another block of forcing myself to check out every side road and person under the age of thirty. Then I turned to Paige.

"I won't say I wanted you guys to be proud of me, because that makes me sound like I'm still a kid, but . . ." A deep breath. "Oh, hell. I wanted you to be proud of me. You and Lucas and Adam."

"We—"

I lifted my hand. "You are proud of me. I know. I also know that you're pretty much obligated to say that because you love me."

"No, we—"

"Let me finish, okay? That's why I didn't want to say it. Not only does it sound lame, but then you have to defend yourself and that's really not what I'm looking for here. I just want to talk. To explain."

"All right."

"I know I'm not living up to my potential. As a witch, yes. As a person, no." I had to raise my hand again against her protest. "Last year, after everything that happened, I realized I needed to smarten up. Shape up. Move out. Start my own life. Part of that was going to college, because it's what you wanted for me, and please don't say you didn't. It wasn't so much a dream as an expectation. In your world and in Lucas's, college is a given, just like going to high school after elementary. Even Adam feels that way. He dropped out, but as soon as he got his shit together, what was the first thing he did? Went back for his degree. That's what I wanted to do. Show you—all three of you—that I'd gotten *my* shit together. I applied to other places because that was the mature and responsible thing to do. Why didn't I tell Adam? Because I don't *want* to go anyplace else. Except once I got the acceptances, I started feeling . . . I started feeling like I *should* go. That if I didn't, I was . . ."

I trailed off and looked back out the window.

"That you were what?" she asked softly.

"Back up," I said.

"To . . . what I said before?"

"No, the car." I gestured. "Back up."

She did, and I directed her to pull up beside a parked SUV.

"Now start parallel parking behind it," I said.

"There's another spot—"

"Parallel park, Paige. I know you can. Stop when I tell you to."

She grumbled but did it. When she was about halfway backed in, I had her stop. From that angle, still mostly hidden by the monster SUV, I could see my target and, hopefully, he couldn't see us.

It was a tall man in his fifties. Thinning blond hair. Dark shades that I knew hid bright blue eyes. People said Josef looked like my dad, only with a thinner build. Beyond the coloring, I don't see it.

In life, Kristof Nast was a son of a bitch. He still is in death. But, like my mom, there's more there. A fierce and loyal heart. Josef

Nast is a stone-cold bastard. If he'd had a heart, it calcified when his son died eight years ago. I could cut him some slack for that, but I won't. My family had suffered too much at Josef's hands, and the only excuse he had was jealousy—he was jealous of my father and later of my brother, both beloved by my grandfather, who was the biggest son of a bitch of them all.

When Thomas Nast died, any remaining hope for Josef died with him, and our uncle had spent the last year showing Sean just how heartless he could be. So, no, I don't see the family resemblance. I can joke about "Uncle Joe," but I'd be no more moved by his death than I'd been by Thomas's, and if that makes me a stone-cold bitch myself, I'll call it hereditary.

"Josef's here," I said. "Can you park farther up?"

"Josef?"

"Yep, the boss himself, meaning Keefer's a bigger prize than we thought."

As Paige parked, I texted a message.

"Lucas?" she said.

I shook my head.

"Adam? Good." She looked at me. "Fix this as soon as you can, Savannah. Don't tell yourself you're giving him time to cool down. Don't slap a Band-Aid on it, either."

"I don't think a Band-Aid will cover this."

"Of course it will. You can tell him you were only testing your admission chances and you didn't want to admit it, in case you didn't get accepted at all, and he'll buy that. But it doesn't fix the core of the problem."

"I know."

She looked over, as if surprised. When I reached for the door handle, she squeezed my shoulder before getting out.

I waited for her on the sidewalk.

"I know we're running out of time for talking," she said. "But I'm going to leave you with one thing you need to know, because as well as you understand Adam, this is something neither of you wants to see. It's the reason he's overreacting right now, because, yes, he is definitely overreacting. He should know you'd never dump him and run across the country. But there's a problem with your relationship. One neither of you likes to admit. The age difference."

I stiffened and she said, "I rest my case."

"We—"

"He's ten years older than you. In twenty years, that won't be a big deal. Right now, it is. To *him*, it's a huge deal."

My gut clenched. "I know I can be immature—"

"And so can he. That part evens out. You've matured enough that, honestly, that isn't a problem. Even Lucas admits it."

"But you just said it was a problem. For Adam."

"The *fact* of it is a problem for Adam. Not the reality. Not the day-to-day relationship with a younger woman. The problem is . . ." She tapped her head. "Up here."

We reached the corner. She checked around it and then said, "Josef's still there. Just standing with his bodyguards. About Adam . . . Do you want me to shut up now?"

"No."

"Good. I'll be quick. You know he's been working out a lot more. You think that's because of his scare with Balaam. I'm sure that's part of it. But the bigger part? Having a gorgeous twenty-two-year-old girlfriend."

I made a face. "Adam has nothing to worry about, and he knows it. My gaze doesn't wander. It's got something damned fine to look at already. He knows that. Confidence in that area has never been a problem for Adam."

"It is now. But that's just a symptom of the bigger problem. This is it for him, Savannah. *You're* it for him. The one he wants to spend the rest of his life with. Has he told you that?"

I shook my head.

"Has he even hinted at that?"

"No, we don't . . . talk about it."

"You need to. He's not saying it because he's worried about scaring you off. That's what the age difference means to him. He's a guy who's found what he wants and is ready to settle down. You're a girl who's just starting life on her own. He's being careful, Savannah. So careful it only takes one hint that this isn't what you want, and he's going to panic." She looked up to meet my gaze. "You can't go on like this. A relationship needs more stable ground."

"I know."

"Good. Put that in your back pocket for now, and go handle Josef."

"Uncle Joe!" I said as I walked toward him, arms wide. "Big hug? No?" I glanced at the two bodyguards stepping my way. "Sorry, guys. No hugs for you. Family only. Unless you're hot, which . . . No, sorry." I turned to Josef and put my arms out again. The look on his face said he'd rather be devoured by alligators.

"If it's family only, then I'm afraid I don't qualify," he said.

"Ooh, snap. Are we going to play this again? Here, let me get it out of the way. *You are not my brother's child, witch-brat.* Yes, I am. He stood right in front of you, in manifested form, and told you— *No, you lie. You and your witch mother. She's cast a spell on him to make him believe he's your father.* Um, then why do I have my father's eyes? And sorcerer powers? *Because she slept with some random blue-eyed sorcerer to further the charade. She is evil. Evil, incarnate.*" I stepped back. "There. Did I cover everything?"

"I'm sure you find yourself very amusing, Savannah—"

"He does, too," I said, pointing at the hulking bodyguard on Josef's left, who quickly erased his smile. "I know what he's thinking: Joe's right. I can't possibly be related to such an unrelentingly boring and humorless old coot."

"If you're done, Savannah . . ." Josef said.

"Nope, not yet. I have a message for you from my dad. Well, from Jaime Vegas, who got it from my dad. Something about manipulating share prices? I don't know exactly. I don't speak corporate. But the upshot is that if Sean and Bryce don't get their fair due in the division of assets, he'll . . ." I paused and looked around. "I'd rather not say in public. It's kind of rude. How about I just pass on Jaime's e-mail?"

Josef glowered at me.

"I'll do that. And now, familial chitchat over . . ." I waved to Paige. "The boss takes the stage for business."

Paige stepped forward. "Get the hell out of my city, Josef."

"Your city? Big words for such a little witch."

"Portland is Cortez Cabal territory. My husband is Benicio's heir. We work together on his Cabal responsibilities. Ergo?" She looked up at him. "My city."

"I'm not sure which is more amusing, that very tenuous logical leap or the fact that, after all these years of fighting Cabals, you're actually claiming a role in one."

"I'm *accepting* a role in one, as Lucas and I both have been for several years. I'm sure you got the memo. You would have also gotten the one from the intra-Cabal regulators, ordering you to stay ten miles away from Savannah while your Cabal assets are being split."

"She came to me."

"We're three miles from her place of employment, which is well within that court-mandated radius."

"Is it?" His brows shot up. "I can't be expected to know where your office is."

"Of course you do," I cut in. "You followed Keefer from it."

"Who?"

I opened my mouth, but Paige cut me off. "As an acknowledged executive representative of the Cortez Cabal, I'm hereby informing you that Keefer Brown is under our protection. If you need a *man's* word for it, Lucas will be here in a few minutes."

Josef pursed his lips. "Under your protection, is he? Then why did he flee your offices not thirty minutes ago?"

"He was taking a walk," Paige said.

Josef snorted.

"And, since you just admitted to following him from our offices, you just admitted to violating a more important boundary rule." She lifted her phone. "Now, I know you normally aren't all that worried about the intra-Cabal regulators, but with your company's assets being split by them, I think a call is in order." She turned to me. "You should go look for Keefer. I'll handle this."

I'd turned to go when Josef said, "Have you contacted Sean about this boy, Savannah?"

I glanced over.

"I'm sure you have," he continued. "You play Sean like a violin, and he's young enough—and weak enough—to fall for it. You called him for information. What did he say?"

I resumed walking.

"Did he react?" Josef said.

I turned back. "To what?"

"News of the boy and his powers."

"If you're asking if he's interested in Keefer, I'm sure he is. Possibly even salivating. A high-powered teleporting demon is a valuable prize, and if he ignored that, I'd think him an idiot. Which he is not. So, yes, he reacted."

"*How* did he react?"

"What?"

Josef stepped toward me. "I know you aren't very bright, Savannah. Further proof that you're not my brother's child. But let me explain this slowly for you. When you told him about young Mr. Brown, could his reaction be construed as more than simple interest? Oh, by 'construed,' I mean—"

"I know what it means," I snapped. I glanced at Paige, but she was on the phone with her back to us. "But I don't know what *you* mean. He was interested—"

"Oh, I'm sure he was interested. *Exceedingly* interested in a teenage boy with genetically modified supernatural powers."

"Genetically—? What the hell are you talking about?"

"Ask Sean. I suspect you'll discover you've just loosed the fox on the chickens. I'd be very surprised if he wasn't already in his jet, on his way here to take young Mr. Brown off your hands. Just being helpful, of course."

Running footsteps sounded behind me. Adam jogged over, his gaze darting between me and Josef.

"No need to run to her rescue, boy," Josef called as Adam slowed. "We're just talking."

Lucas came around the corner then, moving fast, his gaze fixed on Paige. Adam kept walking, stopping when he was still two feet from me but lowering his voice to say, "Everything okay?"

"No," Josef said. "I'm attacking her on a street corner in broad daylight. No wonder you two make such a good pair. Between you, there's a full share of brains."

Adam flinched, but it wasn't at the insult—that was Josef being an ass, as always. He flinched at the part about us making a good pair.

Josef continued, "Now, Savannah, as I was saying. About Sean—"

"Keefer," I whispered.

Josef sighed. "No, *Sean*. Remember him? Your alleged—"

I jogged off before he could continue, though I caught something about my limited attention span. Adam came after me.

"Savannah?"

"He's stalling me. Damn it." I scanned the row of buildings. "Keefer's here, and Josef's men either have him or they're closing in. He was talking about Sean to distract me. Not hard to do right now."

I didn't look at Adam when I said that. Couldn't. I had to focus. As for what Josef said about my brother, I didn't dismiss it. I just set it aside for later.

My gaze stopped on a shop front with a For Lease sign. Adam stepped closer and murmured, "Too small and too open. The front's all glass. Look left, but carefully."

I did and saw a more promising choice, another empty shop front, this one without a front window, likely former offices— medical, legal, something. When I started to move in that direction, Adam whispered, "No, Josef's watching. Let's prove we're as clueless as he thinks."

I walked over to the first storefront. An unlock spell opened the door. This wasn't the kind of neighborhood where they put security systems on vacant shops. As we slipped inside, Josef snorted and resumed talking to Lucas, having dismissed the inept duo who would spend the next twenty minutes searching the wrong shop.

We went in the front and out the back. The lock on the next one proved a little tricky for my spells, so Adam moved in with his picks.

"About earlier . . ." I said.

"Not now."

"It's not what it seemed. I have no intent—"

He met my gaze. "Not now."

He was right, of course, but having him here made my gut twist, added to my distraction, and I wanted to get that out of the way— *I'm not leaving*—so I could focus. Before I could try again, he opened the door, and that was my cue to step inside. A knockback spell can sideline an attacker only temporarily, but it's a lot faster and easier to launch than a physical attack. So I stepped in first with my fingers raised.

The hall was pitch-black. I cast a light ball and tossed it up to illuminate the rear corridor. I do carry a flashlight—I'd learned my lesson about relying too much on spells—but the ball was easier here, leaving us both with our hands free for power attacks.

There was one door at the end of the hall and another to my left. I eased forward with Adam right behind me and pushed open the door on the left. It opened into a dark room. I waved the light ball in. Adam followed it, prowling the room while I guarded. There was no need to discuss the plan. No need to glance at one another before executing it. We'd worked together for years. It came as naturally as breathing. But that day, watching him circle the room, knowing exactly where he'd look first and even how he'd look—the motions, the expression, the regular shoulder checks back at me, making sure I was fine—it all set my gut roiling.

I could say I'd been in love with him since I was twelve, but that's not true. I'd crushed on him since I was twelve. I'd deeply cared about him—as a friend—for years. Now, though, thinking of losing him? It felt like a fist in the gut, knocking the air from my lungs. *This* was love. Complete I-can't-live-without-you love, and that scared the shit out of me.

It was too much. That was the problem I couldn't articulate to Paige. That I was happy—utterly and unreservedly happy. Happy with my job and with my life. Ecstatically happy with Adam. And that was all I wanted. This life with this guy, and nothing more. I felt like that was wrong, like I should want more.

I walked behind him and lowered my voice. "I—"

He lifted a hand, and I started to shake my head, to say *No, I need to get this out.* Then I caught a whisper of sound through the wall. Adam waved me back into the hall. The door at the far end was locked. A quick spell solved that. I pushed it open a crack. Darkness. I caught a muffled thump. No light ball, then. Too risky.

I opened the door another inch and blinked, hoping my eyes would adjust. Adam claims I have better night vision from Balaam, but if I do, it's only the very slightest boost. I peered into the room. After a few seconds I could make out a door on the other side, faint light circling the edges. Another thump sounded from inside.

I turned to tell Adam, but he was right there, looking over my shoulder. I stepped aside to let him past. As he went, I leaned in and whispered, "I'd never go."

He glanced over.

"I never planned to go," I continued. "I just wanted to see if I could get accepted, but when I did, and I felt . . ." I swallowed. "I feel as if I should consider it, but I don't want to. I just want . . . this."

His brow furrowed.

I went on, still whispering. "I don't want to go anywhere else. Be anything else. And I know that's wrong."

"Wrong?"

"I—"

The blow hit Adam in the side of the head. I never saw it coming because there had been nothing to see. Now, as Adam went down, a man lunged for me. I was already casting. My energy bolt hit him in the chest as my kick struck his knee. He dropped. Another kick made sure he didn't land on Adam, who was staggering up. I caught the guy in a binding spell.

"I've got him," Adam said. "Go on."

A kick to the side of the half-demon's head made sure he couldn't use his teleportation power when I released the spell. As he collapsed, I raced past Adam and kicked the door open. That sounds far more impressive—though perhaps more stupid, too—if I don't admit that I'd noticed it was already cracked open. My kick slammed it wide, and the guy inside jumped, which was the point of the dramatic entrance.

I caught him in a binding spell and jogged in to find Keefer Brown trapped inside a ritual circle.

I took a good look at Keefer—and right-hooked his captor in the jaw.

"You son of a bitch," I said. "You get off on hurting kids?"

"I'm not a kid," Keefer mumbled through his swelling jaw. "But there were two of them. One held me down."

"While the other used you for a punching bag?" I kicked the guy in the binding spell hard enough for Keefer to wince.

"Because I bit his buddy."

"No excuse," I said. As Adam walked in, I erased the circle and took the ritual knife that magically held it in place. Then I looked at Keefer. "You want to get out of here?"

"Um, yeah."

"Will you come with us?" I said. "You don't have to. We can't force you. But in light of recent events . . ."

He quirked a smile. "Come with you if I want to live? Sure. Get me out of here. Please."

"I've got the kid," I said into my phone. I was not in the office. I wasn't taking a chance on Keefer overhearing this conversation and deciding to run again. We'd left him with Paige and Lucas. I was making this phone call from a coffee shop while Adam stood guard outside. Lucas and Paige's threats about the division of assets had sent Josef scuttling off, but we weren't trusting that he was actually gone. Or that he'd taken all his men with him.

On the other end of the line, Sean exhaled in what sounded like relief. "Good. He's all right, then?"

"Banged up, but fine. Seems Josef's men subdued him with their fists."

"No, they were showing him why he shouldn't run from them."

"Ah, of course. Intimidation. The lifeblood of any decent Cabal."

"I won't argue. I'll just say there are ways to do it that don't involve beating teenagers. But the boy's safe now?"

"He is. The question becomes: what do we do with him?"

"I . . . have an idea."

"I thought you might."

"It's not what you think."

"What do I think?"

"Recruitment." Sean paused, and I heard him moving on the other end of the line. "No, let me be honest. It *is* ultimately about recruitment. But it's more complicated than that."

"Is genetic engineering involved?"

A hiss of breath. "Can I come there and talk, Savannah? This isn't a telephone conversation. And no, I won't bring along a team to snatch him away from you. I wouldn't do that. Not to you or to him."

"I know."

Which is why I worried about my brother as Cabal leader. As good and decent a person as Lucas was, he had a streak of Machiavellianism that my brother did not. Lucas would never harm a kid like Keefer. But if he thought that kid was in danger, would he consider taking him temporarily against his will? Yes.

In some ways, Sean could come down harder than Lucas. He could make tougher choices. But he had his weaknesses, too. As a person, those "weaknesses" kept him good and decent. But as a Cabal CEO? They were problems, and I could only trust that he was smart enough to work around them and lead his Cabal effectively. So far, he'd been doing fine. Maybe, between him and Lucas, there was still hope for the Cabal institution. A place for reform and humanity and compassion that wouldn't be perceived as weakness.

I agreed to meet with Sean. He'd fly up from LA on the corporate jet and be here before midnight.

After we hung up, I sat there, staring into space, one hand wrapped around the untouched coffee I'd bought to justify taking up a table. I lifted it for a sip.

"That one's cold," said a voice above me, and another coffee appeared—a vanilla latte by the smell of it.

Adam set it down and then slid into the booth seat with me. He sat there, hands folded on the table, before saying, "I overreacted."

"No, I fucked up."

"Yes, you should have told me, but when I saw the letters, I should have known there was more to it. That you weren't going to pretend everything was fine if you were planning to dump me. That's not you. And unless I'm seriously misreading things, that's not *us*. We're doing better than that."

"We are. I hope."

A soft laugh. "Yeah, *I hope*. That's the problem, isn't it? We work together, we play together, we're obviously very happy together, so there shouldn't be any 'I hope.' Not for either of us. It should be clear. This is good, and we're going to make it work. I can say that for my part. Without reservation."

"It's my side you're not so sure of. You don't feel comfortable assuming I feel the same way because we don't talk about that. About where we're going. What we want. Long term."

"Yeah."

"We should."

"I know."

I sipped my latte, then said, "Let's start with the age difference."

He stiffened exactly as I had when Paige brought it up.

"It's . . . significant," I said.

He fidgeted and glanced at the door, as if hoping a Cabal goon would barrel through to save us from this conversation. Then he said, "You mean in size or in importance?"

"Both."

More tensing. "You're saying it's become a significant issue. Big enough that you're wondering if we should—"

"Break up?" I looked at him. "Do you want that?"

"Fuck, no."

"Same here. *Fuck, no*. So let's move that off the table and get through this conversation without either of us raising that possibility again. Because it isn't one. Agreed?"

"Agreed."

"The age difference doesn't bother me. Does *not*. At *all*. I do worry that there might be times my maturity—or lack of it—is a problem, but I think I've come a long way, and I know you wouldn't have ever started this if I hadn't. The bigger problem, it seems, is you worrying that you're moving too fast for me, because of my age. Which is laughable."

He shifted, face darkening. "I don't think—"

"Hear me out. Yes, given that we've been dating a year, living together isn't exactly a big deal. Paige was a year older than me when she moved in with Lucas. When I say it's laughable, what I mean is . . ." I inhaled and looked him in the eye. "You can't move too fast for me. This is what I want. It's all I want. I know you worried that, when we got together, my crush would wear off, but it had already worn off before that. I love you. I don't want anyone else. That hasn't changed. It won't change. And that's the problem, because I know . . ."

I gripped my cup. "I don't want to go to college, Adam. Not out of state. Not even here. I just want what I have. Hell, I joke about getting out of the receptionist's chair, but I'm fine if that's always part of my job description. I know I should want more. At the very least, I should want a specialty. You're the research guy. Paige is the tech whiz. Lucas is the lawyer. I'm the receptionist. But I'm okay with that. We all pull our weight. We all get out in the field. I want to be the best damned investigator I can be, but I don't want more. I just don't."

"You don't need to."

"I feel like I do."

"If I've ever—"

"You haven't. Not you or Paige or Lucas. But I see you guys get excited when I talk about college. About what I want to specialize in. Maybe I'll find it someday. But I'm okay for now. Just like I was okay with moving straight from their house to your building. I would have been fine moving into your place. I wanted an independent life, but . . ." I looked at him. "This *is* my independent life. Being with you. Staying in Portland. Working at the agency with Paige and Lucas. Nothing's holding me back. This is just what I want. What I'm happy with."

"That's all anyone cares about, Savannah."

His arms went around me, and he held me tight as I rested there, feeling like I'd been holding in some deep and shameful secret, and now it was out, relief washing over me.

"So you want to get a place together?" he said as I pulled back.

"I do."

"An apartment or—"

"A place. A permanent place. I'm not saying I want a wedding ring and babies. Not now." I took a deep breath. "Eventually, yes. That's where I'm headed and I know you might not be—"

"I am."

I nodded. "Then I think we need to start being honest about that. Expectations. Timelines. Stop worrying that one of us is more committed than the other or that one is too young to think about things like that."

"I *am* a little young for fatherhood."

I laughed and kissed his cheek. "I know. And I'm *much* too young for motherhood. But we'll begin with a place of our own. And maybe a cat."

"I'd prefer a dog."

"Given how little time we spend at home, maybe we'll start with fish and work up."

He smiled. "Agreed."

"Go get yourself a mocha," I said. "Sean isn't coming in for a few hours, and I'm in no rush to get back to the office."

Two hours later, we were in Paige and Lucas's condo, having deemed it the most private place to meet. Paige and Lucas themselves were still at the office with Keefer. They trusted us to handle this.

"Genetically modified supernaturals," I said as we walked into the living room.

Sean and I don't share a mother and I suspect, beyond the height, blond hair, and bright blue eyes, he takes after his mom more than our father. In temperament as well as looks. So he didn't turn icy blue eyes on me and tell me to give him a damn minute to settle in. He just sighed, lowered himself into a chair, and said, "Good to see you, too, sis. No chance of coffee first, I'm guessing?"

I handed him a can of Coke. Another sigh, but he popped the top and drank half. Adam sat beside me on the sofa. As Sean drank, he eyed us over the can, one brow lifted. When he lowered it, he said, "So which of you will be playing bad cop this evening?"

"Adam is always bad cop. I'm worse cop."

A tweak of a smile. "Of course."

"We have a teenage teleporting half-demon who can take passengers. And the fact that you aren't even raising an eyebrow at that tells me almost everything I need to know."

"Good. Then we can skip all the—"

"Not a chance." I inched forward. "It's the St. Clouds, isn't it?"

One thing Sean *did* inherit from Dad? An excellent poker face. Which would be so much more effective if it extended to his eyes. Those who knew him best could always call his bluff. I only needed to give him a hard look before he said, "Excellent deduction. Or . . ." He glanced at Adam. "Should I say research?"

"We dug up a few rumors," I said. "Now you're going to fill us in and tell us how you're connected."

Silence. Then, "Do you trust me, Savannah?"

"This isn't an issue—"

"I'm afraid it is. Let me put it to you another way. You know I can't be completely trusted in matters of business. I'm CEO of the Nast Cabal. You're my sister, yes, but you're also, effectively, the granddaughter of my rival. There is no question which Cabal you put first, and I don't blame you for that. Maybe, someday, ours will be something you feel you can more fully support, but until then, we cannot trust one another in that arena. But do you trust me as a *person*? As someone who, if put in the position of choosing between a massive corporate advantage and the safety and well-being of teenagers, would find a way to protect both his corporate interests and those teens, with the emphasis on the teens?"

"Yes, but—"

"Then let me give you a hypothetical. Suppose you are right. Suppose the St. Clouds did conduct prenatal genetic experiments on supernaturals. Suppose they handled it poorly."

"Shocker."

A quarter smile. "Yes, I know. So suppose they handled it poorly, and these subjects—now teens like Keefer—broke free only to find themselves—again like Keefer—on the run from every Cabal plus a few independent interests. Hypothetically, is that how you'd see it play out?"

"Of course. If they have modified powers, everyone will want them."

"Can they fight back?"

"Against Cabals? Not a chance."

"So presume, then, hypothetically, that I saw a way to intervene. To give them a safe environment, a community where they can be with their families and grow up as close to normal as possible. While being trained to become Cabal operatives, because as CEO, I'm not about to lose the opportunity to recruit some. Note that I say 'some.' You know my philosophy, Savannah. If Josef had this opportunity, he'd lock them up under house arrest, train them, and forcibly recruit them. I would rather show them that Cabal life isn't so bad if you're a talented and powerful supernatural. I prefer willing employees over slaves."

"So you—"

"Hypothetically."

I rolled my eyes. "Let's drop the—"

"I can't. Because if I do, then you can reasonably ask for details. For names and powers. You might ask to come and see what I'm doing. And the answer would be no. Unequivocally no. For their protection. For your protection. And, yes, for the protection of my business interests, because if Paige found out, she'd make this *her* business, as a member of the interracial council. Then, if we had werewolves or vampires in the group, those delegates would want to get involved, and ultimately it would be a political firestorm that would clearly not provide the kind of safe and stable environment I'd be trying to give these kids." He met my gaze. "Am I right?"

I glanced at Adam but knew what he'd say. The same thing I would. That Sean was right.

Adam nodded and said, "So what do you have in mind for Keefer?"

It wasn't an easy decision or a quick one. But whatever Sean said to Keefer in the hours that they spent talking, it convinced the boy that he could trust Sean enough to at least see what he had in mind.

Convincing Lucas and Paige was tougher. Sean constructed a decent story. He told them he had a place, not unlike a college dorm, for kids like Keefer—powerful supernaturals nearing the age of recruitment. It was private and secure, but would provide enough freedom that Keefer could always contact us and let us know if he wanted out, and if he did, we could come up with a better solution.

Given that Sean was my brother—and that our relationship was valuable on both sides—we knew he'd never make Keefer "disappear" or refuse to release him. Most important, though, we knew Josef wouldn't dare come after Keefer while he was in Sean's custody. The asset split would take years to finalize, and during that time it was the best leverage anyone had over Josef. Interfere with Sean's business and Josef risked losing his share of the spoils.

In the end, though, what counted was Keefer's decision. He wanted to go, so we couldn't hold him. The only alternative we could offer would be to contact the half-demon community and see if someone could take him in until he started college. That

wouldn't just be awkward—crashing in the spare room of strangers—
it wouldn't be safe, either, not with Josef hot on his trail. Paige and
Lucas would have taken him in themselves . . . if that wouldn't be the
first place Josef looked.

No, Sean's plan was best. So by morning, they were gone, heading off to parts unknown with Sean promising to have Keefer call
the next day and let us know what he thought. I had little doubt
the answer would be, "This is fine." Whatever Sean had going on
with these kids, he'd be giving them a good place, and Keefer was
smart—he knew he couldn't survive out here on his own. Better
to take what Sean offered until he was old enough to make his
own choices.

As we drove back from the airport, I stifled a yawn.

"Your place or mine?" Adam asked.

"Which is closer?"

He laughed. "We won't be able to ask that soon."

He said it casually, but I caught the faintly anxious look, the one
that checked on my reaction. I smiled and put my hand on his leg.
"Good."

A few minutes in silence, then I said, "After we get some sleep,
can we look at what's out there to live in together?"

He grinned. "We can. What do you want? House? Town house
condo?"

"We'll keep our options open. It's a first home. We can always
change our mind and move later."

His grin broadened as he took my hand, fingers lacing with
mine. "We absolutely can."

Also by #1 *New York Times* bestselling author Kelley Armstrong

The Otherworld Series

978-0-452-29664-0

978-0-452-29666-4

978-0-452-29722-7

978-0-452-29799-9

978-1-101-59342-4
**Available exclusively
for your e-reader from
Dutton**

978-0-14-219674-8

And the stunning conclusion to the Nadia Stafford trilogy

978-0-452-29881-1

PLUME

— est. 1852 —

www.kelleyarmstrong.com

Explore the World of Cainsville

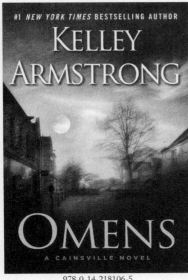

978-0-14-218106-5

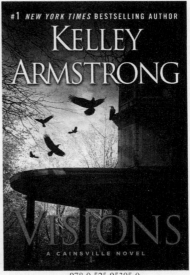

978-0-525-95305-0

Plus
Available for iPhone, iPad, and iPod touch on the App Store:

Appstore.com/KelleyArmstrongsCainsvilleFiles

PLUME

DUTTON
⸺ est. 1852 ⸺